JOLINE'S REDEMPTION

— Land Rush Dreams 2 —

Vickie McDonough

An Imprint of Barbour Publishing, Inc.

Print ISBN 978-1-62836-952-6

eBook Editions:
Adobe Digital Edition (.epub) 978-1-63409-402-3
Kindle and MobiPocket Edition (.prc) 978-1-63409-403-0

All scripture quotations are taken from the King James Version of the Bible.

This book is a work of fiction. Names, characters, places, and incidents are either products of the author's imagination or used fictitiously. Any similarity to actual people, organizations, and/or events is purely coincidental.

Cover Design: Faceout Studio, www.faceoutstudio.com

Published by Shiloh Run Press, an imprint of Barbour Publishing, Inc., P.O. Box 719, Uhrichsville, Ohio 44683, www.shilohrunpress.com

Our mission is to publish and distribute inspirational products offering exceptional value and biblical encouragement to the masses.

Printed in the United States of America.

Chapter 1

Oklahoma City, Oklahoma Territory
Late March 1893

Drifting back to a different time and place, Joline Jensen hummed the words of a long-forgotten hymn, keeping tune with the peaceful organ music wafting through her window. *Softly and tenderly, Jesus is calling. Calling for you to come home.* She sucked in a sharp breath when she realized what she was doing and glanced at her open door, hoping none of the other women had overheard. She wasn't in the mood for their teasing today.

"What's a trollop like you doing singing church songs? You ain't gettin' religious on us, are you? God doesn't hear the prayers of the likes of us." Jo could hear their taunting in her mind.

Long ago, she'd quit singing church songs. They were for decent women—not ones like her. She'd made her choice when she ran away from her family.

She walked to the window of her second-story bedroom and looked down at the field next door. She wasn't the only one who thought it odd that the traveling preacher had selected that particular spot to raise his tent, especially since the nearest church was only a block away. The man must have thought the "ladies" at the bordello needed to hear his revival messages—or perhaps he thought the presence of his tent would keep customers away for the duration of the revival. She quirked her lips to one side. *Not likely.*

The soulful tune haunted her, reminding her of better days—days she'd so easily cast off in the arrogance of youth. If only she could go back. . .

She instantly squelched that thought. There was no room for dreams or what-ifs in this place.

"You're not listening to that pitiful music, are you?"

Jo stiffened at the sound of Ruby's voice and lowered the window. "Of course not. I'm shutting the window so I don't have to hear it." Pasting on a smile, she spun. "Besides, it's getting too chilly in here. I don't want Jamie to catch cold." She crossed to the left side of her bedroom and tugged the small quilt over her son's shoulders. She wanted to tell the other ladies that today was his first birthday, but the less attention drawn to him, the better. Badger would like nothing more than to be rid of him.

"I'm glad to hear that."

Jo stiffened. "I never had much use for churches or their music."

Ruby, still dressed in her silk robe even though it was past one in the afternoon, leaned on the door frame. "Me neither." She snorted and shook her head. "Maybe if'n we had we wouldn't have ended up here."

Jo wouldn't admit there was truth to her statement. She glided closer to the door and gestured for Ruby to move into the hall, hoping the woman would leave before she woke up Jamie. He fussed when he was tired, and Badger didn't like it when he could hear Jamie downstairs. "Did you need something?"

Ruby narrowed her blue eyes and jerked her head toward the stairs, smirking. "Badger wants to see you."

Jo's heart jolted. Badger rarely sent for her except in the wee hours of the morning. She nodded, backed into her room, and squirted perfume—the kind Badger preferred—on her neck. He hadn't sent for her for several weeks, so why now? She tiptoed over to Jamie's little bed and checked on him again. He should sleep an hour and a half still, so there was time, but she hated to leave him, even for a short while. He was her lifeline. The only good thing in her life.

"I'll sit with the boy. Gotta stitch up a ripped hem. You go on."

Ruby seemed coldhearted most of the time, but she had a soft spot for Jamie. Jo nodded and slipped out the door, heart pounding and her blue dress swishing. She used to love blue, because it matched her eyes, but she hated it now. If only she could wear a soft lavender or sunny yellow, but Badger insisted each girl be named for a jewel and that she only wear the color of dresses that matched her jewel name.

She paused outside his door, already smelling the stench of the smoke of his cigar. The first few times he'd kissed her, her mouth had burned as if someone had set it on fire. Shuddering, she sucked in a steadying breath and stepped inside.

Badger lifted his gaze from his desk and caressed her with his steelgray eyes. His lips lifted at one corner. "Have a seat, Sapphire."

She didn't want a seat. She wanted to run upstairs, snatch her son, and flee this horrible place, but she couldn't. Instead, she glided in, pasted on a smile, and cocked her head. "Ruby said you wanted to see me."

He leaned back, tugged the half-smoked cigar from his mouth, and blew out a ring of smoke. "I looked over the books, and things seem to be in order."

Jo nodded. "You know they are. It's why you gave the job of bookkeeping to me."

He narrowed his gaze, setting Jo's heart to fluttering like the wings of a trapped bird. "I don't reckon you'd cheat me like Topaz did."

She worked hard to keep her face neutral. Had he found a

discrepancy somewhere? She thought she had covered her trail well enough that he wouldn't notice the tiny pittance she'd been pilfering for months. If she ever needed to make a quick getaway, she'd have to have that money. Would he strangle her like he did Topaz, a lovely girl with dark blond hair and hazel eyes? What would happen to Jamie if something happened to her?

Badger chuckled. "You worried about something?"

"Um. . .no, just wondering if that's all you wanted."

He hooked one arm over the back of his chair and fiddled with his cigar. "Maybe I'm just lonely for your company."

"You don't get lonely." He could have any of the women in the bordello whenever he wanted, but for some reason, he'd singled her out. As much as she hated spending time alone with him, she was grateful that he rarely made her be with the other men who came nightly. For some reason, he considered her his personal belonging. The only time he shared her now was when an especially high-paying client visited. She was grateful and yet the other women disliked her because of it.

"Would you like me to get you some coffee?" she asked.

He shook his head. "Sarah's getting it."

He stared at her for a long moment then flicked his hand toward a package on the side table. "Open that. I got you a present."

Jo's stomach clenched as if she'd gulped down sour milk. She didn't want Badger's gifts. They always came with expected payment. But she learned early not to disobey and to pretend compliance. She crossed the small room, opened the package, and curiously fingered the blue calico with tiny pink flowers. Badger had never before allowed such a common dress in his establishment. Why now? She glanced at him, brows lifted. "Calico? What's this for?"

He slowly rose and stepped around his desk. "I've made an appointment for four this afternoon. You're to wear that and take that boy with you."

She tightened her grip on the fabric. "What? Why?"

He held her gaze but then looked away. "There's a couple wantin' a kid."

Jo stepped back. She wanted to flee to her room, get Jamie, and leave. "No. I—I can't give him up. You said I could keep him if I did what you wanted." He was her only joy. The only thing in this wretched place that brought her any happiness.

Badger grabbed her throat. "That noisy brat has customers complaining. I want him gone."

"No! Please! I'll do anything."

He shoved her against the table. "You'll get rid of the kid—and you'll still do anything I say. You belong to me."

"Badger, please. Today is Jamie's birthday. I can't give him up today."

Badger glared at her, but a shuffling at the door drew his gaze, and his expression softened. "Put it on the desk."

Jo wiped her eyes and glanced at Sarah. Keeping her head down, the girl slipped in quietly, set the tray on Badger's desk, and then turned to leave. She peeked up at Jo. "Birthday is special day," she muttered as she fled the room.

Badger frowned and stared at the empty doorway. "Go meet them folks. If they like the boy, you can give 'im to 'em tomorrow." He swiveled his gaze to her. "Just make sure to arrange a place and time to meet 'em again and hand over that kid. Am I clear?"

Jo nodded and swallowed back her argument. There was no disagreeing with Badger. She would pay dearly if she did, and she wasn't certain that he was above hurting Jamie. Maybe he would be safer away from this place. She slipped from the room, her heart breaking. How could she bear to give away her son? It was an unconscionable thing for Badger to demand. Heartless.

She wouldn't do it.

She couldn't.

As she dragged her numb body up the stairs, she searched for another solution. There had to be something she could do besides handing Jamie over to strangers. She'd tried escaping before and suffered for it. She'd nearly lost Jamie before he'd been born as a result of the beating she'd incurred, and if she hadn't stayed in bed for two months, per doctor's orders, as she recovered, she probably would have.

Oh, why had she ever believed Badger? Believed he had wanted to take her away from the awful situation she'd found herself in when she learned the truth about Mark Hillborne's deception?

If she'd known then what she knew now, she would have listened to her sister. She'd never have left her family. How could she have known her actions would one day cost her something so priceless—her son?

That afternoon, Jo clutched Jamie tight around his belly as the buggy bumped along the rutted street. The innocent child bounced and gurgled, enjoying the ride that was ripping out her heart. Stoney, one of Badger's henchmen, drove the wagon. There'd be no escape for her with him along. Why couldn't Garnet have driven? She would have been more sympathetic to Jo's plight, but even she wouldn't have allowed Jo to run, because it would have meant a severe beating for herself.

Jo sighed, blowing Jamie's wispy blond hair. While her son had her coloring, his features more resembled his father. She scowled at the thought of Mark Hillborne. Why had she been so enamored with him? Why had she believed him when he'd said he wanted to marry her? He'd been a charmer, wooing her into his store. Into his bed after they'd repeated their vows to one another. It was only later that she learned the man who "married" them wasn't a real preacher. She looked to the side, focusing on a general store, much like the one she and Mark had run together.

The man she thought she loved had deceived her. And he'd lied when she confronted him with the news she'd learned. He laughed it off as a rumor and had coaxed her to believe that he truly loved her and that they were legally married. Didn't his ring prove that? But the last time he learned she was pregnant, he'd boarded up the store and left town. Left her. Left his son.

Jo pushed the morose memories from her mind. Today's troubling thoughts were already more than she could handle. Dressed in the dark blue calico Badger had supplied and riding in a buggy she'd never seen before, she was able to study the town without receiving the censuring glares and huddled whispers she normally endured as one of the ladies from the bordello. Anyone might think they were a married couple. Though only a few years old, Oklahoma City had already surpassed Guthrie in size. One could easily hide among the crowds. She glanced down at her dress, her heart picking up its pace. In calico, she could walk the streets and fade in with the regular folk.

Stoney turned a corner and stopped the buggy at a small park. A couple sitting in a fancy surrey turned to look at them. The woman's eyes lit up as they latched onto Jamie. Jo tugged her son against her chest. He reached up and patted her cheek. She'd never let that woman have Jamie, but she had to play the part now or Stoney would become suspicious and tattle to Badger.

The man helped his wife down then offered his arm and escorted her toward Jo. They were dressed in nice clothing, and their buggy was a newer model. In another situation, she might have liked them. Stoney jumped to the ground then lumbered around and helped

Jo out of the buggy. He gestured with his head for her to go on. Sucking in a steadying breath, she pushed her feet forward. *Just be an actress. Play the part.* Then tonight, she and Jamie would make their getaway.

The couple cautiously approached, both of them looking at Jamie. Jo felt a little sorry for them, since they wouldn't be gaining a son like they hoped. But Jamie was *her* son, and no one would force her to give him up. Besides, this was none of her doing. For all she knew, they'd paid Badger a fee to claim her son.

"Oh, Charles. He's such a comely lad." The woman's gaze shifted to Jo. "The baby is a boy?"

She nodded. "His names is James, but I call him Jamie."

"We'd want to change that, of course." The man glanced at Jo. "I suppose I should introduce us. I'm Charles Willhite, and this is my wife, Cecelia."

He looked at Jo as if waiting for her name, but she remained silent. Her name didn't matter. And neither did Jamie's, so it seemed.

"Could my wife hold the boy?"

Jo shuddered. Would the couple try to steal Jamie away now? They'd be upset when they learned they couldn't have him today. Forcing herself to nod and her arms to loosen, she held out her son, hoping he'd cry and fuss and want her back—but she knew he wouldn't. He'd always been such a good baby, and he was used to different women holding him.

"Oh, look. He has blue eyes like you, Charles."

The man scowled. Maybe he didn't like his wife comparing him and Jamie. Cecelia was obviously taken with him. Jamie reached for the woman's gold necklace, but Mr. Willhite reached out and gently pushed his hand down.

"Mr. Worley informed us the boy is an orphan. Do you know anything of his background?"

Stunned, Jo didn't respond at first. Badger had told them Jamie didn't have parents?

Mr. Willhite lifted a brow.

Jo straightened. "Jamie is not an orphan. I am his mother."

Behind her, Stoney coughed a warning.

Mrs. Willhite's face turned white. "Why would you give away your child?"

Jo wanted to snatch her son from the woman's arms and flee. She wanted to scream that she didn't want to give him up. Instead, she kept her head down, hoping they couldn't tell she was lying. "As much as I'd like to keep him, my circumstances are such that I can't. I only want him to go to a good home."

She peered up, watching the couple look at one another. The woman gave a slight nod and tugged Jamie up, resting her cheek on his head.

Mr. Willhite turned. "All right. We'll take him, but there is to be no further contact from you or Mr. Worley, is that clear?"

Jo stepped toward them. "I understand, but there is one thing. You can't have Jamie until tomorrow."

"Tomorrow?" Mrs. Willhite took a step back.

Jo wrung her hands. "Please understand. Today is his first birthday. I can't bear to give him up today. Please."

Mr. Willhite scowled. "I was afraid of something like this. It's why I didn't like this harebrained idea from the start."

"It's only one more day, Charles. And then we'll have our son."

"Are you sure? What if something happens? I don't want to see you disappointed again."

"The young lady seems sincere. As much as I'd love to take Jamie now, I can wait one more day." But when she looked down at Jamie and kissed his head, Jo noticed her lips quivered. She knew the agony the woman felt at the thought of parting with him.

Cecelia passed Jamie to her husband, and he handed him back to Jo. She clutched him to her.

"Same time tomorrow? Same place?" Mr. Willhite asked.

His wife placed her hand on his forearm. "Could we perhaps meet earlier in the day? I don't think I can bear to wait all day, and it might be easier on Jamie's mother?"

"Ten o'clock?" Mr. Willhite lifted a brow.

Holding her son tight, Jo nodded. She turned and fled back to the buggy, knowing she was going to break Mrs. Willhite's heart. But Jamie was her son—and she wasn't letting him go without a fight.

Chapter 2

Baron Hillborne set his satchel on the steps and stared at the building that housed the store his brother once bragged about. Mark had dreams to make Hillborne's the best general store in Guthrie, and from the tales he told in the few letters he'd written their mother, he had succeeded. But the place had been boarded up for well over a year and a half—ever since Mark had tired of it and returned to St. Louis.

The facade of the two-story building sported a coat of faded tan paint with windows trimmed in dark green. He needed to hire someone to repaint it while he took inventory and worked on getting the inside cleaned up. He blew out a sigh. Once again he was tasked with cleaning up a mess his brother had made.

Baron jogged up the stairs and yanked on one of the loose boards that covered the front door. A splinter from the dry, grayed wood pierced his skin and he winced.

"Can I help you with somethin', mister?"

Casting a quick glance at his finger, Baron turned and faced a tall man with a badge on his vest. "Marshal?"

The man eyed him with a narrow gaze. "Hillborne?"

Baron nodded. "My last name is Hillborne, but I'm not the man you're probably thinking of. That was Mark. I'm Baron, his older brother."

"Ah. . .there is quite a resemblance."

"Yes, but also a difference."

The marshal's expression relaxed. "Do you plan to reopen the store? Your brother did a brisk business here before he up and left town."

"That's my goal. How soon that happens will depend on the condition of things on the inside."

"Well, I ain't doin' nuthin' at the moment, so I can help get these boards off."

Baron smiled. "I'd appreciate the assistance, Marshal."

"The name's Bob Myers. Most folks just call me Bob. I reckon you can, too."

"Thank you. You're welcome to call me Baron." He bit down on the edge of the splinter, pulled it out, and spat it on the ground.

The marshal yanked on a board, creating a high-pitched screech as the nail pulled loose. "That's a might fancy moniker, if you ask me."

Baron chuckled. "My mother was enamored with British royalty. Mark's real name is Marquis, like our father's middle name, but he refuses to use it. He decided he wanted to be called Mark—spelled with a *k* at the end, not a *q*—when he was seven, and it stuck. Of course, Mother stubbornly refuses to call him that."

The marshal tossed down a plank he'd pried loose. "Guess I'm lucky to be just plain ol' Bob."

"You're not a Robert?"

"Nope. My ma believed in short names. My brothers are Sam and Jim."

Working together, they had all the boards down in a matter of minutes. Baron pulled the key from his pocket and unlocked the door with a loud click. He pushed open the door while the marshal attacked the boards on one of the windows. A thick layer of dust coated everything, but the store looked intact. "It's smaller than I expected."

"That's probably because of the size of the town lot," the marshal offered from the back door. "The lots were mapped out prior to settlement."

"I remember Mark writing that in a letter to my parents. My brother was fortunate to win this lot in the land rush." But then, Mark always loved a challenge.

He glanced around the dark store. Clothing hung against the wall opposite the counter, tools and work supplies along the front windows, and canned food, cooking supplies, and other housewares sat on shelves on the rear wall.

He blew out a sigh. Dusting everything and airing out the building would take a while, but he was thankful that no one had broken in and stolen anything. He returned to the porch and started removing the boards from the last window.

Mark had never said why he left Guthrie in such a hurry, especially with the store being a success. Baron thought he'd stayed just long enough to prove to their father that he was capable of making something of himself, but as usual, Mark had started something and not finished the task. If he had to hazard a guess, Baron figured his leaving had something to do with a woman. It wouldn't be the first time his brother had run from an upset female. Baron hoped no fuming father saw him and came after him with a rifle, thinking he was Mark.

"What do you want to do with these boards?" Bob asked.

Baron shrugged. "I guess we can put them out back."

"If you don't need them, I know a family that lives in a dilapidated shack that could put them to good use."

Baron waved his hand in the air. "Help yourself. I'm glad someone else can use them. Once I get the ones off the back windows, you can have those, too."

"Tell you what. I'll take these over to the Borgmans then take a walk around town. If things are quiet, I'll come back and remove the boards myself. I reckon you have plenty to do inside."

Baron's chest warmed. "That's mighty kind of you, Marshal."

"Bob, remember. And you'll find most folks in Guthrie are kind." He leaned against the doorjamb, looking relaxed, but his alert gaze scanned the buildings on the opposite side of the street. "Of course, there are always them that like to cause trouble, and with all the cowpokes that come in town on the weekends, we do get our fair share."

Baron grabbed his satchel, anxious to get busy. The sooner he opened the store, the sooner he could make it profitable again. Then maybe he could sell it and go back to St. Louis. Guthrie was much larger than he'd expected, but it was still a young town. He longed for St. Louis and all the amenities it had to offer, especially its electric lights and indoor plumbing.

He set his satchel inside, found matches and a lantern, and lit it, as well as several others; then he took a walk down the aisles of the store. He had to admit the place was set up better than he'd expected and well stocked with supplies. His brother had done a decent job establishing the store, and he knew from his father that it had made a very nice profit. So what exactly had happened to send Mark packing so quickly that he just up and left everything?

Though Mark had returned to his wife, he and Abigail had never been truly happy together. Mark quickly lost patience with Abigail, saying all she cared about was owning the latest fashion in gowns and jewelry, and she had confided in Baron that she wished she'd married him instead of Mark. Baron shook his head. Women couldn't seem to look past his brother's handsome features and charming personality to see the shallowness of his character. As a Christian, Baron believed character was important, and he always tried to keep his word and treat people with respect. If only his brother did the same, but Mark was cut from a different cloth.

He snatched a feather duster off a hook in the storeroom and attacked the shelves. He and his brother closely resembled one another in looks, but there was no doubt Mark's features were more comely. Baron didn't care, but he despised how his brother used his good looks to charm women and how they all fell under his spell. He'd love to meet one woman who hadn't been taken in by Mark's magnetism. Why couldn't they recognize a snake when they saw one?

Dust clouded the air. Baron coughed and waved his hand. He'd been so lost in thought he forgot to open the windows. Stomping across the room, he unlocked a window and lifted it up, allowing in the cool spring breeze. He did the same with the next one, but what he really needed was to get the back door open and create a cross breeze.

He unlocked the door and gave it a shove. Maybe he could jar the boards loose from the inside. After several hard shoulder shoves, the door moved.

"Hey," the marshal hollered from the outside of the door, "I thought I was going to clear the boards."

Baron chuckled. "The dust was getting to me, so I thought I'd try to break through from this side. I did loosen the boards, but my shoulder is telling me to stop."

A few creaks later, the marshal pulled down the last board and opened the door. A refreshing breeze blew through, cooling Baron.

"Thanks for taking care of that, Bob. Guess I'll return to my dusting." He needed to get the store cleaned and up and running again; then he could place a for-sale ad in some area newspapers.

The sooner he finished things here, the sooner he could go home.

Jo held her breath as she hugged Jamie against her chest and descended the stairs. Moonlight filtered in through the windows, illuminating her way. She'd chosen the wee hours of the morning to make her escape because everyone had finally gone to bed. Even Badger should be asleep by now.

It was now or never.

She avoided the boards she knew would squeak and hoped that all the jostling wouldn't awaken her son. He'd be fussy if he did awaken and would probably cry.

Her heart pounded. Her breath was so ragged she thought certainly someone would hear. She had to make it past Stoney's room near the back door. She didn't dare go out the front, because Badger was sure to notice. If Stoney woke up, she hoped he would assume it was one of the ladies on a trek to the outhouse.

She quietly opened the back door and tiptoed down the stairs and toward the shed where the rented buggy still sat. If she could get the horse hitched, they could easily make their getaway.

A thought dashed through her mind, and she made a quick turnabout. If Stoney was listening, he would expect to hear the outhouse door. Jo tugged it open, gritting her teeth at the creak.

A sharp squeal from inside nearly caused her to drop Jamie. Fearing she was caught, she peered in. The moonlight illuminated Sarah, already dressed for the day, staring back at her, wide eyed.

Jo's mind raced. Would the girl cry out when she learned what Jo was up to?

Sarah's gaze dropped to Jamie. "Why you bring boy to privy?"

When Jo didn't answer, the girl's dark eyes widened further. "You are leaving."

Jo nodded. "I can't give up my son."

Sarah stared at her. "You should not have to. Badger is wrong to tell you to."

Hope surged through Jo. "You understand?"

The girl nodded. "A child should not be separated from her mother."

Jo didn't miss the fact that Sarah said *her*. "Come with me. I was hoping to take you away from this place, too, but I was afraid to tell anyone about my plan. You don't belong here."

The girl shook her head. "I can't."

"There's no future here. You know where you'll end up if you stay."

"Badger would not—"

"He would." Jo stepped closer. "He doesn't care about any of us. All he wants is money. I don't want you to endure what I've had to. Come with us, Sarah. We'll be our own family."

"You would let me stay with you?"

Jo nodded. "Of course. You're like a little sister to me."

Nibbling her lower lip, Sarah glanced at the house. Her expression suddenly hardened, and Jo thought for certain the girl would sound an alarm. But Sarah turned her gaze on her for a long moment as if taking her measure, and then she nodded.

Once again hope warmed Jo's chest. "Then c'mon. Let's go before we get caught." She headed for the barn, silencing the crickets and night creatures. "You can hold Jamie while I hitch the horse to the buggy."

Jo reached for the barn door, but Sarah grabbed her arm.

"We should go in the back."

Jo nodded then followed the girl. She'd been to the barn so few times she hadn't even known there was a rear entrance. The door rattled a bit as Sarah opened it, making Jo grit her teeth. She stayed there, holding it ajar to allow moonlight inside. The horse nickered softly, as if complaining it was too early for a drive. Jo tapped her fingers on the wooden frame, watching the house. If she leaned slightly, she could just make out the edge of the back door. *C'mon, Sarah. Hurry.*

From inside the barn, she could hear the jangle of horse tack and movement. The seconds ticked by like hours. Jamie's steady breaths warmed her face. Jo glanced heavenward. She loved her son enough to do about anything—and that included praying. "God," she whispered. "If You're up there, please help us get away. I can't give up my son. I promise—I'll even go to church if You'll help us escape."

A noise from inside the barn drew her attention. Sarah appeared, leading the same horse that had pulled the buggy yesterday, but this time the horse was saddled. Was Sarah planning on riding off without her?

"Why the saddle?" Jo moved in front of the horse to block him.

"Buggy too slow. We move faster if we ride."

"How can we ride with Jamie?"

Sarah held up a canvas bag and some rope. "I fix." She held out the reins to Jo, and she took them. Then Sarah lifted Jamie from her arms and laid him on the ground. She made quick work of sliding Jamie, quilt and all, into the burlap, leaving only his face showing, and then she hoisted him up. "You hold boy."

Jo held her son to her chest, and Sarah moved behind her and tied Jamie to her, leaving both of Jo's arms free to guide the horse. The concept was rather ingenious.

Sarah helped Jo balance atop the chopping block and held the horse's reins while she clumsily mounted. She knew how to ride, but mounting with a heavy one-year-old attached wasn't easy. Sarah, holding Jo's pillowcase that contained Jamie's diapers and clothing, stepped up on the block and lithely swung up behind her.

A lantern flickered to life in Garnet's room in the closest corner of the house.

"We go." The girl kicked the horse.

Jo barely had time to get situated and gather the reins before the surprised animal broke into a trot. She turned him away from town, and as she did, the back door of the house opened.

Her heart jolted.

For the second time that night, she prayed. *Let whoever it is think we're someone from town. Or better yet, please don't let them hear us.*

Jo guided the horse to the north, keeping the house between them and the person out back. Sarah held on to Jo's waist. She wanted to gallop but feared the horse might stumble. The animal was their lifeline. Without him, they were doomed.

When no one cried out, she allowed herself to relax. The money she'd managed to steal from Badger by manipulating the income records weighed heavy in the hem of her skirt. There wasn't a lot, just enough for food for a few days, but it was something.

Where should they go? Badger knew people in many of the nearby towns. People who would gladly tell him if they saw her because they knew they'd get a reward.

There was really only one place she could go, and it was the last place she wanted to go—her sister's home.

But Guthrie wasn't all that far from Oklahoma City. Would Badger find them there? Or would he expect them to ride straight to the depot, catch the train, and go far away? If only they could. At least Gabe and Lara lived a ways out of town. But dare she go there?

She'd treated her family despicably, especially her older sister. But Lara would forgive her. It wasn't her nature to hold a grudge.

She wasn't so sure about Gabe. He would want to protect his wife from more hurt and might chase her away at gunpoint, because she'd certainly broken her sister's heart with her childish behavior and cruel treatment. To think, she wouldn't even stand up with Lara at her wedding.

She shook her head. If only she'd known then what she knew now.

Gabe wouldn't send her away, not once he saw Jamie—and Sarah. She felt certain he would let them stay.

And if she went home, she could see her nephew, Michael, and Grandpa again—if Grandpa was still alive.

She rounded the corner of the last house before they hit open prairie. She allowed herself to relax a smidgeon. Suddenly, a privy door banged open. The horse jerked, shying sideways and nearly unseating her. Sarah's grip tightened on Jo's waist, and she felt the girl regain her seat.

A disheveled man stumbled from the privy, gawking at them. He rubbed the back of his hand across his mouth, eyes brightening. He staggered toward her. "Well now, what have we here?"

Jo sucked in a breath. She recognized the man from the bordello.

He stumbled and reached for the reins, missing and falling against Jo's leg. She tightened the reins and turned the horse in a sharp circle. The man, obviously still drunk, grabbed for her skirts, but he slid away and fell to the ground. She turned the horse away from town. "Hold on tight," she said, kicking the horse into a trot and then a gallop.

Had the man recognized her? Would he run to Badger and tell him he'd seen them? A bead of sweat trickled down her temple in spite of the cool temperatures.

The sky had already started to lighten, turning a brilliant hue of magenta. Soon the sun would chase away the remaining darkness. No one at the bordello, other than Sarah, normally stirred before noon. But Garnet had awakened. Still, she would have no reason to check Jo's room. By the time anyone noticed they were missing, they should have a good head start—unless the drunk awakened Badger and reported seeing her. She glanced over her shoulder, relieved to see he was still lying on the ground. Maybe he would fall asleep and think he'd only dreamed about her.

Unless disturbed, Badger shouldn't awaken until late afternoon. He had been drinking more than usual last night. He came to her room several times, and each time, she'd been holding or playing with Jamie. In spite of being a gruff, heartless man, he liked her son, but he had ordered Jamie sent away. Although, to be honest, he'd allowed her to keep him far longer than she'd expected.

Still, she didn't owe Badger anything. He'd made promises just like Mark, but he, too, had lied.

She wouldn't believe there were good men in this world if not for her grandfather. She barely remembered her father, but what memories she did have were good ones. And then there was Gabe. He had been a gambler, but he'd won her sister's heart—and that was no simple task.

Jo shook her head. She never wanted another man to touch her. But Jamie deserved a father. She tightened her knees, urging the slowing horse to move faster. Finding Jamie a father wasn't a topic she wanted to contemplate now.

First, she had to get him to safety.

And to do that, she had to go home.

Chapter 3

Moaning, Badger grabbed his throbbing head and rolled onto his side. He enjoyed drinking as much as any man, but he hated how he felt afterward—hated losing control of his mind and body. The guilt at separating Sapphire and her son was eating at him. She adored that boy, as did all of his ladies, but he'd already indulged her far too long. She would hate him for what he'd done, but he was used to women despising him.

Someone pounded on his door.

"Go away," he yelled, clutching his head.

The door creaked open. Badger flipped over and reached for the gun on his nightstand. With a shaking hand, he aimed it at the door. His eyes focused on Stoney, and he lowered the gun. "What do you want? Can't a man get his rest?"

"Sapphire's gone."

"Gone?" Badger bolted to his feet, reaching out to steady himself on the nightstand. His eyes blurred then slowly refocused. "Did you check out back?"

Stoney nodded. "The kid's gone, too, along with most of his belongings."

Sapphire wouldn't cross him. She wouldn't dare. But she deeply loved that snot-nosed kid.

Badger kicked the leg of the nightstand, rattling his bowl and pitcher. "Is the buggy gone? Maybe she went to deliver the boy to that couple on her own."

Stoney shook his big head. "The buggy's still there, but the horse is gone."

Badger lurched to the doorway. He needed coffee, and lots of it, to sober up. "We gotta go after her and bring her back." He stepped into the hallway. "Sarah! Bring me a pot of coffee—and something to eat."

Stoney cleared his throat, drawing Badger's gaze. He shook his head. "Cain't find her neither."

Badger blinked. "What?"

"She's gone, too."

Grabbing the door frame, Badger shook his head. "She wouldn't leave. She knows I have plans for her."

Stoney rattled out a raspy laugh. "Maybe that's why she's gone."

Badger narrowed his gaze. Stoney was a bigger man, but Badger was younger and quicker—at least when he wasn't drunk. He'd never had call to fight the man, but he was sorely tempted to right now. "You know nothin' about Sarah, so keep your trap shut. Go rent a horse and see if you can pick up their trail.

"I'll find someone to stay here and run the place; then once you find their trail, we'll go after them. I'm not losing two females, especially those two."

Stoney lumbered off, and Badger dropped into his chair. The first time he met Jo Jensen, he was attracted to her, even though she had been hot and dirty at the time. Her man had left her, and she had nowhere to go. He was more than a little happy to help her, and once she got cleaned up, he'd discovered she was a beauty, as he had suspected. Her fiery spirit was something else that drew him to her. He knew back then that his customers would pay extra to spend time with a woman as fine as her, but then he'd discovered she was carrying a child. He should have turned her out then and there instead of supporting a woman who couldn't work for months, but he knew how much his customers would like her, so he bided his time until the kid had been born and Jo had recovered. He hadn't counted on being so attracted to her that he would have trouble sharing her, but that would change—as soon as he got Sapphire back. He owned a popular bordello that made good money, and he was foolish for allowing his own physical desires to overrule good business sense. Sapphire would pay dearly for runnin' off.

When she'd first discovered what he had planned for her, she tried to escape over and over. He rubbed the back of his neck, hating that it had taken several beatings to teach her a lesson. He leaned back in his chair, smiling. Jo had finally accepted her plight and agreed to become Sapphire. But he had still coddled her because he fancied her—but no more.

He didn't like beating her, and he'd never wanted to break her spirit. One side of his mouth cocked up. It looked as if he hadn't. She'd simply been playing along and biding her time. If he hadn't pushed her to get rid of the boy, she'd still be here, but people had been talking. Saying he was getting soft. He had to get rid of that kid or people would think he was weak.

If people learned Jo held a place in his heart, they would use it against him. He cursed. His mistake was letting her keep the baby in the first place, but when she turned those tearful blue eyes on him, he was putty in her hands.

But no more.

He needed to find her and show her who was boss. She'd taken Sarah—and stolen his horse. That was still a hangin' offense in these parts.

After watering the horse, Sarah led him to a patch of grass near where Sapphire tended her son and secured him to a sapling so he could graze. She checked the saddle, anxious to start riding again. Every minute they weren't on the move was a minute that Badger was probably closing in on them. He would come, she was certain.

With the horse tended to, she grabbed a fallen tree branch and walked back the way they'd traveled until she reached a fork in the trail. Using the branch, she blended the horse's tracks into the dirt until there was no sign they had come this way. If anyone was following, they'd have to check both trails, and that would give Jo and her more time to get away.

And she had to get away. Badger was a hard man most times, although he had treated her fairly well since he took her from her dying mother, but she didn't know if he would continue to do so. Though only twelve, she was starting to fill out, becoming a woman. How long before he forced her to move upstairs and earn her keep in that horrible way the other ladies did?

She shuddered at the thought. Many times she had considered slipping away while the others slept, but being so young and half-Cherokee, she knew getting by on her own would be difficult. Many people still looked down on anyone with native blood, especially half-breeds like her. Her mother had told her that many men thought they could have their way with a woman who carried Indian blood. Was that what had happened to her own mother?

As she approached Sapphire, the woman spun around. "Sarah, where have you been? I was afraid you'd gotten lost."

Pausing, Sarah glanced at the horse, her heartbeat racing. She'd made a careless error. She hadn't considered that Sapphire could have ridden off without her. She'd have to be more careful in the future, at least until the woman proved that she would keep her word. Bawdy house women weren't exactly known for being honest. "I hide trail so Badger not find us."

Sapphire smiled. "That's a wonderful idea. I'm so glad you thought of it, but come, we need to be off now that Jamie is satisfied and has a dry diaper."

Her stomach rumbled, but she wouldn't complain. She just wished that she'd been able to collect some food before they left, but going back into the house was too risky.

"Could you tie Jamie on me like you did before?"

She nodded and attended to the task then watered the horse again. Mounting was harder without a stump to climb on, but they managed. Back on the horse, Sarah held lightly to her companion's hips. "It is good you wore calico, Sapphire."

She nodded. "Yes, it will help if we run into others. They wouldn't look too kindly on us if I were dressed in a colorful low-cut satin gown." She glanced over her shoulder. "I think it's best if you call me Jo now."

Sarah wrinkled her nose. "That is man's name."

Sapphire chuckled. "My full name is Joline, but no one calls me that except my sister—when she's mad at me—and sometimes my grandpa. Besides, a man called Joe spells his name J-o-e, but mine is just J-o."

"That almost same thing."

"Yes, it is, I suppose. If you'd rather, you may call me Joline."

Sarah thought it was odd to know the real name of one of the painted ladies. Badger always insisted they have a new one when they first arrived, and he never allowed a woman to keep her old name or let others call her by it. She'd been the only one to keep hers. She supposed having the new one made it easier to pretend you were someone else when living such a life.

"Sarah is a lovely name, but it isn't a Cherokee one. Do you mind if I ask how you came by it?"

Sarah stared at the passing landscape. No one had ever asked her that before. "My mother say my father give me name. Same name his grandmother had."

Jo looked back over her shoulder. "Did you know that Sarah means 'princess'?"

Sarah's gaze shot to Jo's. "That true?"

Jo shrugged as she faced forward again. "I believe so. I once heard a preacher talk about it. The name is in the Bible, and it belonged to the wife of a man named Abraham."

Sarah had never known what her name meant. Her father sure didn't treat her like a princess. In fact, she felt as if he was ashamed of her, always making her stay in her room if the women were awake or anyone else was there. She'd lived mostly alone since Badger had brought her to the bawdy house. Working when the others slept as much as possible and staying in her room with the door locked after sunset, with only Jamie for company whenever Sapphire worked.

If only they could make their escape without getting caught, maybe she would no longer have to live that way. She longed to walk the streets of a town and not have people whispering behind her back because they knew she lived at the bawdy house. She'd finally found a way to leave that dreadful place. Dare she hope for a different life with Jo?

Would Jo keep her word? Or would she dump her somewhere, leaving her completely alone?

With each mile closer to Lara's homestead, Jo's stomach churned more. In the rebelliousness of youth, she'd treated her sister despicably. Still, Lara wouldn't turn out her or Sarah, no matter what her living conditions were. Probably by now, Gabe had built her a decent house—at least Jo hoped that was the case. She refused to live in a soddy again, not after having her own room with a feather bed. She'd rather stay in a barn.

Jo sighed, knowing she really had no choice. She'd have to live wherever Lara did, and she couldn't afford to be picky. If she could find some kind of work, maybe she could save enough money so that she, Jamie, and Sarah could move farther away from Badger. Just thirty-some-odd miles was far too close for her liking. And what was she thinking? How could she work in Guthrie when Badger would be looking for her?

The horse trotted down an incline, and Jo pressed her hand against Jamie's back and held on with her knees.

Oh, why couldn't she have been more like Lara? Less troublesome and stubborn? Why had she thought she knew what was best for herself when she was just sixteen? If she'd been more cautious, she wouldn't have fallen for the likes of Mark Hillborne—but then she wouldn't have Jamie, either. She bent and kissed her son's head.

She'd paid a high price for her son. Life with Mark, except for the first few months, had been difficult. She'd thought him so kind and handsome when they first met, and she'd jumped at the chance to work in his store with him when she first left home.

Jo reined the horse to the right, following the trail. She glanced at the clouds, hoping it wouldn't rain tonight. If only she could go back to the snug house Mark had built for them. If only. . .

She had far too many "if onlys."

She thought about how she'd fallen under Mark's charming spell while he was wooing her, but once he'd gotten what he wanted from her, life with him changed. After a few months, he became verbally and physically abusive. It seemed that nothing she did pleased him. Gone was the charmer, and an ogre took his place. Jamie squirmed, as if sensing her distress at the awful memories.

She gritted her teeth, remembering how hard she had worked in his store and how she'd endured his abuse. And then she learned she was with child—at just seventeen years old. She had hoped the news would make him as happy as it did her, but instead, it had the opposite effect. Mark nearly tore up their new house when she told him. Then she lost the baby and things settled back as they were in the beginning. Until she became pregnant again. Life repeated itself until the third time she told him she was expecting. She blew out a breath at the memory of how he packed her a bag and put her out of his home, then boarded up the store and left town.

A cool gust of wind slapped her in the face, yanking her from her thoughts. She had no idea why so many disturbing memories were assaulting her today. Probably because she had little to do at the moment besides think.

Why had Mark just walked out of her life? Most men would be happy to become a father, but not him. Stunned, ashamed, and humiliated, she had fled Guthrie and headed to Oklahoma City. Desperate and penniless, she easily succumbed to Pete Worley's charm. The handsome man offered to marry her, but instead he took her to his bordello where she discovered he was better known as Badger. If not for Jamie, she never would have endured life there for the past year and a half.

She swiped at a tear running down her cheek. She'd never been a crybaby, but she had been sorely afraid those first months. At least Badger had let her keep the baby, once it became obvious she was carrying, but not until after he nearly beat the child from her body. Thank God he hadn't succeeded.

"Why are you shaking?" Sarah asked.

Jo shrugged. "Just thinking about the mistakes I've made in the past and dreading the thought of having to ask my sister for help."

"You do not think she will help us?"

"I do—I know she will. She's a kindhearted woman, but I dread my family knowing how low my life has fallen."

Sarah was silent for a long moment. "You were married. Yes?"

Jo nodded, although she knew now that her marriage wasn't real. The man Mark had stand in as a minister was not truly a man of the cloth. So in truth, she'd never been married.

"You could tell people you are widow."

Jo considered the girl's suggestion. It might pacify Lara for a time, but she would want to know more. Her sister already knew that Mark had closed his store and might have even heard how he put her out. But she'd left quietly, so it was possible that wasn't common knowledge. Jamie would certainly face less scorn if people didn't know. "I like that idea. I won't mention the bordello if you don't."

"I will not."

Jo doubted that Sarah would speak of that awful place, but she felt the warning was warranted, even though the girl rarely talked. In fact, she'd talked more in the past few hours than she had as long as Jo had known her. Badger didn't like for his ladies to socialize with Sarah, and he kept her away from them as much as possible. She always thought that odd. He'd never done that before, even when a new girl arrived. Sooner or later, Sarah would have become an upstairs lady, so why keep her separate from them? She shook her head. It never made any sense.

"How far to sister's house?"

Jo shrugged. "I'm not sure. We won't make it today. I'm afraid we'll have to go to Guthrie first, because I won't be able to find Lara's place unless I go there from town. And I don't want to take the chance of asking too many people for directions, because if Badger gets this far and happens to talk to them, he'll know we came this way."

"We must find place to camp soon."

"I suppose so." Jamie wriggled in his bindings and fussed. When awake, he didn't like being constrained for so long, but she was afraid to ride with him free. What if he fell off the horse?

Her stomach grumbled. She didn't look forward to the long night with nothing to eat except for two dried biscuits.

A short while later, they forded a shallow creek. Jo held tightly to the saddle horn and gripped with her knees as the horse lurched up the incline on the far side. As soon as they reached level land, she relaxed, but Sarah slid off.

"I find place to camp."

Jo followed as the girl headed to the right and away from the trail they'd been traveling on. Although they'd be safer not camping near the trail, she was more than ready to get off this horse for a long while. Too bad that they couldn't have used the buggy, but she supposed it was bad enough that she'd stolen the horse. In her rush to get away, she hadn't considered that horse stealing was still a hanging offense in some places. Jo swallowed the lump in her throat and rubbed her neck. She had no idea what the law was like in Guthrie or Oklahoma City. If she was caught, would she be sent to Arkansas for trial since Oklahoma was still a territory? She sure would hate to end up in Judge Parker's court. He'd sentenced a woman or two to hang.

A branch smacked her cheek, pulling her from her thoughts. She'd better pay attention or she could cause herself or Jamie to get hurt. She caught up with Sarah, who was clearing a small open area surrounded by trees. The girl tossed a big limb to the side and added some smaller limbs. She dusted off her hands, walked over to the horse, and helped Jo dismount. Jamie squealed, as if he knew he'd soon be free. Sarah unfastened the papoose contraption that held him to Jo's chest, pulled Jamie's quilt loose, and spread it on the ground. Jo held on to him as he was freed of his tight bindings, enjoying his big smile. She placed him on the quilt then glanced at Sarah. "Could you watch him while I. . ." She waved her hand toward the trees.

Sarah nodded, and Jo set off to find a private spot. One thing she hoped Lara had was indoor plumbing, although it probably wasn't likely with them living on a ranch. Jo quickly finished her business and turned to head back. A man's sudden yell made her freeze and hunker down.

Chapter 4

Baron dumped the last of the dried-up produce in a pile out back of the store, ready to be burned. He'd wait for a less windy day before tackling the big stack of refuse he'd cleaned out. Taking a moment from his labors, he turned to face the setting sun. If he stood in just the right spot, he could look down the streets and between buildings and see it. Pinkish-orange clouds dotted the horizon, creating an enchanting scene. Watching sunsets was something he rarely got to do back in St. Louis because the tall buildings usually blocked them.

"Hillborne, is that you?"

Baron turned to face the man who stalked toward him. The anger in the stranger's voice surprised him. He had only arrived a few days ago so he hadn't had time to make enemies—not that he was in the habit of doing so—but this man certainly sounded as if he considered him one. He eyed the tall cowboy with dark hair and piercing black eyes and nodded. "My name is Hillborne. Have we met before?"

The man studied him for a moment then seemed to wilt. "You're not Mark."

Baron shifted, a bit amazed at how quickly the starch had gone out of the man's voice. "I'm his older brother, Baron."

The man walked down the back stairs of the store and toward Baron, his expression now friendly. "My apologies. I have some unfinished business with your brother. I'm Gabriel Coulter, but most folks just call me Gabe."

Baron shook the hand he offered.

Gabe studied him again. "You and your brother look a lot alike. From a distance, I was sure you were Mark."

Baron grinned. "This isn't the first time I've been glad I'm not him."

Gabe's eyes twinkled. "You've got the same sandy hair and blue eyes, but I'd say you're a bit taller and broader."

"I'm often reminded of the fact that my brother and I resemble one another, especially from people who are upset at Mark for one reason or another."

Frowning, Gabe looked back at the store. "He does have a way of charming you and then stabbing you when you're not looking."

The man's words were harsh but nothing he hadn't encountered before. "Mark is a rascal for sure, and I don't mean that in a good way. Might I ask what he did to you?"

Gabe ran his hand over his chin stubble. "It's rather personal, and I hope you'll understand if I don't explain it all, since we've just met."

Baron held up one hand. "No problem at all. I know my brother better than anybody, since I'm the one who seems to get tasked with cleaning up his messes."

A smile tugged at Gabe's mouth. "Having met the man, I can imagine there are quite a few. Can you tell me where he is now?"

Baron shook his head. "He came home to St. Louis for a short while to see the family, but then he was off on another escapade after a few weeks. I believe he's in Texas, but I have no idea what town he's in."

Gabe blew out a loud breath and rubbed the back of his neck. "He didn't happen to have a woman with him last time you saw him, did he?"

Baron couldn't help that his brows lifted. "Um. . .no, he didn't." The last thing Mark would ever bring back to St. Louis was a woman. Abigail would have his head, not to mention a nasty divorce, which would scandalize the family. She had gone on a rampage when she found out Mark was leaving town again. Abigail was beautiful, but she wasn't an easy woman to live with. He certainly knew that since she spent most of her time at the Hillborne estate.

"I suppose it was too good to hope that he might have her with him."

"Is she someone related to you?"

Gabe nodded. "My wife's sister." He waved his hand toward the mercantile. "She worked in the store with him. Jo was only sixteen when she met Mark."

Baron sucked in a quick breath and closed his eyes. No wonder the man was angry.

"To be honest, she looked and acted older—at least, most of the time. Mark wouldn't have known Jo was so young unless she just plain told him. She was a charmer in her own rights."

And Mark loved a challenge, especially in a pretty woman, which Baron was sure this Jo was, in spite of her masculine-sounding name. "I wish I knew something that could help you, but my brother never mentioned her."

Gabe studied the ground. "I don't know what I'm going to tell my wife. Where is Jo now if not with Mark? It was bad enough learning they'd left town suddenly and didn't say good-bye, but I expected Mark to be responsible and keep her with him, since they were married."

Baron's head jerked up. "Married?"

Gabe nodded.

Baron shifted from side to side. He had to tell this man the truth—and Mr. Coulter wouldn't like it.

"What's wrong?" Gabe narrowed his eyes.

"I don't know how to tell you, except straight on. Mark lied to your sister-in-law."

Gabe's tense posture relaxed. "I have no doubts about that."

"No, you don't understand. Mark couldn't have married Jo, because he was already married—has been for five years."

Gabe's eyes widened; then he scowled. "I thought of Mark as a friend, even though I had some reservations about his relationship with Jo, but I never expected he'd do something like that. Has the man no conscience?" He rubbed the back of his neck with one hand. "Wow. I can't tell my wife this news—at least not right now. She's about to have a baby, and I don't know how this information would affect her."

Baron hurt for the man and the pain his brother was still causing this family. "I don't plan to tell anyone, so she won't hear it from me—if I ever have the pleasure of meeting Mrs. Coulter."

Gabe blew out a loud breath. "I appreciate that. I'll have to tell Lara, of course, but I think I'll wait until she's recovered."

Gabe Coulter sounded like a wise man. He wouldn't mind being friends with him, but he doubted the man or his family would want anything to do with him after what Mark had done.

Sweat trickled down Jo's temple as the horse trotted across the familiar land. Yesterday evening, she'd thought for sure she'd never make it this far when she'd heard that cowboy's yell. He'd been rounding up horses. Thankfully, he hadn't seen them or lingered in the area where they had been camped. One more hill and she'd be home—no, not home, but rather at her sister's house. This land that Gabe won in the land run had never been *her* home. But her family was here.

Though asleep, Jamie squirmed, as if sensing her anxiety. Finding out that Pete's—or rather Badger's—big home was actually a brothel instead of his private home as he had told her had been a nightmare, but she felt certain facing Lara scared her more. It wasn't that her sister would be mean and turn her out, but rather, it meant she'd failed at living on her own. Her marriage had failed. She'd failed at everything.

Eating humble pie was a lot more difficult than she'd expected. If only she had enough money to travel west—or south—anywhere but here. As she crested the hill, her mouth dropped open. She'd expected a small cottage, not the big two-story house that met her gaze. Gabe had certainly done well.

"Is this it?" Sarah glanced over her shoulder.

Jo heard the bleat of goats, and if she'd had any doubts, they were gone. Even from this distance, she recognized Mildred, Lara's favorite nanny. "Yes, this is my sister's place."

"It is nice."

Nice was an understatement. On the positive side, Lara should have an extra room available for them to use. With a loud sigh, Jo nudged the horse forward. The closer she got to the house, the louder the goats bleated. Some things never changed.

The door opened, and Lara stepped out, shading her eyes. Jo noticed right away that her sister was close to delivering a baby. Jo hoped the shock of her return didn't send Lara into instant labor.

Jo kept her face down as she approached the house. As soon as she stopped, Sarah slid off the back and helped her down. Steeling herself, she glanced at Sarah then stepped around the horse and faced her sister.

Lara's hands lifted to her mouth and she squealed. "Jo?"

The joy and love in her sister's eyes brought unexpected tears to her own. She nodded and stepped into Lara's open arms.

But their arms weren't long enough to stretch around Jamie and

Lara's big belly. They giggled and turned for a sideways hug. Lara's gaze dropped to Jamie, who was waking up from all the jiggling. She gasped and looked up. "Yours?"

Pride soared through Jo, and she nodded. "My son, Jamie."

"Oh, Jo, he's adorable." Lara's gaze lifted, her smile never wavering; then she stepped toward Sarah. "And who is this?"

Sarah ducked her head, as if half expecting Lara to send her away.

Jo walked over to the girl and wrapped her arm around her shoulders. Sarah stiffened, obviously not used to physical touch, but she didn't move away. "This is my sweet friend Sarah. She goes where I go."

Lara nodded and stepped forward. "Welcome, Sarah. I'm happy to have you stay in our home for as long as you'd like."

Sarah glanced at Jo and then offered Lara a rare smile.

"Are you hungry? Supper is almost ready, and Gabe should be back from town soon."

"We're starving." Jo's stomach rumbled as if agreeing, and she and Lara chuckled.

Lara took the reins of the horse from Sarah and tied him to the hitching post in front of her house. "I'll have Michael take care of your horse." She pivoted, keeping one hand on her stomach. "He will be so excited to see you again."

Jo nibbled her lower lip as Sarah untied Jamie's bindings. "Do you think he'll remember me?"

"Of course he will. You won't believe how much he's grown."

"I'm sure he has. He's almost nine by now, isn't he?"

Lara nodded, smiling proudly. "Let's go inside and talk over a cup of tea. It may be warm for March, but it's still too chilly for my liking to be outside without a cloak. Speaking of cloaks, where's yours?"

Jo glanced at Sarah, uncertain how much to tell her sister. "I'll tell you about that later. Right now, we could really use some food. We haven't had an actual meal for several days." She had to keep things as vague as possible. She wasn't prepared to tell her sister the depths to which she had fallen. For all she knew, Lara might still believe she and Mark were together. She probably thought Jo had been living with him since she'd last seen them, nearly a year and a half ago, before she'd left Guthrie. It would be better for Jamie and her if that's what everyone thought—that she was a married woman in town to visit family. That would place a damper on her finding employment and earning money to get them farther away from Badger, though.

Jamie yawned and looked around, obviously curious about their new surroundings. As they walked into the foyer, Jo touched Lara's arm. Her sister turned with one eyebrow lifted. "I have to know. . . . Is Grandpa. . . ?"

Lara smiled. "He's still with us, although he's not as hearty as he was before you left."

Jo nodded, both relieved and a bit apprehensive. Grandpa had probably been upset that she'd up and left town without letting them know. She was sure they'd all worried about her back then. In the past, she wouldn't have cared, but after living in such a harsh environment, it felt good—far better than she expected—to be with family who loved her.

Stepping back, Jo waved for Sarah to enter. The girl seemed to have withdrawn since their arrival. Perhaps it was just the newness of the place. Or perhaps she was still uncertain whether Jo was serious about keeping her. She smiled, hoping to relieve Sarah's fears. "Come on in. Like Lara said, you're welcome here. These are good people, Sarah. They will love you without expecting anything from you."

Sarah cast her a skeptical glance. What had the girl's life been like that she had such fears?

It couldn't have been much worse than Jo's, and yet, she'd known what it was like to live in a loving family and had thrown it all away. Jo swallowed the lump in her throat. Why had she been so stubborn? So inconsiderate of her family's feelings?

Lara walked into the large parlor, and Jo's heart flip-flopped. Michael and Grandpa sat at a table in front of a window on the side of the house, playing checkers. Michael had certainly grown. He no longer looked like a youngster but a half-grown boy. He looked her way then crinkled his forehead, as if he should know her. She stared at the boy, willing him to remember her. A gasp drew her gaze back to Grandpa. He had aged in the time she'd been gone.

"Jo? Is it really you, Punkin?"

She nodded and stepped toward him, unsure of his response.

He pushed up from his chair and started toward her, one hand shaking in the air as if he were rejoicing at a tent meeting revival. "Glory be! The prodigal finally came home."

Jo hurried forward to keep him from walking so far. Grandpa reached for her and enveloped her and Jamie in a hug. After a long moment, he took a step back and swiped his eyes, making Jo's water.

"And who is this bright-eyed little feller?" Grandpa chucked Jamie on the chin, and her son grinned even though he laid his head on her shoulder as if not quite sure what to make of the man. He'd never been around men much, mainly just the women at the bawdy house.

"This is my son, Jamie." Jo brushed her hand over Jamie's hair as she looked at Michael, whose blue-green eyes were wide open. "Do you remember me, Shorty?"

"You're my aunt Jo, ain't ya?"

She nodded and smiled, a bit disappointed when he didn't rush into her arms like Lara and Grandpa had.

"How come you got a kid?"

Jo felt her cheeks warm. Grandpa chuckled as he dropped hard back into his chair. She glanced at Lara, who shrugged and smirked in a playful manner. "Well, I was married, and a baby sometimes comes along after a couple marries."

"I know." He rolled his eyes. "Ma's going to have one. So, where's your husband?" He glanced past Jo. "Who's she?"

"Michael. Don't pester your aunt with questions," Lara said. "Come and give her a hug."

The boy rose, but he didn't look as if he was quite ready to welcome her back to the family. Jo never expected he'd be the one to hold back his affection. He'd always been so free with his hugs and kisses in the past. Had her leaving hurt him, too?

"It's all right. He doesn't have to until he feels comfortable."

Jamie jabbered and waved at Michael, seeming delighted to see someone more his size. Michael studied him, and a tiny grin quirked up one side of his mouth, but then his gaze shifted behind her again. Sarah! She had almost forgotten about her. Jo turned and found her halfway hiding behind the doorjamb. She held the pillowcase with Jamie's clothes in the hand Jo could see. "Come and meet the others, Sarah."

The boy's eyes widened as he stared at Sarah. "Is she an Injun?"

"Michael. That was rude." Lara reached for her son's shoulder. "You need to apologize, and there's a horse out front that needs to be watered, fed, and then groomed. Please take it to the barn and tend to it."

"Yes, ma'am." He lowered his head and shuffled through the room, stopping in front of Sarah. The girl was only a few inches taller than him. "Sorry. I didn't mean nuthin'. I was just wonderin'."

Jo held her breath as Sarah studied the boy.

After a long moment, she nodded. "I am part Cherokee."

Michael's head popped up. "You really are an Injun?" he said with awe in his voice.

Wariness invaded Sarah's expression and posture.

Michael held out his hand. "It's a pleasure to meet you. Maybe me and you can be friends. I ain't never had an Injun friend before."

"I'm so embarrassed," Lara whispered under her breath. "Michael, go on outside."

"Can she come, too?"

Jo glanced at Sarah, who seemed half-interested. "It's nice of you to ask, Michael, but we haven't had much to eat the past few days. I think it's best if Sarah stays inside for now. Maybe later today or tomorrow you can take her on a tour."

"All right. See ya." He gave Sarah a little wave and headed out the door.

Jamie squawked, as if not wanting him to go.

"I think my son is intrigued with yours. Sarah is the only other child he's ever been around."

"I am not child."

Jo's gaze shot to the girl, whose chin jutted up. She hated that her comment had offended Sarah. "I meant that you're the only small person Jamie has ever known. I suspect that's why he's enamored with my nephew."

Sarah nodded. "I understand."

Lara clapped her hands. "Well, now that we've all met, let's get you two something to eat, and after that, I imagine you'd like to clean up and rest a bit." She started for the kitchen then paused at the bottom of the stairs. "Would you rather I show you to your rooms first?"

"Rooms?"

Lara nodded. "We have two spare bedrooms, so you don't need

to share unless you really want to." Her gaze shifted between Jo's and Sarah's.

"Let's eat first. I'm so hungry I could devour a horse."

Sarah shuddered. "Horse is not good to eat."

Jo blinked. She hadn't expected the girl to take her seriously.

"Well, not to worry, I have a big pot of beef stew on the back of the stove, waiting for Gabe to get home. I'll go ahead and dish you up some and then you can get cleaned up and rested. I'm sure you're exhausted after your travels. How long did you say you were on the trail?"

Jo shifted Jamie to her other arm, fully intending to avoid that last question. "It feels as if every muscle in my body hurts after riding that horse for so long and sleeping on the ground last night."

"So, you've been living close by?" Grandpa asked.

"Um. . .yes." Jo glanced over her shoulder, realizing her mistake. She'd have to be more careful. If word got out that they'd come from Oklahoma City, and Badger made it to this area, someone might add things up and send him her way.

"Please have a seat, and I'll get the food. What can Jamie eat?"

The chairs squeaked as she and Sarah pulled them out. Jo dropped down, more tired than she could ever remember being. Now that they had finally arrived, all the things she'd worried about seemed nonexistent. Although she still had to face Gabe, and he would more than likely be the hardest on her. He was within his right to send them packing after the way she'd treated her sister in the past.

Grandpa sat beside Jo, reaching out a finger to tickle Jamie's belly. Her son smiled and grabbed the finger, lifting it to his mouth. "That boy has teeth," Grandpa said, tugging his hand away.

Jo smiled, and the relief she felt at seeing her grandfather again was overwhelming—and surprising. He'd always been special to her, except those times when she was unhappy with him. It warmed her heart that he was still alive to meet her son.

As Lara lifted the lid off the stew, a delicious aroma filled the room, making both Jo's and Sarah's stomachs grumble. She glanced at the girl and smiled.

Lara set a bowl of steaming stew in front of each of them, and they dug in. Jo savored the delicious flavors and the hot biscuits with melted butter. From the way Sarah was wolfing down her food, Jo guessed she felt the same. Lara always was a good cook.

Before Jo's bowl was empty, she heard the front door open and hard steps approaching the kitchen. Gabe was home.

Chapter 5

Jo tiptoed from the bedroom that she and Sarah were sharing. She glanced back at the girl who had crawled in her bed, flashing a nervous smile. Sarah wasn't comfortable enough in the unfamiliar house to stay in a room alone, even though she was used to doing so at the bordello. Jo wondered if Sarah thought she might sneak out and leave her. She had hardly uttered a word since they arrived and seemed more withdrawn than she'd been on the trail. Perhaps it was just the newness of the house and the people.

She started for the back stairs to make one last trip to the privy, but the murmur of voices pulled her to the stairs that led to the foyer. Pausing where the wall ended and the railing started, she peered down. Gabe and Lara stood just inside the parlor, talking.

She couldn't make out Lara's soft voice, but she caught most of what Gabe said. "Wasn't with Mark. . . Lied to you. . . Don't want. . .hurt again. . . Hillborne in town. . ."

Jo sucked in a sharp breath. Mark was back in Guthrie? Why would he return now—just when she did? What would he do if he learned she was nearby? She crossed her arms to keep them from trembling. When thinking of returning to the area, she'd never once considered that Mark also might have decided to come back. But it made sense if the store was still there and stocked as it had been when he closed it. Perhaps he was only in town to sell it.

The voices had quieted. Her sister and Gabe must have gone to the kitchen. She slunk back the way she came and hurried to the rear stairway and went down to the privy. What should she do now? If she only had herself to think about, she'd get Badger's horse and ride off again, but she had Jamie—and Sarah. Both children needed good food and a roof over their heads, and this was the only place she knew where they could get that.

She would have to steer clear of Mark. She'd nearly lost Jamie once. She couldn't risk Mark finding out about him and deciding he liked the idea of being a father.

Back in her room, she huddled under the covers, shivering. With the threat of Mark in town, she wondered if they shouldn't pack up and leave. But where could they go with no money? How would they survive? She had to find a way to make some money. She'd never been one to sew much and didn't like cooking, but perhaps it was time she learned. Her sister would be more than happy to teach her, and one day, if things went the way she planned, she and the children would have their own place, and she'd need to know how to cook for Jamie and Sarah. She sighed, wishing now that she hadn't been such a tomboy. Fishing or trapping had always held more interest than cooking and cleaning. And besides, she always imagined she'd marry a wealthy man and have servants to do those things for her.

But nothing had gone as planned. She'd been so sure she knew what was best for her life, running away from her family when she was sixteen, albeit almost seventeen. And look where it had gotten her. Jamie was the only good thing to come from all the horrible things she'd endured. She supposed she should give herself some credit for helping Sarah escape the awful future she faced.

"Your sister is nice," Sarah said behind Jo's back.

Flipping over, Jo faced her in the bed they shared. "Yes, Lara has always been nice." Except when she was pushing Jo to do her chores or help more. Still. . .in all fairness, now that she'd been married—sort of—and had become a mother, she'd learned how much was involved in keeping a home and raising a child.

"Why did you leave, then?"

"Well, for one thing, she lived in a dugout at the time."

"What is wrong with dugout?"

"Oh. . .they smell, bugs and snakes fall out of the ceiling and onto you, rain sometimes leaks in—lots of things."

"She has nice house now. Will you stay?"

Jo thought for a moment of all the reasons to say no. "I don't know. Until we get some more money, we can't afford to go anywhere else, but I worry that this isn't far enough away from Badger."

"He will come."

Jo felt the same way. Sooner or later, Badger was sure to find them. The man was tenacious, if nothing else. If it had only been Jo who left, he might not search so hard, but she'd taken Sarah. And she had a feeling he wouldn't give up until he found the girl. Knowing that gave her the answer she needed. She must risk going to town to look for work. It was the only way she knew to get the funds they needed to get away.

Lara wouldn't be happy seeing her leave again, but it seemed Jo's lot in life was to disappoint her sister.

Lara stared at Jo, her arms crossed. "I don't understand why you feel you must get a job."

Jo attempted to stand still in the face of her sister's confusion, but her feet insisted on moving. Lara was always nice, but Jo still felt belittled, even though she knew it wasn't her sister's intent.

"I can't explain it, but just accept the fact that I do."

"You can stay with us for as long as you wish. You won't lack for anything here. Gabe has done well in the ranching business and has even bought out several of our neighbors so that he could have more land. We have the funds to buy whatever you all need."

"Maybe I don't want you providing for me. Have you considered that?" The words came out harsher than she intended.

Lara winced. "I, of all people, understand how hard it is to let others help you. I nearly chased Gabe off because I didn't want his help in the beginning." She glanced down and ran a hand over her swollen belly. "Just think of all I'd have missed if he hadn't been so stubborn and persistent."

Jo thought of all the pain she would have avoided if she had listened to her sister before she ran away from home when she was only sixteen, but still. . . "If you have to know, I fear someone is after us. I need to get Sarah away from Oklahoma and somewhere safe."

Lara's eyes widened. "Who is after her?"

"I can't tell you that."

"Why not? You should describe the man to Gabe so he and the ranch hands can watch for him and make sure he doesn't harm Sarah."

The girl wasn't the one Badger would seek to harm. Jo gritted her teeth, remembering the first beating he gave her. "At least now you understand why I have to find employment."

"As I said before, if it's money you need, we can give it to you, although I'm not ready to lose you again."

Her sister's comment touched a lonely spot deep within Jo, but she wouldn't accept money, even from her sister. "I appreciate your offer, although I'm sure you know I can't take it. I'm going to town, but I'll be back by supper. Do you want me to pick up anything while I'm there?"

Lara sighed. "I suppose you could get some flannel for diapers. I should have more for the new baby, and Jamie could also use some."

"That's a good idea. Washing them every day gets tiring."

"I remember those days when Michael was a baby." Lara smiled. "Why don't you also pick out some fabric for a couple of dresses for Sarah, as well as undergarments?"

"She does need some clothing. There wasn't time—" Jo bit her lip, knowing she'd almost revealed something she didn't want to.

Lara frowned but thankfully didn't interrogate her. "Just put those things on our tab at the mercantile. And don't worry about Jamie or Sarah. I'll see to them. Be careful, and make sure to be home well before dark. Not everyone is nice, although most folks are. And I know you're not too familiar with the area."

"I didn't have any trouble finding my way here. I recognized certain landmarks."

Lara smiled and touched Jo's arm. "I'm glad. It's so good to have you here with us."

"Thank you for being so generous." Her sister had always been kind, but Jo had been blind to her benevolence when they lived together before. Maybe she'd grown up in more than one way.

Three days after her arrival at Lara's, Jo rode into Guthrie on one of Gabe's saddle horses. She'd chosen to leave Badger's horse hidden in the barn. The town was bigger, but the original wooden buildings not painted had grayed and lost that fresh-scented newness. And now there were numerous buildings made from brick. Guthrie had been a brand-new town the first time she saw it, ringing with the swishing of saws and the pounding of hammers and oozing with optimistic people. She'd thought Guthrie was the place of her dreams, but it sure hadn't turned out to be.

Jo recognized many of the stores she'd traded at when she lived here previously and easily found her way to the street that boasted Mark's store. Her heart throbbed. She wiped her sweaty palm across the skirt of the burgundy calico Lara had given her and tugged the borrowed cloak across her chest.

She rounded a corner, and there it was. Hillborne's General Store. The place where her dreams had taken wing and then plummeted back to earth. It didn't look too imposing, but then, it wasn't the store that had wrecked her life. She curled her lip. Mark had done a fine job of that.

The facade needed a fresh coat of paint, as well as the Hillborne sign, but everything else looked pretty much the same. A pair of barrels sat on each side of the doors, inviting folks to come in.

Jo rode past several stores then dismounted and tied the horse to the hitching post. She moseyed down the boardwalk, her heart pounding harder with each step she took. She felt as if she were gambling—with her life. She didn't know what to expect from Mark. He could charm spots off a snake or turn around and poison you with his venom. Why was she even here? She'd never work for him again. Never live with him. She didn't want anything he had to offer. She spun around, bumping into a man.

He raised his brows, muttered, "Pardon," and kept on walking.

Jo sighed. She'd come this far. She needed to know if Mark was back or not. Stepping close to the nearest window, she acted like she was looking at the merchandise displayed there. Her gaze flitted toward where she knew the counter stood and then around the store, but because of the sunlight reflecting off the windows, she couldn't see anyone inside. When a couple passed her, she fell into step and hurried past the next window. She might not be able to see in, but Mark could probably see her. At the door, she drew in a deep breath, tugged down the long brim of the sunbonnet she'd borrowed from Lara, and stepped inside, instantly heading to the back of the store where two other women studied the bolts of fabric. Jo had no intention of buying anything here, but she needed to blend in. To purchase something, she would have to look Mark in the eye, and she couldn't. But she also couldn't sleep until she knew for certain if he was back. And if he was, she and the children would be leaving Lara's very soon.

As she studied the stock of threads, she glanced out the side of her eye and spotted him. She ducked her head so fast she nearly dropped the thread in her quivering hand. The women moved on, so Jo pretended interest in the calicos, listening to the clerk's voice. It sounded like Mark's but different somehow. Perhaps his voice was hoarse from a recent illness?

Her being here at this place was dim-witted. She'd worked here day after day, had chosen Mark over her own family, had fallen in love with him, and then out of love after Mark had abused and treated her miserably. She shouldn't have come, and yet she had to. Her nerves suddenly got the best of her, and she held on to the cabinet to stay upright. She needed to leave before Mark saw her and asked about the baby she'd been pregnant with when he left her.

A man behind her cleared his throat, and Jo spun around, staring straight into Mark's blue eyes. She sucked in a sharp breath then realized the truth. This man wasn't Mark, but he looked enough like him to be his twin. He was taller—broader. But he *was not* Mark. Her stampeding heartbeat slowed.

"Are you all right, ma'am? You look a bit pale."

"Um. . .I'm fine. You just startled me."

"My apologies. Is there something I can help you with?"

Jo backed away. She had to get out of there. This man wasn't the one she was married to, but they were obviously related. And if he knew who she was, he might contact his brother and let him know she was in town. Jo sidestepped toward the ready-made garments hanging on a bar, pretending to be interested. When several feet were between her and the man, Jo spun and dashed out of the store. She didn't care what the man thought. She just had to get away from him.

Baron walked to the doorway and stared out as the strange woman rushed away. When she first glanced up at him, his breath caught in his throat, and he'd been a bit stunned by her beauty. Her delft-blue eyes looked troubled. But why? Had he frightened her that much?

And why had she been slinking around the store? Had she been planning on stealing something? It would certainly explain her odd behavior and her reaction when he addressed her. But she didn't have the look of a beggar in her calico that still had a new sheen.

"Um. . .excuse me. We're ready to check out."

At the timid voice, Baron spun around. The mysterious woman had so mesmerized him that he'd forgotten he still had customers in the store. "I'm sorry, ma'am. I'll have you checked out in a jiffy."

Rarely rattled and never one to overlook a customer, Baron quickly tallied the woman's items and helped her carry them to her wagon, but his mind was still on the pretty blond who had turned his day upside down. Why couldn't he quit thinking about her?

"Wish I had time to lollygag all day."

Baron pushed up from the porch railing he'd unknowingly sat on and smiled. "Isn't that what you do most of the time, Marshal?"

Bob's lips quivered as if he were struggling not to smile. "No. I call it keeping an eye on the town. You never know when there might be a robbery or some drunk causing trouble."

"I had a woman in a short while ago who I thought might be a thief."

Bob leaned against the wall. "Sounds like maybe you changed

your mind about her."

Shrugging, Baron gazed down the street. More than likely, he'd never see the pretty blond again. He rubbed the back of his neck. "She looked suspicious, and when I walked up behind her and asked if I could help her, she nearly fainted."

"She does sound as if she was up to somethin'." Bob rubbed his hand across his bristly jaw. "You might want to keep a close watch if she comes back. What did she look like?"

"Pretty. Blond hair and dark blue eyes. Slender. Probably at least six or seven years younger than me."

Bob cocked one eyebrow. "And just how old are you?"

"Twenty-nine." Baron straightened under the marshal's stare, even though there was a spark of humor in his gaze. Bob was his first friend in Guthrie, although the authority he carried sometimes made Baron edgy. He'd never broken the law and never intended to, but a man had to respect a lawman. "How did you end up in Guthrie?"

Bob shrugged. "I was just one of the eighty-some-odd lawyers who set up shop right after the land run. I never dreamed so many would come to town, but with all the land disputes after the run, we were all needed for a time. Someone got wind that I'd been a lawman in the past and asked me if I'd consider being one again. By then, I was ready to shed my suit and get outside again, so I agreed."

Baron swatted at a fly. "How well did you know my brother when he lived here?"

"Not well. I bought a few things from him and that pretty wife of his." He scowled. "What happened to them? They both up and left town so fast, it was the biggest news around until several drunks shot up the schoolhouse one night."

Baron pursed his lips. How could he tell Bob what he didn't

know? And yet admitting he didn't know what happened to his own brother might seem odd. Still, he believed honesty was always the best route to take. He blew out a loud sigh. "I wish I could tell you, Bob, but the truth is, I don't know."

The marshal lifted his hat at two women who smiled at him and then at Baron. The ladies turned into the store. Baron was grateful for the timely reprieve, because he sure didn't want to talk about Mark's Guthrie bride.

Bob nodded and pushed away from the wall then paused and turned back. "You know. . .that woman you described sounds just like the gal your brother married." He huffed a laugh. "Kinda ironic, ain't it?"

Not waiting for an answer, the marshal moseyed down the street. Baron hurried into the store, pondering Bob's comment. He stepped behind the counter, cleaned off the scissors and twine from his last sale, and set them on a shelf below. The two ladies debated patterns of dishes in one corner, not needing his help.

Those haunted blue eyes stared at him in his mind. If the woman Mark falsely married resembled the one he'd seen today, no wonder his brother had been enamored with her and had gone to such extremes to win her heart. He certainly didn't condone what Mark had done in any way, but he could understand how his brother had been tempted. He had been tempted by a woman, too, on occasion, but his convictions and his faith in God helped him keep from making a mistake he'd sorely regret.

He thought of the pretty blond again. It wasn't likely this Jo that Gabriel Coulter had talked about several days ago was the same woman he'd seen today, since Gabe said they hadn't seen her in a long while. No, the odds were highly against it. But where had Jo gone? He'd sure like to know what happened to her. Had his brother done something nefarious to the poor woman?

Baron walked to the window again, not liking that he thought such awful things about his brother.

He would like to meet today's stranger and talk to her again. Something about her tugged at his heart. Something was bothering her. Maybe God wanted him to pray for her. Yes—that must be why she filled his mind so much.

Chapter 6

Jo reined the horse to a stop in front of Gabe's barn and sat there, staring out across the barren field in the distance. She pushed on Lara's sunbonnet until it fell onto her back as she relished the cool air blowing across her warm head. All the way home she'd berated herself for talking to the store owner. She hadn't gotten his name, but he must be Mark's brother or possibly a cousin. What would she have said if he'd asked her name? Lied to him? She couldn't tell him the truth.

As she dismounted, her pulse sped up at her sudden thought. If the man was Mark's brother, that meant he was also Jamie's uncle. He would likely know where Mark was, not that she cared to see him again, but would he tell Mark that she was back in the area? Jo's hands shook as she led the horse into the barn. If Mark returned, she'd have to leave—maybe she should go now and not risk him finding out about their son.

Gabe stepped out of the tack room carrying a saddle. He set it on an empty stall railing and walked toward her. "How was your trip to town?"

She searched for something common to mention—something other than the Hillborne store. "The town has grown. There are brick buildings now."

Gabe nodded. "That's true. Did you find what you were looking for?"

She handed him the reins and unhooked a bag from the saddle horn and held it up. "Got the flannel and fabric Lara asked for." She forced a smile, knowing that wasn't what he was referring to.

He stared at her for a long moment. "Look, Jo. You're family and always welcome here, but Lara's in a delicate condition right now, and I don't want you upsetting her."

She lifted her chin. "I have no intention of doing that."

"Maybe you don't *intend* to hurt her, but you do. I just hope you've changed. You're a mother now, and that has a way of settling a woman down."

Jo didn't know how to respond. Part of her wanted to smack him for the things he said, while the other part knew they were more than deserved. "I'll try hard not to hurt her."

He nodded. "That's all I'm asking." He led the horse into the stall, and Jo turned to leave. "Did you meet Baron Hillborne?"

Jo swung around, surprised. "You've met him?"

"Yes, and he seems like a levelheaded man. He's a lot different from Mark, although there are many similarities."

Baron. . .what an odd name, but then she remembered that Mark's mother was enamored with European nobility, and he had confessed one night that his real name was Marquis, which he hated. "They do resemble one another."

"So, you met him."

"I admit I was more than a little curious to see the store reopened. I had to know if Mark was there." Because if he was, she'd be gone by tomorrow.

"He's Mark's older brother. Did you tell him who you are?"

Jo's eyes widened, and she hugged the bag of fabric to her chest. "Of course not. We didn't get far enough for introductions. I rushed out of the store so fast that I'm sure he thinks I'm a crazy woman."

Gabe chuckled. "I wondered that a time or two myself."

Jo wanted to be upset, but instead, a smile broke loose. She owed Gabe a wealth of gratitude for how he loved her sister and had provided for their family so well. Who knew where Lara, Michael, and Grandpa would have ended up without his help, especially since her sister failed to get a claim in the land run after her horse took a fall. She knew Lara believed God had sent Gabe to help them—and maybe He had. So why hadn't He sent anyone to rescue Jo?

As she reached the front of the house, she noticed Grandpa sitting in a rocker with his eyes closed. She paused, wondering if she should go around to the kitchen door, when his lashes lifted and he smiled. He straightened, staring directly at her. "I just can't get enough looking at you." He reached for the arm of the rocker next to his and patted it. "Come and sit with an old man."

He'd probably lecture her on her behavior, but she couldn't refuse. She'd missed him while she was gone and had worried that she might never see him again. Years of suffering malaria attacks had left him the shell of the man he was when she and her siblings had first gone to live with him and their grandma. She took the seat next to his, wondering if he had something specific on his mind or if he merely wanted to visit.

"That li'l tyke of yours sure is somethin'. Looks a lot like you."

Jo nodded. Her son did resemble her, but she could see Mark in him, too.

"How'd you come by the girl?"

Jo chose to skip that question. "Do you know where she is?"

"She's sitting with Michael while he and Lara work on his reading and arithmetic. That girl sure has a passion to learn. How come she didn't get no schoolin'?"

"I don't know. She doesn't talk much about her past."

"Where'd you find her?"

Jo sighed and leaned her head back against the chair, setting her package in her lap. She should have known he was like a dog with a bone he wouldn't turn loose of. "She was at the last place I stayed. I felt the owner had something odious in mind for her, so I took her with me when I left."

He shook his head, pursing his lips. "You can't take other folks' children, Jo."

"I'm pretty sure the person who had her wasn't her parent. Her mother is dead, and she's never mentioned her father. I couldn't let anything bad happen to her."

"You're right about that, but it makes me wonder what kind of place you were staying at."

"It doesn't matter. We're no longer there, and we're not going back."

Grandpa rubbed his chin. "I reckon you heard that Hillborne's is open again."

"That's part of the reason I went there today."

"I suspected as much. Was *he* there?"

"Mark? No, and I'm glad."

Grandpa turned her way, a worried expression on his wrinkled brow. "I don't know what happened between you two, Punkin, but it pains me to say that I hope you don't plan to get back together with him. I'm not one to believe in divorce, but a man ought not go off and leave his wife."

Jo forced herself not to react. She couldn't very well divorce a man she'd never officially been married to. If Grandpa knew how Mark had tricked her by having a phony preacher marry them, he'd probably go gunning for him, even if it killed him. "I can assure you, Grandpa, that I never want to see Mark again."

"Gabe says the man at the store is his brother. That means he's related to that boy of yours."

"Gabe and I talked about Baron Hillborne, but I fail to see how his relation to Jamie matters."

Grandpa shrugged. "I'd think you of all people would understand, the way your brother up and left us. Family is important."

Jo straightened, scooting to the edge of the chair, more than ready to be done with this conversation. He didn't say anything about how she had abandoned the family, but she felt sure he was referring to that, too. "What Jack did has no bearing on this situation, and Jamie is no concern of Baron Hillborne's. Mark never talked about him, so I have no idea what sort of man he is."

He clucked his tongue and shook his head. "What kind of man did you marry?"

A lying, deceiving snake. Jo rose. "I need to check on Jamie." She bent down and kissed him. "Don't worry about me, Grandpa. I've been taking care of myself for a long while."

As she stepped through the open door, she thought she heard him mumble, "Far too long."

In the kitchen, she paused in the doorway and took in the homey scene. Sarah sat on Lara's left with Michael on his mother's right side. Eight-year-old Michael was reading a sentence from a simple children's reader. She slipped away, not wanting to disturb them, and went upstairs. In her room, she found Jamie still asleep.

She quietly placed the package on the bed and sat in the rocker, thinking about her encounter with Baron Hillborne. What would he have said if she had introduced herself as Mark's wife? Or his kept woman, which was closer to the truth. Would he demand to see his nephew? Or would he despise Jamie if he learned the truth about her sham marriage?

Baron had kind, concerned eyes, not teasing, flirting ones like Mark. From the first time she met Mark, he'd seemed on a mission to win her heart, although looking back, she didn't think it was her heart he wanted. Jo sighed. She hadn't exactly been difficult prey.

No, she'd wanted to be caught. She had wanted an excuse to get away from Lara. She'd longed to walk down the street on the arm of a handsome man, and she wanted a pretty house, not one with dirt floors and ceilings. And pretty dresses that drew a man's eye.

Her throat tightened. She had gotten all that she wanted, only to learn too late that with those dreams came unimaginable nightmares.

Saturday evening, Jo laid Jamie in the bed and spread his blanket over him. Dressed in a nightgown that had belonged to Lara, Sarah sat in the bed they shared, looking at the first grade reader Michael no longer used. With her brow furrowed, she squinted at the letters as if staring at them long enough would cause them to make sense.

Jo had never cared much for school. She'd much rather be fishing with Grandpa and riding one of the many horses he used to own when he still had his ranch. Those days when her grandmother was still alive were good days, once she and her siblings started to get over the loss of their parents. She'd been so young when they died—only five years old. Then Grandma cut her arm on some barbed wire and, not long after, died from a fever. And then Jack left, and she hadn't seen her brother since then. Though they were never close because of their twelve-year age difference, she had looked up to him. Had Jack gone west and become a cowboy like he had talked of doing? She shook her head, wondering what had caused her to reminisce about those sad days.

Sarah blew out a loud breath and tossed the book to the end of the bed. "I cannot learn your words."

Jo walked over to the bed, smoothed out a wrinkled page, and closed the book. "What you need to learn first is the letters; then you can read the words."

Sarah shook her head. "I not smart like white people."

Jo suspected that the girl was probably half-white because her coloring wasn't as dark a reddish brown as most Indians she'd seen. Her hair was lighter, too—dark brown instead of black. "You are smart. You simply need someone to show you how to sound out your letters. Let me show you an easy word." She thumbed through the pages to the middle of the alphabet. "You see this letter that looks like a fishhook? It's a *J*, and makes a sound like *Juh*."

Sarah repeated the sound and nodded.

Jo flipped a few more pages. "This circle letter is an *O*, and many times when you say it in a word, you'll hear its name. Now, if you put the *J* and the *O* together, they say *Juh-O*." She repeated it a bit quicker each time until she caught the moment Sarah understood.

The girl bolted upright, her black eyes brighter than Jo had seen. "*Juh-O*. It is your name."

Jo smiled. "That's right. You only need a *J* and an *O* to spell my name—at least the name most people call me. Tomorrow, we'll write out those two letters, and I'll show you how to spell some other words."

Sarah smiled and then a yawn broke loose.

"I think it's time you go to sleep."

"What about you?"

"I need to go talk to Lara about something, and then I'll be back up."

Sarah slid under the covers, and Jo set the primer on the bedside table, turned down the lamp, and stepped into the hall. She liked the warm feeling of seeing Sarah catch on and realize that she could learn to read. Maybe one day Jo would teach Jamie his letters. It might be good practice to help Sarah, even though Lara had also agreed to help her.

As she walked downstairs, she dreaded the talk that was to come. Lara wanted her and Sarah to attend Sunday services with Gabe and Grandpa. Lara was too far along in her pregnancy to travel to the nearest schoolhouse where the services were held, but she'd encouraged Jo to go and take Sarah. But Jo didn't want to go.

What if she saw *him* again? What if he asked her name?

She found everyone in the parlor. Grandpa slurped coffee while Lara sat with a steaming cup of tea resting on her stomach. Gabe stood at the mantel staring at a window, although it was too dark to see out. Jo was halfway surprised that he would leave his wife for church with her being only weeks away from birthing Gabe's first child. Though he considered Michael his son, Gabe was not his birth father.

She paused just inside the room and took a deep breath. "Before you say anything, I'm not going to church in the morning. I think I should stay with Lara."

Her sister cocked her head and smiled. "That's very kind of you, but my closest neighbor, Marilyn Eastman, is coming over to sit with me."

Jo's heart sped up. Now what? They didn't understand her situation.

"Perhaps you could stay with me next Sunday, if the baby hasn't arrived by then?"

Crossing her arms, Jo stared at the ceiling. Things were getting too complicated. This was why she never should have come back. She glanced at each of her family members, wishing she could tell them the whole sordid truth, but it would crush Grandpa and Lara. She had to try to get Lara to see reason. "What happens when someone asks my name?"

Lara blinked, her gaze innocent. "Just tell them. Why are you concerned about that?"

"I'm worried about *him*."

"Who?" Lara asked, placing her teacup on the side table.

"She means Baron Hillborne." Gabe shifted to face her, one eyebrow lifted. "Isn't that true?"

Jo nodded. "What if—" She paused and swallowed, hoping to get rid of the tightness in her throat. "You do realize that he is Jamie's uncle. And from what I understand, their family is wealthy. What if he tries to take Jamie away from me?"

Both Lara's and Grandpa's expressions changed to surprise. "What makes you think he'd do something like that?" Grandpa scratched his chin.

Unable to stand still any longer, Jo paced to the front end of the parlor. "Mark told me his family was very wealthy, and if I'm remembering correctly, his parents don't have any grandchildren. If they learned of Jamie, I fear they'd try to. . ." She couldn't voice the words again.

"Jo, please come and sit." Lara's sympathetic tone drew Jo's gaze, and she took a seat on the sofa, next to her sister.

"I understand what you're saying, but I think your fears are unwarranted. Gabe met Baron Hillborne and said he seems to be a levelheaded man."

Jo's gaze shot to Gabe's, her heart thundering. What had he told Baron?

Gabe nodded, not revealing anything.

Lara patted Jo's arm. "I would think the most you could expect from Mr. Hillborne is that he might like to see Jamie and visit him on occasion."

And ask lots of questions she didn't want to answer. "Couldn't I just use a made-up name, and then we could avoid all of that unpleasantness?"

Three heads shook in unison. She should have known her churchgoing family wouldn't make things easy on her. They were all too upstanding to tell a falsehood. "People will ask questions."

"And you'll answer them the best you can." Grandpa eyed her with a no-nonsense look like he had when she was young and didn't want to obey.

"Besides," Lara said, "there are bound to be people who will recognize you from when you and Mark owned the store. You can't avoid them."

"I can if I stay here and don't attend church."

Gabe straightened. "We're a God-fearing family, Jo, and everyone living under our roof is expected to go to Sunday services."

She never should have come here. Maybe she should pack up and leave this place with its rules and regulations. She had enough restrictions back at the bordello.

"It will be good for Sarah, too. She needs to hear about God and His goodness, and she'll be able to meet other girls her age. I think it will help her to settle in."

Jo couldn't imagine Sarah doing things that most twelve-year-old girls would do. She'd seen too much and lived too hard a life, but Jo didn't want to cheat Sarah out of going to church in case it might help her in a way it had never helped Jo.

"We're only going for the service, Jo." Gabe caught her eye. "We don't plan to stay for the meal afterward—and that's where most of the visiting takes place. I want to get back home in case Lara needs us."

Jo sighed, feeling surrounded. There were other reasons for her not to go tomorrow, such as Badger, but she couldn't mention him. She hadn't considered that she'd have to go to church if she came back, but she supposed it was a small price to pay to have food and a home for the children. She'd just have to make sure to avoid Baron Hillborne, if he was there. "All right. We'll go."

Chapter 7

Church bells clanged all over town as Badger rode into Oklahoma City Sunday morning. The timing of the clamor made him feel welcomed, as if it were all done in his honor. He smirked at the thought, in spite of his frustration over not finding any clue of Sapphire and Sarah in the small towns east of Oklahoma City. Maybe there'd be news waiting for him at the house from one of the detectives he hired to find them. And he hoped his business was still intact with him being gone for almost a week. If he didn't rule with an iron fist, the ladies would take advantage and everything would fall apart. That was why it was so important to bring back the runaways and show the others what they could expect if they got any harebrained ideas.

He dismounted at the barn, opened the door, and led his horse inside, his thoughts on Sapphire. He'd been more lenient with her than the others because the feisty blond had touched something deep inside him, but he couldn't be the man she had thought he was when they first met. He hated to injure that beautiful body of hers again, but a beating was the only way these women learned.

He uncinched the saddle, tugged it off, and set it on a saddle block. And what about Sarah? The girl had to have gone willingly. Sapphire couldn't have carried that runt of hers and wrestled Sarah into going along, too. But why would the girl leave? Hadn't he treated her well? Taken her from her dying mother and given her a warm place to live?

As he strode to the house, Badger shook his head. He'd never understand females. Give them a nice house to live in, good food, pretty dresses—and they still weren't happy. He opened the back door and stepped inside, shedding his duster and hat.

Stoney's door jerked open, and the man stepped out looking half-asleep and half-ready for a fight. His posture instantly relaxed. "Oh, it's just you, boss."

"Who else were you expectin'?"

Scrubbing a hand across his face, Stoney shrugged. "Never can tell. Might be another of them hussies trying to sneak off."

Badger straightened. "Has that happened? Who left?"

Stoney swatted his big hand in the air like a bear toying with its prey. "Naw. No one else is gone."

Blowing out a sigh, Badger strode to the kitchen. He needed coffee—and food. He paused and turned back toward Stoney. "Did I get any telegrams? Any word of Sapphire or Sarah?"

Stoney shook his head and yawned.

It might be morning, but Badger would be willing to bet the man had only been asleep for a few hours. "Go on back to bed. I'll holler if I need ya."

Half an hour later, his belly satisfied, Badger sat at his desk, an idea for a newspaper ad spinning through his mind. He glanced down at what he'd written.

Missing wife, son, and half-Indian girl. Suspected to be victims of foul play. Substantial reward. Contact. . .

He leaned back in his chair, tapping a finger on his lips. Was that the best angle to use? Sapphire could easily deny being married to him. And the boy certainly didn't favor him, so there was little chance of proving her wrong, if push came to shove. But then, he really didn't need to do that. He just needed to find her. Once he did, bringing her home wouldn't be hard, not even if he had to knock her out and tie her to the back of a horse. Sarah would come along quiet-like as she had before. With Sapphire subdued, she wouldn't have the gumption to fight him. One thing was for certain, they wouldn't be bringing that boy back with them. If need be, he'd drop the kid off on someone's doorstep.

He stared at the ad then ran his pen across the words. He needed something more emotional. *Grieving father searching for missing family.*

Baron muttered amen to the pastor's prayer as the Sunday morning service came to an end. He found the man's message encouraging and inspiring and felt this would be a church he'd enjoy attending while he remained in Guthrie. He rose and nodded at the man across the aisle and waited until the man's family had exited their bench; then he stepped into the aisle. His gaze instantly landed on a blond woman in the back row who'd turned into the aisle with a darker-skinned girl beside her. Behind them, Gabe Coulter followed. Gabe nodded at Baron then stepped outside with a boy with curly blond hair following close on his heels.

He wanted to push and shove his way out to get a better look at the blond woman, who he felt sure was the mystery woman who'd come to his store, but the aisle was blocked. As he reached the door, he shook the pastor's hand and mumbled, "Good sermon," all the while searching the crowd of people talking in small groups. Others were heading toward their buggies.

He found Gabe talking to Elmer Baxter. A short ways past him, the blond woman stood beside a buggy with her back to him while facing the girl. He pushed through the crowd. "Excuse me. Pardon me."

Baron bypassed Gabe, who still faced away from him, and headed straight for the woman. The girl, who looked to be part Indian, widened her eyes, and the blond turned as he neared them. He noted two things at once—she *was* the same woman—and she held a young child in her arms. Her expression turned frantic, and she looked as if she were searching for a place to hide. Stunned, he pulled to a quick stop. What reason did she have to fear him?

The girl climbed into the buggy's rear seat, and the blond handed her the sleeping child and turned to face him, her expression neutral. He studied her, and except for a fleeting flick of her eyes toward the baby, her fearful expression had surprisingly fled. She offered a soft smile. "So, we meet again."

How had she managed to hide her fear so quickly—or had she mistaken him for someone else at first glance?

He shook off his concerns, just glad to talk to her again. "Yes. It's a pleasure to see you."

She didn't repeat the comment, he noted.

"Did you need something, Mr., uh. . . ?"

"Hillborne. Baron Hillborne." Why would the mention of his name cause her to wince?

"As in Hillborne's General Store."

He nodded, searching for a polite topic of conversation. "Good sermon today."

There it was again—that quick spark of fear or apprehension—and just as fast, it was gone. The woman seemed a master at controlling her emotions, which made him wonder about her background. He grappled for something reasonable to say, wondering why it had been so important to talk with her.

The baby wiggled, fighting the girl, and then let out a screech. The blond spun toward him. Did the baby belong to her? If so, she must be married, and he had no business lingering, much to his disappointment. A sudden thought struck him. Was this Gabe Coulter's wife? He'd only met the man once, so it was possible. But she didn't look old enough to be the mother of the eight- or nine-year-old boy who now leaned against Gabe's side. And hadn't Gabe said she was having a baby soon?

He needed to leave. "Um. . .well. . .I just wanted to say good day." He tipped his hat and stalked away, wishing he'd never approached the woman.

Halfway back to his house it hit him—she'd never said her name. Had that been an oversight or on purpose? Was she always so secretive? He turned, looking back toward the schoolhouse, but could no longer see the buggy. He shook his head, wishing he hadn't made an idiot of himself.

Although he didn't have Mark's charm, he'd never had a problem getting women to talk to him, and the fact that this one wouldn't made him more determined to discover who she was. If it turned out she was married, so be it.

He kicked a rock, sending it skittering down the street. He'd never married because he hadn't found a woman who intrigued him enough to make him want to pursue her—at least he hadn't until he noticed the quiet blond sneaking around his store.

There was something about her that drew him. But he had no idea why—or what he was going to do about it.

Glen Haven, Texas

Jack Jensen closed the church doors, relieved he'd made it through another Sunday service. Preaching to a different group of people each week as he had as a circuit rider was much easier than preaching to the same folks every Sunday. In Glen Haven, he felt like everyone was watching him each day, just waiting for him to make a mistake.

His belly grumbled as he walked down the street toward Comstock's General Store. Some folks objected to Abel opening up on Sunday, but Jack thought it was a nice thing to do. Some people who came to town for church also needed supplies, and it saved them a trip if they could shop after church.

Since Abel was only open about an hour, he should be ready to close up shop and eat Sunday dinner. Dining with his parishioners was one perk he didn't mind. As he reached the door to the store, Jack heard a scuffling sound and a squeal. He rushed inside and halted. A stranger held a knife to Mrs. Parnell's throat. Jack held up one hand, mentally searching for a peaceful way to disarm the man. "I'm one of the local ministers. Glen Haven is a peaceful town, and we don't want any trouble."

"I don't want to hurt nobody, but my kids gotta eat."

Jack studied the knife held against Mrs. Parnell's throat. "Take whatever food you need, and I'll pay for it. Just let the woman go."

Mrs. Parnell whimpered and shook so badly Jack feared she might cut herself by moving too much. Behind the man with the knife, the store owner, Abel Comstock, had slipped from behind the counter and held his rifle trained on the stranger. Jack shook his head.

He tried to calm the frightened woman with his gaze, beseeching her to hold still. "Mrs. Parnell has five children, and they need their ma. Like I said, I'm the parson of the small church down the street, and my word is good. Let her go, and we'll see you get some food."

"You promise, Parson? My little'uns ain't had nothin' to eat in more'n two days. I can't stand their cryin' no more."

"I promise, and you can trust my word. Let the woman go."

The man stared at Jack for a long moment then lowered the

knife. Mrs. Parnell cried out and rushed to Jack's side, wrapping her arms around him and weeping on his chest. He patted her shoulder. "I know you've had a fright, ma'am. Why don't you go outside and sit on the bench while I help this man and his children?"

"Pastor Jack, I was so—"

"I know." He patted her arm. "We'll talk later." He gently set her aside and gave her a nudge toward the door. He wanted her out of the way should the stranger get desperate again.

But when he looked back, the stranger had sheathed his knife and looked defeated. Jack eyed the store owner and indicated with a shake of his head that the man should put the rifle away. Mr. Comstock backed quietly into the storeroom and then reappeared without his weapon.

Jack smiled. "So, what's your name, sir?"

"Ralph Beatty."

"Nice to meet you. Folks call me Pastor Jack." He held out his hand, relieved to have the confrontation over with no one getting hurt.

Mr. Comstock slid back behind his counter. "What can I get for you, Mr. Beatty?"

As if nothing had happened, Mr. Beatty moseyed around the store. "I don't cotton to takin' handouts, but my boys is starvin'. Ain't got no choice. I reckon I should get a five-pound bag of flour for starts. My biscuits ain't too bad."

Jack glanced at Abel, glad the man had backed down and seemed ready to help. Abel plucked a bag from under the counter and started filling it with flour.

Mr. Beatty set several cans of beans on the counter then went back and stared at the sections of smoked meat hanging near the window. "A hunk of ham would be nice. I've gone hunting for several days and ain't had no luck."

Abel set the flour bag on the counter with a thud then strode over and took down a smoked ham shoulder and cut off a sizable chunk. He wrapped it in brown paper, tied it, and then rehung the meat.

Mr. Beatty stood in front of the coffee, eyeing it, then shook his head and walked away.

"How many children do you have, sir?"

"Just two boys. One's ten and the other is four. Had a couple of pretty daughters, but they and their ma died of yella fever last year. Them was sad days. Me and the boys left Louisiana after that to get a fresh start in Texas, but we've fallen on hard times."

"You're not the only one. I have others in my church who are struggling." But none of them had resorted to violence. Jack pursed his lips. The man's children needed food, but it bothered him to reward Mr. Beatty's misguided actions. Still. . .he wasn't the judge. That was up to God. "Abel, will you wrap up a half dozen peppermint sticks for the boys?"

"Yes, sir. I can do that."

Mr. Beatty paused in front of a pair of overalls then moved back to the canned goods and pulled several more cans into his arms, including a tub of lard, then set them on the counter. "I reckon that'll get us by for a while."

Jack's pockets weren't too deep, but he wouldn't have any trouble paying for the small amount of supplies Mr. Beatty had selected. He pushed away from the counter and walked down the coffee aisle and selected a pound of Arbuckle, some cornmeal on the off chance the man caught some fish, and a pound of bacon that Abel had wrapped previously, and added them to the pile.

Mr. Beatty's eyes watered, and he smiled for the first time that day. "That's mighty generous of you, Parson."

Jack shrugged. He'd been hungry plenty of times in those early years, when he first left his family, and no one but the good Lord knew what he'd done to survive.

Abel totaled up the supplies and quoted a surprisingly low cost. Jack looked at him and lifted one eyebrow. Abel's neck reddened, and he shrugged. "I figured it wouldn't hurt for me to offer a discount, all things considered."

Jack nodded his thanks and paid for the items. "You got somethin' to carry all this in?"

Mr. Beatty glanced down and shook his head.

"I've got some burlap bags that should work." Abel went to his storeroom and returned with one; then he filled it three-quarters full and tied it off, leaving enough up top for a handle. "That should work."

Jack walked toward the door with Mr. Beatty. "If you need anything, you can check with me or one of the other churches in town."

"I reckon it's best I move on. I feel awful bad for scarin' that woman. If my wife was still alive, I shudder to think what she'd've said to me."

"Everyone faces troubles now and then, but it's how we deal with it that matters. God loves you, and He can help if you call on Him."

"I reckon I gave up on Him after losing so much I care about."

They stepped outside together, and Jack froze at the same time as Mr. Beatty. A group of more than a dozen men, including Zeb Parnell, faced them with rifles drawn. Glen Haven was too small to boast its own lawman, so the men of the town dealt out justice when needed. Jack stepped in front of Mr. Beatty. "What's goin' on here?"

Brody Johnson, owner of one of the town's two saloons, stepped forward. "We don't allow men to pull knives on our women. Step aside, Parson."

"Look, no one got hurt. I realize Mrs. Parnell was badly frightened, but I don't believe Mr. Beatty had any intent to harm her. He's got two boys and they haven't eaten for days." He noticed sympathetic glances from the women, but the men's faces remained hard.

"Most all of us got young'uns, but we don't go knifing women. That man needs to be locked up until we can get a judge to come to town."

Mr. Beatty paled and backed up. "I cain't. My boys are waitin' for me down by the creek. Who'll take care of them?"

Jack held up his hands. Half of these folks just wanted to feel powerful. They didn't really care about what had happened to Mrs. Parnell or that she'd been set free with no injuries. "Think about this. It's the Lord's day. No one got hurt. I bought Mr. Beatty some food for his children, so why not let him go?"

"Can't do that, Parson. Next thing you know, every man in town will be bullyin' women."

That was a fine comment coming from a saloon owner who also had an upstairs area for ladies of the night. He couldn't imagine any worse treatment of females than that.

Someone shoved Jack in the back, and he stumbled forward. His forehead collided with the porch post. Pain shot through his head and neck. He struggled to focus as he pushed up.

"No!" Mr. Beatty screeched.

A shot rang out. Jack jerked, watching in horror as Mr. Beatty clutched his chest. He dropped the bag of food as a crimson circle spread across his faded shirt. Beatty's stunned gaze connected with Jack's.

Though his head pounded, Jack struggled to rise. Giving up, he crawled to the man's side.

"My boys."

Jack swallowed. He was the last person who should be responsible for young'uns—not after he'd run away from caring for his younger sisters years ago. But he was a different person now.

Mr. Beatty's grip on his arm lessened. "Please. . .find my young'uns."

He nodded. "I'll find them and make sure they are cared for."

"Good. . ." Mr. Beatty's eyes closed and his hand fell to his side.

Jack sat back, numb at the senseless killing.

"Looks like the pastor needs the doc," someone shouted.

A doctor couldn't fix the aching pain in Jack's heart. The two Beatty boys were now orphans—and he'd promised to take care of them.

How could he tell them their pa was dead?

Chapter 8

Jo was halfway home before her heartbeat returned to its normal rhythm. Mark's brother had specifically sought her out after church, but why? He barely talked to her. At least one good thing—she hadn't revealed her name to him.

Jamie fussed and gnawed on the fringe of a shawl Lara had loaned her. He was ready to eat, but she'd been so nervous about going to church, she'd forgotten to put a biscuit in her bag. She jiggled him. "We'll be home soon, little man."

Michael, who sat next to Sarah in the backseat of the buggy, stood and leaned over the front seat. "That's what Ma calls me sometimes."

Jo smiled at him. "That's right. I'd forgotten about that."

"Sit down, son." Gabe peered over his shoulder at the boy then at Jo. "So, what did Baron want?"

"You saw that?"

He nodded, watching the trail up ahead as the horse trotted toward home.

"I don't really know. He introduced himself, then stammered 'nice sermon' and then 'good day' and rushed off."

"You must have shocked him when you told him your name."

"Um. . .I never quite got to that part."

His gaze shot toward her again.

She lifted a hand. "Ask Sarah, if you don't believe me. She heard the whole stunted conversation."

Gabe didn't look over his shoulder and seemed to take her word.

"You can't avoid him forever, you know. Sooner or later he'll find out."

"I suppose you'll tell him?"

He shook his head. "It's not my place. You need to be the one to reveal that information."

"But I don't want to." She hated how she sounded like a spoiled six-year-old.

"I know, but the man has a right to get to know his kin."

"Why? Just because he opened the store again and just happens to be in Guthrie at the same time as Jamie and me?"

Gabe seemed to mull over her valid point. "I'll admit the timing is a bit uncanny. The store has been closed the whole time you were gone, until two weeks ago. It's almost as if God brought you and Baron back at the same time."

"God had nothing to do with my return."

"Don't be so certain, Jo. God's ways are mysterious and far above what we can understand."

Nothing she could say would convince Gabe she was right. He might have been a gambler at one time, but he'd obviously changed. God might have brought Gabe into her sister's life, but when had He ever done anything for her?

The night she escaped the bordello flashed back in her mind. She'd been so desperate that she'd prayed that night—twice.

She glanced up at the sky. Maybe she did believe in God, but she still had never seen Him do anything for her. Maybe God had brought Lara and Gabe together, but what possible reason could there be for her and Baron Hillborne to know one another? She couldn't think of a single positive purpose. No, he was a threat to her. And he could tell Mark where she was. Not that Mark cared, but if he knew he had a son. . .how could he not want to know him?

Mark hadn't cared to have a child in the past, so why should it matter now? He'd even beaten her the first two times she'd been with child, causing her to miscarry. But people changed, and she couldn't take a chance that Mark had. Jo kissed the top of her son's fuzzy head. Jamie was the most important thing in her life, and she wasn't going to lose him.

Feeling a bit guilty for ignoring Sarah after Baron's confrontation, she glanced over her shoulder. "What did you think about the church service?"

A warm glow filled Sarah's black eyes. "It was wonderful, especially the music."

"That Maude Potter sure is a good piano player," Gabe said.

Jo remembered seeing Sarah sitting at the bawdy house piano a time or two, plunking keys. The piano was reserved for entertaining the guests early in the evening while they spent their money on Badger's booze. She shuddered at the memory of what followed after that time.

Badger had forced her to entertain some special clients after she got over Jamie's birth, but more times than not, he wanted her for himself. That's why she feared he'd never let her go. What would he do if he caught her? Kill her or take her back? Beat her, for sure.

At least Jamie would be safe with family if something happened to her. She knew Gabe and Lara would raise him with Michael and their new baby, just as if he were their son. But oh, how she would miss seeing him grow up. She hugged him closer.

"Looks like someone's coming this way and fast." Gabe nudged his chin toward a cloud of dust on the horizon. Soon a rider crested the hill and headed for them in full gallop. As he drew closer the man slowed the horse.

"That's Barney."

Jo gasped. "Maybe Lara's in labor."

Gabe reined in the horses, and the buggy slowed. "How could she start so fast? She was fine when we left, other than mentioning some back pain."

"That's how my labor with Jamie started."

Gabe shot her a quick worried glance and stopped the buggy. Barney rode up to them.

"Your wife. . .uh. . .she sent me for the doctor. The, uh. . .baby's comin'." A bright red blush shot up the cowboy's neck, engulfing his ears and jaw at the mention of the delicate subject. "You'd best get on home, boss. Daniel's taken sick, too."

Gabe nodded, tension lines showing around his lips. "Go on and get the doc."

"Yes, sir." Barney flicked a look at Jo, touched the end of his hat, and then clucked to his horse and trotted off.

"Hold on, y'all." Gabe slapped the reins against the horse's back. "He-yah!"

The buggy bolted forward. Jo held on to the side with one hand and Jamie with the other as the buggy careened down the rutted road as fast as possible. She hoped Lara was all right and that her delivery would go well. She'd never before thought of her sister dying, but it happened to women every day in childbirth. Lara had always seemed so strong that it was hard to imagine something going wrong. The sooner they got home and she could see that her sister was all right, the better she'd feel.

Jack sat on the bench outside the store, still numb over all that had happened. The town doc stooped over Mr. Beatty's body, but Jack knew there was no hope for the man now. Doc Vance stood. "Nothing I can do for that fellow." He turned his gaze on Jack.

"That gash doesn't look too bad, Parson. Did you black out?"

He shook his head, instantly sorry. He got woozy for a bit, but he wasn't going to mention that, not with so many of the townsfolk listening. "No."

Doc tugged Jack's bloody hand away from the gash on his forehead and swabbed it with a white cloth. Jack grimaced as pain shot through his head but refused to cry out, even though it hurt worse than the kick he received while branding cattle a few years back. He glanced down at the scar on the back of his hand, remembering his cowboy days. What he wouldn't give to be back there now and to have avoided today's events.

But God had set him on another path—one on which he still was finding his way.

"Looks like you'll live, Pastor. But I want to get you back to my office before I stitch up this wound."

Jack didn't argue with the man. He was ready to get away from the crowd he was still angry with. How was he supposed to teach these folks about loving God and their neighbors when they were so quick to judge a hungry man and pull a trigger?

He pushed to his feet, wobbling, but regained his balance as he held on to the post he'd banged into.

"Let me pass. Please. I need to get through."

Jack closed his eyes. Not now.

Cora Sommers rushed to Jack's side and gasped. "What in the world happened? Did you get into a fight, Jack?"

He narrowed his eyes. Did she have such little faith in him? "Of course not."

Doc looked around. "This man can't walk on his own, and I need to get him over to my office." He snapped his fingers then pointed at two men. "You and you, help me with the parson."

Jack wanted to argue that he could walk by himself, but he

wasn't sure that was true. At least with a man pulling on each of his arms, Cora had to step back. While they were friends, he didn't want the townsfolk suspecting anything more in their relationship. He'd told her several times that he wasn't sure he'd be staying in Glen Haven very long, and he didn't want her getting her hopes up that he would.

He placed one foot in front of the other, trying to keep from losing his breakfast as the ground swirled. He needed to regain his faculties and then go find those boys. They had no one but him now.

As they stepped inside the doc's office, the man turned to Cora. "You'll have to wait out here, Miss Sommers."

"Are you sure you don't need me to assist?"

"I'm sure," Doc grumbled.

Jack suspected Cora wasn't too happy about that, but she didn't protest and he didn't look at her. Cora liked to have her hand in everything happening in the town. It was one thing he both admired and disliked about her. She was always helpful, but she bordered on being a busybody. The men assisted Jack onto the doc's table then shuffled out. The antiseptic odors in the room threatened to make Jack's belly erupt. He pressed his hand against it.

"I'll need to give you something for the pain, but it'll make you sleep for a while."

"No." Jack gently shook his head. "Just sew it up."

"It'll hurt like heck."

He shrugged and flexed his hand. "It's not the first time I've been injured."

"Have it your way."

Jack focused on Mr. Beatty's boys. He couldn't recall that the man ever stated their names. How was he going to get them to come with him? Chances were, they wouldn't believe him if he told them about their pa. In fact, the youngest one was probably too small to even understand it all. *God, what do I do with two orphans?*

Jack hissed as the needle pierced his skin, burning like fire.

"Won't take long. Just hang in there."

Boys—focus on them. Where could he take them? There wasn't an orphanage nearby, not that he was aware of. Even so, the idea of placing them in a home knotted his belly. Was there a family who might want to take them in?

Most of the married couples in his church had a whole slew of young'uns. And he wanted to find a family who really wanted children to love and care for, not just some extra hands to work their farm or business.

The doc wrapped his head and handed him a bottle with six pills in it. "Take one of these every four or five hours if the pain gets too bad, although I suspect you won't need them."

Jack nodded and paid the man for his services then steeled himself to face Cora. She was looking out the window as he slipped from the back room. Her dark green–striped dress looked pretty with her auburn hair, which was pulled back from her face and hanging in tight coils down her shoulders. The dress's color almost matched her pine-green eyes. She must have sensed him because she turned, and he noticed she was holding his hat.

"Jack!" She rushed to his side. "How are you? Does it hurt badly?"

He shrugged. "I'm all right, so don't worry."

"Let's get you home and off your feet. You need to rest and let that wound heal. I'll bring you some chicken soup later on." She reached out and touched his shirt, which was stained with his blood. "I nearly fainted when I saw your head so bloody."

"I can't go home. There's something I have to do."

Her eyes widened. "You can't be serious. You were just badly injured. You could have died."

He would've rolled his eyes if he wasn't afraid that it would cause more pain to his head. "Cora, it's not the first time I've been hurt and won't be the last. Don't coddle me."

She ducked her head, rolling the brim of his hat. "Someone needs to. You sure don't take care of yourself."

He wasn't sure if she referred to the fact that he only knew how to cook beans and ate them most nights, except for when he was invited to someone's home. Or if it was because he slept outside on hot nights as he'd done so often during his days as a circuit-riding preacher.

She blew out a breath. "You need to go home and rest, Jack."

"I can't. I told you, I have something important to do."

She pursed her lips, drawing his gaze. "And just what is so important?"

He reckoned he'd need her help with the boys when he got them back to town, and he could use another person's opinion. He waved toward a chair. Since the doc's office was empty, he didn't figure the man would care if they talked there.

Cora tucked down her brow but took a seat. Jack took the one next to her, turned to face her, and told her about Mr. Beatty. The closer he got to the end of the tale, the more her eyes widened. Her skin paled so that the small smattering of freckles that spread across the top of her nose and spilled onto her cheeks stood out.

"Those poor children. We've got to find them."

"There's no *we* in this. I'm going alone."

"But what if those boys are scared of you? You're a big man, Jack—and a stranger to them. Don't you think you'd have better luck if I went with you? I think a woman's touch is needed in this situation. And you'll need a buggy anyway to bring the boys back to town."

He hadn't thought about that, although he reckoned he could

borrow a horse from the livery for the boys to ride. But if they had much gear. . .

And maybe a woman's touch wasn't such a bad idea. Though used to doing things himself, he wasn't good with children. He'd pretty much avoided them since riding off and leaving his two kid sisters with their grandpa. He clenched his teeth, preferring not to think of those troubling days. He had more immediate issues.

"I don't know what I'm facing there, but I don't see how it could be dangerous. I guess it would be all right for you to go along."

Cora straightened and beamed; then she hopped to her feet. "I'll go pack some food for the boys while you see to the buggy. Just go around back of the house and hitch Dolly to it." She turned to go then paused. "Are you sure you're feeling up to going?"

"I *have* to go. I feel partly responsible that those boys no longer have a father."

Cora's expression hardened. "I'll not listen to such words, Jack Jensen. You tried to help that man—Abel Comstock stopped by and told me what happened and said he'd keep your sack of food until you could pick it up. It's not your fault some of the men in this town resorted to vigilante justice."

She was right. But he still couldn't forget Mr. Beatty's horrified expression when he realized he'd been shot and was dying. Jack had promised to see to the man's children, and he meant to do so.

The moment Gabe set the brake, he was out of the buggy and running for the house. Luke, his foreman, met him coming out of the kitchen, carrying an empty bucket. Gabe took one look at his friend's pale face and raced upstairs, two steps at a time, to the bedroom he and Lara shared, anxious to see how she was faring.

The flowery curtains Lara had made were pulled back, and light was spilling into the room. One window had been opened, even though the temperature outside was cool. Several lanterns had been lit, and a basin of water sat on the bedside table. Marilyn Eastman stood over the bed, wiping Lara's forehead with a cloth. His wife's eyes were shut, and she looked relaxed. Marilyn glanced at him and smiled. "She's doing fine, so don't worry."

A weight fell off Gabe's shoulders. Lara had told him a little about Michael's birth and that delivering a baby could take a long time. Still, this was the first time he'd been through childbirth, and soon he would see his newborn son or daughter. Something in the pit of his stomach warmed. There was a time he'd never have thought such a thing possible. He wished his ma were still alive to share in the joy of this day.

Marilyn rose, pressing her fist in the small of her back. "I'll take a short break since you're here and can sit with Lara. Just holler if you need me."

Gabe's heart jolted. "How will I know if I do?"

Their neighbor smiled. "Lara will tell you."

Moaning, Lara ran her hand in a wide circle over her bulging belly. "Here comes another one."

"Another what?" Gabe glanced from his wife to Marilyn and back.

"Birthing pain." Lara reached for his hand and tugged him down onto the side of the bed. "Don't worry, dear. It's all per—fect—ly nor—mal," Lara said, her voice deepening. She stammered out the last few words as if her teeth were gritted. Her hand moved faster on her stomach, and she drew up her legs, groaning.

"What can I do to help?"

Even in her pain, Lara chuckled. "Not a thing. . .unless you can get a draft horse and chain. . .and pull this little one from me."

Gabe smiled, and some of the tension left his shoulders. If his wife could joke in the middle of such pain, she must be all right.

Footsteps sounded behind him, and he turned to see Jo and Michael standing in the doorway.

"Is Ma all right?"

Lara blew out a loud breath. "I'm fine, now that that is over with."

"What's over?" Michael crinkled his forehead and looked from Lara to Gabe.

"Never mind, Shorty." Jo gave him a playful shove. "You're about to become a big brother."

Michael had assisted Gabe with the livestock births enough to know what was about to happen. Gabe knew the moment his son fully understood. The boy's face went white, and his blue-green eyes widened. He backed up. "I'm getting something to eat."

Jo chuckled as she watched him leave; then she sobered. "Are things truly all right?"

Lara nodded. "Progressing just like last time, only maybe a bit faster."

"Faster?" Gabe rubbed his hand across his nape, thinking of the times he'd aided a cow that had trouble delivering. But this was different. "You're goin' to wait until the doctor comes, aren't you?"

Lara and Jo both giggled. Lara reached over and cupped Gabe's cheek. "Sweetheart, you know things don't always work that way. Marilyn has delivered several babies, and Jo can help if she wants."

"What about me?" Gabe reached for the cloth Marilyn had left on the side of the bowl and wiped his wife's forehead, half-tempted to wipe his own face, too.

Lara shrugged. "I don't know. Men don't usually watch their young'uns being born. Do you want to?"

Gabe considered what she was asking as he watched tension tighten her pretty features. He'd heard a woman screaming during childbirth once at the hotel where he lived then, and he wasn't sure if he could sit by and watch his wife suffer like that. "I think it might be better if I sit with Michael, in case he gets upset."

"Fine." She squirmed under the intensity of the pain. "Oh, my back hurts. Rub it, Gabe."

He slid off the bed onto his knees and crawled toward the headboard. Lara groaned, arching her back while massaging her belly. She couldn't seem to sit still. He hated seeing her hurting. Gabe pulled out a pillow and reached behind Lara, touching her back. She jerked away.

"No! Don't touch me!"

Gabe yanked his hand away, his gaze shooting to Jo's as she walked toward the bed.

"Don't worry. She doesn't know what she wants right now." Jo stood on the far side of the bed and leaned across it, her hand brushing the hair from her sister's face. "This is why men tend to leave. Women's emotions are like a seesaw—up and down—late in the birthing."

"S–sorry, Gabe."

He rose, bent over the bed, and kissed Lara's head. "Don't worry, darlin'. It's not the first time you've snapped at me."

Her light green eyes shot toward his. He loved those eyes—loved her. "I don't snap."

He smiled. "You just did."

She closed her eyes and tucked in her chin. "I need to push."

"Push! Already?" Jo wrung her hands then faced Gabe. "You'd better get your neighbor. I *had* a baby but I've never delivered someone else's."

Gabe looked at his wife a final time. "I'll be praying—for a son."

Lara shook her head. "Girl."

Smiling, Gabe hurried down the hall. He didn't care what the baby was as long as it was healthy—and had Lara's eyes.

Chapter 9

Jack reached the place where the trail dipped into a wide but shallow creek. He guided the buggy off the trail and pulled back on the reins. After setting the brake, he turned toward Cora. "Mr. Beatty never said exactly where by the creek his kids were."

"I can go one way if you want to go the other."

Jack shook his head. "We don't know what we're facing. That oldest boy might have a rifle. I think it's best if you stay here until I find out."

Cora shot to her feet. "I didn't come clear out here on my day of rest to sit alone in the wagon. I'm going with you."

Sighing, Jack jumped down then helped the stubborn woman to the ground. "Just make sure you stay behind me until I assess the situation."

"All right, Jack."

Praying they'd have no trouble with the boys, he turned left, walking along the trail that paralleled the river. How was he going to tell those kids that their pa was dead?

You've gotta help me here, Lord.

They walked several minutes with Cora fighting the tall grass and shrubs on either side of the faint path. Her breathing became more labored. Why couldn't she have waited at the wagon like most women would have been content to do?

Cora grabbed Jack's arm, stopping him. "Did you hear that? It sounded like a big cat's cry."

He heard it, although he wasn't quite sure what to make of the noise. "Not likely a cougar would venture this close to town. Too many people around." Jack touched his hip, wishing for the first time in a long while that he had his gun, but he put it away when he started pastoring the church in town.

An eerie howl raised the hairs on his arms. "That sounds more like a person than a cat." He grabbed Cora's hand and tugged her along with him. The wail could be that of the younger boy. Had something happened to him—or his brother?

A low-hanging branch slapped his cheek, causing a burning sting. He lifted the branch so Cora's bonnet wouldn't snag on it then proceeded forward, his gaze searching in all directions. He spotted a flash of red near the creek and started toward it.

"Stop wailing, Lee, and hand me a branch."

Jack rushed forward at the frantic tone of the boy's voice. At a bend in the creek, he saw the boy called Lee standing near the bank, facing the water. The boy was far too close for his liking. Jack hurried toward him and lifted him.

The boy stiffened and cried out.

"Shh. . .you're all right. I don't mean to hurt you. Where's your brother?"

"Help! Down here!"

Jack's heart somersaulted. "The boy's in the water!"

He passed Lee to Cora. "You two stand back," he ordered; then he held on to a cottonwood trunk as he slid down the bank. He worked his way along the creek's edge toward the older boy, who had clung to the branch of a downed tree. Most of the creek was shallow, but here in the bend, a small lake had formed from the fast-moving waters of flash floods that often came after a bad thunderstorm.

"My name's Jack, and I'm here to help. My friend is watching your brother."

Relief flashed in the boy's eyes. "I was so afraid L–Lee would f–fall in. He c–cain't swim." His teeth chattered.

"What's your name?"

"Nick."

The temperature wasn't overly cool for early spring—he was only wearing his suit that he preached in—but being in the water was something different. Jack surveyed the scene. Nick held on to the end of the tree, about fifteen feet away from the bank. Jack eyed the trunk. If he stepped out onto it, would it hold his weight? If only he had a rope.

"Can you swim, Nick?"

"A l–little."

There was no way to get the boy without getting wet. "Stay where you are, and I'll come to you."

The boy nodded.

Jack removed his frock coat and vest, laying them across a shrub, and yanked off his boots. He searched the bank and found a four-foot-long branch, grabbed it, and waded into the chilly water. He sucked in a sharp breath. In spite of a week of sunny weather, the water was colder than he'd expected.

He waded out farther, gritting his teeth as the chilly water quickly reached his stomach. Holding on to a branch of the fallen tree, he stretched the shorter limb toward the boy. "Can you grab hold?"

Nick worked his way around the tree toward Jack and stretched out his arm. "No."

Jack's teeth chattered as a light breeze wafted across the water. He took another step, but the ground dropped off. He stretched out, holding the end of the limb. "Try to get it now."

Face white and chin bouncing as he shivered, Nick lunged for the limb. His hand touched it, but then he slipped under the surface.

"Nick!"

The boy's head bobbed up, and he was closer now. He reached up a hand and grabbed hold.

Jack's knees nearly went weak from relief. "Hang on. I'll have you out in a moment."

Slowly, he pulled the lifeline his way, drawing the boy nearer. Finally, he reached out and snagged the child's icy arm and drew him close. "I've got you. You're safe now."

Jack waded toward the bank then lifted the skinny, shivering kid into his arms. "Hold on to my neck until we're back on level ground."

Nick nodded, but the only sound he made was his teeth clacking together. Grabbing a sapling halfway up the bank, Jack hauled himself and the boy up. Doing the same thing again brought him to the top.

Cora's relieved gaze heated his belly. He glanced at Lee, feeling awkward being in Cora's presence with his clothes clinging to him. Nick loosened his chokehold on Jack's neck, and he set him on the ground. The boy rushed to his brother, kneeling down and hugging him.

"You're gettin' me all wet." Lee squirmed.

"We need to get you fellows back to town." As her gaze wandered from Jack's face to his torso, Cora's cheeks turned red.

He spun around and found his boots, tugging them on even though his socks were soggy. It probably would have been smarter to remove them first, but the expression in Cora's gaze flummoxed him. He glanced down, wondering if he had mud or something on his shirt. What had she been looking at?

Glancing at his frock coat and vest, he decided against donning them. It was the only coat he had good enough to wear on Sundays. He held them by the collar and turned around.

"Where's our pa?" Nick asked, his arms clasped around him.

"Do you have any blankets at your camp?" Cora asked, obviously trying to change the subject.

Nick nodded. "It's just over there."

"Let's get them so we can wrap you in them. We need to get you to town so Dr. Vance can look you over."

"We ain't goin' nowhere." Nick's chin shot into the air. "Pa won't know where to find us."

Cora glanced at Jack, her gaze pleading.

He didn't want to broach the topic of their pa now, but he could tell the boy wouldn't budge. "Nick, come here. I need to tell you something."

Jack nudged his chin at Cora in the direction of the boys' camp.

She frowned for a moment; then her gaze lit up. "Lee, will you show me where your camp is? We need those blankets."

The young boy looked at his brother, who nodded.

"All right. It's this'a way."

When the pair disappeared around a curve in the trail, Jack bent down. "I met your pa in town."

Nick's eyes brightened.

Hating to hurt the boy, Jack lowered his gaze to the ground. How much should he tell him about his pa's death?

"What happened? Is he hurt? That why you came out to get us?"

Jack blew out a sigh, shaking his head. "There's no easy way to tell you. Your pa was killed in town."

Nick backed up a step; then his gaze hardened. "I don't believe you."

Jack held out his hands. "I'm the town preacher, son. I have no reason to tell you a falsehood."

"I ain't your son."

Jack's heart ached as he watched the boy struggling with his emotions and confusing thoughts.

"Where is he? I want to see him."

He couldn't blame the boy for that request. He'd felt the same when his own parents died, but with a raging fire, there was no chance of seeing their bodies. If not for him, they might still be alive. He cleared his tight throat and squatted on his toes, ignoring the squish in his boots. "I lost my folks before I was fully grown. I understand what you're feeling."

"No, you don't. Me and Lee ain't got nowhere to go."

"I had two younger sisters to care for." But he didn't. He could only think of his own pain back then.

"What did you do?"

"Well, we were fortunate that we had grandparents to go live with."

"We ain't got none."

"You've got me. I'll make sure to find you a good home with a couple who'll take good care of you."

Nick studied him with watery eyes—eyes that had seen too much for a child his age. "You married to that pretty lady?"

Feeling his ears redden, he shook his head. "No." But he had a feeling she'd like to be.

Nick dropped his head, sniffled, and then wiped his nose with his sleeves. "Lee will be sad."

"It's the nature of things when you lose someone you love, but I'm sure you'll be a big comfort to him."

"I'll try."

Jack stood, surprised that Nick didn't cry over his pa. Maybe he would when he and his brother were alone. "Let's get you two to town, cleaned up, and get a good meal down you."

Nick nodded then looked up. "How am I going to tell Lee about Pa?"

Jack offered a somber smile and held out his hand. "I'll help you."

"Can we stay with you—at least for now?"

Jack's heart clenched. He hadn't thought much further than finding the boys. He wasn't cut out to be a father. He'd abandoned his whole family—and killed his parents. Just being a pastor was really pushing the edge of what he was comfortable with. If God hadn't saved him and changed him from a two-bit rustler and thief and given him a reason to live, he doubted he'd even be alive today. How could he refuse this soggy orphan? "I reckon I've got enough room. You and your brother can stay with me for now."

Holding Jamie, Jo paced the hallway. She hoped to get him down for another nap, but he must have sensed the tension in the house, because he refused to let Sarah hold him, which was a rare occurrence. He fussed and she patted his back, murmuring softly.

Nearly an hour had passed since she left Lara's bedroom. She thought for certain the baby would have arrived by now. Was her sister having trouble?

The pounding of someone rushing up the stairs drew her attention. Sarah appeared first, followed by the doctor. A gush of relief washed through her at seeing the man. Sleepy eyed, Jamie rose up and waved at Sarah, who showed the doctor to the door and then stepped back. Jo hurried to her side so that she could peek in.

The neighbor, Mrs. Eastman, bent over the end of the bed. "I see the head. Go ahead and push when you feel the urge."

"Howdy, Mrs. Coulter. Looks like things are progressing well." The doc turned to Gabe, who had tried to stay away but couldn't. "I need to wash up, and I think it's time for you to step out."

"But—"

The doc raised one hand. "Ever since a husband took a knife to me, thinking I was hurting his wife, I've never let another one in the room during a birthing."

Gabe glanced at Lara, whose sweaty hair stuck to her cheek. "I'm fine, dear. Please make sure Michael is all right."

He nodded and turned toward the door, but Jo could tell he wasn't happy about it. Gabe closed it and stood there a moment, breathing hard as if he'd been helping Lara. His hair was mussed, shoulders drooped. "I never knew birthing babies could be such hard work. It seems much easier when animals do it. Where's Michael?"

Jo shrugged and glanced at Sarah.

"Luke took him to barn."

Gabe rubbed the back of his neck. "I think a walk would do me good."

"Just don't be gone too long. Babies come quick at this point," Jo said.

His hand froze in midair. "You think I should stay?"

"I would imagine the baby will be here within the next five or ten minutes."

"I guess I'll go freshen up a bit and then get a cup of coffee."

"It is hot on stove," Sarah offered then ducked her head. She still wasn't comfortable near Gabe, even though he'd only been kind and courteous to them. "I fix you cup."

"Thank you, Sarah. I would appreciate that. I prefer mine black."

The girl nodded and rushed toward the stairs, as if eager to get away from Gabe, who turned and headed down the hall. He paused at the top of the stairs and turned, looking at her. "I'm glad you're here, Jo. It means a lot to Lara to have you here when the baby is arriving. Thank you for the help you've been."

She nodded, more stunned at his gratitude than she would have been if he'd walked up and slapped her. Thinking back to the rebellious days of her youth and how she hated Lara bossing her around, she probably deserved the latter. Gabe's gratitude created a warm feeling in her chest that took hold and made her want to experience it again.

Jamie grew heavy in her arms, and she glanced down, glad to see he'd finally fallen asleep. As she walked into her room to put him to bed, she thought about the men she'd known. Most of them had been nice to her—even charming—but few were courteous. Baron Hillborne had been considerate and polite, even though she noticed caution in his blue gaze.

She laid Jamie in bed and covered him then walked to the window. Why had Baron sought her out at church? He must have recognized her from when she visited the store, but what could he want? Had he learned her name somehow?

She needed to stay away from the man—and yet a part of her wanted to know more about Mark's brother.

But getting to know him could be dangerous.

A quivering cry broke the quiet, and Jo spun toward the door. Lara's baby had arrived.

Three days after the birth of Elizabeth May Coulter, Jo sat in Lara and Gabe's bedroom, rocking her tiny niece. Lara had smoothed down the baby's fuzzy blond hair with a bit of hair oil, and the baby's long lashes rested against her rounded cheeks. Her pink lips moved in sleep as if she dreamed of nursing. "She's beautiful, you know."

A proud smile graced Lara's lips as she sat on the end of the bed. "Gabe certainly thinks so. I've never seen him so proud." Her smile faltered. "Tom was never this happy over Michael—and he got a son."

"Your first husband was a louse." Jo smiled, helping to soften the words even though they were true."Does Gabe mind that you had a girl?"

Lara shook her head. "No. Not at all. He's just thankful we're both healthy." She huffed out a laugh. "He said the next one could be a boy, but I'm not ready to journey down that path yet."

"I should think not. I'm not ready to consider it, either." Jo ducked her head, realizing how awful that must have sounded since she wasn't married. But Lara didn't know that.

Jamie crawled over to Lara's ankle boots, which lay under her dresser, and tugged one out. He banged it on the wooden floor and grinned, revealing his new front teeth.

"He's such a happy boy." Lara rose slowly and went to rescue her shoes and handed him a rattle she'd taken off the dresser.

Jamie shook it and jabbered when it made a jingling sound; then he stuck the end in his mouth.

Lara reclaimed her spot on the bed and slipped one of her boots on and then tied it. Jo noted that her sister's taste in shoes had changed—or maybe it was simply the fact that she had money to buy a nice pair now. After donning both shoes, Lara stared at the floor for a long while.

When her sister got thoughtful, often a lecture followed. Feeling the sudden need to flee, Jo attempted to rise, but her bulky skirts and the baby in her arms hampered her.

"Do you want me to take Beth?"

"I thought you were calling her Lizzie."

A teasing smile lit her sister's face. "That's what Gabe says, but I prefer Beth."

"This may be one confused little girl." Jo flashed an ornery grin. "I think I'll call her Liza—or Bess—just for the fun of it."

"Don't you dare." Lara glanced at Jamie. "How did you come up with your son's name?"

Jo shrugged. "It was hard. I finally remembered a boy back in grade school that I was sweet on—James 'Jamie' Roberts—and named him that."

"And Mark didn't mind?"

It was the first time her sister had mentioned him. How could she tell her sister that he had been long gone by the time Jamie arrived? "He didn't really care what we named him."

"That's a shame. I thought Gabe and I would never settle on a name for Beth."

Jo chuckled. "It doesn't sound like you have."

Jamie crawled out the bedroom door, and Lara hopped up and went after him. She hauled him back into the room and gave him the rattle again.

"You shouldn't be lifting him."

Her sister shrugged. "I feel fine except for being a little tired from waking up several times a night to feed Beth."

"I remember those days." Days when she was so alone and locked in a bordello, worrying about her future and Jamie's. Life here was so much better, but she couldn't afford to get settled. Badger might find her. She had to make plans for the future, and that included finding a job and making some money—and unfortunately, the only place she could think of to do that was in Guthrie.

"Jo, will you tell me where you were? What happened to Mark? I've been worried sick over you ever since the store closed and you left town."

And there it was—the question she'd been dreading. "All I can say is that I was living in the Oklahoma City area."

"So close?"

The disappointment in her sister's eyes made Jo squirm. Jamie crawled over to her and pulled up, standing beside her chair. He mumbled some baby talk, which Jo assumed meant he wanted her to hold him.

Lara rose and crossed to her. "Let me take Beth. It looks like someone needs you."

She handed the baby to her sister then picked up her son, who felt so heavy compared to the baby. "I think he's ready for some lunch, isn't that right, son?" She tickled his belly, receiving a giggle.

"If you ever want to talk about things, I'm always willing to listen. Sometimes it helps to share and get another person's perspective. I don't care what happened or what you did. You're my sister, and I love you, no matter what."

Jo nodded, warmed more than she cared to admit by Lara's comment. She wasn't fooling her sister by pretending to be distracted by Jamie. Once again, she was running away.

Would there ever come a time when she'd learn to stand her ground and not flee?

Chapter 10

Baron stood with the rest of the congregation at the minister's request. After a short blessing upon the church members, the minister finished his prayer with a hearty, "Amen. I hope to see all y'all next week."

Baron picked up his hat from the seat, placed it on his head, and looked toward the back of the church. Two weeks had passed since Baron last saw Gabe Coulter in church. The Indian girl was with him today but not the pretty blond. Had she been a relative simply visiting the family—or perhaps she was a neighbor?

"Excuse me." He worked his way through the crowd, hoping to catch Gabe before he left for home.

Outside, he scanned the area and found the man talking with someone else. Baron moved in his direction, squeezing past chatting churchgoers until he reached Gabe's side. Gabe glanced his way and nodded then finished talking with Mr. Hemphill, a local business owner. When Mr. Hemphill walked off, Gabe turned to face him and held out his hand. "How are you doing?"

Baron shook it. "Fine. Business is growing."

"I'm glad to hear it. Lara's been making a list, so I reckon I'll be in one of these days."

Baron nodded. "If you need me to, I'm happy to open the store for you after church. I imagine getting to town isn't always easy."

"I appreciate that. We do stay busy, especially with a new baby in the house." Gabe beamed proudly.

"So the rumor is true." His mind scrambled to remember if the blond had been with child. Surely he would have noticed such a thing. "Congratulations."

"Thanks, but what's the frown for?"

Baron rubbed his hand across his jaw, more than a bit embarrassed for what he'd been thinking. "It's just that I saw a blond woman with you two weeks ago, but she didn't look—" He waved his hand in front of his abdomen, feeling his ears burn. "You know."

Gabe looked confused; then his eyes sparked and he laughed. "That's my wife's sister. She's stayin' with us for a while. Lara—my wife—has been too much in the family way to travel as far as church for the past few months. You'll probably get to meet her and our little Lizzie next month."

The relief Baron felt at learning the blond wasn't Gabe's wife was so overwhelming, it took him off guard. He struggled for something to say. "So. . .you have a daughter. That's nice."

"It is, especially since we have a son already." Gabe smiled. "Hey, I've got an idea. Why don't you ride out and join us for Sunday dinner? I can show you my place, and you can meet my wife and daughter."

Pursing his lips, Baron shook his head even though he wanted to agree. If he went, he'd get to see the mysterious blond and learn more about her—find out if she was married. "I'm not sure that's a good idea, not since your wife so recently—you know."

"She won't care. She's doing wonderfully. You'd hardly know she gave birth two weeks ago if we didn't have a new baby."

Shuffling his feet, Baron watched the people walking to their buggies and wagons. Having babies wasn't a normal topic of conversation, especially for two men—one of whom was a bachelor.

The blond boy he'd seen with Gabe rushed up to him. "Pa, c'mon. I'm starvin'."

Gabe struggled with a smile and gave the boy a somewhat stern expression. "Mind your manners, son. Mr. Hillborne and I were talkin'."

The boy's cheeks turned red and he ducked his head. "Sorry. But I'm dyin' to eat, Pa."

Gabe waved toward the buggy where the Indian girl quietly sat. "Go on. I'll be right there." He turned back to Baron. "You comin' or not? I'm about as anxious to get back as Michael is, but for a different reason. It's the first time I've been gone from home since Lizzie arrived."

He shrugged. "I'd love to, if you're sure I won't be in the way."

"I'm sure." Gabe clapped him on the shoulder.

"A home-cooked meal will taste good. I'll need to rent a horse from the livery, though."

"All right. I'll get my buggy and meet you there."

Excitement coursed through Baron as he jogged to the livery. He'd get to spend the afternoon with the mysterious blond, whose name he still didn't know. Lara must have two sisters. One had been married to Mark, but Gabe had said she was gone, and the family didn't know where. The woman in the store had to be the other sister. She certainly was pretty enough to have gained his brother's attention. He blew out a frustrated breath. For all he knew, the woman was married. She did have a child. He was getting excited for no reason.

He paid the fee for the rental horse then led the animal outside and found Gabe waiting.

"Why don't you tie him to the back and ride with us?"

The Indian girl sat in the rear seat with Michael and looked less than thrilled to have him along, but Baron did as his friend asked.

The buggy creaked and leaned to one side as he lugged his big body up and onto the bench.

Gabe clicked to the horse, and they started moving.

They chatted about the store and what his plans were for it; then they talked about Gabe's ranch. Gabe told him how he met his wife, even the part about killing her husband in a dark alley when the man tried to rob him.

Baron was a bit stunned at Gabe's tale of being a gambler and killing someone. God certainly had changed the man. Maybe there was still hope for Mark to change his ways, although he'd be mighty surprised if that ever happened. He knew God could change Mark, but he had trouble envisioning his brother yielding to God's guiding hand.

They crested a hill, and spread out before them was a better than average two-story house, a big barn, and several other small buildings. He let out a long whistle through his teeth. "This is your place?"

"Yep. Won the land in the rush of '89. It wasn't nothing but virgin prairie then."

"You sure have proved it up well."

Gabe nodded. "I also bought out two of my neighbors' claims, so we own close to a square mile of property."

No wonder he was doing so well. Baron suspected Gabe must have had some money stashed before the land run in order to have built such a nice home. Many farmers in the area were still struggling to make a go of things. Gabe had been smart to take up ranching instead of trying to farm the hot, dry land. Everyone needed horses.

As they pulled up in front of the house, Baron realized two things: the girl in back hadn't said a single word on the long trip to the house—and he still didn't know the name of Gabe's sister-in-law.

Jamie sat in a high chair and banged on the table with a spoon as Jo mashed the potatoes. Gabe and the children would be home from church anytime, and Lara wanted to have a hot meal ready for them. Beth had other ideas, so Lara was upstairs feeding her. Jo was left with the overwhelming task of not burning their Sunday dinner. And she needed to check on Grandpa, who had taken to his bed with another bout of malaria.

Sweat trickled down her temple, and she stepped back from the stove to wipe it. Her apron looked as if she'd worn it all week instead of to prepare one meal. She added a pinch of salt to the potatoes and started mashing again. She eyed the fancy stove with its high shelf and double compartments for baking as well as a large reservoir that Lara had called a water jacket. The kitchen had never been her domain, not even at the bordello. How had Lara made meals when they'd lived at the soddy in Caldwell where she had cooked over an open fire?

Cooking definitely wasn't her favorite task, but she was a mother now and needed to learn so that she could prepare meals for Jamie and Sarah. At least Sarah knew how to make basic meals, since she'd assisted the cook.

Jamie screeched at the same time the water on the black-eyed peas boiled over. Jo jumped, dropping the masher into the pot. She grabbed the corner of her apron to protect her hand and moved the peas to a back burner. A quick glance at the clock that sat on a shelf told her it was time to remove the ham from the oven.

The spoon Jamie had been playing with sailed through the air, hit a chair, and clattered onto the floor. He squealed. Jo carried a plate of sliced bread to the table, tore off a corner of one piece, and gave it to him. He smiled, slapping his empty hand against the table as he shoved the treat into his mouth. She watched him for a moment as he enjoyed the bread. Her son did love to eat.

She was hungry, too. *Oh! The ham.* She rushed to the oven, yanked open the door, and searched for a towel. Fragrant scents wafted through the kitchen, making her stomach gurgle. She hoisted the heavy pan out and set it on top of the stove then closed the oven. Lara had prepared and seasoned the ham, but Jo still felt a sense of accomplishment. After removing the masher and placing a lid on the potatoes to keep them from cooling, she glanced around to see what else needed to be done. Lara had suggested redeye gravy would taste good with the meal, but she had no idea how to fix that.

Footsteps sounded on the porch, signaling the family had arrived home—just in time. Jamie squealed, excited the others were back. Sweat trickled down Jo's bodice, and she turned away from the door to scratch it. She probably should go ahead and slice the meat, but she'd wait until she knew how much longer Lara would be.

"I built the place with the help of my ranch hands and another crew I hired."

"It's incredibly nice and well built."

Jo spun at a man's unfamiliar voice. Gabe brought home company? Smoothing some sweaty wisps of hair, she glanced down, horrified at how she looked. Three colors of stains marred her apron.

Michael hurried into the kitchen and went straight to the pail reserved for washing. "Smells great, Aunt Jo! I'm starved."

"When are you not? Who's with your pa?" She reached for the ties and pulled, just as Gabe—she gasped—and Baron Hillborne ambled into the room. Jo stared at the man, then at Jamie. There was no way to snatch up her son and get him out of the room. Mr. Hillborne had already seen him. She had a feeling this day would come, but she hadn't expected it so soon. She could only hope that the kindness she'd seen at the store in Baron Hillborne's eyes meant he was a different kind of man than his brother.

"I believe you two have met." Gabe's expression bordered on a smirk. "Baron Hillborne, this is my sister-in-law, Joline. . .uh. . ." His gaze shot to hers as he obviously struggled with her last name.

"Joline is fine." She narrowed her gaze at him. Had he deliberately set her up so that she had to talk with Mark's brother?

"I'm. . .uh. . .gonna run upstairs and check on Lara and the baby. Have a seat, Baron. I'll be right back." Gabe shot out of the room as if she were chasing him with a long-bladed knife, as she was sorely tempted to do.

Baron stood just inside the kitchen, looking quite unsure of himself. Jo grabbed another set of silverware and a napkin and set a place next to Michael's. "You're welcome to sit here."

"Thank you, but I believe I'll remain standing until the rest of the family arrives."

Jo nodded and glanced at Michael. "Where's Sarah?"

The boy shrugged and snagged a slice of bread, quickly buttering it. "She ran upstairs as soon as we got home."

Jo was certain the poor girl must have felt terribly uncomfortable on the long ride home with three males in the buggy and no other women. She glanced at Baron, wishing he looked less like his brother. The similarities made it difficult for her to relax around him. "I hope you'll excuse me while I get the food dished up."

He glanced past her to the stove, his forehead crinkled as if he were wrestling with a thought. "Is there something I can do to help?"

"You gotta wash up first," Michael offered. "Ma don't let no one help in the kitchen 'less they wash first." He pointed to the bucket that sat on a small table near the kitchen door. "Over there."

Mortified at her nephew's command, Jo wished a hole would open up and swallow her and Jamie.

As if he didn't mind being ordered around by a child, Baron

crossed the room and washed his hands. Jo busied herself by dishing up the potatoes, but when she turned to take them to the table, Baron was right there. She stiffened and looked up, not sure what she expected.

He smiled and glanced at the bowl. "May I?"

"Um. . .sure." She handed it to him, making sure their fingers didn't touch. She turned back to the stove, sucked in a deep breath to calm her shakiness, and removed the lid from the ham.

"That smells good."

"It sure does. Hurry, Aunt Jo. My belly's rubbin' against my backbone." Michael hopped up from the table and scurried over to the stove and looked in the pot.

"Shorty, could you please tell everyone I'm dishing up the meal?"

"Sure!" The boy raced from the room and thudded up the stairs, with Jamie fussing that he was gone.

Jo realized too late that she was now alone with Baron Hillborne. She glanced at him, and he was staring at Jamie. She didn't want to tell him about her relation to his brother—about his relationship to Jamie—but there was no getting around it now. She would have words with Gabe later.

Baron glanced at her, eyebrows furrowed. "Could I ask you something?"

Heart jolting, Jo nodded as she dished up the black-eyed peas. She spilled some juice on the counter and tightened her grip on the quivering spoon. Right now, she wished she'd never come to her sister's house.

"Gabe told me that his wife's sister was married to my brother, Mark, and he mentioned her name being Jo." He rubbed his hand over his jaw. "He introduced you as Joline. Am I safe in assuming you go by Jo at times?"

"Yes," she whispered.

"You were married to Mark?"

"Yes."

His gaze shot to Jamie, and Jo knew he'd made the connection. "This is probably encroaching the bounds of polite conversation, but I have to know—is that boy Mark's son?"

Blowing out a loud sigh, Jo closed her eyes and nodded. Whatever came from his knowing would come, and she was helpless to stop it.

Baron gasped, and when she looked at him, she saw his blue eyes had filled with wonder. "That means I'm an uncle."

"What's his name?"

"It's James, but I call him Jamie."

Unfathomable joy billowed through Baron as he stared at the child—his nephew. The boy looked a lot like Jo, but he thought he could see Mark in him, too. As far as he knew, Mark wasn't aware he had a son—and maybe that was for the best. Abigail would go on the warpath and run the family name into ruin if she learned about Jamie. He wasn't sure how Mark would react.

Wouldn't his mother be delighted to hear the news? Baron frowned. No, she wouldn't, not when she learned the child was illegitimate. There were numerous people who would be happy to bring down the Hillborne family if they learned of the boy. And yet, Jamie was their blood relative. As thrilled as he was to be related to the boy, he needed to tread carefully. Would Jo expect him to help her? Not that he wasn't willing. . .

"Why are you scowling?" Jo crossed her arms, glaring at him.

Footsteps sounded on the stairs as Baron rubbed the back of his neck. "We need to talk, but not now."

"I have nothing to talk to you about."

"Maybe not, but there are things I need to tell you." He

couldn't blame her for being apprehensive, not after she'd lived with his brother. Who knew what Mark had done to the woman? He remembered a pretty brunette who'd come to the estate, badly beaten. She claimed Mark had done the deed and threatened to run down the family name if he didn't help her. At his father's orders, he'd paid for the woman to see a doctor and then gave her enough money to leave town and get a fresh start somewhere else.

He glanced at Jo, whose back was to him at the moment. Even with her hair kinking around her red face and wearing that stained apron, he could see what had attracted his brother to her. It wasn't just her pretty face, but that fiery spark in her gaze. Hadn't Gabe said she'd only been sixteen when his brother first charmed her? That had to have been just before the land run in '89. That meant she was only about twenty now. Gabe was right when he said she looked mature for her age. He would have guessed she was closer to twenty-three, but she wasn't. That meant she was nine years younger than he, not that it mattered.

Gabe walked in, beaming, with a lovely woman on his arm, who somewhat resembled Jo, except she had darker blond hair and eyes less vivid than Jo's blue ones. Both women were the same height, about five foot five, he guessed.

"This is my wife, Lara." Gabe's wide smile sent a shaft of unexpected jealousy coursing through Baron.

She smiled at him. "Welcome to our home, Mr. Hillborne." Her gaze lingered on his for only a moment before she shot a worried glance to her sister, who was slicing the meat.

"Thank you for having me, Mrs. Coulter. You have a most impressive home." He hoped to lighten the tension and assure them he was no threat to their family. Why had Gabe invited him? Baron could imagine how awkward his presence must be for them, especially Jo. Her odd behavior at the store now made sense. She must have been scouting him out—or perhaps she'd come to see if Mark had returned. Did she still pine after him?

He certainly hoped not, because she was bound to be distraught when he told her that her marriage to his brother was not official since Mark was already married. Or had Gabe told her? If he hadn't, Baron hoped she didn't fall apart, weeping and wailing. He'd never been good with women's emotions. He often dealt with Abigail's when she was upset with his brother, and he never knew how to console her. Women always gravitated to Mark, and Baron didn't want a woman who'd rather be with his brother. The idea that Jo had turned his stomach.

"Where's Sarah?" Jo asked as she set the meat platter on the table.

Her sister smiled. "She offered to sit with Beth while we ate. I'll take her a plate when I go upstairs after dinner."

Jo nodded and took her seat next to her son on the far side of the table. Baron had a hard time keeping his eyes off them, especially Jamie.

He sat down when the rest of the family did. It was hard for him to be upset with Jo for her relationship with Mark when he just learned he had a nephew. Smiling, he closed his eyes while Gabe said the prayer for the meal. Baron thanked God for the unexpected blessing He'd bestowed on him today. At least Jamie was an unexpected gift. He wasn't so certain about the child's mother.

Chapter 11

Jack stood in the front part of the doctor's office while Nick helped Lee get dressed in the new clothes that Cora had purchased at the store. He glanced at her, glad he'd let her come along and help. She'd done a wonderful job of calming little Lee.

Dr. Vance stepped out from behind the curtain separating the waiting area from his examination room and blew out a loud breath. He walked over to where Jack stood by the front window, shaking his head. "Those boys are in sad condition," he said, keeping his voice low. "They must not have had much to eat lately, and they're covered in mosquito bites and scratches."

"I aim to fix the food problem." Jack shifted his feet, wondering if the boys would be happy with his passable cooking skills.

"They should only have some broth or chicken soup today. If that doesn't upset their stomachs, then you can feed them eggs or porridge for breakfast, but no bacon or anything else greasy. If they hold that down, then whatever you have to feed them should be fine. Be sure to send word if they have any problems."

Jack nodded. "All right, Doc. Thanks for letting the boys have a bath here. We sure hated putting them in new clothes with all that grime on them."

Doc shrugged. "No thanks needed. It was necessary. I couldn't very well examine them in that state, either."

Cora stepped forward. "So, other than what you mentioned and suffering from a lack of good food, you didn't find anything else wrong with them?"

"The bigger boy had some fresh scratches that he probably got when he fell in the creek, but unless he comes down with a cold, he should be fine. The younger boy had a few old scratches on his hands and arms but nothing I wouldn't expect from a child his age."

Cora smiled, creating odd tingles in Jack's belly. Then again, he'd missed lunch, so maybe that was the cause.

"You let me know if either boy takes sick."

"Will do, Doc."

"I'd best make sure they aren't getting into anything back there. You know how children can be." Doc turned and slipped behind the curtain.

"What are we going to do with the boys, Jack?"

"I promised them they could stay with me, so I reckon they will."

"But for how long? And are you sure the church leaders will even allow that since you live in the parsonage?"

"How could they refuse two orphans?"

Cora glanced toward the curtain and lifted a finger to her lips. "They can, and they might, so you should be prepared."

He leaned toward her. "I already decided that I won't put those boys in an orphanage."

"Not all of them are bad places."

He straightened. "I know that, but the officials would more than likely separate them because of their age difference—and they've lost enough already. They need each other." He thought back to how he and his sisters had been sent to different homes right after the fire that killed his parents. No one wanted to take in three youngsters at once, but at the same time, no one stopped to consider that maybe they needed to be together. The man who took him only wanted him for the work he could do. No matter that he was grieving the loss of his parents while suffering the overwhelming guilt of knowing he was responsible for their deaths. He'd wanted to protect and care for his little sisters, but well-meaning churchgoers had said it wasn't proper for a youth his age. And besides, they had no home to live in. Jo wailed when Mr. and Mrs. Olander had taken her and Lara away. He gritted his teeth. He could still hear her screams. Thank the good Lord his grandparents had come for them a week later.

"Did you hear me, Jack?" Cora tapped her foot. "I said we'll just have to pray for God to send a loving couple who will take both boys and raise them to be their children."

Jack gave her a quick nod. The curtain parted, and Doc stepped back into the room. He held open the white linen so Nick could pass through with Lee behind him. The younger boy held tight to his brother's hand. Jack was amazed at the difference in them with the dirt scrubbed off and new clothes on their backs. Both boys' hair was still damp and combed to one side.

"Are you two ready to get something to eat?" Cora walked forward. "My mother made chicken and rice soup for Sunday dinner, and I think it's just the thing you youngsters need."

"That sounds wonderful, ma'am." Nick glanced at his brother and smiled.

Jack took Cora's cue, glad he didn't have to go home and scramble to prepare a meal. "That sounds delicious. I never had lunch myself."

Cora shot him a surprised look. "I'm sure there's enough for you, too, Pastor."

He smiled. "I'm right glad to hear that."

She turned to the doctor. "Have you eaten? I'm sure Mama has plenty."

Doc held up one hand. "Thank you kindly, Miss Sommers, but I did eat—at the café."

"Thanks for checking over the boys." Jack held out his hand, and Doc shook it.

An hour later, with their bellies sated and having said his farewell to Cora and her parents, Jack bent over a checkerboard in his parlor, playing a game with Nick. The boy was good and had already beaten him once, partly because Lee distracted him when he got into the kitchen cupboard.

He rubbed the back of his neck. What had he gotten himself into?

He knew nothing of entertaining children. At least he didn't have to figure out where they could sleep since the house had an extra bedroom. Evidently, pastors often came with families.

Jack studied the board then reached to make his move when someone knocked on the door. "Hang on, pardner. I'll be right back."

He rose and ambled across the room, but when he saw three men from the church board, his hackles rose. They didn't look to be in a benevolent mood. He stepped outside, nodding at the men, and closed the door. "What can I do for you gentlemen?"

Ted Sizemore glanced at the other two then cleared his throat. "Is it true you're housing the children of the man who drew a knife on Mrs. Parnell?"

"It is." Jack crossed his arms over his chest.

Burt Gladstone crossed his arms. "Well, Zeb Parnell came to us, madder than a rooster whose henhouse had been upset by a thievin' weasel."

Jack suspected the weasel he referred to was Mr. Beatty.

"He said it ain't right that them boys stay here when the church owns this house and pays your salary." Burt shifted his feet, as if not completely comfortable relaying the news.

Jack narrowed his gaze, annoyed at the men's lack of compassion.

"The Beatty boys are children—young ones at that. Just what does Mr. Parnell think they will do?"

"It ain't so much that," Bill Arnold offered. "It's what their pa did."

"So, the boys are guilty because their father did the wrong thing, when all he wanted was to get food for them?"

All three men stared at their feet.

"They are not guilty of any crime," Jack said, taking advantage of the silence. "And you should see them. Those poor orphans are as scrawny as fence wire."

Mr. Sizemore looked up. "Zeb said he'd quit giving to the church if you don't get rid of them."

"Fine! Let him, because they are staying until I find them a proper home."

"No, they're not." Mr. Sizemore lifted his chin. "The church board has decided. You have two weeks to find a place for them or else."

"Or else what?"

Mr. Sizemore glanced at the others, who nodded. "Or we find us a new preacher."

Carrying Jamie, Jo reluctantly led Baron into the parlor while Gabe and Michael helped Lara clean up. Right after the meal, she had escaped to check on Grandpa, but he was sleeping. She blew out a sigh, dreading her talk with Baron Hillborne. What could she say? That his brother was a charming snake who told her what she wanted to hear at the time she had been most vulnerable?

She took a seat on the sofa and placed Jamie next to her. Baron sat in a chair at a right angle from the sofa, his eyes on her son. What would he expect of her? Would he want to be part of Jamie's life? Would he *demand* to be part of Jamie's life?

Baron looked at her and smiled. "I have to say this is quite a pleasant surprise. When I got up this morning, it was just a regular day. . .and now. . .I'm an uncle. I can't seem to quit smiling."

At least his smile was different from Mark's. He only had one dimple where Mark had two.

Jo's hand shook. Why was she afraid of him? What could he do?

Dumb question. She of all people knew what men were capable of.

"Do you think Jamie would let me hold him?"

She wished she could say no, but Jamie had always been a congenial child. The ladies at the bordello had passed him around so much it was a miracle he knew who his mama was. She hadn't expected him to be so friendly with Gabe, but he had been. With a sigh, she nodded. "Probably."

Grinning, Baron scooted to the end of his chair. "Hey, little guy. You want to sit with me?"

"You'll have to pick him up. I doubt he'll just come to you."

Baron rose, hovering over her. Then he surprised her and bent to his knees. From his pocket, he pulled a leather strap with several keys attached and jingled them in front of Jamie. The boy's gaze lifted, and he babbled something then reached for the keys, taking them from Baron. He shook them, making them clink together, then lifted his gaze to Jo, grinning.

Baron reached out and patted Jamie's knee. "That makes a fun noise, doesn't it?"

Jamie's excited chatter warmed Jo's heart, but having Baron so close did little to soothe her taut nerves.

Baron clapped his hands together. "You want to come to me, huh, Jamie?"

The boy shook the keys again, and they flew from his hand, landing on the floor. Baron reached down and picked them up, jiggling them. Jamie squealed and lunged for them. Jo started to grab him, but Baron beat her to it and picked up her son. He stood, shaking the keys, and Jamie claimed them.

"He closely resembles you, but I see Mark in him, too." His brow furrowed and his gaze shot to hers. "He doesn't know about Jamie, does he?"

Jo stood. "No, and I hope you won't tell him."

"Why not? He has a right to know, don't you think?"

Evidently, he thought her marriage was a legitimate one. Jo lifted her chin. "No, I don't. I told him I was carrying his child, and do you know what your brother did?"

Baron shook his head, his interest obvious.

"He boarded up the store and left town—without me."

His mouth dropped open for a moment, and his eyes widened. Then he pursed his lips and blew a loud breath from his nose. "I'm so sorry. I wish I'd known. I would have helped you."

Jo hadn't expected his sympathy. If anything, she thought he'd side with Mark. "It wasn't your responsibility."

He ran his hand over Jamie's head. Her son had leaned back against him, his eyes drooping, the keys lying in one hand in his lap.

Baron looked toward the window. "I've been cleaning up Mark's messes all of my life."

Jo stiffened. "Jamie is not one of your brother's messes. He's my *son*."

His apologetic gaze shot back to hers. "I was thinking of the store, not Jamie. Please forgive me for not making that clear."

Jo felt as if her emotions were churning at the speed of a runaway train. "All right. I understand."

"What happened after Mark left? Did you return here?"

Jo tensed. This was the part she didn't want to talk about. "Um. . .no, I didn't."

"But where did you go?"

"Oklahoma City." Jo winced. Maybe she shouldn't have told him the truth in case Badger or one of his cronies came to the store, asking about her. Jo reached for the hand Baron held across Jamie's stomach, touching the back of it. "Please, you can't tell anyone we're here—if someone should ask. Sarah's life could be in danger if you do." Not to mention her own.

His eyes widened, and he obviously wanted to ask another question, but he was quiet for a long moment. Finally, he nodded. "I don't see as it's anyone's business."

Relief washed through her. He *was* different from Mark. If Mark thought he could earn a coin, he would tell people anything they wanted to hear, no matter the cost to others. He'd use a person and then toss that person out, just like he'd done with her.

Baron glanced down at Jamie then lifted his head, a look of wonder on his face. "He fell asleep."

"I guess he feels safe with you."

Baron caught her gaze. "He *is* safe with me—and so are you. I'm not the man my brother is."

Jo nodded. "I can tell, even though I don't know you well."

"Thank you. That means a lot."

"Was Mark always the way he is?"

"As far back as I can remember. I was my father's favorite, I suppose because I was the oldest. He groomed me to help in his business. Mother latched onto Mark, spoiling and babying him. He always had a quick smile with big dimples and learned at a young age to wield them like weapons."

Jo remembered the first time she met Mark, and that description fit him perfectly. If only she'd known then what she did now about him, but knowing her stubbornness and her desire to find a wealthy man, it wouldn't have mattered at the time.

"I want to do whatever I can to help you, Joline."

"You can call me Jo, like everyone else, but I don't want your help. I'm not one of Mark's messes, either." In truth, she was, but she didn't want his help because he felt obligated. She wouldn't let herself get indebted to another man. They only wanted one thing from a woman, and she was done paying their price.

"Then let me help Jamie. He'll need clothes as he grows, shoes, all kinds of things. It would please me to provide for him."

"It's my place to take care of my son, not yours. If you really want to help, you can give me a job."

Sarah stuck a bite of eggs in her mouth as she glanced around the table, still amazed at how the Coulter family had welcomed her into their home. She almost felt as though she were a member of the family. Even Luke, Gabe's foreman, always sought her out whenever he came into the room and flashed his warm smile at her. He always joined the family for breakfast so that he and Gabe could plan their day. He ate with the ranch hands at the other meals, although Sarah rather wished he could join the family for lunch and supper.

As she reached for a biscuit, the ruffle on her sleeve nearly touched the butter. She lifted her arm higher, not wanting to soil the pretty calico dress that Lara had sewn for her, as well as an apron to wear over it when she did her chores. It still amazed her that Lara hadn't demanded anything in return for the dress. In fact, it seemed to have pleased her to make the dress. She said it was a gift—and she was working on a second one, a gold-and-brown-striped fabric that Jo had said would look good with her eyes. Not since she lived with her mother had she felt cared for—maybe even loved.

When they'd first left Oklahoma City, she'd figured Jo would dump her somewhere, but she had more than kept her word. That wasn't something she expected white people to do, especially for her. But Jo and the Coulter family weren't most people. Her Indian blood did not matter to them.

Luke cleared his throat. "I reckon y'all heard there's talk that the government will be opening the Cherokee Strip for settlers, probably by another land run."

Sarah glanced at Luke then ducked her head. She enjoyed the way the handsome cowboy's blue eyes twinkled. He was always happy and friendly.

Gabe nodded. "I read about that in the *Guthrie Ledger*. There may be more land than was available in the rush of '89."

"How much more?" Luke shoved in his last bite of food.

"Don't know yet."

Luke pushed his plate back. "I'm hoping to take a shot at some of that land."

Gabe frowned. "You're my right-hand man. I'd sure hate to lose you, but you know I won't hold you back from gettin' your own place. If things don't work out, you'll always have a home here."

"I appreciate that more'n I can say."

"Can I go with you, Luke?" Michael, his blue-green eyes dancing, rose up to sit on one leg.

Lara shook her head. "Of course not. You're much too young."

"There was kids in the other land runs."

"Only because their parents had no place to leave them during the race." Gabe pointed to Michael's plate. "Eat your breakfast, son. There are chores to be done."

"Aww. . ."

"Michael?" Lara lifted one brow.

Her son ducked his head. "Yes, sir. Sorry, Pa."

Jamie squealed and tossed a gummy biscuit halfway across the table, eliciting a snicker from Luke. Jo turned toward her son. "No. No. We don't throw food."

Jamie puckered up, but before he could start crying, Jo grabbed her spoon and slid a bite of apple butter into his mouth. His expression instantly softened, and his eyes lit up as he smacked his lips.

Sarah smiled and focused on finishing her own meal. She enjoyed the antics that occurred with a baby at the table. Meals at Badger's house had been so different. The women mostly talked about the guests they'd entertained the night before. Sarah preferred to eat in the kitchen with the cook or out on the back porch alone. She'd hated that place and had even started praying to Lara's God that He would let her stay here and not have to return. But if Badger found her. . .she shuddered to think what he would do.

She wanted to keep learning to read. Already she could sound out easy words, and the thrill of that achievement was more than anything she'd ever done. She might never have learned to read if she'd stayed with her mother. Although many Indian children were attending schools these days, *Etsi* hadn't wanted her to suffer the insults she would face for being a half-breed. So Etsi had kept her home. . .until the day Badger arrived. Her mother had called him Pete, but she was the only one.

She stirred her eggs with her fork, not really hungry anymore. Thoughts of how Badger had taken her from her dying mother always ruined her appetite. She hadn't wanted to leave Etsi with no one to care for her, but even Etsi had agreed she should go. What would have happened to her if she had stayed once Etsi was gone?

Maybe she should be more grateful to Badger, but she found it difficult. Her mother said he was her father, but Sarah had never seen him before. She wouldn't have known him if she had passed him on the street. If he cared for her, why hadn't he been there when she was small? Why hadn't he helped Etsi? And what purpose could he have for her now that she was nearly an adolescent? She shuddered to think he'd make her do what the other women did.

No, she would never go back. No matter what.

Chapter 12

Jack stood outside Comstock's General Store, listening to Mildred Yates rattle off a list of her ailments. Her grandson, Seth, sat on the nearby steps next to Lee, tossing clods of dirt into the street. Jack looked for Nick but didn't see the boy.

Mrs. Yates rubbed the small of her back. "These cloudy days make my rheumatism worse. I tell you, Parson, it's gonna rain before the day's over."

He suspected as much just from looking at the pewter sky, and there was a bit of chill to the air but not enough to don a duster.

"And my Henry, why, you should see the size of the boil on his. . .um. . .you know." She swatted her hand in the direction of her backside, her cheeks turning bright red. She snapped her fingers. "Seth, it's time we was gettin' home. C'mon, now."

"Yes'm." The child, who looked to be a year or so older than Lee, rose and gazed down at the boy. "Nice throwin' dirt with ya."

Lee grinned and waved but didn't say anything. Jack's heart warmed at seeing Lee smile. The boy had been quiet and withdrawn for nearly the whole week he'd stayed with Jack. He looked for Nick again. Where had that boy gotten to?

A shout and then rapid footsteps made him turn around. Nick ran smack into him. Jack lifted his arms, catching the boy, and took a step back for balance. Nick squirmed, trying to get loose, but Jack held on to him.

Abel Comstock rushed out the door, his gaze harried. "Hang on to him. He stole something from my store. I turned to see him snatch something from the glass display. He stuck it in his pocket."

Jack pushed Nick back to where he could see the boy's face, but Nick hung his head. "Look at me, son."

Nick's head jerked up. "I told you before—I ain't your son."

The anger in his gaze slashed Jack, but he shook off the pain. He'd been Nick at one time and had made bad choices, too. "What did you take?"

The starch left Nick's shoulders, and he tucked his chin to his chest and shrugged.

"Show me."

With a loud sigh, Nick reached into his pocket and pulled out a folding knife. Jack ground his back teeth together. He couldn't fault Nick for wanting a knife, especially that one with its shiny silver and inlaid bone. But stealing was wrong. He'd learned that the hard way. "Nick, give the knife back to Mr. Comstock and apologize."

Nick scowled and shot Jack an angry glance then turned and shuffled toward the store owner. He passed the knife to Mr. Comstock, but not before running his thumb across the bone. "Sorry."

"I accept your apology, but I think it's best you don't come in my store again." Abel glanced at Jack, gave a curt nod, and strode back inside.

Jack wondered if he'd have any friends left by the time he found a place for the boys. "I'm of a mind to take you home and feed you bread and water for a week."

Nick's gaze flicked to Jack's, probably checking to see if he was serious. "Pa always said we have to watch out for ourselves 'cause no one else will. I need that knife."

"If a man needs something, he works until he has the money to buy it. He doesn't steal it. Understand?"

Nick nodded. Lee shuffled over to stand beside his brother then took his hand.

"You're the oldest, Nick. It's up to you to set a good example for Lee. Do you want him to steal from others and get into trouble?" He wanted to say, "Like what happened to your pa," but he didn't.

"Naw, I reckon not."

"Good. Remember that he's watching everything you do, and your example is the one he's most likely to follow." Jack's belly grumbled, and Lee smiled. "Now, let's go get some lunch."

As they crossed the street and angled for the café, Ted Sizemore and Bill Arnold exited the Hungry Cowpoke Café. The men were deep in conversation when Mr. Arnold noticed them. He poked his friend and nudged his chin in their direction. Ted Sizemore turned, placing his hands on his hips, and frowned. Jack wished there were some other place to eat, but the Hungry Cowpoke was it.

He nodded to the men as he and the boys drew near. "Afternoon."

Mr. Arnold nodded back, but Ted Sizemore just stared at the boys. Lee backed up until he bumped into Jack's legs. Jack placed a hand on the youngster's shoulder to comfort him.

"Why don't you two go inside and get us a table. I'll be right in." He glanced at Nick, who nodded and took Lee's hand.

Mr. Sizemore stepped aside to let them enter, but his frown remained. As soon as the door closed, he set his sights on Jack. "We don't want their kind in Glen Haven. Them boys is trouble."

"They're just kids. They need to be guided and trained like any others." Jack was thankful the duo hadn't witnessed Nick's escapade at Comstock's. "I think you're being awfully hard-nosed about this situation. Where's your Christian compassion? Those boys already lost their ma and two sisters to illness, and now their pa is dead."

Mr. Arnold looked somewhat chastised, but Mr. Sizemore continued to glare at Jack.

"You've only got another eight days to find a home for them hooligans—and I sure hope it's not in this town." What he didn't say—that Jack might be out of a job—hung as heavy in the air as the moisture from the coming storm. A bolt of lightning zigzagged across the southern sky, as if to emphasize the point.

"I'm doing my best, but it's not easy to find a place for two kids."

"Then separate them. Shouldn't be too hard to place that bigger boy. Lots of folks need help on their ranches."

"I'm looking for a home where they will be loved and treated like family, not like workhorses."

"You'd best just take the first offer that comes along, or you may be sorry."

"Those boys are more important than my job."

Mr. Sizemore frowned. "I'm right sorry to hear you feel that way. Folks like to think their pastor cares about them more'n some raggedy orphans."

Jack's anger grew at the pompous man's declaration. "I do care about the people in my church, but those orphans have the same right to my time as my parishioners. James 1:27 says, 'Pure religion and undefiled before God and the Father is this, to visit the fatherless and widows in their affliction.' Besides, I haven't neglected my church duties to care for those kids, and I won't."

Mr. Sizemore shrugged. "It may not matter if you don't find them a home soon. Y'all will be on your way out of town—together."

Jack nodded and ducked into the café before he did something he'd regret. Uncompassionate and insensitive men like Mr. Sizemore who felt they had more say than others because they had deeper pockets had no call to be leaders in the church.

On her first day to work with Baron, Jo walked around Hillborne's General Store, noticing the subtle changes he had made. He'd moved the fabric section to the wall beside the windows where the ladies would have more light to view the selection but the sun wouldn't fade the wares. The canned goods were now on the wall opposite the ready-made garments, and the farm tools were still at the back of the store.

The familiar scent of spices, leather, and the pickles that sat in a big barrel near the front door lulled her to a contented state. She'd always enjoyed working in the store around so many new items, except for when Mark was in one of his moods. She shook off the thought, not wanting to dampen the day.

She glanced down at her shaking hands. She hadn't thought about how much she'd be alone with Baron when she'd blurted out that she needed a job. But he wasn't like the other men she'd encountered—the ones who raked her body with their leering gazes and looked at her as if she were a delicious meal to be devoured. Baron's eyes were kind, and although she thought she'd noticed attraction in his gaze, there was nothing improper in his manner or actions. Maybe he was a man she could be friends with. Time would tell.

She pulled her eyes off him and studied the store again. "I like the changes you've made."

Baron cocked his head. "It doesn't bother you?"

"Why should it?"

"Well. . .you worked here with my brother."

She shrugged. "Mark was always changing things around. I'd

put something one place, and two days later, he'd move it back or to a new spot. He said people came in the store more often if things looked different."

"That is true, but I'd like to hear your opinion. If you feel we need to move things, especially the women's items, please tell me."

Jo nodded. Mark had wanted her opinion at first, but she soon learned that he rarely listened and would do what he saw fit. Would Baron be the same?

"What would you like me to do first?"

He turned, looking around the room. "I always seem to be fighting the dust that's so prevalent here."

Jo nodded and walked to the counter, retrieving the feather duster; then she moved to the canned goods area. As she tended to the task, she thought about last Sunday when Baron had arrived unexpectedly at the ranch. She'd feared him finding out about Jamie, but it would seem her worries were unfounded. The man was enamored with her son and thrilled to be an uncle.

Baron carried a crate in from the storeroom and set it on the counter. "What duties did you attend to when you worked here before?"

"I generally assisted the women who came in while Mark helped the men, and I did the book work. I'm good with numbers, where Mark hated paperwork."

Baron nodded. "He never has liked sitting at a desk or doing menial work, as he called it." His lips pursed as if he were remembering something.

"But I'll do whatever you need me to. I just have to leave here by four to get back to my sister's place before dark."

"I don't mind closing early if we aren't busy. That way I can escort you."

Jo swiped the duster over some boxes of crackers. "That isn't necessary. I'm a good rider. That's why I rode one of Gabe's horses instead of bringing a wagon." And she had a pistol her grandpa had given her for protection, but Baron didn't need to know that.

The door opened, ringing the bell above it. A woman walked in, holding the hand of a girl who looked to be about six.

Jo glanced at Baron, and he nodded for her to assist the customer.

"Welcome to Hillborne's," Jo said as she approached the woman. "Can I help you find something?"

"I need some thread and a new sewing needle."

Jo stepped back and held out her hand toward the fabric area. "They are right over here."

"Thank you." The woman smiled at Jo then glanced down at her daughter. "Come along, Pamela, let's see what pretty threads we can find for your sampler."

Jo walked over to the counter where Baron was unpacking the crate. She picked up a plate with a lovely blue-and-pink floral pattern that he set down. "These are pretty."

"My mother selected them."

Jo glanced at him. "She picks out your wares?"

"Not normally, but I'm. . ." He looked away then back, his neck red. "Well, the truth is, I'm sort of color blind. Have you heard of that? It used to be called Daltonism."

"Oh. Is that why you always wear clothing in shades of brown?"

He glanced at the customer then down at his clothing. "Mother thought it would make things easier for me since all the various pieces would match."

"It does make sense, but I could never stand to wear the same color all the time." Instantly her thoughts jumped to the deep blue silk dresses she'd been forced to wear at Badger's bordello. Mark had once said the color brought out the blue in her eyes. Now she could hardly stand the shade.

"Fortunately, you don't have to worry about that."

"So. . .can I ask what you do see? Is everything black and white, or do you see some color?"

"I have no trouble with blues and yellows. It's the red and green shades that make me pause."

"Why don't you wear blue—or yellow?"

He shrugged. "Blues weren't in style when I was younger. I've always had brown clothes made; then I never had to worry about matching colors."

She glanced around the store, appreciating the variety of colors, and felt a bit sad for him. She loved looking at a field of wildflowers or a rainbow in the sky. Jo turned back to face him. "Just let me know if you need my help with any things with color."

He smiled. "I appreciate that."

"So, are we going to remove some of the dishes you currently have on the shelves to make room for these new ones?"

"I was considering putting these in the window—at least some of them." He lifted up a plate with an ivy pattern. "What do you think about that?"

She liked that he asked her opinion, but would he do what she suggested? Most of the time Mark didn't.

The woman and child came up to the counter, and while Baron checked them out, she studied the current window display. On one side were several cast-iron skillets with a trio of pancake mix boxes beside a mixing bowl. The other side sported a sack of horse feed, a fancy saddle, and a bridle.

The bell rang as their customers left.

"So, have you been having more male or female customers?"

Baron glanced toward the ceiling for a moment, and Jo followed his gaze, noticing a cobweb that needed to be knocked down.

"Since I've been here, there have been more women coming in."

"In light of that, how would you feel about removing the tack and feed from this window and making the whole thing geared toward women?"

She held her breath as he contemplated her suggestion; then he nodded. "It makes sense. Let's do it."

Her breath whooshed out. Smiling, she spun around and snatched the bridle from the display. Baron walked to the window, lifted out the saddle, and carried it to the supply room.

Jo studied the stack of tablecloths then pulled out a cornflower-blue one with tiny white dots. It would go perfectly with the dishes. After Baron removed the sack of feed, she dusted the window display area and then spread out the tablecloth, leaving parts of it poofed up. She placed a stack of three plates in the center with a saucer and coffee cup on the right. Tapping her finger against her lip, she tried to think what else was needed. More color?

Jo crossed the store and studied the collection of glasses, settling on one that was clear at the top and a pinkish red at the bottom. She filled it with water from a bucket in the storeroom then set it down. "I'll be right back," she said as she hurried out the rear door. She was certain she'd noticed some wildflowers near Baron's barn.

As she walked behind the fancy house Mark had built for her, it amazed her that she didn't miss it. She'd always wanted a pretty home with wood floors and ceilings that weren't made of dirt and didn't have varmints crawling in them. She shuddered at the memory of living in a sod house. The dugout they stayed in when they first arrived at the section of land Gabe had won in the land run hadn't been much better—just a bit bigger.

Her gaze latched onto a patch of white daisies growing alongside the barn. She checked on her horse, making sure it still had water, then picked a handful of flowers. Back in the store, she heard Baron talking to someone while she arranged the flowers. Eager to see the final effect, she returned to the window and placed the cup on the right side of the plates. She hurried out the front door and stared at the display. All it needed was a backdrop of some sort on the two-foot-high wall at the back of the display area. That crocheted tablecloth would be just the thing.

The bell rang as she entered the store. Baron, and a woman with a baby in one arm and a toddler in tow, glanced at Jo then looked away. Suddenly the woman's gaze shot back to Jo, and her eyes widened.

Recognition hit her. "Alma Lou?"

Baron watched as delight engulfed Jo's pretty face. The women squealed so loud that the toddler and baby both jumped and started crying.

The woman Jo had called Alma Lou patted the baby and looked at the little girl. "Hush now, Charlotte. You're fine. I simply got excited when I saw my old friend. We went to school together when we both lived in Caldwell."

Baron filed that information away to look up later. He had no idea where Caldwell was. He couldn't help smiling at seeing Jo so happy. Most of the time, she only smiled around him when she looked at her son, and that was a different kind.

"What are you doing in Guthrie?" Jo asked. "And look at you with two children."

Alma Lou beamed. "This is Charlotte Ann and this is JJ. Short for Jerry Jr."

Jo waved at the little girl and ran her hand over the baby's dark hair. "They're both so sweet. When did you move to Guthrie?"

"We didn't. We live in Wichita, but we're here visiting Jerry's older sister, Eloise."

"How long will you be here?"

Alma Lou frowned. "We're leaving tomorrow. If only I'd known you were here."

Baron dusted the packing straw off the counter and set the crate the new dishes had been shipped in by the back door. He tried not to listen, but he was curious about Jo's former life. Alma Lou was a fair-looking woman, but not nearly as pretty as Jo. He grabbed the broom and swept up the straw then emptied it into the yard out back.

As he returned, Alma Lou touched Jo's arm. "Tell me all about what you've been up to since I last saw you! Are you married?" Her eyes flicked in his direction. She leaned in close to Jo and whispered something he couldn't make out.

Jo's surprised gaze shot to him and back to her friend. Her cheeks turned a becoming rose color. "Um. . .no. Baron is my brother-in-law."

"Oh. So where's your husband?"

Jo shifted her feet, obviously wrestling with her response.

"He's gone," Baron offered, sounding a bit sad.

Alma Lou's eyes widened as she gasped. "Oh, Jo. I'm so sorry. You're so young to be a widow."

Jo ducked her head. "Thank you."

"If there's anything I can do, you let me know."

"I will, but it's been a while now."

"I'm sorry, but I have to run. I was hoping to find some teething cream for JJ. But you don't carry the brand I like." She tugged her daughter away from the glass front of the counter. "We'll be back at Christmas, so I hope to see you then."

Jo nodded as she walked with her friend to the door. "It was good to see you again."

They hugged, and the moment the door closed, Jo spun

around. "Thank you for coming to my rescue. I didn't know what to tell her about Mark."

"Glad to help." He walked down to the far end of the counter and polished away the fingerprints Charlotte left behind. "Vagueness is probably the best option. I merely said he was gone, but she made the assumption that he was dead."

"True, but I do feel bad lying to Alma Lou. We were best friends once."

"Care to tell me what happened?"

Jo shook her head and walked over to the spools of thread and straightened them.

Curious, Baron put the broom away and looked around the supply room for a new project. Whatever had caused the rift between friends must not have been too bad from the way they were acting today. Too bad the woman didn't live here. It would be good for Jo to have a friend in town.

He couldn't help wondering how many times Jo would be questioned about Mark. A number of the townsfolk had already inquired about him. Many would recognize Jo and remember that she was married—so they thought—to Mark and ask about him. He hadn't thought how hard that might be for her when he agreed to let her work for him and hoped most people wouldn't recognize her, but then she wasn't exactly forgettable. He'd hate for nosy customers to drive her away. Realizing he was staring, he stooped down behind the counter and rearranged the knives on the top shelf. Baron enjoyed having Jo here, having someone to talk to and discuss ideas with. Glancing at her, he watched her examine one of the ready-made dresses. He didn't know what would become of their relationship, such as it was. He only knew he wanted it to last a long time.

Chapter 13

Relief washed through Jo as she rode over a hill and saw Lara's home. She'd stayed much longer than planned, and with it being early April, the sun set by 6:45, but she'd made the long ride safely. Supper would be over, although Lara had probably saved her a plate. Though famished, she ached even more to see Jamie. She hadn't been separated from him for this long before and worried how he'd done. Sarah had agreed to keep him so that she could work and make money for them to go somewhere farther away, but tending a baby who wasn't yours all day could be a chore, even though Sarah loved Jamie.

Luke strode out of the barn as she rode up. He tipped his hat. "Evening, ma'am. I'll tend your horse for ya."

Jo slid to the ground, her legs a bit shaky from the long ride. Luke McNeil was a good-looking cowboy, but he didn't interest her. Most times he was cocky, and his blue eyes twinkled, reminding her of Mark—a man she didn't want to be reminded of. "Thank you. It's been a long day."

She entered through the kitchen door and washed up. Everything had been tidied, but the aroma of cooked beef still lingered, making her stomach fuss. Jamie first, then food. She started out of the kitchen, but her belly grumbled again, and she spun back to the stove where a plate covered with a towel sat. She lifted the edge and snagged a biscuit then hurried up the stairs.

An excited squeal came from her bedroom. She hurried toward it then paused at the door and peered in. Sarah sat on the floor with Jamie and Michael, in a circle. Michael stacked several squares of wood, and then Jamie knocked them over, giggling with delight. He grabbed a block, lifted his hand, and flung it toward Michael.

Sarah gently grabbed Jamie's hand. "Do not throw blocks."

Jamie's lower lip stuck out, and his chin quivered. Jo could tell that his feelings were hurt and any second he'd burst out in a wail. She stepped forward, hoping that seeing her would distract him, but Michael clapped two blocks together, drawing her son's attention. Jamie smiled and bounced, waiting for Michael to restack the blocks. Then her son sent them flying once again, leaving Jo wondering how many times they had repeated the same action.

She smacked her lips, drawing the attention of all in the room.

"Ma–a!" Jamie cried.

Jo smiled, even though his name for her sounded more like something a baby goat would utter than a child. She rushed forward and picked him up, holding him close. "Yes, son, Mama's home."

Jamie placed both of his chubby hands on her cheeks and gave her a damp, openmouthed kiss.

"He is happy to see you." Sarah rose.

Michael placed the blocks in a wicker basket.

"Where's your ma?" Jo asked.

"In her room, feeding Lizzie."

Jo flashed him a teasing look. "Her name is Beth."

"That's not what Pa calls her," the boy said as he left the room.

Jo sat down in the rocker. "How was Jamie today?"

"He miss you. Fussy some. Happy some."

She kissed his fuzzy head. "I missed you, too—both of you."

Sarah's gaze jerked to hers, as if surprised. "How did work go?"

"Good! And I saw an old friend."

Sarah frowned as she crossed the room to the window. "You are not. . .afraid. . .for people to see you?"

She was, but how else could she earn the funds they needed? "I am, but I don't see that I have a choice."

"You be careful. Badger hurt you if he find you."

Sarah spoke the truth. Working at the store was risky, but it was her only option. Would Baron have hired her if he knew the money she was making would one day take her—and Jamie—away from him?

Jack paced across his small living room then turned and crossed it again. He paused by the window and looked up at the sky. They'd had a toad soaker of a storm, but it had passed and now the skies were clear, a rainbow decorating the horizon. *Lord, those boys need a home, and I know there's a family who needs those boys to love. Help me find them—and soon. I can't fail Nick and Lee like I did my sisters.* The memory of how he rode away from Lara and Jo and never returned still haunted him.

As he passed his desk, he glanced down at his sermon notes scrawled on a piece of paper. There wasn't much there, and the thoughts weren't flowing. All he could think about was the boys. He hated failing his church and being cast out like a leper, but God would take care of him—He always had. But he didn't want to have to hit the trail, not knowing where he was going, with those little boys in tow. They deserved a home. People to love them. If he had a place of his own, he'd keep them, but he didn't. All he owned could be packed in a set of saddlebags and a satchel.

Jack padded through the house to the back porch where the boys were supposed to be washing off. He tiptoed to the open back door and peeked out. Lee squealed as Nick poured a pitcher of water over his head.

"I guess you're as clean as I can get you. Get outta that tub."

Lee shimmied out of the round metal washtub, shivering, and Nick wrapped a towel around him.

Jack leaned against the door frame. "Good job being a responsible big brother."

Nick's gaze shot to his, and a rare smile lifted one side of his mouth.

"I can take this little rascal in and help him dress if you want to go ahead and take your bath."

Nick nodded and nudged Lee toward Jack. He picked up the light youngster and threw him across his shoulders. "Look at this sack of potatoes I got."

Lee giggled. "I ain't no tater."

Holding tight to Lee's skinny legs, Jack carried him to the spare bedroom and lowered him to the bed. He dried off the child and helped him into a nightshirt that Cora had bought. Lee yawned and rubbed his eyes.

"You think you've got enough energy left for some milk and cake before you go to sleep?"

Lee instantly perked up and nodded his head.

Jack smiled. Maybe one day he'd have himself a fine boy like Lee. "Then let's head to the kitchen."

Before he'd sliced the cake that a kind church lady had brought him, Nick sauntered in, his hair damp. The boy had washed in record time, but at least the dirt was off his face. "Have a seat. You're just in time for a snack."

He poured two glasses of milk and a cup of lukewarm coffee

then sliced three pieces of cake and set them on the table. As he reached to pull back his chair, someone knocked on the door.

His gut churned, but he smiled at the boys. "Looks like we've got company." But company at this hour generally indicated something bad.

Jack opened the door and smiled. He didn't recognize the couple. The man yanked off his hat while the woman tried to peek past Jack.

"Can I help you? Are you lost?"

The woman's gaze jerked to his. "You're the pastor, are you not?"

Jack nodded. "Yes. I'm Pastor Jensen. What can I help you with?"

"We—"

The man gently clutched the woman's arm. "Let me talk, Emily."

She smiled. "I'm sorry, Phillip. I'm just anxious."

"I know." The man caught Jack's eye again. "I'm Phillip McGrady, and this is my wife, Emily. We're from over near Pine Gulch. We heard you were looking for a home for a couple of boys, and we—" He placed his arm around his wife's shoulders. "Well, the good Lord hasn't blessed us with any children. We were hopin' we could meet the boys and see if they might be a good fit for us."

Jack noticed the couple's clothing—though a bit damp—was of a fine cut, and their buggy was a newer model surrey with padded seats and a fringed top. They looked to be able to support a family, but he knew nothing about them. Could he give the boys to strangers?

Mr. McGrady pulled an envelope from his inside coat pocket. "Here's a letter from our pastor, Reverend Joseph Gilmore, explaining to you what kind of people we are. He's known us both since we were little'uns."

"Please, Pastor." Mrs. McGrady reached out and touched Jack's arm. "Could you at least tell me if the boys are spoken for? Did we waste our time and get our hopes up for nothing?"

Jack smiled. "You're the first to ask for them."

She gasped and turned to her husband. "Did you hear that? I just knew it was meant to be. Are they already in bed? Could we see them? I know it's late, but we only arrived in town a short while ago. We've been traveling most of the day—even through that storm."

"Emily. . ." Her husband shook his head.

It was late, but Jack didn't have the heart to turn the couple away. "We just sat down to eat some cake before the boys head to bed. Why don't you join us for a short while and meet them, but let's not mention why you're here. If things go well, we'll tell them tomorrow."

Mrs. McGrady quietly clapped her hands and bounced on her toes.

Mr. McGrady eyed him. "You're sure we won't be imposing?"

"I wouldn't have asked if you were. Come in. Afterward, I'll point you to the boardinghouse since we're filled up here."

"Oh, thank you so much, Pastor. I've been so worried that we'd be too late."

Just in the nick of time was more like it. Jack led them into the kitchen, and both boys' eyes widened.

"This here is Mr. and Mrs. McGrady, and they just arrived in town. I offered them some cake for refreshment. You two don't mind, do you?"

He read the caution in Nick's eye, but the boy shook his head.

"Have a seat, and I'll dish up the cake. There's coffee, but it's just a little warm, or we have milk."

"Milk—or water—is fine for both of us," Mr. McGrady said. "Thank you."

Jack turned toward the cake and cut two more slices, his hopes higher than they'd been in a long while. It seemed God had seen fit to answer his prayer.

Jo kissed Jamie's cheek and handed him to Sarah. He puckered up, making her heart ache, and he broke out into a loud wail as Sarah carried him up the stairs. She wished she could stay and comfort her son, but she had a job to do, and she knew, too, that once Sarah distracted him with a toy or something else, Jamie would be fine. She put her straw hat on and tied the ribbons as Sarah reached the top and disappeared from view. Grandpa ambled out of the kitchen, holding his coffee cup and looking a bit pale after suffering with a malaria attack for several days.

"Don't you have time for a of cup coffee or a little breakfast?"

Jo shook her head. "I'm running late and need to get to town."

Lara jogged out of the kitchen with a cloth napkin and held it out to her. "There's a biscuit with an egg in here. At least take this and eat it on your way to town."

Jo accepted the gift. "Thanks." She turned to leave.

"Be careful." Grandpa nodded at her and returned to the kitchen, not waiting for a response.

Jo opened the door.

"Jo, wait." Lara touched her shoulder.

Closing her eyes, she held on to the door latch. "I need to go."

"I know, but can't you find a time that we can talk? I missed you while you were gone and worried about you every day. I'd like to hear where you've been and what you were doing all this time. How you got by without Mark."

Jo stiffened. The last thing her kindhearted sister needed to know was Jo's recent past. It would devastate her. But she had to say something to pacify her. "Um. . .sure. Soon."

She rushed outside, grateful that Gabe had saddled a horse for her as he'd promised when she'd first come downstairs to feed Jamie his breakfast.

The door opened as she reached the ground, and she sighed. Was Lara going to fuss at her again?

"You forgot your cloak."

Jo glanced down. She'd been so focused on getting out the door and avoiding Lara that she'd forgotten her outer garment. Now she noticed the chilliness of the morning. She hurried up the stairs and took the cloak from her sister. "Thank you."

"Be careful." Lara smiled. "I love you, sis."

Jo flashed her a tighter smile than her sister deserved for her kindness. She donned her cloak and stuffed the napkin and biscuit into her pocket. She untied the horse and led him beside the stairs; then she stepped onto the lowest one, helping her to mount. Giving Lara a brief wave, she nudged the horse to a trot and then into a gallop.

The cool breeze chilled her, and she tugged her cloak around her and tucked the edge under her legs as best as she could with one hand.

As she rode for town, she thought of her talk with Lara. What could she tell her that would satisfy her? She couldn't admit that she'd lived at a brothel. Her sister was a good Christian woman in all ways. And it wasn't something Jo could voice, for it was far too embarrassing to admit. It shamed her. She was nothing like her pious sister. She was tainted—filthy. No decent woman would associate with her if they knew about her past. If not for Jamie, she'd still be in that dreadful place and might never have had the courage to escape. She shuddered at the horrid memories of smelly, demanding men.

At a big bend in the road, she slowed the horse to a trot. She passed section after section of land that had been won in the land rush. Most only had sod houses or ones made of stacked stones. None were as nice as Gabe's. The first time she saw him in Caldwell, Kansas, she thought he must have money. He wore fine clothes and was handsome, but at the time, she'd only been sixteen and thought him too old for her. Who would have thought Lara would end up marrying him?

She was happy for her sister, and glad Lara was free of the lout she first married. Jo shuddered as she remembered the times Tom had tried to charm her—and had even stolen a kiss. She'd slapped him, of course, but the fact that she had secretly enjoyed it had proved that she was a bad girl—far different from her sister.

Why couldn't she have been more like Lara?

The sun had risen over halfway in the sky by the time she reached town. People were milling around everywhere, tending to business or chatting. The streets were lined with horses, buggies, and buckboards. There was something about the busyness of town that she loved.

At Baron's barn, she dismounted, tended to her horse, and then washed her hands at the pump behind the store. She dried them on her cloak and hurried inside, eager to begin working. Three people were already shopping. Baron talked with a man in the corner by the tack. Two women stood shoulder to shoulder in front of the rolls of fabric. Jo quickly donned her apron and rushed over. "May I be of assistance?"

Baron must have heard her, because he glanced over his shoulder and smiled. Her stomach flipped a somersault, and she pressed her hand to it, forcing herself not to react to the unwanted feelings of attraction.

For the next half hour, she busied herself helping the women pick out fabric, thread, ribbon, and lace for two evening dresses they were planning to make. Baron finished up with the man he sold a bridle to and was straightening the tack when the women left the store. Jo scurried back to the fabric area and tidied it as well.

"How was your ride this morning?"

"A bit chilly, but nice. The sun kept me warm enough."

Baron crossed the store, his boots thudding on the wood floor. "And how is little Jamie today?"

"He's figuring out that I'm leaving after he eats breakfast, and he got a bit fussy today when Sarah took him upstairs."

"I can see that bothers you."

Jo shrugged. "Nothing to be done about it. I'm sure he's forgotten about me by now."

Baron took hold of her shoulders and gazed down at her. "Don't say such a thing. A child could never forget his mother."

Her mouth went dry at his nearness and the intensity of his dark blue gaze. But memories of her own parents, whom she barely remembered, overwhelmed her, and she turned back to the thread case. Everything was perfectly straight, but she rearranged several colors anyway. "I can't remember what my mother's face looked like."

"What happened to her?" Baron's warm breath brushed her neck.

"Both she and my pa died in a fire when our house burned down."

He returned his hands to her shoulders, gently tightening his grip, anchoring her to him. "I'm so sorry. How did you and your sister manage to escape?"

"We were away on an errand. And there are three of us. Lara and I have an older brother named Jack."

"I didn't know about him."

"We don't talk much about Jack. He rode out of our lives about a year after we went to live with our grandparents—and right after my grandma died. We haven't seen him since."

"You've faced so much loss in your life. No wonder you're tough."

She turned to face him. "You think I'm tough?"

"Maybe *tenacious* better illustrates what I mean. And you're a hard worker."

She warmed under his compliment. She caught his gaze, holding it for a long moment. Her heartbeat stampeded. How could this gentle, considerate man be related to Mark? She suddenly realized she was still gawking at him and turned away, searching for some other task.

The doorbell dinged, and Jo started toward the woman, who glanced up at her and suddenly halted, halfway in.

"I remember you. Didn't your husband own this store?"

Jo wanted to run but held her ground and nodded. "Yes, ma'am, he did. My brother-in-law is now overseeing the operations of Hillborne's."

Mrs. Scott's gaze shot to Baron and back to Jo. "I see." She closed the door and looked around. "I was so delighted to see that the store had reopened. I wanted to come sooner, but a bout of rheumatism kept me close to my bed. So where's that handsome husband of yours?"

Jo ducked her head and shook it. "I'm sad to say he's gone."

"Oh my heavens. I'm so sorry. But you're young enough to find another man."

Jo looked up, stiffening as if a steel rod were running down her spine. "I don't need another man, Mrs. Scott. I'm perfectly able to take care of myself."

"I'm sorry. I didn't mean anything by that. Perhaps it's best that I be on my way."

She spun around and raced from the store before Jo could say a thing. Baron would probably be furious with her for chasing away a customer. She mentally prepared herself for a lashing, but from behind her came a chuckle. Jo turned to see Baron struggling to hold back his amusement.

"You thought that was funny? You do realize I just chased away a potential customer."

"It was worth it to see her expression."

"Even if she never comes back?" She turned to face him.

"I don't want her business if she's going to question you and make you uncomfortable. You don't owe anyone an explanation about your past."

She stiffened but then realized that he was referring to his brother, not the bordello. "Thank you."

"I mean it, Jo."

The door opened again, and they both looked in that direction. A thin man with an odd hat slipped in and looked around. When his gaze found Baron, he moved toward him. "You Baron Hillborne?"

"Yes, I am."

The man pulled something from his pocket. "You've got a telegram."

Jo sucked in a breath. Telegrams generally brought bad news. Had something happened to one of Baron's parents or the family business?

He collected the paper and handed the man a coin. "Thank you."

Jo could read the tension in his expression and the way he held his body stiff. The telegraph man closed the door and briskly walked past the store window.

The paper rattled as Baron opened it and scanned the brief missive.

A muscle in his jaw ticked, and he lifted a worried gaze to her.

She stepped forward and placed one hand on his arm. "What's wrong?"

She saw him swallow. Several emotions crossed his face; then he handed her the telegram.

Heard you reopened store. Am returning to Guthrie on the 14th. Mark.

Chapter 14

"No!" The paper fell from Jo's hand as she felt the blood drain from her face. She touched her fingertips to her forehead. "What am I going to do? I can't face him again. He can't know that I'm in town." She reached for Baron's arm. "Please. You can't tell him."

Baron laid his hand over Jo's. "You have my word. You must not come to the store again until I manage to get rid of him."

"But I need the work."

"You can work after he's gone. I know Mark. He's only coming back to taunt me."

"Why would he do that?"

Baron's jaw tightened, and he turned toward the window, staring out. "Because he enjoys the fact that I'm tasked with cleaning up his messes. In a way, he thinks he's controlling me—if that makes sense. He thinks of me as my father's lackey. Mark believes that the reason I want to please Father is so that he'll leave his fortune to me, but that's not what motivates me. I'm a Christian, and as such, I believe that I should do my best no matter what the task is. It pains me to say it, but Mark has no idea how satisfying it feels to do a good job and serve others."

Baron was right about his brother, but at the moment, all she could think about was Mark's return. All manner of thoughts raced through her mind. She should leave town right away, but she couldn't. Not yet. Maybe if she stayed at the ranch, Mark wouldn't know she was there. But people talked—and what if one of those women she had helped came in the store when he was here and asked about her? What if Alma Lou returned looking for her when Mark was here? What if—Jo reined in her runaway thoughts and noticed Baron's troubled expression. A bolt of compassion surged through her. "I'm sorry that Mark has caused so many problems that you've had to deal with."

Baron shrugged. "I'm used to it."

"I'm still sorry." She'd been so adrift when Mark left her that she had never considered how his abandoning the store might affect his family. But it was her family she needed to think of now. She nibbled her lip, wondering if she should voice her thoughts. Talking things out often helped, but she wasn't used to relying on others—and she didn't want to sound like a frantic mother. Still. . . "I'm concerned that if Mark learns he has a son, he will decide to take him from me."

Baron's eyes widened for a moment. "I honestly don't believe he would do that, but I know more than most what means my brother will go to in order to get what he wants. To be safe, you need to go back to your sister's ranch and stay there. I'll pay you for the days you were supposed to work, but I don't want you here where anyone else can see you until Mark leaves town."

"While I appreciate your generosity, I can't accept it. But I do think it's a wise thing to stay away from the store for the time being. The fewer people who question me about Mark, the fewer there will be to mention me to him."

"I'll do my best to get rid of him."

"How? What will you say to him?"

He shrugged. "I don't know yet, but I'll think of something. He won't want to hang around here unless he has a good reason."

"What do you think he'll do if he finds out about Jamie?"

Baron rubbed his hand over his clean-shaven jaw. "I don't know for certain, but I imagine he will be enamored with him at first, but then as usual, he'll probably run away from his responsibility."

"That sounds like Mark." And running away was exactly what he'd done when he learned she was carrying his child. That was better than what he'd done the first two times she'd told him she was pregnant. She tensed at the painful memories.

"Jo, look at me."

She did as asked and was touched by the compassion in Baron's eyes.

"I know how to deal with Mark. Trust me to take care of him and to protect you and Jamie."

Tears blurred her eyes. No man other than her father and grandpa had protected her and asked nothing in return. But then, who was to say he wouldn't ask something of her later? No, she didn't want to believe that, but she'd been wrong before—with devastating results. She backed away, not wanting to think how protected she'd felt, if only for a moment. "Thank you. I suppose I should get back to work."

"Why don't you go home?"

She shook her head. "I can't. I need the money too bad."

"Might I ask why?"

She realized that she'd said too much. Of course he'd be curious. She scrambled for a response. "I. . .uh. . .can't stay at Lara's forever. She has a growing family and doesn't need the three of us underfoot."

"From what I've seen of your sister, I think she enjoys having you there."

"Maybe so. But haven't you ever heard the saying, 'After three days, fish and family stink'?"

Baron chuckled. "Fish always stink."

Jo smiled. "True, but they are fun to catch. Grandpa, Michael, and I used to fish the creek near our house in Caldwell."

"That's an interesting concept—a woman fishing. I'd like to see that sometime."

Jo warmed under his stare then realized she was still gazing into his eyes and pushed her feet into motion. Mark's brother was the last man on earth she should be exchanging glances with. She hid away in the supply room for the next hour, unpacking several crates of new supplies and listing them in the inventory ledger.

The front bell dinged, and she heard footsteps as more than one person entered. Jo stiffened.

"I'm tellin' you, Hank, you really oughta consider riding in the land run. My cousin, Buster Holmes, got him a nice claim in the run last April."

"I'll think on it, but Bertha doesn't wanna move again. She likes it here. And there's no guarantee I'd win a claim."

As Jo listed the last item, her pen paused. If not for the run of '89, she probably never would have met Mark. She thought back to the day she'd first met him, back when she lived in Caldwell. He was handsome—enchanting—and he told her that her red dress looked good with her complexion. But then she had turned and looked him fully in the face, and when he saw her eyes, he changed his mind and stated that blue was her best color. She'd been young then and upset with her sister. And she'd just learned that Alma Lou was getting married and chose someone else to be her maid of honor. That both hurt and angered her. Mark had charmed her and made her forget her troubles for a time. Later, when she left her family and went to Guthrie, looking for work and a place to live, she'd run into him again in his store, which was housed in a tent at the time. She gladly accepted his job offer, and only a week later, they got married.

The snap of her pencil breaking jarred her from her thoughts. What a naive fool she'd been. Pushing the ledger aside, she reached for a lantern she'd just unpacked and a cloth she'd previously set on the desk. She wiped off the glass and base. The globe rattled as she set it on the base. Jo stared at her shaking hand. Mark had done this to her. Could Baron get rid of him as he vowed? Or would Mark discover she was nearby and force himself back into her life? Why did life have to be so uncertain?

Why couldn't she have been more like Lara? More genteel and less stubborn? Quieter and happy rather than dissatisfied and adventurous? Why did she have to fall for two men who had charmed her, used her, and then battered her if she displeased them? Tears stung her eyes, igniting her ire. She batted at them. Tears never helped a thing, and she hated them.

"Jo?"

She jumped and turned away.

"Are you all right?"

"I'm fine." She cleared her throat. "Just finished listing the new stock in the ledger."

"Well, if you're certain you're fine, I'll head back out front." Baron stood there a moment then finally left.

Jo blew out a loud sigh. She probably would be better off if she went home, but she wasn't a quitter.

Baron's footsteps strode her way again.

Jo slid off the stool, swiped her damp lashes once more, and bent over a crate.

"I've been thinking of something. It's not like Mark to let me know he's coming. Normally, he just shows up. It's got me wondering if he might be trying to trick me into thinking that he's coming on the fourteenth."

Curious, Jo straightened and turned to face him, hoping her nose wasn't beet red. "Trick you?"

Baron nodded. "It wouldn't surprise me if he arrives in town sooner than he indicated in the telegram."

Jo's heart jolted. "How much sooner?"

He shrugged. "I have no idea, but I don't think you should come to work tomorrow—just in case."

"You don't think he'll arrive today, do you?"

"Not if he comes by train, which is his normal mode of travel. There are no arrivals today, but there's one due tomorrow."

Jo squeezed her hands together, trying to decide what to do. The last thing she wanted, next to running into Badger, was encountering Mark again. Maybe she should return to Lara's. But then, she couldn't make the money she needed if she didn't work. Lifting her chin, she looked Baron in the eye. "I'll go ahead and finish out today."

"If you're sure."

She nodded. "I am—although I may spend more time back here."

"That's a good idea. The storeroom could stand a good straightening and cleaning. I've been so focused on the front of the store that I've hardly done a thing back here."

Jo smiled. "Thank you. You're a kind man, Baron Hillborne."

He returned her smile as he stood a bit taller. "Thank you. Let me know if you need anything."

"I will. And when no one's in the store, I'll probably set some things that need to be stocked on the end of the counter."

"Sounds good. I think I'll get one of the ten-pound bags of rice and resize it to one five-pound and the rest in single-pound bags. The ammunition case needs refilling, so you might check what we're low on and pull out those boxes as you find them."

"All right." She watched him turn and disappear into the other room. He was a kind man—unlike anyone she'd met in a long while. The gentle way he spoke to her reminded her of Grandpa, not that their voices were the same, but the tone was similar. Too bad she hadn't met Baron before Mark, but then she would have been far too young for the man. He must be at least ten years older than she.

She stamped her foot. What in the world was she thinking? She wasn't interested in any man—especially Mark's brother.

After the Sunday service, Jack sat on the front bench of the McGradys' buggy, along with Phillip McGrady, while his wife sat in back with Nick and Lee, telling them a story about the first time she rode a horse. Jack glanced over his shoulder to check on the boys. Nick was actually smiling, and Lee had laid his head against the woman's arm.

Jack turned around, feeling more at peace than he had since first meeting Mr. Beatty in Comstock's General Store. He'd prayed last night and again this morning and truly believed the boys were meant to go with Phillip and Emily.

Jack pointed toward the street they approached. "Turn left up there, and then Cora's house is the third on the left."

"It was nice of your lady friend to invite us to dine with her."

"She's merely a friend, not"—he waved his hand in the air—"a lady friend."

Phillip glanced at him. "Forgive me for saying this, Pastor, but I'm not sure she feels that way."

Jack peeked at the boys again, glad they were fully engaged in Emily's passionate tale. He leaned close to Phillip, keeping his voice low. "What do you mean?"

Phillip grinned. "You really don't know?" He shot Jack a quick glance then focused on turning the team.

"Know what?"

"And Emily thought I was blind when it came to romance." Shaking his head, Phillip chuckled softly. "That woman is in love with you."

Jack felt as if someone had walloped him in the chest with a fifty-pound bag of feed. Was that why Cora seemed to show up every time he stepped outside? Why she brought him goodies and wanted to spend time with him? He blew out a sigh.

"It's not a death sentence, you know. Unless you don't feel the same."

He liked Cora—a lot—but did he love her? He wasn't even sure what love felt like. The only people who'd ever loved him had been his family, but he ran away from them when the pain of what he'd done had become overwhelming. He rubbed the back of his neck with his hand. "I don't have anything to give a woman. Don't even have a house of my own." He couldn't tell the man that his job was in jeopardy, too. Nor could he talk about the restlessness he'd felt of late. There was something God wanted him to do, but he didn't yet know what it was or where that task might take him. How could he commit to a woman with that hanging over his head?

"A home is important, but your relationship with the woman is foremost. If you truly love her, you'll find a way to make things work."

But did he love Cora? He did enjoy her cooking and appreciated her help with the boys. She was a good woman, whom any man should be proud to call his own, but was she the woman for him? And that remained the crux of the matter. He didn't know.

"Emily and I were dirt poor when we first started out. All we had was the homestead my uncle sold me the rights to. But now we have a nice house, a barn, and over a hundred head of cattle. We're doing all right for ourselves—except that we haven't been able to have children."

"I think you've solved that problem this weekend."

Phillip's gaze shot to his. "Are you saying what I think you are?"

Jack nodded. "I am." He pointed to a light yellow house. "That's the Sommerses' house."

A wide grin spread across Phillip's face as he slowed the wagon in front of Cora's home. "Whoa, Fred. Sadie."

Jack tied the team to the hitching post while Phillip helped Emily and Lee from the buggy. Nick hopped out on his own. Jack winked at him, but the boy's expression remained sober. He was smart enough to know what was happening. Maybe he needed to have a talk with the boy.

After he knocked, Cora opened the door, her wide smile welcoming. "Come in, everyone. We're excited to have all y'all join us."

Jack stood back to allow the McGradys to enter with the boys; then he followed, locking eyes with Cora. She flashed him a special smile, which sent his innards into turmoil. "Cora." He removed his hat. "It was good of you to invite us for dinner."

"Mama suggested it when I told her what you told me this morning about"—she glanced toward the others—"you know."

"Still, I do appreciate it."

She closed the door and shifted into hostess mode. She approached the McGradys. "In case you don't remember, I'm Cora Sommers."

Cora's mother glided out the dining room door. "Welcome to our home. Dinner is ready, so let's move into the dining room."

Lee gazed up at Mrs. McGrady then slid his hand into hers. Nick frowned, crossing his arms, but he didn't say anything.

"Something sure smells delicious." Mr. McGrady held out his arm, and his wife looped hers through it. Then he looked down at Nick. "Would you like to go first?"

The boy's solemn expression turned to surprise, but he nodded and followed Mrs. Sommers into the dining room. He started to sit but then pulled out a chair and shyly smiled at Emily.

"Why, thank you, Nick. What a gentleman you are."

Nick took the chair next to hers, his cheeks red.

Lee scrambled into the chair to Emily's left, leaving Mr. McGrady the chair at the end. By his pleased expression, Jack doubted the man minded sharing his wife. He stood behind a chair on the far side of the table, waiting for the women. Mr. Sommers moseyed in from the kitchen, carrying a platter heaped with sliced ham, and greeted everyone. Jack's mouth watered. Most Sundays, he was invited to the homes of his parishioners and enjoyed a wholesome meal, but the rest of the week, he had to endure his own cooking. A man could only tolerate so many meals of brown beans and burned corn bread.

As the meal progressed, Jack learned more about the McGrady family as Cora and Mrs. Sommers guided the conversation, and the more he heard, the more he felt at peace with the couple taking the boys. God had been faithful to answer his desperate prayers by supplying a kindhearted Christian family as parents for the Beatty boys.

Emily sliced Lee's meat for him and wiped his face a time or two and engaged Nick in conversation. The boy's eyes lit up when he learned they had horses on their small ranch, although Lee was more impressed with the fact that the McGradys had two dogs and three barn cats.

After dinner, Jack took a walk with Phillip and Nick while the women entertained Mrs. McGrady. Lee remained behind, asleep with his head on Emily's lap.

As soon as they were clear of the house, Nick looked up at Phillip. "You came for us, didn't you?"

Phillip stopped suddenly and nodded. "We were hoping that you boys would still be unclaimed and that you might like us and want to come home with us."

Nick scowled. "How come you don't got no kids of your own?"

Jack touched the boy's shoulder. "That's a rather personal question."

Phillip held up a hand. "It's a fair one, given the circumstances, and I don't mind answering it. My Emily has not been able to have children. We've longed for some for years, but God hasn't seen fit to bless us. I think maybe He had other plans."

"You mean like me and Lee?"

"Yes. We'd be good to you boys, and I would expect you to be kind to Emily. She's a sweet woman with a big heart. I think she's already falling in love with you and your brother. I don't want to see her get hurt."

"I wouldn't hurt her. I can tell Lee already likes her. . .and, well . . .I reckon I do, too." The boy shrugged. "Been a long while since we had a ma."

Jack bent to look Nick in the face. "So are you saying you *want* to go home with the McGradys? It's your choice to make. No one is going to force you to go if you don't desire to, but you understand that I can't keep you, even if I'd like to."

Nick studied Jack then Phillip and nodded. "I guess so."

"You *guess* you want to go with them?" Jack asked. "It's a big decision, and you need to know for sure."

Nick looked up at Phillip. "Can I have a horse of my own?"

Phillip looked to be fighting a grin. "Every man who works on a ranch needs his own horse. But first, I expect you to go to school and get an education. It's important that you know how to read and cipher. You need those skills to run a ranch, and mine will be yours and Lee's one day, if you decide you want us for your parents. But a horse shouldn't be the basis for your decision."

"I know. I think y'all will be good to us and treat us fairly."

"We will." Phillip grinned. "So, you've made the decision, then? Do you want to come home with Emily and me and be a family?"

Nick nodded. "Can I still remind Lee about our other family? I'd hate for him to forget."

"Of course you can. We'll always be grateful to your parents for having you."

Nick blew out a loud sigh. "All right. We'll go with you."

Phillip stuck out his hand, and Nick shook it. The boy finally grinned.

Jack fully relaxed for the first time since meeting Mr. Beatty.

Less than an hour later, Jack and Cora waved good-bye to the new family. She turned toward him. "I think they'll be happy together. Did you see how Lee couldn't take his eyes off Emily?"

"I did. And it was nice of Phillip to allow Nick to drive their surrey, even if it's for a short while."

"So, what are you going to do now?"

Jack frowned. "What do you mean?"

"I suppose your place in the church is secure since you found a home for the boys."

Jack shrugged. "I reckon, but the fact that they were willing to boot me out for such a thing still bothers me." He stared off down the road, unable to see the buggy any longer. "And I feel like there's something God wants me to do, only I don't know what it is."

Cora was quiet for a long while. "I think I might know."

His gaze shot to hers, hoping she wasn't suggesting they marry. He couldn't do that until he was certain of his feelings for her and he knew better what his future held. Her sad expression took him off guard. "What are you talking about?"

She ducked her head, her hand going into her skirt pocket. "I should have given you this the day I found it, but I was. . .scared."

"Scared?"

"Never mind." She tugged out a scrap of newsprint and shoved it at him. "Here."

Curious, he unfolded the tiny paper and stared at an ad for horse liniment.

"The other side."

He turned it over, and his eyes instantly latched onto his name. His heart jolted as he scanned the paper. *Searching for Jack Jensen of Kansas. Living near Guthrie. Ask for us at post office. Lara and Jo.*

Chapter 15

Jo stirred the peas on her plate as she waited for Jamie to eat his mashed potatoes. What was she going to do? Things had been going so well at the store, and then Mark had to go and ruin everything—again—and he wasn't even in town yet. Worrying about Badger finding them was bad enough, but now she had to be concerned that Mark would learn she was at her sister's and come looking for her.

She mashed some peas with her fork and mixed them with a dab of potatoes then fed a bite to Jamie. The boy eagerly took it then frowned and spat it out. The glob ran down the towel she'd tied around his neck.

"He not—uh. . .does not like peas." Sarah fought back a smile. "He smart. You not trick him."

"You're right. Maybe I need to smash them up better. He noticed the skins, I think."

"You're not eating much. Aren't you hungry?" Lara took a bite of stewed chicken.

Jo shrugged. "I am, but I have a lot of things on my mind right now."

"What kind of things?" Lara lifted one brow at Michael. "It's not polite to reach across the table, son. Ask for someone to pass something if it's that far away."

Michael ducked his head. "Yes, ma'am."

Gabe pushed his plate back. "That was a fine meal, sweetheart." He glanced at Sarah. "And thank you for your help with the meal, little lady."

Her cheeks turned a deep reddish brown, and she ducked her head. "I like to help Miss Lara."

Sarah's speech was definitely improving. Either Lara was helping her or the girl was listening and trying to mimic them. Whichever, Jo was glad.

"Sarah is quite the student." Lara patted Sarah's hand. "She is already reading short words."

Jo smiled at the girl. "That's wonderful. I'm proud of you."

Sarah stared at her, and if Jo wasn't mistaken, moisture dampened her eyes. Once again, Sarah looked at her lap. Had no one ever told her they were proud of her?

"Before you know it, she'll catch up with Michael." Lara glanced at her son, as if the challenge might stimulate him to work harder.

"Huh-uh." He drew the syllables out to make one long word.

"Huh-uh is not a word, son." Gabe sat back in his chair.

"You say it."

Gabe frowned. "I do?"

Michael nodded.

Gabe looked at Grandpa. "Is that true?"

He made an exaggerated effort of rubbing his jaw and appearing to be thinking; then he grinned. "Uh-huh."

"Ha! Grandpa is old, and he still needs to work on his manners."

Everyone at the table chuckled at Michael's observation. Jamie squealed, as if enjoying the light atmosphere. Jo smiled, but it did little to remove the heaviness from her spirit.

"Guess we all need to work on that." Gabe gently elbowed Michael. "I challenge you and Grandpa to a checkers game as soon as you're finished eating. Whoever wins the most games is the winner."

"I'm done." Michael shoved his plate away.

"Finish your peas first." Gabe pointed his fork at Michael.

Jamie grunted and tugged at the towel tied around his neck, indicating he was done.

"Looks like Jamie wants to play checkers, too," Michael said.

Grandpa pushed back his chair. "I'll take the li'l squirt."

After wiping off her son's face and hands, Jo lifted him up to Grandpa and watched them leave the room. She rose and started stacking the empty plates then carried them to the dry sink counter. She would actually miss her family when the time came for her to leave again. When she'd first run away from home, she'd been in such a foul mood that she hadn't missed them in the least. Well, maybe Michael and Grandpa, but certainly not Lara or Gabe.

Sarah scraped the plates into the slop bucket. "This is full. I will take it to the hog."

Once the kitchen door shut, Lara rounded on Jo. "What's wrong? And don't bother denying it. Ever since you got home from work, your lips have been puckered like a hem with the thread pulled too tight." She crossed her arms. "Did Baron do something that upset you?"

She didn't want to answer, but she couldn't let her sister think badly of Baron. "No, not at all. He's always been a perfect gentleman."

Lara's posture relaxed. "Well, I'm glad to hear that. So what is it that's troubling you?"

She set several cups on the counter then went back for more. Lara's hand stopped her.

"Sometimes it helps to share our problems. You've nothing to fear from me, Jo. I love you no matter what, and I always will."

Jo hung her head. She didn't deserve that love. If only Lara knew how far she had fallen. She never would, not if Jo had her way, but still, maybe she could help with the current problem. She looked at her sister. "Baron got a telegram today stating that Mark was returning to Guthrie by the fourteenth."

Lara frowned. "So, that's not good news?"

Jo blew out a loud breath. "I knew you wouldn't understand. Mark left me. He found out I was pregnant again, and instead of battering me so I'd lose the baby like he did with the others, he simply left town."

The color drained from Lara's face. "Oh, Jo. I had no idea things were so bad for you. Why didn't you come home?"

"Because I couldn't face you, especially with you and Gabe so happy." She crossed her arms, wishing she hadn't revealed so much. When people knew your weak points, they often used them against you.

Lara pulled out the nearest chair and dropped into it. "I'm so sorry. What are you going to do?"

"Stay here until he's gone. I will not see him."

Fingering a frayed place on a napkin, Lara shot her a glance then looked away. "Did you. . .divorce him?"

Jo sniffed a sarcastic laugh. That certainly wasn't necessary. "No."

"So you're still married to the man."

She hated seeing her sister hurting. Unsure what to do with the odd feelings, she pulled out a chair and sat. A part of her wanted to tell Lara everything. If she couldn't tell her sister, who could she tell? And yet, some parts were too heinous for Lara to hear. "I have something to tell you, but it's not easy to hear." She drew in a strengthening breath. "I found out that the preacher Mark hired to marry us wasn't a real one."

Lara sucked in a gasp. Jo could see her patching together what that meant. Tears glistened in Lara's eyes, and she reached out and clasped Jo's hand. "I'm so sorry. I know how much you loved him."

"Thank you." Jo tugged her hand free. "I'm not sure I really did love him. Oh, I was charmed by him and in love with the dream of marrying a handsome, well-to-do man, but I don't know that I ever truly loved Mark."

"Your life must have been so hard after you found out."

"I didn't find out until after he left town. The 'preacher man' found out Mark was gone and took delight in informing me of their little secret."

"You must have been devastated."

Jo nodded. "I was at first, but now I'm glad I was never truly married to the louse."

Lara was silent for a long while, and Jo could just imagine what she was thinking. "If you feel that having me stay here—a woman who had a child out of wedlock—will affect your reputation, we can leave."

Lara's gaze shot up. "I won't hear of it. You're far more important to me than my reputation."

Touched by her sister's passionate tone, she shook her head and fought not to show how much Lara's confession meant to her, especially after all she'd done. "You have to think of your family."

"It's nobody's business who I host in my home, so get that thought out of your mind."

Jo nodded, unable to talk because of the tightness in her throat. She'd been so wrong about her sister in the past. Why hadn't she noticed years ago? It would have saved her so much pain and sorrow. And to think how much she'd hurt her family. Footsteps sounded outside, signaling Sarah's return. Jo jumped up. She had to get out of there before she started blubbering like a baby. "I. . .uh. . .need to check on Jamie."

"Just remember. . .you're safe here. Gabe and I won't let anything happen to you."

She nodded again and fled the room, but instead of heading to the parlor where the men and boys were, she turned and rushed up the stairs.

Baron stared at the calendar. Today was Monday the seventeenth. The train on the fourteenth had come and gone, but Mark wasn't on it. Had the telegram merely been a joke to rattle him, or was it for some other purpose? Or had something happened to his brother? Baron had waited at the depot until the train had prepared to depart again, but Mark did not get off.

He walked to the window and stared out. It bothered him that he was glad Mark hadn't arrived. He shouldn't feel that way toward his own flesh and blood, but he and Mark had never been close. When they were young, he'd tried to develop a relationship with him, but Mark saw everything as a game—or competition. Their mother had no qualms about spoiling her younger son and showing he was her favorite. That hadn't bothered Baron too much since his father favored him, but it seemed to have affected his brother in negative ways.

Mark saw every pretty woman as a challenge—something to be conquered. It was a wonder he ever married Abigail, but that was probably because their father threatened to cut him from his will if he refused. His father was tired of Mark's gallivanting and besmirching the Hillborne name. Life would have been far better for his sister-in-law if he had refused—and maybe Jo, too. But there was a part of him that was glad Mark had no claim to her. He gritted his teeth at his train of thought. He needed to stay focused where Jo was concerned. She was the mother of his nephew. That was all.

He might be attracted to Jo, and he liked her, but he couldn't—wouldn't—lose his heart to a woman his brother had been involved with. Mark would never let him live that down. He'd always be rubbing it in his face and reminding him that he was playing second fiddle to him.

There was another train due today, but he wasn't going to close the store again and risk losing business. If Mark was on it, he knew where the store was located and could come on his own.

He sure wished he knew if Mark was coming or not. Jo couldn't return to the store until they knew for certain. He straightened several cans of beans then turned another can so that the label was facing forward, like his father taught him. Then he continued to the other vegetables.

Jo needed money, but she'd never stated what it was for. He suspected that she wanted to get a place of her own, maybe a small cottage in town or a room at the boardinghouse. He could hardly blame her. His permanent home had always been the Hillborne estate, but he thoroughly enjoyed times when he was working in another town and had his own place like the house Mark had built. The only thing he didn't like about it was the cooking and cleaning, but he was too neat to let things go for long.

The door rattled. He forced a smile on his face and spun to greet his customer. His smile drooped, and he blinked his eyes to make sure of what he was seeing. "Mother? Father? What are you doing here?"

His mother's lips quivered, and she rushed to him, falling into his arms. "Oh, Baron."

Patting her back, he looked to his father for an explanation and noticed the lines of tension creasing his face. "Your brother is dead."

His mother's sobs filled the store. He didn't know what to do other than continue to hold and pat her. He nodded toward the door. "Would you mind locking the door and flipping the sign to Closed? You might even draw the shade to give us some privacy."

His father did as requested then joined them. "Maureen, get ahold of yourself."

His mother suddenly pushed away. "How can you say that? My baby is dead!"

"Mark hasn't been a baby for many years."

"That hardly matters. Why aren't you more upset?" She dabbed her nose with her lace handkerchief.

"Hysterics accomplish nothing." His father looked at him, his expression stern.

Baron knew his father would grieve over Mark in his own way, but he wouldn't miss all the problems his son created. "I suggest we go to the house. It's just behind the store. You'll be more comfortable there."

"I told the porter to bring our luggage here."

"If the store isn't open, he'll know to come to the house. I imagine you're tired from your travels." And the stress of losing their son, but he left that unsaid.

"I'm exhausted, but I could use a cup of tea."

Baron strode to a shelf and snatched three boxes of tea he thought his mother would like. "Follow me, and we'll get you situated."

As they crossed the short distance from store to house, Baron searched his mind, trying to remember how clean—or not—the house was. But they were already on the porch, so it hardly mattered now. He opened the door, allowed his parents to enter first, and then followed and shut the door.

"This is nicer than I expected, although it could stand a good scrubbing." His mother walked into the parlor and gazed at the furnishings.

Baron hadn't considered before that Jo more than likely had a hand in picking them out, if not doing it solely herself. The thought warmed him and made him appreciate everything in a new way.

"There's one bedroom downstairs, which you and Father can have. I'll need to change the bedding and, um. . .tidy up a bit."

"Don't you have a housekeeper for that?" His father removed his hat, revealing his thick white hair. At one time, his hair had been blond, like Mark's, but not anymore. His mother's hair was still brunette, with becoming silver highlights. She was still a pretty woman, although she'd gained weight in the past few years.

"I haven't lived here long enough to hire one. I mean, I guess I could have, but I didn't feel I needed one. I'm not here much, and I often take my meals at the town's small café. The food is quite delicious and reasonably priced."

"Maybe you should consider it." His father's tone left no room for argument.

"Have a seat, and I'll stoke up the stove and set the water on to boil." He showed his mother the boxes of tea he'd taken from the store, and she selected one.

Once he'd seen to the task, he sat in a wingback chair near the sofa. He could hardly believe his brother was gone. "So, tell me what happened to Mark."

His mother sniffed and lifted her handkerchief to her nose. She shook her head. His father pursed his lips and stared out the window for a moment, as if gathering strength to talk about it. Baron wondered why he didn't feel more upset. His little brother was dead. Yes, he'd been a burr under his saddle most of his life, but he was still his kin. And Mark had died not knowing God unless he'd become a Christian since Baron last saw him. As much as he wished that were true, he doubted Mark would have yielded his life to God.

His father blew out a loud sigh. "Your brother got involved with a married woman, and her husband didn't take kindly to the idea. He went after Mark and gunned him down at the train depot." His chin trembled, but he stiffened it. "Word was sent to us, but he was dead before I arrived."

His mother moaned and leaned her head on his father's arm. "Oh. . .my poor son."

"Shh. . .Maureen." He shifted his shoulder, and she sat up. "If he hadn't been consorting with a married woman, he'd still be alive. I should have trained him better." He jumped up and strode to the window, hands on his hips.

"It's a sad day. Where is Abigail?" Baron wanted to comfort his mother, but he knew his father wouldn't like him coddling her. Still, he reached over and patted her hand.

She smiled and moved hers to squeeze his. He straightened before his father turned around. Wilfred Marquis Hillborne II was a hard businessman and had little place for excuses or compassion. He'd ruled the roost of the Hillborne home with an iron fist, or so he thought.

"Abigail has returned to her parents' home. I doubt she will return to ours, now that—" His mother's voice broke, and she dabbed her eyes with her lacy handkerchief.

Baron's heart ached for her. He had learned the mercantile business well, but it was his mother who illustrated the softer side of life. Where his father was organized and strict, his mother was frivolous and carefree, most of the time.

"Our family name is ruined." She shook her head. "Whatever will we do?"

His father spun around. "No, it is not, and I won't have you thinking it is. Mark isn't the first young man to get caught cavorting with a married woman. Give it a little time and things will quiet down. It won't be long before something else takes its place in the news."

"But what about the funeral?" she asked.

"There won't be one."

His mother gasped. "You can't be serious, Marq."

"I am. I gave the mortician permission to go ahead and bury Mark in the family plot. When we return, we'll have our own private time to remember him."

Baron rose and went into the kitchen to check on the water. Hearing his mother call his father Marq always bothered him. For some reason, still unknown to him, she'd talked her husband out of naming him, their only son at the time, after his father. Most of the time he never thought about it, but obviously it still bothered him. He should have been the one to carry on his father's name, not the younger son. Instead, he bore the name of European nobility—the lowest degree of royalty, at that. Ah well, there was no sense dwelling on that touchy topic.

Pushing aside his troubling thoughts, he prepared the tea, added some cookies to a plate, and set it on a tray, which he carried to the parlor. The silence and his parents' stiff posture indicated they weren't talking to one another.

Baron thought of Mark. He should have done more to try to reach him—to get him to see the error of his ways. He should have hauled Mark to church when he started going, even though his brother didn't want to attend. If only he and Mark had been closer.

His father laid his head back, staring up at the ceiling. The man hurt on the inside and rarely showed any emotion, but Baron didn't doubt his pain. Though Father was often strict and grumpy, Baron never doubted his love, unlike Mark.

He handed a saucer and cup to each parent then took his seat again. "How long do you plan to stay in Guthrie?"

His mother waved her hankie in front of her face. "Until the scandal dies down, of course."

Baron's heart bucked. If they stayed, how could Jo work? He couldn't very well go out to visit and leave his parents alone on Sunday. How long would it be before he could see her and Jamie again?

And how was he going to keep them a secret from his parents?

Chapter 16

Jo hung a diaper on the line and stared at the hill she crossed each day she went to town. "Why hasn't Baron sent me word? I'm dying to know whether Mark showed up or not."

Lara removed the wooden pins from her mouth. "I imagine, if Mark did arrive, it would be hard for Baron to get away for any length of time."

Jo grabbed another clean diaper and sighed. "I suppose that does make sense. Still, he should be able to send me a note."

"Be patient. You know he will when he can."

"If only it didn't rain so much on Sunday and Gabe had been able to go to church. He could have talked with Baron there."

"Well, it did, so there's no point in moaning about it." Lara pinned a pair of socks to the line.

"You don't suppose Gabe could spare Luke long enough for him to ride into town and find out, do you?"

Lara stepped out from behind the diapers on the line and lifted one brow. "I doubt it."

"Well, it was worth a try."

Lara chuckled. "I wouldn't expect anything less from you."

The teasing tone of her sister's voice took the sting from her comment. "I've been thinking, now that the ground has dried, I might ride to town and see if I can find out anything."

Lara pinned another diaper to the line. "Only if you want to run the risk of Mark seeing you. He's not likely to stay in the store, you know. What if he saw you riding down the street?"

"I hadn't thought of that, but this waiting is driving me loco. And I need to be working."

"Can I ask you why? You must have a good reason that you need the money since you're willing to be gone from Jamie for so long."

Because horrible men are after me. Because a man probably wants to kill me. What could she say to pacify her sister? "We can't stay here forever, you know."

"It's fine with me if you do."

Lara had always been generous and kind. "I know, but one day you'll need the room, and I'm sure Gabe doesn't appreciate having three extra mouths to feed."

"Gabe doesn't care as long as I'm happy, and having you and Sarah and Jamie here makes me ecstatic. Grandpa has even been livelier since you arrived."

"You're too kind. One of these days someone is going to take advantage of your generosity."

"God has been good to Gabe and me and blessed us so much. How can I not share all that I have?"

"Just be careful. There are people who love preying on others."

Lara frowned. "You speak like you know what you're talking about. Has someone done something to you?"

Jo huffed a sarcastic laugh. "Look at what Mark did. Isn't that enough?" And if not, there was always Badger—or rather, Pete Worley, as he'd called himself when she first met him. Once again, she'd been charmed by a snake of a man and poisoned by his bite—a poison that had touched every part of her life except for Jamie. Jamie was the one unblemished thing in her life.

She needed to change the subject before she confessed her

horrible past to her sister. "Sarah seems to be doing well in her studies."

Lara lifted one eyebrow again, as if indicating she knew Jo had changed the subject. "Yes, she's a delight and such a smart girl. She's so sharp. I'm surprised she hasn't taught herself to read before now. She's almost caught up with Michael."

"She sure likes to learn. Back at the bord—boardinghouse she was always quiet." Sweat trickled down Jo's temple. She'd almost said *bordello*. "That's the last of the diapers. I'm going to empty the wash water."

With the laundry basket on her hip, she scurried toward the house. She had to be more careful. Lara might not throw a stink if she learned where Jo had been, though she'd certainly be disappointed, but Gabe would probably toss her out of the house. But then, he'd once been a gambler, so maybe he'd be more understanding than she thought.

"Well, howdy, Punkin."

Jo glanced up to see Grandpa sitting on the back porch. She smiled and waved. He'd aged a lot in the years she'd been gone, but she was glad he was still living. He pretty much raised her, at least until Lara was old enough to take over the task. Why had she resented them so much? The reasons had faded away so that she could barely remember.

She set the basket by the door and took the rocker next to Grandpa. "What are you whittling?"

"I thought I'd make your little Jamie a set of animals like Gabe and I made for Lara's boy."

"That's so sweet of you, but he can play with Michael's. You don't have to make a whole new set."

He shrugged and kept on working. "I don't expect that you'll stick around here forever."

She tried not to squirm. Had he overheard her talk with Lara the other day? "What makes you say that?"

"You may have been gone a long while, but I know you." He flashed an ornery grin. "You won't be content to stay here at Lara's place for too long. I reckon you still have itchy feet."

He knew her better than she'd thought. "If things were different, I might stay, at least for a while."

"What things?"

She'd done it again—said more than she meant to. "I have Jamie now and Sarah. They deserve their own home."

"It'll be mighty hard to raise two young'uns while working enough hours to make the money you'll need. Where's that husband of yours?"

"Jo! Jamie needs you." Sarah's call from an upstairs window as well as Jamie's sudden wails were exactly the excuses she needed.

Jo jumped up. "Sorry, Grandpa. Gotta run."

"Don't think I don't know you're runnin' away again," he mumbled as she hurried into the house.

Later that afternoon, Baron walked his father around the store, explaining the changes he'd made.

Marq nodded. "I like what you've done here. You seem to be focused on the specific needs of this town, which will result in more sales."

"That and the fact that we can offer items at a lower price on most things, since you buy so many at one time to supply all of our stores."

"So, are you turning a big enough profit that we should consider keeping the place? Or should we sell it?"

Baron's thoughts instantly shot to Jo. She needed the work, and he wasn't ready to cut his ties with her and Jamie. But he could hardly tell his father that. "We're doing well enough. It was a slow start, but people are realizing our prices are better than other general stores and are venturing in and buying more."

"Good." His father stroked his chin. "The front of the building could do with a fresh coat of paint."

"I know, but I've been concentrating on getting the inside straightened and restocked. I've been planning on painting the facade one evening, but I seem to always be working late on something else."

"Hire someone to do that work. You don't have to do it all, son."

Baron stared at his father. The man had changed. Six months ago, he would have told him to paint it himself in order to make sure it was done right and to save money. Had Mark's sudden death been the catalyst that caused the change, or was it just age and growing wisdom?

Footsteps echoed on the boardwalk.

"I think I'll go check on your mother. She's taking your brother's death hard."

Baron patted his father's shoulder. "It wouldn't hurt you to rest a bit, too. You've worked hard your whole life. Take time to grieve the loss of your son."

His father's gaze jerked to his, and after a moment, he nodded. "You're getting wise in your old age. Now, if only you could settle down and find a wife."

Baron turned away, his lips tight. That was the father he knew. The one always poking and prodding for more, although the topic of a wife usually came up when he talked with his mother.

The bell rang, and a tall man dressed in a blue plaid shirt and what Baron thought were probably black pants strode in. He pushed a slouch hat that Baron recognized as a model from several years ago off his forehead and squinted as his eyes adjusted to the dimmer lighting inside.

"Afternoon. How can I help you?"

"Well, the truth is, I'm looking for some people—Lara and Joline Jensen."

Baron's heart slammed against his chest. What could this man have to do with Jo and her sister? "Might I inquire why you're looking for them?"

The man lifted his brow. "Not that it's any concern of yours, but they're family."

"My name's Baron Hillborne." He held out his hand, hoping to learn the man's name.

"Jack Jensen."

Recognition ignited within him. "You're the long-lost brother?"

Jack smiled, and his posture relaxed. "Ah, so you do know them."

"I do, but you never can be too careful, especially where women are concerned."

"I like that philosophy. Can you tell me where to find 'em? We've been separated for so long, and now that I'm gettin' close, I'm gettin' more anxious than a calf separated from its ma for the first time."

Baron chuckled at the odd analogy. "Lara's married, and she and her husband have a ranch a ways from town. Wish I could offer to escort you, but my parents arrived unexpectedly today, and I can't leave them."

"I understand. Could you give me directions or draw me a map?"

"That I can do." Baron smiled, knowing how surprised the sisters were going to be. He wished he could ride out and witness the reunion, but then, that was a private affair for family. He tugged a large piece of paper from a basket, licked the end of a pencil, and drew a map, indicating landmarks to help Jack find his way. He finished drawing, wondering why he felt bad that he wasn't more a part of the family. Maybe it was his unusual connection to Jamie. Knowing Mark and Jo were never married but they parented a child would turn most folks against her. They would look down on Jo because she was an unwed mother. Somehow, he had to find a way to protect her. He owed it to Jamie—and maybe even Mark. He slid the map toward Jo's brother.

Jack waved the map in the air. "Thanks for this. I appreciate it."

"You're welcome. I hope the reunion is all you're hoping it will be."

Jack sobered. "Me, too. But it's been a long while, and I left rather suddenly at a bad time."

Baron's heart went out to Jack. "I think you'll be pleasantly surprised. Lara and her husband are very friendly and welcoming." He wanted to tell Jack of his connection to the family, but it wasn't his place.

Jack headed for the door. "If you're a prayin' man, say one for me."

Baron walked to the window, watched Jack mount, and smiled. Jo, her sister, and Daniel sure were in for a surprise.

Anxiety gnawed at Jack's gut. He'd traveled a long way, not so much in miles as in years, to finally be at a point where he was able to reunite with his family. Would they be happy to see him, or did they hate him for running out on them? Grandpa was probably the one he'd hurt the most, but he doubted he'd have a chance to apologize since it was unlikely he'd still be living, given the fact that he suffered from malaria, which he caught during his years fighting in the War between the States. Too bad. He'd sure like to see him again. If Grandpa was still alive, he'd have to make a trek up to his ranch in Kansas to see him.

Jack doubted he'd recognize Lara and Jo, all grown up and

married. At least that store owner had said Lara was. Jo was, too, he imagined. She was such a pretty little girl, although headstrong. He smiled at how she never did anything the easy way. Was she still hardheaded, or had she mellowed with age? What was she now—twenty? He shook his head at the thought of his feisty five-year-old sister now a mature adult.

As he reached a fork in the road, he glanced down at the map then took the trail to the right. The temperature here was a tad bit cooler than down in Texas, but from the looks of the green grass and multitude of wildflowers, the Oklahoma Territory got more rain than down south had.

He muttered a prayer as he rode up another hill. "Lord, let this be a happy reunion. It will break my heart to find out the girls hate me." But his sisters wouldn't have posted an ad in the paper if they didn't want to find him.

A good-sized ranch spread out before him with one of the nicest houses he'd seen since entering the territory. He clucked to his horse, which trotted down the hill. Jack's stomach churned. He'd anticipated this reunion for years. Why had he waited so long?

Jo swept the pile of dust off the front porch and turned to go back into the house when she spotted a rider heading her way. Mark?

She rushed inside, shut the door, and slid the lacy curtain aside so she could peer out. As the man drew near, she realized he couldn't be Mark. He looked taller and leaner, and had a more humble bearing, if one could tell such a thing without actually meeting a person.

"What are you doing?"

Jo jumped at Lara's voice. "Someone's coming, and I was afraid it might be Mark."

Lara hurried to her side and looked out through the curtain. "Is it him?"

"No. But it's not Baron, either." She hated the disappointment in her voice. Had she actually been looking forward to seeing him again?

"I don't recognize him," Lara said.

"Me neither. What should we do?"

Lara stepped back. "Open the door."

"Just like that? What if he's a thief?" What if he was one of Badger's men sent to find her?

"Yes, silly. Open the door."

Jo backed up. "You do it. I'm going to get the rifle from the parlor, just in case."

"Oh, pshaw. Most folks out here are friendly. Besides, the Bible instructs us to welcome strangers, because they might be angels sent from God."

Jo rolled her eyes as she hurried into the parlor. "If you say so. I'm still getting the rifle."

Lara didn't respond but opened the door. Jo reached up and was barely able to get the rifle down; then she rushed to the door her sister had left ajar.

"Howdy. Can I help you?"

Jo watched the man gawking at Lara as if she'd suddenly sprouted a tail. He dismounted and walked to the bottom of the steps but didn't move up them. He just kept staring.

How odd.

The man cleared his throat. "Lara?"

"Yes, I'm Lara Coulter. Are you looking for my husband, Gabe?"

He grinned. "No, I'm looking for you and Jo."

Lara sucked in a gasp as Jo tightened her grip on the rifle. Badger didn't know her sister's name, did he? As far as she could remember, she'd never told him, so who could the stranger be?

Suddenly Lara gasped. "Jack? Is that you?"

Jo's heart turned a somersault, and she peered out the door. It had been nearly fifteen years, but she remembered how her brother's eyes squinted when he smiled—just like this man's were doing. Unexpected tears blurred her eyes.

"It's me, sis."

Lara squealed and ran down the steps and launched herself into Jack's arms. Jo set the rifle down, knowing the young'uns were upstairs, and rushed out the door. Jack's eyes lifted to hers, and a warmth she hadn't known in years flooded her. But she refused to make a spectacle of herself like Lara had and remained on the porch.

Gabe and several of the ranch hands raced out of the barn and toward them, obviously having misinterpreted Lara's caterwauling.

Jack swung Lara around in a circle then whispered something in her ear, and she nodded and released him. Gabe rushed to her side, his gun drawn, a worried look on his face.

"Put that away this instant." Lara shoved her hands to her hips. "You're not about to shoot my brother when he's finally come home."

Gabe slid to a halt and stared. "You're Jack?"

Nodding, Jack slid his hand forward. "I am. Pleased to meet you."

Gabe holstered his gun and shook hands then hauled Jack into a bear hug. "I'm Gabe, Lara's other half. I'm sure glad to meet you, too."

A flash flood of emotions raged through Jo as she watched the reunion. Jack had returned. She'd never expected to see her brother again, and now that he was standing here in front of her, she didn't know how to react. She was thrilled but angry. She'd clung to him after their parents died. But he left her, just like her ma and pa. She crossed her arms and stayed where she was when she longed to run to him. Besides, he had a crowd around him already.

She heard him ask, "Where's Jo?"

Everyone turned toward her, and Lara pointed. Jo backed up, bumping against the door. Jack started in her direction, and she reached behind her for the door latch. Before she could move, he jogged up the steps in a lithe, long-legged gait. When did he grow so tall?

He stopped three feet from her, his hands twisting the brim of his hat. "Howdy, Jo. My feisty little sister has grown up into a beautiful woman." He shook his head. "I can hardly believe it."

"What? That I'm grown up or pretty?"

A broad grin made him look more handsome than before, and his blue eyes nearly disappeared into a squint. "There's the sassiness I remember."

She hadn't realized that she'd missed him so much until he was right there in front of her. Her chin wobbled, and her throat grew tight. Unwanted tears stung her eyes. "Why did you leave us?"

He hung his head. "I was too afraid to stay and face the consequences of what I did."

Jo blinked the tears from her eyes. "What do you mean?"

He shook his head. "Let's save that for another day. I don't want anything to mar my reunion with you and Lara. Can you forgive me for leaving?"

A part of her wanted to stay mad, but she couldn't. She'd wanted to see her brother again for so long that her joy overpowered her anger. She nodded and a smile pulled at her lips.

Jack straightened, opening his arms, and Jo fell into them, relishing his strength. Maybe she could never hug her pa again, but Jack was a close second. His arms wrapped around her, and for the first time for as long as she could remember, she felt safe.

For a brief moment, she allowed herself the luxury of enjoying the feeling, but the truth was, she wasn't safe. Not until she could get far enough away that Badger couldn't find her. California sounded like a much less dangerous place to live than the Oklahoma Territory.

Jack loosened his arms but didn't let go. "I just can't believe that you and your sister are so grown up."

"Not only are we grown up, but we're both mothers."

He blinked. "Wow. I don't know why I hadn't considered that, but I'm happy for you." He stepped back and glanced over at Gabe. Luke and another hand were walking back toward the barn. "Which one of those yahoos is your man?"

Jo crossed her arms over her chest again. "He's not here. He's. . .gone."

"Gone away or gone. . .as in dead?"

"I'd just as soon not talk about him." She flashed him a smile, hoping to distract him. "I'd rather hear what you've been doing for nearly fifteen years." She knew she hadn't fooled him by changing the subject, but she didn't want to ruin his homecoming with talk of Mark.

The door jerked open, and Jo jumped.

"What's goin' on out here?"

Jack made a gurgling sound, and Jo glanced up to see his face had gone white as he stared at Grandpa.

"Who are you, and why's everyone standin' around?" Grandpa stepped out and shut the door.

"Grandpa. . . I thought. . ."

Sucking in a loud breath, Grandpa stared at his grandson. "Jack? Is it really you, son?"

Jack regained his senses and smiled. "Yes, sir. It is."

Pure delight engulfed Grandpa's face in a way Jo hadn't seen since the day she returned. She stepped away, overcome with emotion as the two men embraced. How was it that Jack had returned almost at the same time she had? She'd fought coming here so badly, but she had no other option. And now her family was whole.

More than a little amazed, she dropped into a rocker. She knew what Lara would say—that God had brought them home. Jo glanced up at the sky. Could it be true that God brought her here? And if He had, what was the reason?

Chapter 17

In all the years he'd been gone, Jack had never cried, but being here with his family again, and finding out that his grandpa was still alive and doing fairly well, was unbelievable. Tears swelled in his eyes as he hugged Grandpa. The man was no longer strong like he'd been when Jack lived with him, but at least he was still here and hadn't followed Grandma to heaven yet. Jack released his grip and stepped back. "I owe you a huge apology for runnin' off like I did."

Grandpa rested one hand on Jack's shoulder and wiped his eyes as he shook his head. "A man's gotta do what he's gotta do, son. I reckon you had to take the path you did so you could become the man God wanted you to be today."

He rolled that thought around in his mind. "You know, I've never considered that before. Do you reckon it's really true?"

Nodding, Grandpa removed his hand. "I do. C'mon in and meet the rest of the family, and let's all sit down at the table and get filled in on all that's happened in the past years."

Jack laughed. "That will take a long while."

"We've got all day."

"Not me. As much as I'd like to join you, I've gotta get back to work." Gabe grasped one of Lara's hands and leaned in to kiss her. "See you at supper, sweetheart."

"I'll be looking forward to it."

Jack glanced at Grandpa and lifted a brow. "Newlyweds?"

Grandpa surprised him by shaking his head. "Nah. They been married nearly four years. They's just lovey-dovey like that."

"I heard you." Lara lifted her skirt a bit and climbed the stairs. "I can't help it if I still love my husband as much as the day I married him. Nothing wrong with that."

Jo huffed a breath, rose from the rocker, and opened the front door. "I'll put on a new pot of coffee."

Jack offered Lara a hand up the last step, and she took it. He cast a concerned glance at the door Jo just hurried through. "What's wrong with her?"

"We're not certain." Lara shrugged. "She married a man in Guthrie several years ago. He owned a mercantile. One day, less than three years after she married Mark, Gabe went to town and discovered the store was closed. No one he asked seemed to know what happened to either Mark or Jo. Then a few weeks back, she arrived here with her son, Jamie, and a girl a few years older than my son. She's been closemouthed about where she's been since she left Guthrie. I'm not telling you anything she wouldn't."

Grandpa rubbed his chin. "You might not want to ask her too many questions, though."

Jack held up his hands. "I've done some things in the past I'm not proud of. I reckon most folks have their secrets."

Grandpa slapped a hand to Jack's upper arm and shook it. He grinned wide. "It sure is good to see you. I can't tell you how many times I prayed for this day to happen."

Jack's eyes teared up again, and he tugged the others to his side. "You have no idea how great it is to be with y'all again."

"Is that a Texas accent I'm hearing?" Lara gazed up at him, a twinkle in her unusual light green eyes.

"Why, yes ma'am. I reckon it is."

The door jerked open, and a half-grown boy stood there, gazing up at him in wonder. "Are you really my long-lost uncle Jack? I kinda thought Ma made you up."

Jack and the others chuckled. "That I am, son."

"Wow! Where ya been all this time? Fightin' Injuns? Rustlers? Huntin' for gold?"

"Whoa there, son. Let's get inside and give your uncle a chance to relax, and when he's ready, he can answer your questions. This is Michael, my son, by the way. Gabe and I have a daughter, too, but she's upstairs sleeping."

"I hope you won't be disappointed when you hear my story." Jack wondered just how much he should tell. Would his family be shocked to learn he'd been an outlaw for a short time, before he met a man who took him under his wing and set him straight? That he got fired from being a pastor in Glen Haven when he asked for time off to visit his sisters whom he hadn't seen in fifteen years?

It might help the boy or someone else to know how far he fell before God lifted him from the quagmire he'd been in. He drew in a deep breath as he followed his sister and grandpa inside. It wouldn't be an easy story to tell, but he believed God had a purpose in his sharing it.

Sarah sat with the family, listening to Jo's brother as he rattled off the long, winding story of his past. When she first sat down, there had been a sense of joy among the family members, but now that he'd told them he'd been an outlaw, everyone except for Michael had grown sober.

"What kind of outlaw was ya? Train robber? Rustler?"

"Michael!" Gabe shifted his baby daughter to his other arm and gave his son a stern look. "If you can't be quiet and let your uncle talk, you'll have to leave the table."

"Aw. . .I just wanted to know."

Jack looked to be holding back a smile. "It wasn't anything so glamorous as that."

Sarah rose and took her plate and Jo's to the kitchen counter and scraped them. Most of the time she felt like a member of the family, but tonight she felt like an intruder.

"Sarah, come and sit." Lara gestured for her to return to the table. "This is a special night. The dishes can wait."

"I don't mind. You talk with family."

Jo rose and came to her side. "You're as much a part of our family as any of us."

Sarah stared at her, longing for the words to be true. For so many years, her family consisted of only her and her mother. Then Badger had come as her mother was near death and had taken her to live in his house. But it wasn't the type of place she'd hoped for, and he wasn't much of a father. But this family was all she'd dreamed of.

She nodded and took her place at the table. Her place. . .a warm sensation filled her insides. She'd finally found a home.

But what would happen when Jo wanted to leave?

The warm feeling dulled. She'd better not get too comfortable, because she knew Jo planned to leave as soon as she had made enough money. But how long would that take? For some reason, she'd stopped working at the store, but she hadn't explained why.

And lately, Jo had been more skittish than she had since they first arrived. Sarah thought that Jo and Lara were doing better and mending their relationship, even though Jo was often closemouthed. She didn't want her family to know where she'd been living, and Sarah could hardly fault her for that.

She studied Jack as he told how he'd met a man who took him in and told him about God. He was a comely man with blue eyes like Jo's, but his hair was browner than either sister. He looked about Gabe's age, but she suspected he might be a year or two older. Did he have a wife and family somewhere?

"Once I gave my heart to God, I never returned to my old ways. In fact, I was the preacher at a small church in Texas when someone showed me the ad you placed in the newspaper."

Lara drew her hands to her chest and smiled. "I'm so glad that you saw it. I can't remember how many ads we've placed, hoping to find you."

"Me, too. So how did you end up here in the Oklahoma Territory?"

Gabe started telling the story of how he'd been a gambler in Kansas and how he'd come to Caldwell and got caught up in the excitement of the upcoming land run, how he'd sold horses to those participating in the run, and how he'd met Lara and fallen in love. He shared a special smile with her that made Sarah duck her head. Having grown up with her Cherokee mother, she wasn't used to people showing emotions—and this family certainly had their fair share of them.

For a time, she got caught up in Gabe's exciting tale of following Lara during the land run and how his heart had nearly stopped when her horse stumbled and she flew over its head. He told of stitching up the wound and lifted the hair on Lara's forehead to show how nice a job he'd done. Sarah smiled. Living here gave her hope that she could grow into a respectable woman like Lara and maybe have a husband and family of her own one day, but first, she had to keep learning to read, cook, and tend a home.

She dreaded the day she would have to leave this place.

Jack started talking about God and how He'd changed his heart, washed him clean, and made him a new man. She didn't understand all he said, but it intrigued her. Could God change her? Make her clean and a child of God instead of the daughter of a man who owned a house of ill repute?

She'd heard all the different names the people of Oklahoma City had murmured as she and the other ladies went to do their shopping: floozy, strumpet, harlot, hussy. She had no idea what they meant, but she suspected it had something to do with the way the town's men cavorted with the ladies of the house. At her father's house, she had felt she had to keep quiet and remain in the shadows, but here, she was part of the family.

A smile lifted her lips. If she had her way, she'd never leave.

Jo fed Jamie while she listened to the end of Jack's story of where life had taken him. He'd been an outlaw for a time, but now he was a preacher. She started to shake her head at the notion but remembered in time and concentrated on spooning applesauce into her son's mouth.

"I fell a long ways before God found me and changed my heart. If He can change me, I reckon He can change just about anyone."

Gabe leaned back in his chair. "I can testify to how God also changed my life." He glanced at Lara, who held Beth, then at Michael. "I wouldn't have this wonderful family if He hadn't." He shook his head. "I sure didn't know what I was missing."

Jack nodded. "I know. Giving your heart to God is the easy part, but trusting Him with your life can be scary. I never thought I'd be a preacher." He ducked his head. "Guess I'm not too good of one since I got fired after only a month. But when I found out where y'all were, I had to come. Job or not."

"Did you never marry?" Lara asked.

An odd look engulfed Jack's face for a moment; then he gave a brief shake of his head. "Nope."

Jo suspected there was more Jack wasn't saying. As far as she knew, Baron had never married, either. But then, she didn't know him well. Perhaps he had a wife back in St. Louis.

Sarah watched Jack with interest. If not for the huge age gap between them, she might think the girl was sweet on him, but she suspected Luke held that place by the way Sarah watched him and ducked her head when he spoke to her.

While the others talked, Jo wondered if Mark was still in town. Had he come for only a visit, or did he plan to stay? Did it bother him that his brother was now in charge of the store he founded so he'd returned to take over? Mark had been proud that he'd managed to win a town lot in the land run of '89 and had the foresight to order several trainloads of supplies, which the new town desperately needed. He'd thought the Guthrie store was his way of getting out from under his father's stern thumb and had talked about it many times. She hadn't expected him to walk away from it as easily as he had. But then, it was her he wanted to be free from, not the store.

Did Baron feel the same toward his father? She'd never heard him say a negative word about him. She fed Jamie another bite then wiped the dribble off his chin. It looked like Baron wasn't going to contact her about Mark's status. She was going to have to ride to town if she wanted answers.

"I never knew that serving God could make a person feel so clean and whole. I was lost for so long, and I never even knew it. If only I'd stopped fighting and had turned to Him sooner." Jack pursed his lips and blew a breath out his nose. "All those wasted years."

Grandpa reached over and patted Jack's arm. "The important thing is that you're walking with Him now. It's so good to see again."

Tired of all the God talk, Jo rose and wet a cloth in the bucket of clean water then wiped off Jamie's face and hands. "I think this little guy needs a fresh diaper."

Jack gazed at Jamie, smiling. "He sure is a comely lad. He looks a lot like you."

Jo pretended to be annoyed and shot her hands to her hips. "Are you saying I look like a boy, Jack Jensen?"

Chuckles bounced around the table, and Jack held up his hands in surrender, but his eyes still twinkled. "You know what I meant, sis."

Jo smiled and lifted her son from the high chair. "It's good to have you back."

"Good to be back." Jack winked at her, reminding her of the cocky brother she had looked up to when she was small.

She climbed the stairs, holding the rail with one hand and hanging on to Jamie with her other one. Back when she was young, she hadn't understood why Jack had left them. She'd only been five or six then, but she'd seen the hurt in Grandpa's and Lara's eyes. As she carried Jamie upstairs, she thought about how almost everyone she'd ever loved had left her—Jack, her parents. . .Mark.

Her heart clenched. She'd also run away—and she had never before considered the consequences of that action. Back then, she'd seen the pain in Lara's eyes, but she had hardened her heart. Jo had known what she wanted in life, and she was certain she wouldn't find it on this little speck of the earth. She glanced around the comfortable room. The irony was that Lara lived in the house Jo had always dreamed of. Somehow, after all she'd been through, a house no longer mattered half as much as it once had. She only wanted her son to live in a safe place.

She laid Jamie on the bed, smiling when he shook his head and rattled off a stream of unintelligible chatter. He was such a happy boy. If he ever ran away, it would break her heart.

The same way Lara's and Grandpa's hearts had been broken when she left?

Jo blinked her eyes at the sting burning them. Why hadn't she considered the pain it would cause them before she left? Why had she been so stubborn? So selfish?

Jamie squealed, pulling her from her troubling thoughts. She quickly changed him and then set him on the floor and handed him his rattle and a block. He pounded the block against the rattle then giggled. Jo smiled and sat in the rocker. In her contemplative state, she wasn't ready to rejoin the others.

She'd known what she wanted and she'd gone after it, and for a short time, her life had been wonderful. But then Mark changed from a charming and loving husband to a beast. She couldn't do anything right. He started yelling at her, saying she was the cause of all his problems. She hadn't understood the source of his anger. As far as she could remember, she hadn't done anything to deserve it.

And then one day, his anger grew so uncontrollable that he hit her. She closed her eyes, not wanting to remember how he'd raged at her. Blamed her for his problems. Said she was the problem, but when she tried to get him to see reason, he'd told her to shut up and slapped her hard in the face, nearly wrenching her head from her neck. She lifted her hand to her cheek, rubbing the spot. It was the only time he hit her in the face. For two weeks, she had to use face paint to hide the redness and then the bruises. But that hadn't been the worst of it. After that, he pounded her in places that others wouldn't see—her back and stomach—and he kicked her legs. She glanced down at her flat stomach, remembering the two tiny babes she'd lost as a result of Mark's abuse.

Jamie pulled up on her skirt and patted her knee. Needing comfort from her troubling thoughts, she lifted him to her lap and kissed his fuzzy head. Oh, how she loved this boy.

Had Lara loved her as much? If so, her heart must have broken when Jo ran away.

And she was preparing to do it again. She couldn't let Mark get his hands on her son.

She sighed and laid her head back as Jamie relaxed in her arms. She didn't want to leave. The thought slammed into her with the force of a locomotive. She'd finally realized the value of family.

If only Badger wasn't looking for her—and she had no doubt he was. They were far too close to him for comfort, and sooner or later, he'd track them down. She had no choice but to leave—to protect Jamie and Sarah. To protect the rest of her family. Badger didn't care who he hurt to get what he wanted.

Soft footsteps padded down the hall, and Sarah paused in the doorway. "You are not coming back?"

The girl's speech was getting better—less choppy. Jo shrugged. "I planned to, but then I started thinking of many things and got stuck here." She glanced down at her son. "And it looks like he's almost asleep."

Sarah sat down on the bed. She moved more quietly than anyone Jo had ever known. Had she learned to do that from her Indian mother, or did she acquire that skill at the bordello in her efforts not to bother anyone or incur their anger for something petty?

Sarah stared at the floor, her eyebrows dipping then relaxing, as if she struggled with her thoughts.

"Got something on your mind?"

The pretty girl glanced up. "Do you believe in God?"

Jo struggled not to wince. She'd never doubted there was a God, even though she'd seen little of His hand in her life. "I do."

"What your brother say—said. . .it is true?"

"What part are you talking about?" Jo glanced down to see Jamie had fallen asleep. She rose and took him to his bed and laid him down, taking a moment to gaze at his sweet face. She'd come so close to losing him—forever.

Straightening, she motioned for Sarah to follow her out to the upstairs sitting area, and they sat on the settee.

"The part where he was outlaw and God change him."

"I don't believe Jack would tell a falsehood about such a thing, especially since he is a preacher now. So I guess it must be true."

"Would God change me? Make me clean?"

Jo jerked, taken aback. "What in the world could you have done?"

"I run away. And pastor at church said all people have sinned."

That included herself. She'd sinned far more than most—even broke several of the Ten Commandments. If God could save an outlaw, would He save a fallen woman?

Jo almost shook her head. She glanced at Sarah, not wanting to say the wrong thing, but she knew so little about God and the Bible. "Why don't you talk to Jack about it?"

The girl's eyes widened, and she shook her head.

"He's a nice man. He'd probably be happy to chat with you about God."

Sarah stared at the floor. "I cannot."

"Are you afraid of him?"

She shrugged. "My mother say to not trust men."

Too bad Jo's mother hadn't lived long enough to teach her about that. "Some men, like Gabe and Grandpa, and I suspect Jack, are good men who care for and protect women." *And Baron,* her heart told her. "Those are the kind of men you can trust. They don't purposely hurt women."

"But Badger, he does."

Jo thought of how charming he'd been when she first met him. She'd fallen under his spell as fast as she had Mark's. But she was older and wiser now, and no man would ever take advantage of her again. "Yes."

"I thought him nice or I not go with him."

Jo scooted closer and gently put her arm around the girl. "Did he ever hurt you?"

She shook her head again. "Not me, but you and the others."

"Some men like seeing women cower before them. They take joy in hurting those who aren't as strong as they are. Those are the kind of men you want to steer clear of. Do you understand?"

"Yes." Sarah glanced up, confusion filling her black eyes. "But how do I stay away from Father?"

"Your father?"

Sarah nodded.

Jo frowned. "Who is your father? I didn't think you knew him."

Sarah stared at her. "You know him."

"No, I don't. I haven't any idea who he is."

Sarah nibbled her lower lip, looked away and then back. Jo saw her swallow, as if she was trying to work up the courage to tell her.

Suddenly, Jo gasped as it all became clear. "Badger is your father."

Sarah stared at her lap. "Yes. My father is bad man."

Jo sat back, stunned. No wonder Badger had taken her in and treated her so nicely—at least as nice as a man like him knew how. She wanted to say something to make Sarah feel better, but what?

"Lara would tell you that God is your Father. Your heavenly Father. If you have Him in your life, you don't need Badger." She blew out a breath, hoping she'd stated the truth correctly.

Hope flamed in Sarah's pretty eyes.

Chapter 18

Jo rode into Guthrie, looking all around for Mark. She'd worn one of Lara's ugly sunbonnets to help keep her face hidden. Mark wouldn't recognize her unless he looked her straight in the face or heard her voice.

Now she must decide what to do next. Dare she walk into the store like any other customer? Too bad she couldn't have brought Sarah and pretended she was her daughter, but she needed to stay home to watch Jamie when he awoke from his nap.

Her heart pounded almost as much as it had the morning she ran away from Badger. She guided the horse to the street the store was located on, watching the activities of the lively town. Buggies and wagons were parked to the side, while men on horseback moseyed down the street to their destinations.

Jo relaxed. She'd always liked town life much more than living on a ranch, even though she was partial to horses. She enjoyed the town events, dances, and special performances by singers and poets. Shortly after they'd married, Mark took her to hear a famous opera singer, and that night when they'd returned home, they'd laughed so hard they'd gotten tears in their eyes as Jo mimicked the singers. It was one of her favorite memories of her time with Mark—before he changed.

Losing a bit of her courage, Jo guided the horse down the alley behind the store, dismounted, and tied him at the back of Baron's barn. Mark shouldn't have reason to go out there. Heart pounding, she tiptoed across the yard, hoping desperately that Mark wasn't in the house watching her.

The back door was open since the day was warm, and Jo tiptoed in. She took a quick glance around the storeroom to make sure Mark wasn't there then quietly moved to the open door that led into the store. She cocked her head and listened. Someone was moving around, but no one was talking.

She started shaking. This was a dumb idea. If it was Mark, he'd certainly stop her and question her if he saw her. Losing her nerve, Jo backed away toward the rear entrance and ran smack into a body. Someone clutched her shoulders, keeping her from moving.

"Just what are you doing sneaking around here?" A deep voice she didn't recognize boomed.

Baron rushed in from the store, his blue eyes wide. "Jo? Father? What's going on?"

The harsh grip on her shoulders relaxed. "You know this woman?"

"Uh. . .yes, sir. She works for me."

The hands instantly released her. "Then why is she sneaking around?"

Jo spun to face the man, more than a little relieved that Mark hadn't found her, but he likely would if the man kept up this ruckus. Then Jo paused. Had Baron called him Father?

She gazed at the man and saw an older version of Baron. His eyes were hazel and his hair white, but they had the same height and bearing. Jo flashed a smile. "I'm pleased to meet you, Mr. Hillborne."

"This is Jo. . .uh. . .Father."

Mr. Hillborne lifted one eyebrow. "Does she have a last name?"

"Uh. . ." Baron glanced at her.

"Jensen. Joline Jensen. Your son has been very gracious to allow me to work here when he needs assistance."

"Has he now, Miss Jensen—or is it Mrs. Jensen?"

Jo ducked her head. How did she respond to that? In truth, she was Jo Jensen and always had been. But she had a son. Smiling again, as if he'd told a joke, she cocked her head. "It's Miss, sir."

The man's mouth lifted in a smile; then he looked at his son. "Your mother is trying to lose herself in a book. I've a hankering to stretch my legs and see more of Guthrie." He turned back to Jo. "A pleasure to meet you, Miss Jensen."

He strode out the door, and Jo joined Baron. "So, where's Mark?"

Baron's smile disappeared in a frown. He walked back into the store and leaned both hands on the counter. Jo followed, surprised by his unexpected reaction. "Is something wrong?"

He maintained his stance for a long moment then straightened. A muscle twitched in his jaw. "Mark is dead."

Jo gasped. "What? How?"

Baron shook his head. "That's not important. At least you won't have to worry about him returning to town."

She wasn't sure if he meant that sarcastically or seriously. Although she was greatly relieved to know Mark would never bother her—or Jamie—again, she was sad for Baron's loss. Jo laid her hand on his arm. "I'm sorry, Baron. I cared deeply for Mark at one time. I want you to know that."

"What changed? I mean, you once loved him but now you don't want to see him."

Jo crossed her arms and walked to the window. "I don't think you truly want me to answer that."

Baron walked over to where she stood. "He was my brother. I, of all people, know the extremes of which he was capable. One moment he could charm a person into happily handing over his wallet and then stab the man in the back the next. I tried hard to love my brother, but it wasn't my love he wanted."

Jo ran her hand down Baron's arm, stopping short of grasping his hand. He was so different from Mark. "I'm so sorry. I fell under his charm, too. But then things changed."

Baron grabbed her hand. "Tell me, Jo. What changed?"

Her stomach clenched at his touch, but she ducked her head, embarrassed to voice the hateful deeds out loud.

Baron gently squeezed her hand. "You're safe with me, and you can't tell me anything Mark did that I haven't heard before."

She looked him in the face. If he wanted to know, then she'd tell him. "Mark was wonderful at first. Kind, sweet, charming, but things slowly began to change several months after we married. He would get angry. . . ." She swallowed the lump that rose to her throat at the memory of his cruelty. "And then he hit me."

Baron's grip tightened. "I'm so sorry. Did he. . .hurt you?"

"His abuse started with a slap when I said something cocky he didn't like. Things became the worst when I told him I was carrying his child." Embarrassed to be talking about such a subject with him, Jo turned back to the window, gripping the top of the short door to the display area. "I thought the news would make him happy, but he was anything except that. He called me names, pushed me down, and then hit my belly so many times that I lost the baby." Tears burned her eyes. She'd been in so much pain and so devastated by Mark's behavior that she'd barely grieved the loss of her first baby. She'd felt the loss of his love so much more.

Baron gripped her shoulders, his breath heavy. "I don't know what to say. I knew Mark had a cruel side, but to cause you to lose his child. . ." As much as she wanted to believe there was good in Mark, she knew now there wasn't. How could Mark be so cruel as to cause the death of his own child?

Jo shrugged. "He did it twice. I suspect that's why he ran away when I told him I was pregnant with Jamie."

"Thank God he did."

A woman walked by, looking in the window, and Jo realized they were making a spectacle. "I should go."

"Not yet. Please." He strode to the door, locked it, and then turned the sign to Closed. "Let's go to the back, where people aren't watching. I need to tell you something important."

He held out his hand, indicating she should go first, and she walked to the storeroom. Baron followed then shut the connecting door to the store. The rear door was still open, but no one was outside.

"I can't tell you enough how sorry I am for what Mark did to you, but as much as it pains me, I have to tell you something else."

Jo couldn't imagine what would have him so tense. She could believe Mark would do just about anything to get what he wanted—the fake minister was proof.

Baron drew in a loud breath then blew it out, as if gathering his strength. The pain in his expression made her heart ache.

"Your marriage to Mark was never legal, because he was already married."

Jo's mouth dropped. She'd never once considered that could be a possibility.

Baron clutched her shoulders again. "I'm so sorry, Jo. Mark was such a fool. But I fully understand why he wanted to be with you."

She glanced up, surprised by his comment. Her eyes locked with his, and she couldn't look away. Was it possible *he* cared for her?

Baron stared at Jo, his heart galloping faster than a horse running a race. He hadn't realized until that moment how much he was starting to care for her. He wanted to pummel his brother for what he'd done to her, but that would never happen. He glanced at her lips, wanting to kiss her.

Suddenly, he sobered. She was Mark's castoff, and he'd vowed long ago to never pursue a woman his brother had been with. He released Jo and stepped back, ending the precious moment.

As much as he wanted to kiss her, he wouldn't. Not just because she'd been Mark's woman, but he wouldn't take advantage of her like his brother had.

She ducked her head. "What was Mark's wife's name?"

"Abigail."

Jo huffed out an unexpected laugh. "Well, it doesn't surprise me that he was married, now that I've thought about it. I found out after Mark left town that the minister who married us wasn't a real preacher. He was just some man Mark paid to pose as one." She faced the open door, staring out. "The man who told me took great delight in the joke Mark had pulled over on me, and then he propositioned me."

Baron sucked in a sharp breath. "What did you do?"

"I pointed the pistol that I had in my pocket at him, and his smile died on his lips. He took off, and I left town."

"Where did you go? To Lara's?"

Jo shook her head. "That's the last place I wanted to go then. I couldn't face her or Grandpa and admit how badly I'd messed up my life."

Baron wanted to pull her into his arms and offer her comfort, but she might misunderstand. "I wish I knew what to say."

She shrugged, still not turning around. "There's nothing anyone can say."

"One thing I know, God can heal the wounded places in your heart."

Jo didn't respond for several long moments. "I would have laughed at that comment not too long ago, but I'm starting to think it may be true."

"It is. Talk to God. He loves the brokenhearted. He can help when no one else can."

"I should be getting back."

"Jo, look at me."

She sighed then turned, her expression cautious.

"I'll help you however I can."

She lifted her chin. "I won't accept charity."

"As far as I'm concerned, you're family."

She blinked, obviously surprised by his statement. "Thank you, but I still feel the same. If you're willing, I'll return to work since. . ."

Since Mark was no longer a threat.

"You may return whenever you want."

"But won't you close the store and return to St. Louis?"

"For what?"

"The funeral, of course. You couldn't have already had one since Mark died so suddenly and you've been here."

He tightened his lips, remembering what his father had said. "There won't be one."

"But how can that be? Surely your parents will need to honor him."

Baron gazed up at the ceiling, shaking his head. "Mark's death happened in questionable circumstances. Mother is concerned Mark's actions will besmirch the Hillborne name, so Father ordered that Mark be quietly buried in the family plot. We're going to have a private ceremony as soon as my parents feel up to doing so."

"How do you feel about that?"

His lips flattened, and he lifted one shoulder. "It doesn't matter how I feel. It's my parents' choice. But to be honest, I think it's a wise thing to do. Mark has traveled around so much that he didn't have many friends left. Abigail returned home to her parents, who never cared for Mark." He closed his eyes, trying to remember a happy time spent with his brother. They were few and far between.

"I'm truly sorry, Baron. I was never close to Lara, but I would miss her if she were gone. I was more like Mark as a child, refusing to do what my sister asked. Grandpa was the only one who could get me to obey, and even then I often did it begrudgingly."

"I suppose you do know how I feel." He smiled softly. "And I wish I could have known that ornery little girl."

"Trust me, you're better off not having witnessed how dreadfully I behaved." She glanced out the door. "I need to be going. I didn't tell Lara I was leaving."

"Ah. . .still the wild child. Well, not a child but. . .you know."

"I'm trying to change, but it's hard."

He reached out and tucked a loose strand of hair behind her ear. "Don't change too much. I rather like the woman you are now."

Her pretty eyes widened, and her mouth opened slightly. Once again, the thought to kiss her overwhelmed him. He stared at her lips, and when she licked them, his pulse tripled its pace.

Then reason returned. "Ah. . .I was wondering." He cleared his throat, hoping to get rid of the huskiness. "Now that Mark is gone, Jamie is the only connection my parents have to him. I think it would bless them greatly to know he has a son. Would you be willing to let them meet Jamie?"

Jo's face instantly paled. "You can't ask that of me. What if— No! I can't do that."

As Jack walked out of the barn with Gabe, he couldn't help feeling a bit envious. This spread was the kind he always dreamed of owning. But he'd made too many bad choices in his life, and now he had few worldly goods to show for it. The only smart thing he'd done was to realize his need for God and to ask Him into his heart.

Helping the Beatty boys had felt good, too. He hadn't failed them, at least. He muttered a quick prayer for their health and happiness and for the couple that took them in.

"So, what are your plans now?" Gabe rested his arms on the top rung of the corral fence. A black horse with a white diamond on his face moseyed in their direction and nibbled some fresh grass below the fence. Gabe reached through the rungs and scratched the gelding's neck.

Jack lifted his foot to the bottom rail and rested his arms on the top one. "I don't know. Part of me thinks I should go back to Glen Haven"—*and fight for my job*—"but another part doesn't." And then there was Cora. He missed her, but did he miss her enough that he should return and court her? Maybe he was just scared. He'd been moving around since he left home, and setting down roots somewhere seemed so—permanent.

"What? No woman in the picture?"

Jack's gaze zipped to Gabe's. Had the man read his thoughts? "There is. I just can't decide how I feel about her."

"I remember feeling the same with your sister."

"How did you decide she was the one you should marry?"

Gabe's eyes took on a dreamy look, and his lips turned upward in the smile of a man in love. "When I couldn't stop thinking about her—couldn't stop worrying over her welfare. Of course, that happened just a week or two after I met Lara."

Jack's heart warmed, glad that Lara had married a good man who cared so much for her. "She always was a sweet girl. Always trying so hard to keep the family together, even when she was small." Jack shook his head. "I must have broken her heart when I left. Lookin' back, I feel bad about that."

"I can tell you that she never stopped searching for you or

praying you'd come home one day. You've made her very happy by doing that." Gabe tightened his lips. "I hope you stick around for a while. In fact, if you'd like to live here, we have room. I can't pay a lot, but you'd have food, shelter, and family."

"A man couldn't ask for much more than that." But the issue of Cora still remained. He actually missed her. That thought surprised him. Now that he'd found his sisters and Grandpa, he was hesitant to leave. He'd missed them all so much and never thought he'd get to see them again. The fact that he had was a special blessing from God.

He thought of Jo and how she'd gone upstairs yesterday evening after supper and hadn't joined the rest of the family in the parlor. She was hiding something. Jack had a feeling she might need him. "I guess I should spend some time in prayer and see what the good Lord wants me to do."

"Always a wise thing to do. I noticed that mount of yours looks like he oughta be turned out to pasture. Help yourself to any of the horses in the barn or corral if you'd like to ride out and spend some time alone. With a houseful of women and young'uns, I sometimes do that."

"Good idea. I enjoy takin' a ride on a pretty day and prayin'. Of course, I'd like to help you, too. Earn my keep."

"There's no rush on that. Spend some time with your sisters." Gabe pushed away from the fence. "Like I said, take your pick of the horses—all except for the black here. His name is Tempest, and he's my mount." The horse lifted his head at hearing his name.

"Thanks."

Gabe slapped Jack on the shoulder. "I'll be praying God shows you what to do."

"I appreciate that."

Jack watched his brother-in-law walk away, tall and confident.

Lara had married a fine man, but what about Jo? She'd said her husband was gone, but did that mean he was dead or merely away on a trip?

He turned and walked back to the barn, ready for a long talk with his Maker. Something about Jo bothered him, but he didn't know what it was. Maybe she needed his prayers.

He saddled a gray gelding then turned the horse toward Guthrie—the same direction he'd seen Jo ride out over an hour ago.

Chapter 19

Jo hurried out the back door of the store. She couldn't believe Baron would almost kiss her—not that she'd let him—and then pull away to ask something so difficult of her. If his parents met Jamie and learned he was Mark's son, they'd want to see him all the time. And if she left town as she planned, it would break their hearts. It was better they didn't know about him at all.

"Jo! Wait. Please." Baron rushed after her and stopped her with his hand to her arm. "I know what I'm asking isn't easy. But think of my parents and their loss. Jamie—"

"Jamie is not a bartering tool. He's my son."

"And my nephew—and my parents' only grandchild. He's all they have left of Mark."

For a split second she wavered. Would it be so bad for Jamie to have a grandmother to love him?

But she wasn't staying. And their leaving would only bring his parents more grief. She shook her head. "I can't."

Baron dropped his hand, his gaze narrowed. "Why not?"

What could she say to appease him?

"Jo—"

She held up her hand. "Your parents would want nothing to do with Jamie if they knew where he was raised. You talk about scandal."

"What?" He frowned. "I don't understand."

"Never mind. I have to get back."

She rushed down the steps, but he continued to follow her.

"You can't make a statement like that and then run off."

She spun around. "I don't owe you an explanation of my past."

He held up his hands. "You're right, of course. But I beg you to reconsider. My parents are getting older, they're hurting, and knowing about Jamie would breathe new life into them."

"And what's in this for Jamie?" She crossed her arms.

"Think about it. My parents are wealthy. Father owns dozens of stores in various cities. I imagine Mark's half of our inheritance would belong to Jamie."

Jo hadn't considered that, but she wouldn't sell out her son for money. "But in return, they'd want Jamie to be part of their lives." She shook her head. "It wouldn't work. I'm headed west, not east."

Baron's forehead crinkled. "West? What do you mean?"

Jo suddenly realized he'd gotten her so flustered she'd blurted out more than she intended. "I have to go."

She started for the barn again, but he ran past her and blocked the way. "You're leaving? Why? I know your sister would let you stay with her."

It seemed there was no way to make Baron understand unless she told him the awful truth. And he'd hate her when he knew. That thought saddened her. At some point, she'd started to like Baron Hillborne, and the idea of never seeing him again left her feeling hollow. No matter. He'd soon be done with her and Jamie.

"I can't stay here. There's someone who is after me—and Sarah."

"A man?"

Jo nodded. "His name is Badger. And he runs. . ." The starch fled her shoulders. Telling him was so much harder than she had expected. She didn't want him to despise her. She wanted what she could never have—him. The sudden thought surprised her.

He took hold of her hand. "Tell me who he is. I can protect you and Jamie."

Tears burned her eyes. "No. You can't. You won't want to once you know the truth."

"Then tell me. And let me be the judge."

And he would. He'd judge her just like everyone else who knew the truth. It was best to get this over with. She lifted her chin. "Jamie spent the first year of his life in a bordello."

Baron frowned. "I don't understand."

"You truly don't—or you don't want to?" Anger burned through her. "When Mark left me alone and pregnant, I had nowhere to go. I stayed at the house you're living in for a few weeks, until I was out of food. I knew I had to leave—and I wasn't about to go crawling back to Lara's, although in hindsight, I wish I had."

"What happened?"

"I met Badger—a charming man like Mark. He wanted a wife and family and offered to marry me. He said he would take care of me." She bit her lower lip and looked away. She'd been such a fool. So desperate that she'd listened to another deceiving snake charmer. "He didn't marry me, but he did take me home with him." She looked Baron full in the eyes so he'd have no doubts. "He took me to his bordello—the whorehouse he ran—where I've lived for the past year, until I managed to escape."

Baron's mouth dropped, and his eyes widened. Jo couldn't bear to see the look of disgust she knew would come, so she turned and ran past the barn to her horse. She mounted quickly and trotted down the alley.

Baron didn't follow or call out this time.

Baron couldn't have chased after Jo if he wanted to, because his body felt frozen in place. Numb to the core. Had she meant what she said about living at a bord—the thought was too horrible to even consider.

It certainly would explain her secretiveness.

He leaned against the back porch railing. Disgusted at the thought of her in such a place. No respectable woman—

Baron gritted his teeth. Mark had done this to her. What a maggot his brother was. Deceiving Jo. Getting her pregnant—and then leaving her alone with no means of support. If Mark hadn't lied and tricked Jo into thinking they were married, she wouldn't be in such a fix. And who was this hooligan who was looking for her?

Baron bent forward, resting his head on the rail. So many emotions swarmed him that he didn't know what to do. He wanted to chase after her again, but he couldn't ignore everything she'd told him. Not only had she been with his brother, but other men, too. His stomach swirled. Thank God he hadn't told his parents about her and Jamie. Talk about a scandal.

Guilt riddled him as if he'd been shot a dozen times. The pain of it made his heart clench. He hadn't realized that he was so attracted to Jo. He thought himself gallant for offering her a job when he didn't really need the help. But she had neglected to tell him that the money she made would take her and Jamie away. More than likely, he would never see his darling nephew again, especially now.

He dropped onto the top porch step and sat with his elbows on his knees. What a mess this whole situation was.

He'd vowed long ago to never fall for one of Mark's castoffs, but then Jo came into his life and slipped under his guard. Sure, he was attracted to her because of her beauty and spunkiness. But she'd proven to be a hard worker at the store and a loving mother to her son. She and Jamie had stolen part of his heart, but he couldn't—wouldn't—court a woman who'd given herself to other men. It was unconscionable. Unscriptural.

His decision made, he rose. His heart hurt, but he had to toughen up. This wasn't his first disappointment, nor would it be the last.

Good thing he found out what Jo was truly made of before he did something foolish like ask her to marry him. His stomach churned at the thought.

At least Jo had the sense not to tell his parents. If word got out that the Hillborne heir had been raised in a brothel—

"What are you doing out here, son?"

Baron jumped. He'd been wallowing in his thoughts so deeply he hadn't heard his father's footsteps. "I. . .uh. . ."

"Ahh. . . It finally hit you that your brother is dead?"

"Something like that."

Jo was dead to him.

Jo was drowning. She felt as if she were being pulled under in a never-ending whirlpool. Confessing her past to Baron had taken more out of her than she'd realized, and it had ended the first real friendship she'd ever had with a decent man.

But her pain went deeper. When had she started caring for him?

Knowing she'd wounded him so badly made her innards wither. She felt dirty. Alone.

And she'd most certainly lost her job before her first payday.

She wanted to cry, but she'd learned long ago that crying never accomplished a thing.

She wanted to rush back to the store and beg Baron to forgive her—to not hate her.

If only she'd made better choices—

A man lunged out from behind a shrub and snagged her mount's reins. The horse jerked up its head and squealed, but it couldn't get free. The man stared at her, sending Jo's heart ricocheting in her chest. She knew him—from the bawdy house.

He cackled, making the hairs on her nape rise. "I knewed it was you at that store."

"Unhand me this instant, or I'll scream." She fumbled in her bulky skirts for her gun.

"Come on down, Sapphire, and let's have us a good time." He held the horse with one beefy hand and dared to run his other hand along her shoe until he touched her stocking-clad calf.

Jo lashed out, kicking him in the chin. The man stumbled back but held on to the reins. Her hand raced through the folds of fabric, hunting for her pocket. A burst of hope surged through her as she found it—but her gun wasn't there.

The man growled and shook his head. He grabbed hold of her skirt. "Why, you little—"

The cock of a gun silenced him. Jo looked up to see Jack aiming his gun at the man. Relief like she'd never known made her weak.

The man released her and the reins and stepped back. "We was just havin' some fun."

"It doesn't look to me like the lady was enjoyin' herself."

The man snorted. "She ain't no lady."

"She's my sister," Jack ground out, his eyes narrowed. "I suggest you get out of my sight before I give you another belly button."

The man's eyes widened; then he glanced at Jo. "We ain't done."

As he lumbered off, Jo rode up to Jack, both glad to see him and embarrassed.

"Did you know him?"

Jo nodded. "I've seen him before."

"You shouldn't be riding alone."

Jo resisted rolling her eyes. "I normally have a gun in my pocket, but I was in such a hurry that I guess I forgot it."

"That's a dangerous mistake for a woman who insists on riding by herself."

"Don't worry about me. I've been taking care of myself for a long while."

Jack stared at her for several moments. "How's that been workin' for you?"

Horrible. Disastrous. "Fine."

"Uh-huh."

She stared at him. Did he know something? "What are you doing in town?"

He looked down the street. "I went for a ride, and God led me here. He must have known you needed help."

The thought that God might have sent her brother at just the time she needed him took her off guard for a moment, but she didn't want him to know it. She fluffed up her bravado. "While I appreciate your help with that lout, I could have managed him on my own."

He lifted one eyebrow as if challenging her statement. "We all need others, Jo. No one should have to live all alone."

She snorted. "That's a fine comment coming from a man who ran away from his family."

As soon as the words had left her mouth, she realized she was guilty of the same crime.

"I'm not proud that I left you and Lara with Grandpa. It grieved me for a long while—still does."

"Then why did you wait so long to find us?"

A muscle in his jaw flexed, and he looked down. She thought he might not answer, but then he finally looked up. "Because I knew that if you knew the truth, you and Lara would hate me."

"What truth?"

"I'm the one responsible for Ma and Pa's deaths."

"How are you responsible?" Jo nudged her horse, ready to be away from Guthrie.

Jack turned his mount, riding alongside. A muscle ticked in his jaw. He flicked a glance at her. "I was smokin' in my room when Pa hollered at me to come down and do chores. I thought I'd gotten the cigar put out, but I must not have."

All this time she'd thought her mother had started the fire. "You don't know for sure that's what caused it."

"There was smoke coming out my window."

"Just yours or all of them?"

"Well. . .I don't remember."

"There's no way that you can know for certain you started the fire. Ma might have done it. The ash bucket might have caught fire—the kitchen curtains. Lots of things might have happened. You need to forget about it and get on with your life."

They rode along in silence, and Jo could tell by Jack's shifting expressions that he was wrestling with the idea. After a long while, he looked her way. "Thanks, sis. I've convinced myself all these years that I was at fault, but now I'm not so sure."

"Even if you were responsible, it was an accident. From what I've heard you say, God would want you to forgive yourself."

A grin broke free, and Jack shook his head. "You just keep surprising me, sis."

She knew he'd be shocked once more to learn she was gone. And she would be as soon as she could. At least she got to spend this time with Jack.

As soon as they reached Lara's house and Jack headed to the barn with their mounts, Jo rushed inside and up the stairs. Voices echoed from the kitchen, but she ignored them. She'd finally remembered the last name of the man who confronted her—Slaughter. She had seen him at the bordello several times. The weasel would run straight to Badger in hopes of getting a reward. It wouldn't take Badger long to get here—no more than a day or two. Her time at Lara's had come to an end. They had to leave—right now.

If only she'd been able to collect her pay from Baron. She had no idea where to go or how they'd get by, but they couldn't stay here any longer.

She tugged the pillowcase she'd taken from the bordello out of the wardrobe then stacked half of Jamie's diapers on the bed. She needed all of them, including the new ones she and Lara had hemmed, but there wasn't room. Next she stacked Jamie's gowns and socks. All she needed for herself was a change of clothing.

Sarah walked in with Jamie on her hip. Her eyes widened, and Jamie grinned and waved. "What are you doing? It is not wash day."

Jo knew Sarah wouldn't be happy about leaving. "A man in town recognized me. He's been to Badger's place before. We have to leave—now."

She turned back to the wardrobe, took out the dark green dress Lara had sewn for her, and removed it from the hanger. Folding it, she spun toward the bed and found Sarah in the same position. "Hurry. You need to pack your things."

"I do not want to go." She shook her head and coughed several times. "It is nice here. I like Gabe and Lara—and Luke—and Michael."

Jo laid the dress down, walked around the bed, and took Jamie. She kissed his cheek then laid her hand on Sarah's shoulder. "I know. Honestly, I don't want to go, either, but we have to. Badger probably already knows we're in the Guthrie area, and it will be a simple matter for him to find out where we're staying. I won't go back to that dreadful place, and I don't think you want to, either, do you?"

Sarah shook her head. "But if we stay, there are others to protect us."

Jo shook her head. "We can't stay. I'm sorry."

Frowning, Sarah crossed her arms.

"Do you know what Badger did last time I tried to run away?"

Sarah shook her head, but Jo could see the curiosity in her eyes.

"He ordered Stoney to beat me. So bad it took weeks to recover."

Sarah's dark eyes widened.

"I won't go through that again—and I don't want to take a chance on you facing the same horrible mistreatment."

"Badger will not hit me—at least I don't think he would." She covered her mouth and coughed again.

Jo barked a laugh. "He certainly had no problem using his fist on me whenever I angered him."

"I am sorry."

"It's not your fault."

Sarah shrugged and sat on the bed. "I not know my father is such bad man until he came and took me from my sick mother." She blew out a sigh. "I think he does not know what to do with me."

Jo checked on Jamie. He'd crawled over to the closed window, pulled up, and was looking out. She sat next to Sarah and put an arm around her thin shoulders. "You must have been frightened to death. No wonder Badger kept you separate from us. He was trying to protect you."

"You and other ladies would not hurt me."

Perhaps it was her innocence he was safeguarding by keeping her to herself. Maybe there was more to Badger than she'd realized. But she still couldn't let him catch them. He'd probably kill her for taking his daughter, even though Sarah had come along of her own free will. The girl had changed so much in the short time they'd been here—not only was her speech improving, but she was also advancing in her reading and writing skills. "You can see now why we have to leave. If he finds us, he'll most likely kill me—and he'll take you back with him. Then what will happen to Jamie?"

Sarah lifted one shoulder as if still not convinced.

Jo had been so busy caring for Jamie and trying to earn money that she hadn't noticed the girl was putting down roots and developing into a child whom Gabe and Lara would be proud of. "I know leaving here will be difficult, but we can return someday, once Badger stops looking for us."

Jamie dropped to the ground and crawled to Jo. She lifted him to her lap, instantly sorry. "Oh! He's soaked."

"I can change him. You must pack."

Jo smiled, glad Sarah was finally seeing things her way. "Thank you. You should pack, too. Just take one extra dress and a change of undergarments."

Sarah shook her head as she unfastened Jamie's diaper. "I not go. I want to stay here."

"I'm sorry, but you can't. If Badger comes here, Gabe and Lara will have to turn you over to him since he's your father. Besides, don't you remember that I promised to keep us together? We're family."

"Lara is your family, but you would leave her."

"That's different. She has Gabe and this fine house, and their children. They don't need me."

"This is better place for Jamie than the trail."

Jo gazed up at the ceiling. Each moment they wasted was a moment Badger could be closing in on them. "I'm going out to the barn to saddle the horse we took from Badger. I don't want it here if he comes. He'd know for certain that we'd been here. Please get your things packed and keep an eye on Jamie. I won't leave you after I promised we'd stay together."

Jo didn't wait for an answer but hurried from the room, feeling so alone. She rushed down the back stairs and out the rear door. Last time she'd left home, she'd been eager and excited to discover what life held for her. This time she'd like nothing more than to stay, but that choice had been taken from her.

There was little doubt that Lara and Grandpa would tell her to stay if they knew her situation, but she couldn't risk that Badger might hurt one of her family members in his effort to find her. Grandpa's regular bouts of malaria left him far too frail to fight off a grown man, and Gabe and the other ranch hands were often gone much of the day, as they were today. Jack had said he would join them after getting a fresh horse, so he should be gone from the barn by now.

One thing she hadn't counted on was Sarah jumping ship. How had that happened? During the time Sarah sat in on Michael's lessons? Or when Sarah was with Lara while Jo was working all day at the store?

She could hardly blame the girl. Traveling was never fun, especially when you didn't know where you were going and had no money to buy the things you needed or to stay in a nice place like a hotel or boardinghouse. Her only option was to travel from town to town and plead help from the local ministers. Church leaders were almost always willing to help a woman in need. But then that left a clear trail for Badger to follow.

Running away wasn't the best choice, but what else could she do? Walking through the open barn doors, she searched the stalls for the horse she'd taken from Baron's barn, but it wasn't there. She blew out a loud sigh. Now what?

Dare she take one of Gabe's horses? She knew he'd give her the animal if she asked, but then he'd know her plans and would stop her. She paused at the stall of a pretty gray horse, but it tossed its head and moved away to the back of the stall, eyeing her. They needed a calm horse that would put up with children, so she moved past several empty stalls to the next one. A brown-and-white pinto nickered to her and stuck its head over the gate, looking for attention. She scratched the animal's head and made her decision. "You ready to go for a long ride, fellow?"

Chapter 20

Badger tried reading about the land run that was to take place this summer, but he stared at the newspaper in front of him, not seeing the words. How had Sapphire managed to sneak away and disappear so well? And had Sarah gone with her, or had she seen Sapphire's success in sneaking off and decided to do the same? He'd been looking for them together, but what if they'd gone in different directions? One of them could be in west Texas by now, and the other. . .who knew?

With a loud sigh, he sat back in his chair. They'd been gone for weeks, and he'd not had a single solid lead as to where they were. He didn't want to quit looking, but Stoney told him when he was gone the other women thought they could get away with things, like refusing customers, pretending to be ill, and whatever else the dim-witted females could think up. If he wasn't careful, he might lose his business, and then where would he be?

He stared up at the ceiling, wishing he'd gotten rid of Sapphire's kid right after it had been born. Then he wouldn't be in this mess.

He muttered a curse and slammed his fist onto his desk—mad at Sapphire, mad at Sarah, and mad at himself.

Stoney pounded on his door. Only his assistant beat on it like it was a foot thick.

"What d'you want?"

The door opened, and Stoney peered in, unfazed by his bluster.

"Someone's here t'see ya."

Badger shook his head and poured himself another glass of brandy. He swigged it back and slapped the glass on the desk. "Don't want to see no one."

"Ya might wanna see this one. Says he saw Sapphire."

Badger sat up. "Why didn't you say so in the first place? Send 'im in."

Stoney nodded and left. Badger grabbed the bottle and set it on the floor beside him then dropped the empty glass over the top of it. No sense lettin' his visitor know it was there.

Unable to sit still, he rose and strode to the door. He recognized the man walking toward him, but he couldn't remember his name. The man had spent more than one night here.

Stepping back to allow the man to enter, Badger gestured toward the chair that sat against the wall. "Have a seat."

The man nodded, licked his thick lips as if he expected something, and then plopped onto the edge of the chair.

Badger took his seat behind his desk, leaned back, and steepled his fingers across his belly. He didn't want to appear too eager because then the information would cost him more. The man sure looked like he could use a coin or two. His faded overalls had more patches than the crazy quilt his ma made when he was a boy. "Who are you? And what do you want? I'm a busy man, you know."

The man nodded. "Ernie Slaughter. I heard you was lookin' for one of your gals what upped and ran off."

"Maybe. Stoney said you'd seen someone who looked like my missin' lady."

"Not looked like. It *was* her. . .Sapphire. I'd'a knowed her anywhere with them big blue eyes and that yeller hair. Whooowee! She's a looker."

Excitement churned in Badger's gut, but he kept his expression neutral. "There are lots of women around these parts with blond hair and blue eyes."

"Maybe so, but they ain't got the attitude Sapphire has. She can pert near slice a man in two with that blue fire blazing from her eyes."

Badger rubbed the stubble on his chin and studied Mr. Slaughter. The name sure didn't fit the pudgy bum.

The man frowned. "I'd have had her if'n some cowpoke hadn't come and helped her."

Badger grunted. The notion of Sapphire taking up with a cowboy didn't sit well with him. "Did she have a young boy or a half-grown half-breed girl with her?"

"Nuh-uh. She was by herself, riding astride on a fine-lookin' horse."

Badger described the horse Sapphire had taken from his barn. "Does that sound like the same horse?"

"Naw, that wasn't the one she rode."

Where would Sapphire have gotten another horse? From that cowboy? He picked up a pencil, gripping it so hard it snapped in two. Probably from some besotted man she'd taken up with. "Where was this?"

The man lifted a brow. "I reckon that info'mation is worth somethin'."

Badger stared at the man. Slaughter might be stringing him along. Since the man had been here before, he would know enough about Sapphire to describe her as he had. He might be wasting his money, but then again, this was the first potential lead he'd had. He tugged open a drawer, withdrew a pair of Morgan silver dollars, and pushed them across the desk.

Greedy eyed, Slaughter watched them move his way. He

reached for them, but Badger laid his hand over them. "*Where* did you see her?"

" 'Twas over in Guthrie, just yesterday. I hopped the train back here last night so's I could tell you. Spent my last dollar on that train. I don't reckon you could pay for my fare, huh?"

Sapphire was in Guthrie? Taken off guard, Badger fell back against his chair, and Slaughter snatched the coins. She had been only thirty miles away all this time? How could she have been so stupid as to stay someplace so close? Surely she knew he'd be looking for her. "You say you saw her in town?"

Slaughter nodded.

"Do you know where she went after that?"

"Nah. That cowboy looked like he could fight, so I just hurried back here. I knowed you'd wanna know I saw her."

Feeling generous and a bit lucky that Slaughter had run into Sapphire, he tossed the man another coin. "Thank you for your information. Come back tonight for a free visit with the lady of your choice."

Slaughter's wide mouth lifted. "That's right kind of ya."

Badger nodded and waved his hand for the man to leave. As soon as he heard the outer door close, he yelled, "Stoney, get in here."

The big man lumbered into his office. "What you need, boss?"

"Got my first real lead on Sapphire. Saddle up my horse. I'm going to Guthrie."

Stoney lifted a brow. "How come you ain't takin' the train?"

Badger unlocked his gun case, grabbed a rifle, and started loading it. "The train arrived yesterday, so there won't be another one for several days. I can be in Guthrie by then."

"Guthrie? I'm surprised she's that close."

"That was my first thought when Slaughter told me. She

should've run a whole lot farther." He grinned for the first time in weeks. "I'm gonna get her and bring her back."

"After you teach her a lesson?"

"Nope. I'll do that here so the other gals will learn from her mistake."

Baron sat at the table, sipping his coffee, feeling worse than he had in as long as he could remember. He'd tossed and turned the night before, thinking of Jo and dreaming of her being hurt or in trouble. Why couldn't she leave him alone? He'd made his choice. He refused to be attracted to a woman who'd slept with other men—even if that woman was the mother of his nephew.

He stared into the liquid blackness of his cup. Why did it fail to revive him this morning as it normally did? Perhaps it was his lack of sleep.

Why did he feel as if he'd made the wrong choice where Jo was concerned? Even God had used harlots—he winced at the thought of Jo as a loose woman—in the Bible to accomplish His purpose. But he certainly wasn't God. And having special feelings for the woman his brother had lived with in a matrimonial way didn't sit well with him.

So why was he so miserable?

Footsteps came his way, but he'd noticed them too late to slip away. He continued staring into his cup as his father walked into the kitchen. He paused on the other side of the table and gazed at Baron. "Rough night?"

"You could say that."

His father poured himself a cup then sat down. "What seems to be the problem, son? Are you still upset about Mark?"

"Shouldn't I be?"

"Of course, but then, you two were never very close. I guess it surprises me that you're taking his death so hard." He took a sip of his coffee, and Baron could feel the man's eyes on him. "If I didn't know better, I'd think a woman is at the root of your sleeplessness."

Baron glanced up. "How do you know about that—that I had trouble sleeping, I mean."

His father lifted one eyebrow. "Because it sounded as if there was a herd of buffalo wallowing in a mud puddle above our bed all night."

"My apologies, but that's the only room upstairs with a bed. I suppose I could move it to the other room."

His father waved his hand in the air. "That isn't necessary. I had trouble sleeping, too."

"May I ask why?"

He shrugged. "I'm struggling with the fact that I wasn't a very good father."

Baron straightened. "You were a fine father."

"Perhaps I was where you were concerned, but not so much with Mark. I never understood how your mother could coddle that boy so much."

"Mark learned at a young age how to get what he wanted." Especially where women were concerned.

His father wrapped both hands around his coffee cup. "I can't pretend that Mark's latest escapade and the news of his death won't hurt business, because they will. The Hillborne reputation has been severely tarnished. Your mother is afraid to show her face in St. Louis."

He understood. His parents were members of the wealthiest class in St. Louis, and news of Mark would make its way to each house, to the gentlemen's parlors, the ladies' tearooms, and the country clubs. "Perhaps it's time for you to take Mother to Europe like you've wanted to do for so long."

His father's eyes glimmered. "You know, I think that is a grand idea. We'd be gone for months, and by the time we returned, this awful news of Mark's affair with a married woman will have died down. Perhaps you should come with us. I know it would make your mother happy."

He shook his head. "Someone has to keep an eye on our business affairs."

"Don't say *affair*. Just the thought of it makes me shudder. Poor Abigail."

"I suspect her parents will send her away somewhere, too." Baron rose and refilled both cups then sat down again.

"To be honest, I think in the long run Abigail will be better off without Mark. In truth, she's been without him for a long while. She'll be free to remarry a man who will appreciate her more than Mark ever did."

"That's true." Baron hoped she didn't turn her eyes his way. She'd said more than once she wished she'd married him instead of his brother. When he thought of marriage, Jo was foremost in his thoughts. Was that because he hated how Mark had taken advantage of her when she was so young and naive? Or perhaps he merely cared for her because she was the mother of his nephew.

"Why don't you tell me what's got you so bothered? Somehow, I don't think it's your brother."

"Telling you would only hurt you more—and I don't want to do that."

Several expressions crossed his father's face; then he tapped his index finger on the table several times—a signal that Baron learned long ago meant he'd made a decision. "Why don't you tell me and let me be the judge?"

Baron considered doing that, but he'd promised Jo not to tell his parents about Jamie. Still. . .he didn't promise not to tell them about her connection to Mark. His stomach quivered.

"I could use some advice." And his father had always given him good advice. He told him about meeting a woman who believed she was married to Mark, but he didn't say her name. Then he told how the woman discovered that the man Mark hired to marry them wasn't a real preacher—that he merely pretended because Mark paid him to. "So you see, she thought she was legally married to Mark, but he tricked her."

His father shook his head. "I never realized your brother was so depraved. How could you and he come from the same source yet turn out so different?"

Baron thought it had to do with his mother's pampering Mark so much, but he wouldn't point fingers or say anything to make his parents hurt more than they already were. How awful it must be to birth a child and spend a good part of your life raising him, only to have him turn out to be so self-centered and cruel.

Lord, please don't let me ever be so selfish or mean.

His thoughts shot straight to Jo. Was he treating her wrongly? Hadn't he offered her a job? Offered to help with Jamie?

But he'd been selfish in not offering his heart. Mark was no longer around to shame him for caring for the same woman. He barely knew Jo, and yet she tugged at his heart like no woman ever had.

"We need to do right by this woman." His father tapped the table again and stared at him. "It's that woman you introduced me to, isn't it? What was her name?"

"Jo." He didn't bother to deny it, because he wouldn't lie to his father.

Nodding, his father said, "It's good that you offered her a job. I'm proud of you, son. Many people would have shunned her or turned her out. You did the right thing in giving her employment."

Humbled, he hung his head. His father's compliments were few and far between. "Thank you. That means a lot."

For a long moment his father remained silent, just looking at Baron. "You have feelings for this Jo, don't you?"

Baron lifted one shoulder and lowered it. He ran his hand through his uncombed hair. "I don't know."

His father grinned. "Well, I certainly do. If you had no feelings for the woman, you wouldn't be so distressed. Only a woman, business, or your children can keep you wrestling at night like you were—and you don't have any children. And the business is going well, so that only leaves a woman as the source of your distress." He chuckled. "They usually are."

Baron sat back, marveling at his father's wisdom. "So, what do I do? You do understand that Jo lived in sin with Mark?"

"Was it living in sin if she truly thought she was married?"

But she wasn't married when she lived at the bordello. And yet, what other choices were there for a woman who'd been taken advantage of as she had? Even most churches probably would have turned her away. And she had a son, which made things even harder.

A verse in the Bible rushed through his mind. *"He that is without sin among you, let him first cast a stone."*

"I need to talk to her."

His father smiled. "That would be a good place to start."

Relief warmed Baron's bones. He couldn't hold Jo responsible for ending up at a bordello when that Badger fellow had lied to her and tricked her. God would have him forgive her. He needed to. Wanted to. And talking to Jo was definitely a good start. He swigged down the last of his coffee, ready to be on his way. "Do you mind if I go now and leave the store closed for a while?"

His father rose. "No need for that. I'll tend it. You run along and talk to that gal of yours."

Baron smiled at the thought of Jo being his. Knowing her personality, she probably wouldn't even talk to him today. She'd make him wait a week or two and stew on his behavior—or lack of it.

Footsteps sounded out front, followed by hard pounding on the door. Baron hurried to it, not wanting his visitor to awaken his mother. He pulled open the door, surprised to see Gabe so early.

"Morning. What brings you here at this hour?"

Gabe stepped inside without invitation. "Is Jo here? Did she come in early to work?"

Baron shook his head. "No. I haven't seen her since yesterday."

Gabe yanked on his hat and slapped his leg, sending a cloud of dust to the floor. He heard his father walk up behind him. Gabe's eyes shot to him. "This is my father, Wilfred Marquis Hillborne, the second." Baron held his hand toward his father then in front of Gabe. "And this is Gabriel Coulter, a friend and Jo's brother-in-law."

"Nice to meet you." Gabe nodded; then his gaze jerked back to Baron's. "There's no time for visiting. Jo, Sarah, and Jamie are missing."

Heading south, Jo pressed the horse hard. They still had several hours of daylight, and she meant to make the most of them. Sarah hadn't said a word since they'd left Lara's, and Jamie squirmed and cried at being bound to her again until he finally fell asleep. She hated taking them from Lara's comfortable house into a world of unknowns.

Why was it that when she was ready to be with her family—to stay and make amends—she had to run away again? But she couldn't put them in danger. Gabe and Lara had their own children to be concerned for. They didn't need to be worrying about her, too. But she knew they would as soon as Lara found the note she'd left. She shouldn't have let Sarah talk her into waiting until early morning to leave. She had to get far enough away that anyone following her would lose their tracks.

She checked the sun, half-hidden behind the pewter clouds, to make sure she was still heading toward Texas. It made the most sense because the temperatures would warm the farther south she went. In the Oklahoma Territory, you never knew whether to expect warm, sunny days in April or cold weather with a slim possibility of snow or ice. Fortunately, this spring the weather had leaned to the warm side. Still, tonight would be chilly. The wool blanket she "borrowed" from her sister would help keep them from being too cold.

Behind her Sarah coughed. Jo had noticed her doing that earlier. She hoped Sarah wasn't taking sick. If things went well and she didn't miss her mark, tomorrow they would be in Kingfisher. Badger would head north from Oklahoma City to Guthrie and probably spend several days hunting for them, only to discover they were gone. She smiled. Once again, she'd outsmarted him. He'd never control her life again—no man would.

Baron's image intruded into her mind. She might have been willing to pursue a relationship with him, but he made it clear that he wanted nothing to do with a woman who'd lived in a bordello, no matter that it wasn't her choice. She was tainted.

Men could force themselves on a woman, and she was the one who ended up with the bad reputation. But as Grandpa often said, life isn't fair.

The pastor at Gabe and Lara's church had talked about how God had used several harlots in the Bible to do good works. Rahab even saved the lives of several Hebrew spies, and in a roundabout way, saved her whole family from destruction when Jericho was destroyed. Why, of all the people in Jericho, had God chosen to use a harlot?

She didn't understand, but if God could save Rahab, couldn't He save her?

Hadn't Jack said something about that? He'd told her that he had to stop running from God—whatever that meant.

She reined the horse down into a shallow creek, allowed it a short drink, and then nudged his sides with her heels. He moved on, and she allowed him to walk for a time, even though she wanted to gallop. They had to get away before someone found them and made them come home.

Too much was at stake.

Just before the sun sank below the horizon, she reined the horse to a stop. Sarah slid off the back of the horse and curled up near a tree. After dismounting and changing Jamie, Jo pulled out some biscuits left over from breakfast, as well as some ham slices and cheese. Sarah ate very little then lay down on the blanket and was asleep before Jamie. Jo nursed her son, and then he, too, fell asleep.

She cleaned up their supper mess, watered the horse, and then washed off in the nearby creek before lying down. Tired as she was from the stress of the day, sleep evaded her. She worried that she'd upset Lara and Grandpa. Worried that Gabe would come gunning for her for upsetting Lara. And she couldn't help thinking about Baron. The one time she was truly honest with someone, it had come back to bite her. If she'd never told him about her past or Mark's trickery, maybe she and Baron would have had a chance together. But she'd lied so much that she couldn't stand telling falsehoods to a man she admired. She hadn't meant to care for him, but he'd been so kind and understanding, and genuinely happy to be an uncle.

But his kindness only went so far. She couldn't blame him for letting her leave without stopping her. What man would want to have a meaningful relationship with a former strumpet? Tears stung her eyes, and she batted them away.

No man would ever want her for his wife.

She'd said as much to Jack, but his response was that God would want her—would love her. She could come to Him as she was. Lara had told her the same thing when they were younger, but Jo was too stubborn to listen. As far as she was concerned, God had been the one to take her parents away, but now she knew that wasn't true. Jack had confessed that he'd been smoking in his bedroom, and when Pa hollered that he should be out doing chores, he'd rushed to the barn and had possibly forgotten to put out the cigar. Maybe her parents would still be alive if he'd remembered it. Maybe her life would have been much different.

She glanced at her son. As hard as her life had been with Mark, she wouldn't change a thing if it meant she wouldn't have Jamie. He alone gave her life purpose.

And yet, he wasn't enough. She wanted more, but she didn't know what that more was.

All the things that Lara, Grandpa, pastors she'd listened to over the years, and even Jack had said bombarded her. She was tired of living as she had, fearing men and being used by them. Feeling worthless, like dirt swept from a floor. She was tired of running. She needed to change—for herself and for Jamie. Her son needed a good example if he was going to turn out well. Jo sniffled. Jamie would have been far better off if she'd left him with Lara—and that truth cut her deeply.

She gazed up at the sky, lonelier than she could ever remember. "Is it true what Jack said, God? Do You truly love me? In spite of all the horrible things I've done? Could You save me, like You did Rahab?"

She thought of the Bible stories of Jesus. How God had given His only Son so that she could be saved. She'd never before thought of how it must have pained God to see His Son suffer for the horrible things she'd done—for the sins she'd committed. "I'm truly sorry for everything that I've done, Lord. Forgive me. Please."

At first, she didn't feel a thing—only the chilly breeze as night settled across the prairie. But then her chest warmed, and she felt a peace she'd never before experienced. The tears that had filled her eyes before tumbled down her cheeks, and she was helpless to stop them. Maybe it was God's way of washing her clean.

Chapter 21

Jo's eyes fluttered open to the sound of birds singing. The last thing she remembered was praying and crying out to God. She must have fallen into a deep sleep. Rolling over, she was relieved to see Jamie still sleeping. Sarah was normally an early riser, but today she was still curled up under the blanket they'd shared with Jamie.

Jo sat up and rubbed the sleep from her eyes then tended to her morning ablutions. By the time she returned, Jamie was stirring. She smiled and lifted him up, cuddling him to her chest. He uttered some unrecognizable words that ended with *mama*. Smiling, she kissed his head, laid him down, and changed his diaper. Tomorrow evening, she'd have to wash them out and hope they dried overnight.

She nursed Jamie then gave him a chunk of biscuit to gnaw on. Going to Sarah's side, she knelt down. How odd for her to sleep so late. Other than coughing, she hadn't made a sound. Jo shook Sarah's shoulder, snatching back her hand at how hot she felt. While Jo slept so peacefully, Sarah had taken a fever.

Jo rose and looked at the sky. She'd hoped after her talk with God last night that things would get easier. "What do I do now?"

Jamie babbled off a string of baby talk as if answering her question. She picked him up, untied the horse, and led the horse to the stream. She only had three options. Continue to Kingfisher, but strangers wouldn't be too welcoming when they found out she had a sick girl with her. They could stay here until Sarah got better, but they had little food and no medicine with which to treat her. She stared across the prairie, back to the north. They were much closer to Lara's than Kingfisher, so it made more sense to return there. But she'd be putting her family within Badger's reach.

The more she thought about returning to Lara's, the more positive she grew. As much as they needed to get away, she wouldn't take a chance with Sarah's life. Guthrie had doctors, and Lara would know how to keep Sarah comfortable until the doctor could arrive. And what if she or Jamie caught what the girl had? She couldn't risk getting sick herself and leaving the two children to fend for themselves.

Going back was risky, but it was the only choice that made sense.

Baron arrived at the Coulter ranch less than an hour after Gabe had told him that Jo and the children were missing. He'd been stubborn—stupid—to let her ride away yesterday without stopping her. But he'd been so shocked at her confession. In the short time he'd known her, he'd grown to care for her far more than he'd realized. The way Mark had used her then tossed her aside disgusted him. He hated that some man she'd met had done something similar by forcing her to stay at his brothel. He shuddered at the thought of the horrible things she'd gone through.

Yesterday they had mattered, but today, all that was important was finding her and making sure she and the children were safe. At the house, he dismounted, raced up the stairs, and pounded on the door. He was relieved to hear footsteps hurrying his way. The door opened, and Lara, red faced from crying, looked up at him.

"Gabe told me what happened. I'm here to help search for

Jo—and the children."

"Thank you for coming." She shook her head. "I was so shocked to find her note. I thought she was doing better. Jack said she had an encounter with someone in town." She closed her mouth suddenly. "Sorry, I'm babbling."

"An encounter with whom?"

"Some man she knew from Oklahoma City, but Jack took care of him—at least we thought so."

"Do you know his name?"

Lara shook her head.

"I think I know why she left."

Lara stepped to the side. "Please, come in."

Baron shook his head. "Thank you, but I need to go. I just wanted you to know that Jo believes a man named Badger is after her. I'm sure that's why she left. She's probably worried she'll bring trouble to your door."

Lara surprised him when she smiled. "My sister has been trouble from the day she was born, but I don't love her any less for it. Thank you for telling me about this Badger. I'll be sure to let the men know so they can watch for him."

"Good." Baron crimped the brim of his hat. "I should go. Any idea which way I should search?"

Lara shrugged. "I think the men have gone out in all directions. If I had to guess where Jo would go, I'd say west or south. We lived in Kansas, and I really doubt she'd go back there where it's colder than it is here."

"I appreciate the information. I should be going."

"Feel free to help yourself to a fresh horse, if there are any left in the barn. My black mare might be the only one. She's a good horse, and you're welcome to her."

Baron slapped his hat on. "Thanks."

"Stop back here before you ride out. I'll fix you some food to take with you."

He nodded his gratitude and rushed down the steps. He felt an urgency to find Jo. Were they in some kind of danger? Or perhaps Badger was already on her trail? He untied his horse and ran toward the barn. The sooner he found them, the better he'd feel.

Ten minutes later, mounted on Lara's mare and with a sack of food and a canteen of water hanging from the saddle horn, Baron faced west. He nudged the mare forward and rode out of the ranch yard, but as he reached the edge, he had a feeling in his gut that he was going the wrong way. "Lord, show me the correct way."

Even if he went in the right direction, he wasn't assured that he'd find her. In fact, he could pass by her, separated by a lone hill, and never see her. "I need Your help, Father."

An overwhelming sensation made him turn south. He urged the horse to a lope and kept his eyes moving, searching as far as he could see. He had to find Jo and Jamie. Bring them back. They needed more time together. He needed time to figure out what his feelings for Jo were. Was he willing to turn loose of his long-held vow to not be attracted to the same woman as his brother?

He blew out a sigh. Who was he fooling? He'd been attracted to Jo since he first met her. But could he truly overlook her past?

He reined the horse to a stop atop a hill and searched in all directions but didn't see a soul. Guilt nibbled at him. Hadn't God forgiven his sins?

Of course He had, but he'd never done anything like Jo had.

His thoughts wrestling with one another, Baron tapped his heels, and the horse moved forward. In the eyes of God, sin was sin, no matter the type. It was man who thought there was a difference in committing murder versus lying—or being a loose woman.

His grip on the reins tightened. He cared for Jo and needed to forget her past. God would wash her clean if only she asked Him to, so who was he to judge her?

Baron sighed. He had no right at all to judge Jo. He had sinned, too. Jo—and Jamie—were what mattered. Not what he or she did before they met.

His heart finally at peace, he nudged the horse to a gallop again as they reached a long valley. Several minutes later, he crested another hill and paused to give his horse a rest. He searched from west to east, and his gaze latched onto a slow-moving horse crossing the next valley. But it was coming his way, so he skipped over it and continued his search. When he saw no one else, his gaze snapped back to the rider. Tugging his hat low over his eyes, he stared. The woman rider looked as if she were with child. Surely it couldn't be Jo. Still he nudged the horse forward. Perhaps the woman had seen Jo and the children.

As he narrowed the gap, his pulse kicked up its pace. Then his heart slammed against his rib cage. *Jo!*

He quickly reached her side. The bundle in front of her was Jamie, who had fallen asleep in her arms. Sarah was slumped against Jo's back and didn't look up as he approached.

"Baron?"

He reined his horse beside hers. "I'm so glad I found you. Why are you headed north?"

"Sarah is sick. I had to turn back to get help for her."

"Thank God you did."

Confused by his outburst, she glanced down. "Could you take Jamie? My arm feels like it's about to fall off."

He smiled. "Gladly." He lifted the boy into his arms and cuddled him against his chest. A powerful desire to protect this woman and her child welled up within him. They were his family. He kissed Jamie's head, noting how hot the boy felt. "He's not sick, too, is he?"

Jo shook her head. "I think he's just sweaty from leaning on me for so long."

Baron stared at the woman he'd grown to love—and as much as he might deny it, that was the truth. Thank God he'd found her. "Are you ready to continue the ride home?"

She nodded. "I need to get Sarah in bed and send for a doctor."

"Do you want me to ride with you or go on back and have someone get the doctor?"

She glanced at her son as if not wanting to let him out of her sight.

"Jamie is safe with me."

As she gazed into his eyes, he read the questions there.

"Let's get the children settled; then we can talk. All right?"

After a long moment when he thought she would order him to give Jamie back, she finally nodded. "That sounds like the best idea. I'll be there as soon as I can. I'm having to take things slowly because I'm afraid Sarah will fall off."

The girl moaned at the mention of her name.

"Would you rather I take her than Jamie?"

Jo shook her head. "It might frighten her, and besides, my arms are sore from holding Jamie. He's heavy when he's sleeping." Her loving gaze at her son left little doubt as to the depth of her feelings.

If only she'd look at him with such love.

"I'd best get going. Just keep heading due north, and you'll reach the ranch before too long."

She captured his gaze and held it. "Thank you for coming after me."

He nodded, reached over, and squeezed her hand; then he reined his horse around. As he rode to the Coulter ranch, he knew he'd done the right thing. He'd put aside his disdain for his brother's former lover and saw her for who she was—the woman he cared for.

Jo watched Baron ride away with Jamie, her heart warmer than it had been in a long while. He had actually come looking for her. What had changed in his attitude?

Something most certainly had. It made her want to hope that they could have a future together, but hope had never been her friend. Hope was dangerous for a woman who'd lived as she had. And yet, ever since she'd prayed last night, she'd felt different. Cleaner. Less worried.

Sarah leaned to one side, and Jo reached behind her to steady her. She wrapped both of the girl's arms around her waist and held on to them with one hand while guiding the horse with the other.

For the first times in years, she looked forward to going home. Not that Lara's house was *her* home, but her family was there. And that's what made it home. At least for now.

She didn't know what the future held, but she wanted to believe for Jamie's sake that it would be better than her past. Badger was still after them, but even he didn't seem as scary as he had yesterday.

Could asking God to help her—save her—actually have changed her outlook on life?

It didn't seem possible, and yet something was clearly different. She should be more concerned about Badger, worried more about Sarah. . .and she'd let Baron take her son. And still she felt at peace. Lara would certainly be happy.

An hour later, Sarah began mumbling unintelligible words. Jo thought they might be Cherokee, but she'd never heard Sarah speak it before. She nudged the horse into a trot and prayed she could keep hold of the girl. The horse slowed as they crested yet another hill, and Jo's heart started. Someone in a buckboard was coming their way. She squinted her eyes and saw that it was Gabe. Relief flowed through her.

He waved and smiled as he approached then drew the wagon to a stop. Jo expected him to lash into her for once again disappointing Lara, but he didn't.

He climbed down and strode toward her. "Lara made a bed in the back. She thought Sarah would be more comfortable lying down."

Jo turned loose of Sarah, and Gabe lifted her into his arms and carried her to the back of the wagon. Then he waved at her. "Come ride with Sarah in case she wakes up. She'll want to see a familiar face."

She would have preferred to ride alone but did as he bid. It made sense. As soon as she was seated in back and Gabe had tied her horse to the rear of the wagon, he climbed up onto the bench and turned the horse for home.

"Luke rode to Guthrie for the doctor."

"That's good. Thank you for coming for us. I wasn't sure if I could keep her on that horse much longer."

"Happy to do so."

Jo felt that he wanted to say more, but he didn't. He loved her sister and would do anything to protect Lara. Jo had to admit that Gabe had turned out to be a far better husband and rancher than she'd expected. He'd lost some weight, and his skin had darkened under the hot Oklahoma sun. Gabe was a handsome man with his black hair and eyes almost as dark as Sarah's. But it was a man with sandy blond hair and blue eyes who tugged at her heart. Was there a chance they could ever be together?

Not likely. What man in his right mind would choose to be with a woman who'd done the things she had?

She glanced at Sarah and pulled the blanket up to the girl's neck. *Please, God. Let her live.*

Jo couldn't afford to hope for a life with Baron. Yes, he'd seemed more accepting today, but she needed to focus on the children. They were her first responsibility.

She beseeched God to make Sarah well and to keep Jamie from catching whatever Sarah had. He'd slept right beside the girl last night. Jo bit her lip. He was so young. Would he have the strength to fight off the sickness if he got it? She couldn't lose him.

"We're home."

Jo looked up, and her heart picked up its pace at seeing the big house again. Had it only been yesterday when she left?

Gabe pulled the wagon to a stop at the front porch steps and jumped down. "If you'll get the door, I'll carry her upstairs."

Lara rushed out the front door with Beth in her arms. "Oh, thank the good Lord you're home."

Jo couldn't help smiling. "You'd best take Beth and put her in your room. We don't want her catching whatever Sarah has."

"That's a good idea," Gabe said as he hoisted Sarah into his arms.

Jo had expected to see Baron come to the door. "Where are Baron and Jamie?"

"In the kitchen. That little man of yours was starving." Lara smiled. "I've prepared the extra room for Sarah. We'll put her in there." She backed into the house, and the screen door banged closed.

Gabe had Sarah upstairs and into bed in short order. Jo wanted to take a bath and rest—to see Baron and Jamie—but caring for the girl came first. As she pulled the covers up to Sarah's chin, she prayed again. "Please, Lord, make her well. Don't take her from us. She deserves a chance to live a happy life—and she can do that here."

Badger rode into Guthrie, his gaze landing on each woman he saw. The town was much bigger than he'd expected—as big or bigger than Oklahoma City, he suspected. He searched the streets he could see for Sapphire, but he didn't expect to find her so easily. First thing, he needed to rent a room at a hotel or boardinghouse; then he'd go from business to business until he found her.

Too bad Ernie Slaughter hadn't mentioned which store he'd seen her at, because it looked like Guthrie had more than its fair share of them. Badger blew out a sigh. He'd thought finding Sapphire would be easy, but he'd certainly underestimated the size of the town—just as he had the woman.

A man caught his eye, and Badger slowed his tired horse. "Can I help you find somethin', sir?"

"Could you tell me where I can find a good place to stay?"

The man rattled off several names, embellishing the finer points of each hotel, and finally pointed him in the right direction. Five minutes later, Badger stopped outside the Windsor Hotel. The place looked decent enough, so he stepped inside and headed to the counter. Off to his left was an elaborate dining room, with enticing aromas drifting into the lobby even though it was only midafternoon. He was tired of eating the same food over and over. The woman he hired to fix meals wasn't much better than his gals at cooking. He needed to find another cook, but decent women with the proper skills for preparing meals wouldn't be seen dead in his place of business. Maybe he could hire a male cook.

He paid the clerk and took his key, anxious to deposit his bag and start looking for Sapphire. On the second floor, he unlocked his room and stepped in. The place was actually nicer than his room at the bordello—probably got cleaned a whole lot more often, too.

With Sarah gone, his rooms hadn't been cleaned in weeks. He tossed his satchel on the bed, strode to the window, and lifted the lower half. Businessmen and several women with children in tow walked along the streets. None of them in a sapphire-blue satin dress.

Sapphire was smart, and she wouldn't wear something that would attract unwanted attention like her blue gown would have. Garnet told him that the ugly calico he'd scrounged up for her to wear to meet the couple that wanted her boy was missing. More'n likely that's what she wore. He remembered it—dark blue, as Sapphire should always wear the color that highlighted her eyes most.

Heaving a sigh, he turned and strode out of the room. He didn't like the task at hand, but if he didn't use her as an example, he'd have no control at the bordello and would soon have his other girls sneaking away. He couldn't allow that.

And he had to get Sarah back. He didn't know what he was going to do with the girl. She couldn't stay with him much longer or he'd have clients asking about her, and he'd probably kill the man who did. Still, he couldn't send her just anywhere, not with her being half-Injun. Too many people looked down on them and mistreated them. He had to find a school where she'd be accepted and not belittled. But that was a tall order. First thing he had to do was get her and Sapphire back; then he'd decide what to do with them.

Badger skipped the barbershop and doctor's office that were located next to the hotel and stepped inside a millinery shop. The woman standing behind the counter working on a fancy lady's hat with feathers and fruit paused and looked up. She frowned right before she forced a smile.

He removed his hat. "Afternoon, ma'am. I'm, uh. . .looking for my wife. 'Bout your height with blond hair and deep blue eyes."

The woman shrugged. "That sounds like many of the women I

know. What's her name?"

The name "Sapphire" was on the tip of his tongue to say but he caught himself in time. "Jo—Joline."

The woman shook her head. "I'm sorry, but I don't know anyone with that name."

He slapped his hat back on, nodded, and then stepped outside. He should have thought that Sapphire wouldn't have the money to buy a fancy hat. He continued down the street until he'd reached the depot; then he started up the far side. With so many buildings in Guthrie, his search could take a week or two. So be it. Someone in this town had seen Jo, and he'd know when he'd found the right person.

He wouldn't give up until he did.

Chapter 22

Jo held her hand to her nose as she watched the doctor apply the onion poultice to Sarah's chest. He'd given her the instructions, and now that she had watched him prepare one, she felt she could do it the next time.

Sarah winced. "It is hot. Stinks."

"Yes, but it will help you get better, young lady." Dr. Crabtree smiled. "You need to get lots of rest and let the fine ladies of this home care for you. I'll return in two days to see how you're doing."

Sarah pulled her pillow over her face and barked a muffled cough into it.

Dr. Crabtree rose, wiping his hands on a towel. "Give her the cough syrup three times a day, as much chicken soup and hot tea as she'll consume, and some fresh air if the temperature outside is not too chilly."

"Thank you so much for coming, Doctor." Many physicians would have refused to treat a half-breed, making Jo especially grateful to Dr. Crabtree for treating Sarah as he would any other patient.

"I'm happy to be of help." He smiled and closed his bag.

Jo escorted him downstairs to the front door. "Are you sure you wouldn't like a cup of coffee before you go? Or something to eat?"

"Thank you, but I need to head back to town and check on Mrs. Yates again, down on Fifth Street. Her baby is due any day now."

Jo closed the door after he walked down the porch steps toward his buggy. When she turned, Baron strode out of the parlor, holding Jamie. The boy squealed and lunged for her, jabbering up a storm.

Baron chuckled. "I think he missed you."

She hugged Jamie close and kissed him then glanced around at the empty house. "Where is everyone?"

"Your sister took her baby upstairs. She said after the events of the morning, she and Beth both needed a nap. Gabe went back to work and took Michael with him."

"Where's Grandpa?"

"In here, Punkin."

Jo lifted her brows at Baron then walked into the parlor and found her grandpa sitting in a chair with his feet on a wooden footstool.

He smiled at her and patted Jamie's back. "These two fine gentlemen have been keeping me company."

Jo wondered what Grandpa and Baron had been talking about, but she didn't dare ask. Both men knew more about her than she cared to talk about.

Grandpa slowly pushed up. "Now that my lunch has settled, a nap sounds mighty good." He winked at Jo as he walked past. "Don't go runnin' off again, Punkin."

Jo walked up to him and gave him a hug. "I won't." *At least not for a few days.* She closed her eyes, wishing he wasn't so frail, but she still enjoyed the feel of his arms around her. When he stepped back, he winked then walked into the foyer and down the hall.

She suspected he was purposefully leaving her alone with Baron. She wasn't sure they had anything to say to one another, at least not unless he'd come to grips with her past. But she could hardly blame him if he didn't. Most men wouldn't be able to.

Jo set Jamie on the floor so he could play. She would be happy when he learned to walk, but then she'd have a whole new set of worries.

Baron leaned forward, elbows on knees, and let out a loud sigh. "I owe you an apology."

"No, you don't. You reacted as any man would, given such despicable news."

He looked up with a pained expression. "But I'm not any man. I care for you, Jo. I realize I haven't acted like it, but I do."

Her heart tripled its pace. He cared? How could he after learning of her past? Unable to believe he meant what he said, she rose and walked to the window, staring out.

Baron followed and stood behind her. "I'll admit what you told me was a shock, but I partly blame Mark. If he hadn't gone off and left you, none of the rest would have happened."

She barked a laugh. "How can you say that when he was married to someone else? I was merely a pastime for him—someone to entertain him while he was stuck in Guthrie. I was dumb and naive, and thought I knew what I wanted, but I was wrong."

"What was it you wanted?"

Jamie tugged on her skirts, and Jo bent to pick him up, needing someone to hold on to. She shrugged. "I thought pretty dresses and a house with wooden floors and a roof that wasn't made of sod would make me happy. But I found out that you can have those things and still be desperately sad and alone."

"I'm sorry that your life has been so hard. I wish you'd met me first instead of Mark."

She turned to face him. "It wouldn't have mattered. No one could have made me happy, because I was a miserable, selfish person." Jamie patted her cheek as if sensing her distress, and Jo kissed his cheek then focused on Baron again. "I didn't know what to do when

I discovered Sarah was so sick and we were far from home. I finally realized that the only One who could help her—and me—was God. I asked Him what to do and felt He told me to come back here."

He stuck his hands in his pockets, jingling some coins. "You left because of that Badger fellow?"

She nodded. "He will find me, probably sooner than later."

Baron gripped her shoulders. "I want you to stay here and not come to town anymore. It's too risky. I'll talk to Gabe about leaving a guard. And I'll talk to my father and see if he can run the store for a week or two so I'll be free to stay close in case Badger shows up."

Jo couldn't believe he wanted to protect her after what she'd told him. "Why would you do that?"

He gave her a gentle shake. "Weren't you listening? I care about you. I don't want anything to happen to you or Jamie. Or Sarah, either. I hope that we can get past this difficult time, and then maybe I can court you properly."

She stared at him, unable to believe what he said. "You want to court me?"

Suddenly, he looked unsure. "Well, yes, unless I misread you—and you're not interested in me."

She sucked back a sob and hugged Jamie to hide the tears stinging her eyes. This was more than she ever could have hoped for.

"Did I misinterpret things between us?" Baron's voice deepened.

Still too overwhelmed to look at him or speak, she shook her head.

"Jo, look at me."

When she didn't, he lifted her chin with two fingers. Jamie looked at him and lunged into Baron's arms. He juggled the boy then held him in one arm, his gaze latched onto Jo's. "Why are you crying?"

Her vision of him blurred even more. "Because I don't deserve someone good like you."

A look of relief softened his worried expression. "Don't say that. In the eyes of God, my sins are just as bad as yours. I'll admit at first I was stunned by your confession, but even though I tried to put you from my mind, I couldn't. I realize we haven't known one another long, but I care for you. Do you think we could take things slow and see how it goes?"

She wiped her eyes, embarrassed that he'd seen her crying when she rarely did so. "I'd like that, but what about Badger?"

"I think I need to talk to our family attorney. The truth of the matter is that Badger kept you against your will. Did he ever give you the chance to leave?"

Jo huffed a harsh laugh. "No. In fact, I tried several times, but he caught me and—" She turned her face away.

"And what?"

She shook her head. "It doesn't matter now."

"Yes, it does. What did he do?"

"He beat me."

Baron's eyes widened. He reached for her and pulled her to his chest. "I hate what he did to you. I'm so sorry."

Jo leaned into him. She felt like she'd finally come home. A good man cared for her. Suddenly, she thought about her past and how it could sully the Hillborne name, and that fast, her hopes dimmed. She tried to step back, but he wouldn't let go.

She dared to glance up. Jamie had laid his head on Baron's shoulder. "Have you thought how a relationship with me could tarnish your family name?"

He sniffed a laugh. "Our family name can't be stained much worse than it was by Mark."

"That's not true. If people knew about my past. . .well, I'm sure you know how people can be."

"None of that matters to me."

"It has to matter. You're the oldest son and only heir. You have to consider everything."

He was quiet for a moment. "You're right. And I promise that I will think through it all, but that still doesn't change how I feel."

Jo smiled, still finding it hard to believe he cared so much for her that he was willing to risk his family name.

He gazed down at her. "When a person asks Jesus into his—or her—heart, He washes our sins away and makes us as pure as fresh snow. Think of it like opening a brand-new ledger book at the store. All the pages are empty, waiting to be filled in. That's how I see you, Jo. You need to look at yourself the same way. If you didn't ask God into your heart, please consider it."

Her tears started again. "I did. Just last night. I feel different, but I suppose it will take time to change the way I think about myself."

Baron smiled. "That's wonderful news." He stared at her, his eyes roaming across her face and then down to her lips. He captured her eyes with his. "I'd like nothing more than to kiss you right now. May I?"

Tears stung her eyes again. "No man has ever *asked* to kiss me before."

"Good. I like being the first. Just let me put this little guy down." He laid her sleeping son on the sofa then started toward her, his eyes locked with hers. "You didn't answer my question. May I kiss you?"

Her eyes twinkled. "Yes, you may."

He took her hand then leaned in slowly, giving her time to object, but she didn't.

His warm lips were soft—gentle—against hers. Almost tentative. So different. She kissed him back, leaning into him but letting him take the lead. He wrapped his arms around her and deepened his kiss. When he pulled back, a look of wonder filled his eyes.

Jo smiled, still amazed that this good, kind man cared for her. God certainly worked miracles.

Jo glanced up as Lara entered Sarah's bedroom. "You shouldn't be in here."

"I thought you could use a break." She nudged her chin toward the bed. "How is she doing?"

Jo rose and crossed the room. "Better, I think. She's not coughing as much. How's Michael doing with Jamie?"

"Fine, but he misses you."

Jo glanced at the dark window. "I probably should get him ready for bed."

"Gabe is playing with Beth. You go on, and I'll sit with her for a while."

Jo nodded and took a step toward the door, but she paused and faced her sister. "I'm sorry for running away again. I know you must have been worried."

"Of course I was, but I've had to learn to entrust you to God." She smiled. "And this time He brought you back."

"There's more truth in that than you realize."

Sarah rolled over. Jo motioned for her sister to follow her out into the hall. She walked over to the upstairs sitting area and perched on the edge of the couch. Lara sat next to her, turning so their knees bumped.

"I've been running for a long while. Ever since Ma and Pa died, I think. I'm not proud of my life, but out on the trail, God and I had a chat, and I believe things will be better from now on. Well, except for one thing."

Lara enveloped her in a hug. "I'm so glad to hear that, Jo. I've prayed for you to find peace for so long." Lara released her and sat back. "But what one thing are you talking about? When God saves us, He saves us all the way."

Jo studied her hands, not wanting to tell Lara how far she'd fallen, but she knew she had to. She explained to her how Mark left after he learned about her being pregnant. Then she told her about Badger—and her awful days at the bordello. She hated the tears that formed in Lara's eyes.

"Oh, Jo. I'm so sorry. I wish you would have come home."

"But that's just it. . .this is *your* home."

Lara squeezed her hand. "That's not true. You'll always have a place with us. Jamie and Sarah, too."

"Thank you for saying that." She squeezed Lara's hand. "I think Sarah is putting down roots. Do you know that she didn't want to leave with me?"

"Maybe she was feeling ill."

"No, it's not that. I think she feels at home here. When I actually leave again, I'm not sure she will want to come."

"I don't want to hear about you leaving, but when that day comes, Sarah is more than welcome to stay with us. Michael has become a better student because he doesn't want her to pass him in skills."

Jo smiled. "That sounds like him."

Lara joined her in a private smile, but then it dimmed. "So, you think this Badger will come after you?"

"I'm sure he will—as soon as he learns where we are."

Lara pursed her lips together and was quiet for so long that Jo grew fidgety. "What are you thinking?"

"You won't like it, but we need to tell Gabe so he can be prepared."

"I know. Baron said the same thing."

Lara's gaze jerked to hers. "You told him? Everything?"

Jo nodded.

A slow smile engulfed her sister's face.

"What does that look mean?"

"Oh, nothing."

"Uh-huh. We're taking things slow."

"That sounds wise, especially since you don't know what will happen with this Badger fellow."

"It seems that I can't get away from my past."

Lara squeezed her hand. "You will. One day you'll be married to a good man and have a family, and all those bad days will be a distant memory."

"I pray you're right."

The odor of burned hide filled Jack's nostrils once again as he pressed the branding iron against another calf. The animal bawled, as did its mother. Luke flicked his wrist, releasing the calf's hooves, and it rose and trotted back to its mama.

"Looks like that's the last one." Luke curled up his rope then looped it over one shoulder. "I'm gonna have me a herd like this one day."

Jack looked at the young cowboy, who he guessed was around twenty. "You worked for Gabe long?"

"Over four years." Luke wrestled the lid off his canteen and took a long swig. "I started working for him before the land run of '89 when Gabe was selling horses to those hoping to ride in the run."

"I thought about doing that—racing in the land rush—but I was working up in Nebraska at the time at a good spread and didn't want to risk my job."

Luke fastened the rope to his saddle and hung the canteen over the horn. "I rode in it, but I didn't win land. Gabe has always been lucky."

"Maybe it's God's blessing and not luck."

Luke stared at him then grinned. "You know, I never thought about it that way, but you might be right. Although I don't know why God would want to bless a gambler."

"God works in mysterious ways. Just look at how I found my sisters after all these years." Jack kicked dirt over the fire and stuck the branding irons in a bucket of water, enjoying the loud hiss they made. It reminded him of bacon cooking.

"Why do you think God would bless a gambler?"

"God looks at a man's heart. Gabe told me about his troubled youth. He needed God's love and His help to forgive his stepfather and become the man he is today. I suppose, too, God knew Lara needed Gabe and blessed him so that he'd be able to help her once they met."

Luke seemed to be stewing on that thought; then he smiled. "That does make sense. You reckon God has a woman out there somewhere for me?"

Jack's thoughts raced to Cora. "I reckon He does, but you need to look at how you live your life and become the man God expects you to be, so you can be a wise and kind husband."

Luke leaned back against his horse and rubbed the light stubble on his chin. "I don't think I've even considered that before."

Jack walked over to the younger man and rested one hand on his shoulder. "You're a good man, Luke. I like your quick smile and your happy-go-lucky attitude, but don't neglect your spiritual life. A good man is still a lost man until he asks Jesus to save him and forgive him of his sin."

Luke nodded. "Thank you. I'll think on what you've said. Gabe has told me almost the same thing."

Jack nodded as he checked to make sure the fire was out and put the branding irons in a crate in the buckboard. He emptied the bucket of water over the hot ashes then set the pail in the back of the wagon. "I guess we're done for the day."

Luke mounted and drew his horse next to the wagon. "How does a lost man get found by God?"

Jack climbed aboard the wagon then slapped the reins against the rumps of the horses. "Start by readin' the Bible. Do you have one?"

He shrugged one shoulder. "Not me myself, but there's one in the bunkhouse. If I read it, though, the other guys will poke fun at me."

Jack understood the man's reticence. "I felt the same way when I worked at the Lazy S Ranch. Our boss was a godly man who often talked about his faith. I'd heard plenty about that when I was a kid and attended church with my folks. What I did was sneak the Bible out one day when no one was in the bunkhouse, and then I'd read it after supper in the barn before I turned in for the night. Once God got ahold of me, I started reading it to the others while they played cards."

Luke chuckled. "I bet they didn't care much for that."

"Not at first, but later on some started askin' me questions. Before I came here, I was a preacher of a small church in Texas."

Luke whistled. "No wonder you know so much about God."

Jack guided the horses off the trail onto the road that led back to the ranch. "A good man took me under his wing and taught me much of what I know now. If you have questions, you're welcome to ask them anytime."

"How long you plan on sticking around?"

"Don't know. I've got some decisions to make."

"We could use a preacher in these parts. There are several in Guthrie, but that's a long drive for some, especially those who live farther from town than us."

Jack nodded. Gabe had said he could stay if he wanted. And he did. He longed to spend time with his sisters and grandfather. And he'd like to see his niece and nephews grow up. There was a time he wanted nothing more than to get away from his family, but now he'd like to stay. Was God calling him to preach here? And what about Cora?

He pretended he knew all the answers, but he didn't. He wasn't even sure where God wanted him.

"Have you heard there's probably gonna be another land run? People are pushin' the government to open up the Cherokee Outlet, up in northern Oklahoma Territory. If'n they do, I plan to ride in it."

The idea appealed to Jack. If he won a claim, he could finally have a place of his own—but was that what God wanted him to do?

A man of thirty-two ought to have his life all mapped out by now. His parents had three young'uns by that age. If he hadn't accidentally started the fire that killed them, they might still be alive—and his life and his sisters' would have turned out far different. Lara's life had turned out well, but not so with Jo's. Was he responsible for that?

"That's some mighty heavy sighing going on over there." Luke's eyes twinkled, but Jack could read the concern in his voice.

"I'm just thinkin' on some troubling things from my past."

"You Christians ain't supposed to do that, are you?"

Jack stared at the young man. "You're right. We're supposed to pray and give our burdens to the Lord. But sometimes I tend to forget that and lift them back on my shoulders and try to carry them myself. Thanks for the reminder to pray."

Luke scratched his temple. "I didn't say nothin' about prayin'."

Jack grinned. Not directly, but the message had gotten through to him. God wanted him to pray over the decisions he needed to make for his future and not dwell on his past.

Chapter 23

Jo softly kissed Jamie and laid a light blanket over him. So far God had answered her prayers to keep him healthy. She tiptoed from the room and checked on Sarah. The girl sat in her bed, sounding out words in a second grade primer. Lara had been right about her soon passing Michael, who was at the same level. Sarah glanced up and smiled.

"I'm so glad you're feeling better."

"Me, too. I'm also glad you came back here." Her smile dipped. "What if Badger finds us?"

Jo shrugged. "There are usually several men around here to protect us, and I'm praying that God will keep us safe and not let Badger find us."

Cocking her head, Sarah stared at her. "You are different."

Jo smiled. "I had a long talk with God, and He and I are friends now."

"Ah. . .Lara tells me of God. She says He wants to live in my heart."

"That is true." Jo wished she knew more to explain it all to her, but her own relationship with God was so new. "Would you like me to read to you from the Bible? Maybe we could both learn something from it."

"You can later, but now I need to rest." Sarah closed the book and laid it on the nightstand.

"That's a good idea. Later, then." Jo closed the door and went downstairs to meet Baron, who stood at the front window.

"Still on guard." She sent him a teasing smile.

"Yes, ma'am." He turned to face her. "Did you get that little fellow down?"

"He was worn out from playing with you."

"I enjoyed my time with him. He's a good boy."

Jo nibbled her lip. So many times she'd dreaded that her past would affect her son in a bad way. "I hope he'll grow up to be a good man, like you and Gabe."

" 'Train up a child in the way he should go: and when he is old, he will not depart from it.' "

"Is that from a poem?"

Baron gazed out the window again. "No, it's from Proverbs 22:6 in the Bible."

Jo joined him. "Did your parents do that—train you up according to the scriptures?"

"I wish they had. Even though we attended church, as was common among people of our stature, I don't believe my parents began to take God's Word seriously until Mark and I were nearly grown."

"I went as a child, but I can't see how it helped me. I still made bad choices." Footsteps sounded overhead, drawing her gaze toward the ceiling. Sarah must have decided she needed to make a trek to the privy before falling asleep.

He reached down and took her hand, turning to face her. "You also endured a horrible tragedy when you lost your parents and your home at such a young age. That had to have affected you."

"Why didn't it affect Lara as well?"

"I'm sure it did, but she was twice your age when it happened. I'm sure that made a difference."

"You're probably right. I'm glad she was able to attend church with Gabe today. She hasn't been since before Beth was born. I would have liked to have gone, too, now that I'm a new believer, but someone had to stay home with Sarah."

Luke rode by and waved his rifle at them. He continued around the side of the house and out of view.

"It's best if you stay close to home until we know for sure what Badger will do."

Jo crossed her arms. "How long are we to wait? What if he never does anything?"

"I wish I knew, but I don't." He stroked her hand with his thumb.

She gazed up at him, still amazed he wanted to have anything to do with her. For the past four days, he'd ridden over early and spent the day, helping to guard her and the children. "How is your father doing with the store?"

"Fine. Mother has started helping him. I think she's enjoying it even more than he. Back in St. Louis, people would have frowned upon her working in one of our stores, so she never did. It's good for them to spend time together."

A loud thump sounded overhead. Jo's heart thudded. "I'd better check on that. Jamie has never crawled out of his bed yet, but there's always a first time."

"All right. You know where to find me." He pushed away from the window and followed her into the hallway. "I'm going to double-check and make sure all the doors and windows are locked."

Jo started up the stairs. "I imagine the noise was merely Sarah's book falling off the nightstand. I'll be right back."

She headed to the girl's room first, convinced she was right, but the book was in the same spot as when Sarah had laid it down. Closing the door, she crossed to her bedroom and opened the door. Nothing looked out of place. She walked over to the bed and stared down. It was empty!

"Jamie!"

Baron reached for the back door to check the lock but startled at Jo's scream. He turned and raced for the stairs. Jo's cry had been frantic, not a normal mother's call to her child.

His footsteps thudded up the stairs, but when he reached the top, he realized the impropriety of his actions.

Down the hall to his left, Jo ran out of a room, her face white. She looked away from him then toward him. She gasped and rushed into his arms.

"What happened?"

"I can't find Jamie. He's gone."

Baron took hold of her upper arms and pushed her back to look in her face. "What do you mean he's gone?"

"Gone! He's not in his bed—and he's never climbed out before. And he's not in our room. Where could he be?"

"We'll find him. He has to be here somewhere." Holding her hand, he headed for the room she'd just exited.

The door opposite that room opened, and Sarah peered out. "Did I hear a scream?"

Jo rushed to her. "You don't have Jamie in there, do you?"

The girl's eyes widened. "No. He might take sick."

"He's missing. I put him to bed and went downstairs, but now he's not there."

Baron turned into the bedroom Jo had been in and walked straight to the small railed bed in the corner. It was possible Jamie could have climbed out—the boy was always on the move. He turned his back to the bed and searched the rest of the room. He opened the wardrobe but quickly closed it when he caught sight of Jo's dresses.

As he peeked under the bed, he heard Jo ask Sarah if she'd walked down the hall a few minutes ago.

Baron's chest clenched when he found nothing under the bed, not even dust balls.

"I never left my room."

"Baron." Jo hurried through the door.

He rose from the far side of the bed. "He's not in here. Let's check the other rooms."

Jo's expression wilted. Her chin wobbled, and tears ran down her cheeks. "He won't b–be there."

He walked around the bed and joined her, taking her hands. "Why would you say that?"

She sniffled. "Because I heard footsteps when we were talking downstairs. I thought it was Sarah, heading down to the privy, but she never left her room. Someone came in the house and took my son."

Baron glanced past Jo to where Sarah stood at the door, peeking out but keeping her body hidden. Her face was as pale as he'd ever seen it.

"Badger found us." Jo hurried to the window and looked out.

Sarah shook her head. "I do not think Badger would take Jamie. He wants me or you, but not the boy."

Jo spun around, her frantic gaze jumping from him to Sarah and back. "Then who would? Why would anyone have a reason to take him?"

"I don't know. Jo, you get Sarah back to bed while I search the other rooms on this floor. We have to make certain Jamie didn't climb out and crawl somewhere, looking for you."

Jo moaned, and he couldn't help taking her in his arms. He hugged her, kissing her on the top of her head. "Shh. . .we'll find him. We all need to pray for God's help to show us where he is."

"But he's so little. He'll be crying for me. I can't stand the thought of not being there for h–him." She melted against him, sobbing. "H–he won't understand why I'm not there to c–comfort him."

Baron lifted his gaze to the ceiling, praying for God's help. *Bring Jamie back, Lord. And keep him safe until then. Comfort Jo.*

Baron suddenly thought of Luke and set Jo back from him. "Take care of Sarah. Then search the rooms upstairs thoroughly. I want to find Luke and tell him what's happened. Maybe he saw something."

Jo nodded and sullenly walked into Sarah's room.

Baron headed to the door at the end of the upstairs hallway. He'd seen the side stairs leading up to the second floor of the house while touring the yard with Gabe. If the door had been unlocked, it would have been a simple thing for someone to sneak in and take Jamie. His gut churned at the thought. What kind of heinous man would steal such a young child?

Baron clenched his fist. He'd come here to keep Jo safe while the family attended church. How could he have known some callous soul would take Jamie? It never occurred to him. He should have checked this door when he first arrived, but he'd gotten caught up in playing with his nephew.

He sucked in a sharp breath. The door was ajar. If Jamie had crawled this far, he might have fallen down the steps. *Please, God. No.*

Bracing himself, he pushed the door open and stepped onto the landing. Relief washed through him that Jamie hadn't fallen down the stairs. He jogged down the steps and ground his back teeth together when he found the outside door wide open. He hurried out and looked around, doubting Jamie could have gotten this far on his own.

He walked around the side of the house, searching for Luke and signs of an intruder. When he rounded the front of the house, he looked toward the barn. Luke's palomino stood near the barn door, his head down. Baron narrowed his gaze as his eyes latched onto what looked like a pair of boots—with legs attached—lying in between the barn doors. He broke into a run and soon reached the horse. The animal jerked its head and stared at him as Baron skidded to a halt. "Easy, boy."

Luke lay on the ground, unconscious. Baron looked around for signs of anyone else then knelt beside the man. The other work hands had gone to church in Guthrie with Gabe and Lara, so he hadn't expected to find anyone. He inspected Luke's head and body but didn't see any wounds. *What happened here?* He nudged the man's shoulder. "Luke. Wake up."

He groaned. His eyes fluttered open for a brief moment but closed again. Baron rose, pulling his handkerchief from his pocket. He ran over to the trough, dunked the hankie, and then hurried back to Luke's side and wiped off his face. The coolness of the water must have helped because Luke squinted open his eyes. "W–what happened?"

"Looks like someone knocked you out."

Luke bolted up then grabbed his head and groaned.

"Easy now." Baron saw a bloody lump on the back of Luke's head. "Looks like someone clobbered you from behind."

Luke reached back to feel the walnut-sized lump. "I've had worse." His hand paused; then his concerned gaze jerked to Baron's. "Is everyone all right in the house?"

Baron pursed his lips, shaking his head. "Jamie is missing."

Luke sucked in a loud breath. "Help me up."

Baron did as asked. Luke motioned toward his hat, and Baron picked it up and handed it to him. Luke smacked it against his leg then set it on his head, wincing as he did.

"Tell me everything that happened." Luke staggered toward his horse.

"Shouldn't you lie down?" Baron followed him, staying close in case the cowboy stumbled.

"Nope. Gotta find that kid. I promised Gabe I'd keep watch on his family. I can't let 'im down." He gathered up his palomino's reins then faced Baron. "I remember now. I heard something at the barn and came to investigate."

"Looks like whoever took Jamie got in the rear door and went upstairs. Jo mentioned hearing footsteps, but she thought they belonged to Sarah."

"How long ago was that?"

"Not long—ten minutes, perhaps."

"Did you check for footprints?"

Baron nodded. "I saw some hoofprints near the back door, but they could be old ones."

"Show me." Luke managed to mount his horse in spite of his wobbliness. He rode toward the house while Baron followed. "I want to see if I can find the man's trail. We've gotta get that boy back."

As they walked past the front of the house, something flapping on the front porch caught Baron's attention, and he started toward it. "Hey, look. There's something near the door."

He ran up the steps, yanked up the paper held down by a rock, and scanned it. His heart dropped to his feet. "The note says he'll swap Jamie for Jo."

Luke's expression hardened. "We're not making that trade."

"Jo will agree in a second. We have to tell her."

"How are we supposed to make the trade?"

"He says to fire two shots then send Jo to the windmill."

Luke shook his head then grimaced. He pressed on the back of his head. "Then he'll have them both."

"If the man is going to swap Jamie, he's got to be around

here close." Baron searched the landscape but saw no sign of the kidnapper.

"That's true."

"I need to show this note to Jo."

Someone yanked open the front door. Jo stepped out, her frantic gaze searching in all directions. "Did you find any sign of Jamie or the person who took him?"

"Just some hoofprints." Baron walked closer to her, dreading what she'd say. He didn't want to lose Jo, just when he realized how much she meant to him. "And this."

Her gaze latched onto the paper as he held it out. "What's that?"

"Read it." He watched the blood drain from her face as she read the missive. The note referred to Jo as Sapphire, but it was clear who the kidnapper wanted.

She looked up, determination on her face. "I have to go."

Badger crawled to the top of a hill, staring at the house that should belong to Gabe Coulter, the husband of Sapphire's sister—if the directions he'd gotten were right. At least the two-story clapboard looked like the house the man at the saloon in Guthrie had described. It was the nicest one he'd passed since leaving town.

A man on horseback talked to another man who stood on the porch. He'd expected to see more people moving about the ranch this time of day. Maybe it was because today was Sunday, and ofttimes ranchers gave their hands the morning off to recover from their Saturday night trip to town. That meant there could be a bunch of cowhands in the bunkhouse.

He gritted his teeth.

The front door opened, and a woman came out. He squinted his eyes. Was that Sapphire?

His heart pounded as he watched her. The roof of the porch blocked the woman's face, but she was about the right size. Hard to tell from this distance, though. He needed to get into the house.

Backing down the hill, he formulated a plan. He'd ride around the far side of the house and see if there was an unlocked door or open window. He mounted his horse, leading the one he'd rented for Sapphire and Sarah to share, and rode in a wide arc around the house. He made sure to keep out of sight behind the hills to the north of the Coulter home. Once he reached his destination and had secured both horses in a copse of trees, he hunkered down and ran to the back of the outhouse. Listening for sounds of others, he paused and caught his breath. He peered around the side of the small structure so he could see the back of the house. A smile pulled at his lips when he noticed a rear door.

He waited several minutes, hoping to see the cowboy who had been at the front of the house ride off, but he was running out of time. He needed to find the girls and get out fast—if they were even here.

With gun in hand, he dashed out from behind the privy and ran to the back of the house. To his surprise, the back door wasn't locked. He slipped inside. At the bottom of the stairway was an inside door. He tried to open it, but the door held firm. His only choice was to go up the stairs.

Badger tiptoed, hoping none of the steps creaked. He kept his gun aimed at the top of the stairs until he reached a landing and another door. When it opened, he breathed out a loud sigh. He found himself in a hallway with four doors. At the far end was another staircase. A brown-and-tan decorative carpet ran down the middle of the wide hall. Halfway down was a comfortable sitting area. At least his daughter—if she was even here—lived in a nicer place than he did.

He stepped into a bedroom that looked as if it belonged to a boy, but one older than Sapphire's kid, from the looks of the clothing hanging on pegs and the slingshot on the dresser.

He crossed the hall into a bigger room with a full-sized bed. This room must belong to Sapphire's sister and husband. Quick footsteps sounded on the other stairwell, and he pressed himself against the wall of the bedroom. He heard someone open one of the doors he hadn't reached yet.

"Sarah. . ."

Badger's stomach clenched at the sound of Sapphire's voice—and the girl's name. He ground his teeth together as he stepped into the hall then hurried to the open door. He leaned slightly and peered inside.

"Why are you dressed? You should be in bed," Sapphire said.

Bed? What had they done to her that she should be abed this time of day? Anger boiling, he moved into the room and shut the door.

Sarah's eyes widened. Sapphire spun around, gasped, and then rushed straight at him like an angered hen. Surprised, Badger lifted his gun.

Sapphire halted in the middle of the room, fire blazing from her eyes. Her fists were clenched, and anger engulfed her face. "Where's my son? What have you done with him?"

He frowned at her comment, but he could hardly take his eyes off his daughter long enough to glare at Sapphire. Sarah wore the simple calico dress of a schoolgirl. Her unbraided hair hung loose to her waist, and a brush hung from one of her hands. She'd filled out in the weeks she'd been gone. He'd always thought her far too thin, but she hardly ate a thing. Jo mentioned she should be in bed, but he'd never seen her looking so healthy.

Sarah walked toward him. "Where is Jamie. . .Father?"

He realized his mouth had dropped open. Sarah had refused to call him that when she lived with him. He stared at his daughter, stunned at the changes in her. Then her words registered. "Jamie? I haven't seen the boy since you left."

Sapphire's eyes narrowed. "I don't believe you. He only went missing less than an hour ago—and now you're here. That's too much of a coincidence." She reached in her pocket.

"Easy there." He lifted the gun and aimed it at her chest. "And coincidence or not, it's the truth."

"I'm just getting the note you left on the door." She unwrapped a wadded-up piece of paper and thrust it at him.

He glanced at the note, not bothering to read it. "That's not my handwriting. You oughta know that. You've seen my signature plenty of times."

Her forehead crinkled, and she stared at the paper for a long moment. "You're right. It isn't."

Sarah walked over to Sapphire and laid her hand on her arm. "If my father did not take Jamie, who did?"

He blinked at the difference in Sarah's speech. She had improved in three weeks far more than in the year that she'd lived with him. And she'd changed in other ways. She seemed more self-confident. He lowered his hand, pointing the gun at the floor.

Sapphire glanced at it for a moment then looked him square in the face. "Did you tell Stoney to take my son?"

"No. He's back at the bordello."

Hiking her chin, Sapphire glared at him. "I know you came for me—us. But I can't go with you. Someone has my son, and I have to get him back."

Badger rolled his neck, caught in a dilemma unlike any he'd ever encountered. "You're right. I came for the both of you." He narrowed his gaze at Sapphire. "If you'd just left and taken your kid, I'd probably have let you go, but why did you have to take my daughter?"

"I didn't know she was your child, but I took her to protect her—from you."

He blinked, confused. "I'd never hurt her. She's my own flesh and blood."

"You sure didn't treat her like family."

"I. . .uh. . .didn't know how." He rubbed his forehead, trying to make sense of it all. "I sure didn't expect to find Sarah in such"—he waved his hand in the air—"fine. . .condition."

Sapphire shoved her hands on her hips. "What did you think I'd do to her? She's only a young girl."

"But she's half-Cherokee. Most whites—"

"That doesn't matter to me." She wrapped her arm around Sarah's shoulders. "I love her like I do my own family. In fact, she is part of our family now. You can't have her."

Sarah slipped from Sapphire's hold and stepped between him and Sapphire—no, Jo. For she was no longer a painted lady.

"Father, Jo's family has been very kind to me. Her sister teaches me to read and write. They treat me like family. I want to stay."

Badger shifted his feet. He'd come here ready to take Jo back, teach her a lesson, and free his daughter, but nothing was as he expected. When Jo had taken Sarah, in a way, she'd rescued the girl—from him. And the life he lived. He was no good for Sarah. As much as he hated to admit it, she was far better off here. From the sound of things, they'd treated her better than he had.

Jo had given Sarah the chance to live a normal life, which wasn't something he could offer her. He owed Jo his thanks, not revenge. He pocketed his gun. "I can see I've made a mistake in comin' here."

Sarah's eyes—black like her mother's—lit up. "I can stay?"

He nodded. Sarah leaped into his arms. And for the first time ever, he hugged his daughter. Tears stung his eyes, and his throat tightened. He loved Sarah but never knew how to tell her. Ever since he learned her mother was carrying her, he'd sent Awinta money to make her life easier, but he doubted Sarah knew that. He could show his love now by letting her stay, even if it meant he might never see her again.

Jo stared at him, obviously as surprised as he. Suddenly, her expression changed. "I have to go. My son needs me."

Sarah stepped back and wiped her eyes, but a smile lingered on her face. Jo turned to her. "I'm sorry to leave you now. Please go back to bed."

The girl shook her head. "I feel fine. The doctor's medicine helped me."

Jo nodded then looked at Badger. "You won't take her? Please. She has a life here and a family who loves her."

"I said she could stay."

"Thank you." She slid past him and hurried down the stairs.

Badger stared at his daughter. "I can hardly believe you've changed so much in such a short time."

"Jo's family. . .they do not see my Indian blood."

"They see it, but like Jo said, it doesn't matter to them."

"I like it here."

"Good. I'll send you money so you can get the things you need."

Sarah stared at the floor. "Thank you."

He felt at a loss for words. Jo's kindness toward his daughter, especially after the despicable way he'd treated her, moved him in ways he hadn't expected. No one had ever treated him that kindly except Sarah's mother—Awinta. She'd found him shot after he'd been robbed and had taken him home, nursing him back to health. He should have stayed, but he got wandering feet. He was such a fool.

And here he was again, ready to walk away from his daughter. "I. . .uh. . .would you be willing to let me visit you. . .once in a while?"

Sarah looked hesitant, but she nodded. "If you promise to never harm Jo or her family."

"I realize now that I owe them my gratitude for how they've taken care of you. I no longer want to hurt her."

"That is good." Sarah tugged on his sleeve. "You should help Jo find her son."

"What?"

"You help."

He huffed a laugh. "I'm the last person she'd want helping."

"She will not care if she gets Jamie back."

Badger shook his head. "I think the best thing I can do for Jo is to leave." He stared at his daughter for a long moment, but he knew the time to go had come. "I'll be in touch."

Chapter 24

Baron was still waiting when Jo returned to the porch. He pushed up from a rocker and walked to her, giving her a lopsided smile. "You took so long that I thought you might have changed your mind."

"I had a little distraction—or perhaps I should say a huge distraction."

"Like what?"

"You wouldn't believe me if I told you."

He fell into step with her as she headed toward the windmill in the pasture closest to the house. "Care to share?"

She blew out a loud breath, knowing he wouldn't take this easily. "When I went upstairs to tell Sarah about the note, Badger came into her room."

"Wait! What?" Baron grabbed her arm, stopping her. "Badger is in the house?"

Jo nodded. "He is, but he's no longer a threat."

Baron narrowed his eyes. "How is that possible?"

"I don't have time to tell you now." She started moving again, searching the landscape ahead of her for a sign of Jamie.

"You can't drop a cannonball like that and not explain. Should I get Luke to chase him away? I thought you said he would take you back if he could."

She stopped at the edge of the yard. "When he saw the changes in Sarah, he, oddly enough, realized that she's better off here than with him. And it helped that she pleaded with him to let her stay."

"And it doesn't flummox you that he's willing to walk away after everything he's done?"

"Of course it does. But right now, Jamie is foremost in my mind. I'm just thankful Badger didn't haul me away before I could save him."

"But if Badger doesn't have him, who does?"

Jo shook her head, struggling with the same question. "I have no idea." She glanced toward the barn. "Where's Luke?"

"He climbed up in the hayloft with a telescope and is looking around to see if he can find the kidnapper. We figure he has to be close if he plans to swap Jamie for you."

"I have to go—and the note said to come alone." She gave a little push backward on his chest. "This is as far as you come."

He reached for her hand. "I don't want to lose you when I've only just found you." He ran his fingertips along her check. "I'm ninety-five percent certain that I'm falling in love with you."

She lifted one eyebrow, fighting a grin in spite of everything. "Ninety-five percent?"

He smiled. "It's probably more like ninety-seven." He tugged her to him. His eyes roved her face, settling on her lips. He leaned down and placed an achingly sweet kiss on her mouth. Then he drew back. "Be careful, Jo. Luke and I will be watching."

"Just have a horse ready and hurry out to the windmill and get Jamie. I don't want him left alone for long."

"We'll come for you both." He gazed at her for a long moment then let go of her hand.

Jo nodded. She pulled her pistol from her pocket and fired off two quick shots. Jo wished she could stay and explore his confession more, but her son needed her. She stiffened her resolve. She didn't know what she was walking into, but at least Jamie would be safe. "Please, God. Protect my son. And if You could get me out of this situation, I'd be forever grateful."

The whooping of the windmill blades grew louder the closer she got to them. After several minutes, she reached it. There was no sign of Jamie or anyone else. She walked around to the far side and found another note. She grabbed the paper and tossed aside the rock that kept it from blowing away.

"Walk straight into the woods ahead."

Baron hated watching Jo walk away to face an unknown enemy, with her life and her son's at stake. He clenched his fist, feeling more helpless than he could ever remember. There had to be something he could do to help Jo—and Jamie.

He spun and ran to the barn and looked in the loft for Luke. "Do you see anything?"

"Not yet. Why's she goin' into the trees?"

"She picked up something on the far side of the windmill. I'm guessing it was another note."

Luke clambered down the ladder and headed to his saddled horse. "I can't help her if she's in the trees." He shoved his rifle in the scabbard attached to his saddle and mounted his horse. He glanced at Baron's waist. "You know how to use that thing?"

He rested his hand on the handle of his gun. "I do."

"Good. Then saddle another horse. I'm riding out behind the barn; then I'll head west for a bit and try to ride out past the kidnapper. Then I'll cut back this way. Pray I find them. You go the same way, but then turn north. Maybe one of us will get lucky and find the culprit."

"I'm praying we do."

Luke nodded and rode his horse out of the barn; then he clucked to his horse.

Baron glanced at the remaining horses and decided on Gabe's black. He figured Gabe wouldn't mind his using the animal to save his sister-in-law. The horse eyed him, but settled as Baron stroked her neck and talked softly. He quickly saddled the big horse then led him outside.

He hoped Jo wouldn't be upset that he didn't stay with Sarah, but the girl's father was with her—and he wasn't a man Baron looked forward to meeting. Not after what he'd done to Jo.

He tapped his heels against the horse's side and nearly lost his seat when the frisky animal shot forward. He hadn't thought to adjust the stirrups, but he and Gabe were close in height, so his feet reached them well enough.

He checked the area around the windmill, hoping to find Jamie, but when he didn't, he rode west as Luke had said, keeping an eye out for any sign of a person. Everything was new to him since the Coulter ranch was as far west as he had traveled. He wasn't sure at what point he should turn north, but since Jo was on foot, she couldn't go very far. "Help us find them, Lord."

Feeling in his gut that it was time, he reined the horse to the right and wove in and out of the trees. Much of Gabe's land was cleared, but in this area alongside the creek, the trees were fairly thick. He stopped the horse, listening and praying. If he went too far, he might go past the spot where the kidnapper was hiding.

A screech rang out. *Jamie!*

Baron dismounted and tied the black horse to a sapling. He made his way through the trees, moving slowly and trying not to step on a branch that would alert the kidnapper to his presence. Though just April, most of the trees already had a new growth of leaves. Redbuds and wildflowers dotted the area, which would be pretty any other time.

He peered through the tree trunks, hoping to see Jo. His heart hammered in his chest and ears.

"No!"

Baron's head jerked in the direction of Jo's voice. He pushed his feet into motion. She was close.

He caught a glimpse of her yellow dress up ahead. About fifteen feet from her, a stranger held on to Jamie with one arm wrapped around the boy's belly. Wailing, Jamie tossed his head back and kicked his feet.

"Just let me take him back to the windmill; then I'll go wherever you want. He's too small to leave here by himself."

"He's stayin' right here. I ain't as stupid as you think. If I let you take the boy back, you wouldn't return."

"I will. I promise." Jo's voice sounded frantic. "Just don't hurt him. Please, give him to me."

"I reckon it won't hurt to let you say your good-byes. Just make it quick." The man looked away from where Baron was hiding.

He ducked down, expecting the man to search his direction, too. Fortunately, he was slightly behind the kidnapper. He wasn't certain, but he thought the man might have come into the store in the past week. Who was he? What could he want with Jo?

Baron's heart ached as he watched Jo comfort Jamie and kiss him good-bye. He wrestled with what to do. The kidnapper had his gun trained on Jo, and she was blocking his view of the man. He told Luke he could shoot, but his aim wasn't all that great. If he tried to shoot the kidnapper, he might hit Jo.

And what about Jamie? Should he go to Jamie if they left him alone and hope that Luke would find Jo and her captor?

The answer became clear. Jo was able to protect herself, but Jamie wasn't. With Jamie safe, Jo would be more likely to attempt escape on her own. He wanted desperately to save her, but he couldn't take a chance on a wild animal or snake crossing paths with the one-year-old. *God, protect Jo. Help her to get away. Help Luke to find her.*

"Put the boy down."

"Here? But my family won't know where to find him."

"Down. Now. Or I'll shoot 'im."

Jo did as told, though Baron could tell that her heart was breaking. Jamie whined and reached for her.

The stranger yanked Jo away from the boy and pushed her toward his horse using the barrel of his gun to prod her. When she mounted, she looked at Jamie, her expression devastated. Jamie sobbed and crawled toward her, obviously confused.

"We can't leave him." Jo looked back over her shoulder, her desperate expression tearing at Baron's heart.

He wanted to show himself to ease her pain, but he didn't dare. The man swung up behind Jo and reached around her to gather the reins.

Jo elbowed him. "I won't go."

"You want me to shoot that kid?" One hand reached for his gun.

"No! Fine. Let's go."

The man grinned then reined the horse westward and crossed the creek.

Good. Luke had gone that way, too.

Jamie's wails gutted Baron, but he had to wait. The moment Jo was out of sight, he rushed forward. Jamie sat and turned toward him. When the boy saw him, he puckered up and screamed.

Baron hurried to his nephew and scooped him up. "Shh. . .it's all right, Jamie. Remember me?"

The boy cried, reaching toward where he'd last seen his mother.

"You're all right, Jamie. Your mama loves you. Shh. . ."

Jamie clutched Baron's lapels and slowly calmed. He breathed in a ragged breath. Splotchy red patches covered his face. The poor kid.

Baron pulled out his handkerchief and wiped Jamie's eyes and nose. He kissed the boy's cheek and cuddled him, patting his back. He needed to get Jamie back home so he could go after Jo.

"Lord, I don't talk to You near enough, but thank You for letting me be here to help Jamie. Please protect Jo. Let me find her and bring her home. She needs some happiness in her life."

Jo looked over her shoulder, trying desperately to see her son, but the trees blocked her view. Everything within her wanted to rush back to Jamie, but Ernie Slaughter might follow through with his threat to kill him. *Please, God, send someone to find Jamie, and keep him safe until they do. Help me to get away.*

Not that she deserved to get away. *Punish me, if You need to, but Jamie is innocent. Please protect him.* The day was warm, but her son sat on the ground in only a thin gown. He had done nothing to deserve what happened to him, but she had.

She thought again of how she'd hurt the ones who loved her, and how her bad choices had landed her in the pit of hell—a place no woman should have to dwell. If only she'd listened to Lara and Grandpa and hadn't been so stubborn. She once heard someone say hindsight made things look sharper—and it was true. She'd been a miserable person most of her life, but God had changed her, and if He saved her from Ernie Slaughter as He had Badger, she planned to live a better life.

But first, she had to get away.

She listened for Jamie but could no longer hear his cries. Her heart clenched. Was he scared? Hurt? Jo squeezed her eyes shut. Those kinds of thoughts helped no one.

She could only hope—pray—that Baron and Luke were out looking for her and Jamie. She'd learned Luke was tenacious and very loyal to Gabe. Certainly he'd come looking for her. But she wasn't so sure about Baron. Would he try to find her or stay at the house with Sarah?

Jo focused on her immediate problem. She had to figure a way to escape. Distracting her captor was her best resort. "Why are you doing this?"

Slaughter chuckled. "I aim to get a whole passel of money for bringing you back to Badger."

She wanted to tell him that Badger was no longer a threat. That, in fact, he was back at the farmhouse, but doing so would mean she'd have to explain why he was there. And she wouldn't tell him about Sarah's connection to Badger, for fear it would endanger the girl somehow.

"If we're going back to Oklahoma City, why are we headed west?"

"You don't think I'm fool enough to ride across your sister's land, do ya? We're takin' the long trail back to Oklahoma City."

A very long trail since they were headed in the opposite direction. And with each step the horse took, they were getting farther away from Jamie.

Her thoughts raced. What could she do? How could she get free from her captor?

The whisper of Ernie's gun sliding into his holster boosted her determination. As he brought his right arm back around her, Jo grabbed the saddle horn and screamed, kicking the horse in the sides as hard as she could.

"Hey—"

The surprised horse leaped forward. Unprepared, Ernie Slaughter fumbled, grasping her waist with one hand. Jo grabbed one of the reins, jerking the horse to the left, and the sudden shift caused her captor to tumble off the back of the horse. Jo wrestled for the rein he'd taken with him. The frightened horse shook his head and jerked free of the man's grasp then trotted away. Jo couldn't reach the dangling rein and hoped that Ernie didn't get up too fast.

The sound of someone crashing through the trees spooked Jo's horse again. He trotted away from the noise. She ducked under a low-hanging tree and looked back over her shoulder.

Luke held a gun on Ernie Slaughter!

"Thank You, God!"

"You all right, ma'am?" Luke slid a quick glance her way but then refocused on his prey.

"Fine. Thanks!" Filled with new inspiration, Jo tugged the horse in a sharp circle, until the confused animal had no choice but to stop. She slid off, keeping hold of the rein, then snagged the other one and cooed to the horse, hoping to calm him. When he settled, she led him back to where Luke was tying up Ernie Slaughter. The man glared at her.

"I hope you like living in a jail cell, because that's where you're headed, buster." Luke yanked Ernie to his feet and helped him mount Luke's palomino.

"I'm going back to get Jamie." Jo mounted Ernie's horse and told Luke where they had left her son.

"I'm pretty sure Baron was headed that way."

Jo's heart leaped at Baron's name. "I sure hope he found Jamie." She watched Luke climb up behind Ernie, so grateful for his help.

Luke glanced over at her, and Jo nodded her thanks. There'd be time later for a more formal expression of gratitude. She reined the horse back in the direction she'd ridden, praying the whole way. "Please, God. Let Jamie be safe."

She rode for several long, tense minutes, and then a noise to her right grabbed her attention. She saw a man and horse through the trees—*Baron!* "Hey!"

He spun around, his gaze snapping to hers, and he started toward her, carrying Jamie. Jo's heart exploded with love, and for the first time, she knew what true love felt like. She slid off the horse and ran to her men. Baron slowed his pace then wrapped his empty arm around her, pulling her close to her son.

Jamie looked up, and his expression crumpled. Tears started anew, as if he were upset at her for leaving him. "Mama!"

She laughed and took him from Baron, whose arms enveloped her and Jamie.

"Thank God you're all right. I've never prayed so hard in my life." He kissed her forehead then her temple.

Jo tilted her head up to receive his lips, and he pressed them against hers in a kiss so precious she would always remember it.

Baron held her as close as possible with Jamie in between. His breathing and his kiss deepened. Jo found herself lost in his embrace. She'd never felt so safe except for the night she'd cried out to God.

Jamie squawked and pushed at her chest. Jo stepped back, laughing. "We must be squashing him."

Smiling, Baron ran his hand over Jamie's head. "The poor little guy has had a rough morning."

"Him and me both."

"We should get you two home."

He ran his knuckles down Jo's cheek, his look making Jo feel cherished—special.

"I was so afraid I'd never see you again."

Her chin wobbled as she pressed her hand to his chest. "I know."

"This isn't the greatest place and probably a terrible time to ask, but will you marry me, Jo? I can't stand the thought of life without you by my side. I'm so sorry for my stubbornness and not chasing after you the other day."

She blinked, stunned by his question, but her heart sang. This was what she truly wanted. Marriage to a good man—a kindhearted man who served God and respected others. A man who loved her son. A man who loved her in spite of all she'd done. But she had to be fair to him. "You do understand that Ernie Slaughter might not be the only man who will recognize me from Badger's place, especially if we stay in Guthrie."

He nodded, reaching for her hand. "I do. I've thought about that a lot, and if that does occur, we can close the store and go somewhere else. All that matters is that you, me, and Jamie are together."

"What about Sarah?"

"She's welcome to live with us, too, if that's what you want. Even with my parents at the house, it's plenty big—" He stopped and stared at her, his mouth partly open. "I. . .uh. . .would you want to return to the house you shared with. . .um. . .Mark?"

She hadn't considered that. Could she return to the house that held so many bad memories? In that moment, she knew she could. The house didn't matter. It was the people who lived in it. But the house did boast many of Mark's particular likes. "Could we make some changes? Make it ours?"

He smiled. "Of course. That's a grand idea."

She longed to say yes, but there was one more thing she had to know. "You understand about my past?"

He nodded.

Her cheeks warmed at the idea of voicing her thoughts, but she was nervous about performing her marital duties. What if she couldn't after all she'd been through? "I. . .it might. . .um. . ."

He squeezed her hand. "We'll take things as slow as you need them to be. I know your past was hard on you, sweetheart, but I'm not like Mark." He cleared his throat. "Or those others you've. . .been with."

"I certainly know that." She smiled, hoping her expression conveyed how much she cared for him. Baron's neck and ears were as red as the cardinal that just landed in the tree behind him. He was such a good man—and he deserved to be with a woman who'd never been with a man before. But God *had* changed her. She wasn't the woman she used to be. The Bible said that she had been made as pure as snow. It was a hard concept to comprehend, and she desperately longed for it to be true.

"I just wanted you to know that your past doesn't matter to me, but I do understand there may be issues we'll have to face in the future because of it."

Jo's eyes burned. "You're so much more than I deserve."

His smile widened. "Is that your roundabout way of saying yes to my proposal?"

Jo laughed—and it felt so good to be truly happy. "Yes, Baron. I'd love to marry you."

Chapter 25

As Jo rode back into the ranch yard, she couldn't believe all the changes that had occurred in a few short hours. Her life had completely changed. And she was getting married!

She couldn't stop smiling.

But she still had to face Badger again—and doing so in Baron's presence would be awkward. Perhaps she'd get lucky, and he would be gone. How could sweet Sarah be his daughter? It wasn't until she knew the truth of their relationship that she could see Badger in the shape of Sarah's eyes and her rounded chin.

She glanced over to check on Jamie, who'd fallen asleep in Baron's arms on the ride home. It warmed her heart that he was so comfortable with Baron, especially after the traumatizing day he'd had. Baron would be a wonderful father and a great example for him.

Gabe and Lara's wagon crested the hill on the other side of the yard. *My, oh my, do I have some stories to tell them at dinner.* She hoped the roast that was still in the oven wasn't burned to a crisp.

The door of the house opened, and Sarah rushed out. When she locked eyes with Jo, a joyous smile spread across her pretty face. Jo realized then that she'd come to love Sarah like a sister in the short time they'd been together.

"Whoa. . ." Gabe pulled the wagon to a stop in front of the

house and helped Lara down, casting curious glances at them. The cowboys who'd gone to church with them reined their horses toward the barn.

Lara hurried around the wagon and made a beeline for Jo. "Did you go for a ride?"

Jo chuckled. "You could say that."

Lara frowned and looked at Baron and then Jo. "Did something happen?"

"Many things have happened. Let me get Jamie into bed, and I'll explain. And sorry about dinner."

"What about it?"

Jo slid off her horse. She walked over to her sister. "I'm so sorry for all of the trouble I've caused you."

Lara's eyebrows popped up. "Oh my. Now I've got to know what happened."

Gabe strode toward them with Michael on his heels. His gaze shot past her to Baron. "Why are you riding my horse?"

"It's a long story. Could you take the boy?"

Gabe reached up, and Baron passed Jamie to him.

Jo glanced at Baron, feeling suddenly shy—something she wasn't sure she'd ever felt before. She looped arms with her sister. "Have I got a tale to tell!"

Jo crawled into bed beside Sarah, completely exhausted after the day's events, but she doubted she'd fall asleep for a while. Sarah was still awake, with McGuffey's Second Reader in her lap. "Crazy day, wasn't it?"

"Yes. I am glad Badg—my father—did not stay to see you again."

"Me, too. His presence would have been extremely awkward."

She wrapped an arm around the girl's shoulders. "But I'm so grateful to God things turned out so well. I never could have dreamed they would."

"Nor I."

"Have you always known Badger was your father?"

Sarah nodded. "He came to visit my mother and me every few years. When he bring me home with him, he told me not to tell you and the other ladies back at—you know. He think you not treat me nice."

Jo thought Badger had probably been more embarrassed to admit that he was her father than he was worried about his daughter. The ladies lived a rough life, but they weren't cruel. "I wish he had told us, but then, if I'd known the truth, I doubt I would have encouraged you to leave him."

Sarah turned and looked up at her. "I am glad you did. I learn much here."

Jo smiled. "I'm glad, too. You're like a second sister to me."

Sarah ducked her head. "I not know what big family is like before coming here."

"I don't think I did, either. Remember, I ran away from this."

"Why?"

Jo leaned her head against the wall. "I was young, dumb, and thought I knew what was best for me. Kind of like when you told your father that you wanted to stay here. Only I made bad choices where you made a good one."

Jo hoped that Sarah would make another good choice. She longed for her to find God like she had. "You know when we left here and you got so sick?"

Sarah nodded. "I remember most of that time."

"I was so worried about you. I knew we had to get away, but I was afraid you might die if I didn't get help. I cried out to God and told Him I didn't know what to do."

"He help—and He change you."

Jo sucked in a sharp breath. "You can tell?"

"Yes. You are much different. More at peace. More happy."

Jo smiled. "You know, you're right. Even with the awful events of today, I felt more at peace than I can remember. God certainly was with us today."

"I think so, too. I also want God's peace."

Jo's heart leaped. "You do?"

"Yes." Sarah ducked her head. "But I don't know how to get it."

Jo slid off the bed, retrieved the Bible Lara had given her, and returned to the bed. "Lara gave me a list of verses to look up. I haven't read them all, but two of them will help you."

She thumbed through the pages until she found Romans 6:23. " 'For the wages of sin is death; but the gift of God is eternal life through Jesus Christ our Lord.' " Then she flipped to Romans 10:9. " 'That if thou shalt confess with thy mouth the Lord Jesus, and shalt believe in thine heart that God hath raised him from the dead, thou shalt be saved.' "

"This is same Jesus the man at church talks of?"

"Yes."

"I want to be able to read God's book for myself."

Jo hugged her. "You will."

"I will give heart to God after you read some more."

Jo smiled. "You and your father have made peace, and soon your heart will be washed clean like God did with mine, and then you'll be at peace with our heavenly Father. I'd say you've had a big day, too."

Sarah nodded, her serious expression remaining. "That is true. Now read more."

Guthrie, Oklahoma Territory
July 2, 1893

Jo stared at herself in the bedroom mirror of the house that Baron's parents had rented in Guthrie. At Baron's request, she'd chosen a light blue dress to get married in. He'd want a shade that matched her eyes, a darker blue, but she couldn't yet bring herself to wear anything close to a sapphire shade.

"You look lovely." Lara tugged on a turned-under place at the hem of Jo's skirt. "Baron won't be able to take his eyes off you, not that he has the past few months."

"Blue is definitely your color," Cora Sommers said.

Jo worked hard not to wince at the same words Mark had once told her. "Thank you." She liked Cora, who had come for a visit at Jack's request. She suspected another wedding was soon on the horizon for her family.

"It's about time for the wedding to start." Lara glanced out the window. "It was nice of Mr. and Mrs. Hillborne to let you use their house to dress in since it's so close to the church."

"Yes, it was." Jo smiled. After she'd agreed to marry him, Baron had ridden out to the ranch as often as he could during the months he courted her and had brought his parents out on Sundays after church. She'd finally agreed to tell them the whole story about Mark and all that happened, with the exception of her time at the bordello. She smiled at the memory of how overjoyed Mr. and Mrs. Hillborne had been when Baron told them they had a grandson. They'd decided to stay in Guthrie, at least for now, and had rented this house so Baron and she could have privacy in their own home.

Something banged against the side of the house, and Michael

peered in the window of the bedroom. "Pa says it's time for the weddin' to start. Y'all c'mon."

Sarah crossed the room and handed Jo the bouquet she had made from the flowers they'd picked earlier. Her black eyes shimmered with unshed tears. "I am very happy for you, but I will miss seeing you every day."

Jo took the bouquet, handed it to Lara, and then pulled Sarah into her arms. "I love you as if you were my own blood. No matter where you live or I live, you will forever be my little sister."

"I am not little. Beth is little."

Chuckles filled the room.

"You are, too," Michael hollered through the window. "I'm nine and almost as tall as you, even though you're already twelve."

"Shh. . ." Lara gestured for her son to leave. "Tell your pa we're on our way."

Michael pushed away from the window, skipped a step, and then broke into a run. "They're comin', Pa! They're comin'."

Lara shook her head. "That boy only has one speed, except when it comes to doing chores and schoolwork."

Jo laughed as she took one final glance in the mirror. She wanted everything to be perfect today.

Lara opened the bedroom door. "Are you ready, Jo?"

Jo considered her sister's question. She'd never expected to be a blushing bride, but God had taken her ruined life and washed her clean. He was giving her an amazing man to marry—a man who was willing to overlook her past and see her potential. A man who would be a wonderful father for Jamie.

"Let's go." Sarah started for the door. "I am sure Baron is eager to get the wedding started."

Jo smiled and followed the two out the door. "I sure hope Jamie is being good for Baron's folks."

Lara nodded. "They certainly are taken with him."

As they exited the house, Jo's heart rate kicked in as if she'd run a race. In a way she had—a long, winding race that had finally brought her to the place she truly believed God wanted her to be.

They stepped into the back of the church, and Grandpa was there to meet them. His glistening gaze latched onto hers. "My, my. Don't you look pretty."

"Thank you—" Jo's throat caught as emotion overwhelmed her. She murmured a prayer of thanksgiving that God had allowed her grandpa to be here today so he could escort her down the aisle. She looped her arm through his.

Jo peered down the aisle and saw Baron, looking so handsome in the blue suit he'd had made special for today. He straightened as their eyes locked.

Lara slipped in front of her with Sarah behind her, breaking her view of Baron. The piano began, and Lara stepped forward. A few moments later, Sarah moved toward the front of the church.

Jo glanced around the almost-full sanctuary. There were more people in attendance than she had expected. Her heart was filled to overflowing, and she couldn't stop smiling.

Grandpa patted her hand, and then they stepped out, moving toward the man she'd spend the rest of her life with. Jack stood at Baron's right side, ready to marry them, with Gabe and Marshal Bob smiling broadly on his left, but she only had eyes for one man. As she approached, Baron's gaze never left her face.

She made the same pledges to Baron that she'd made to his brother, but this time they were filled with love and promise instead of lust and selfishness. And her brother married them, so she had no doubt as to the authenticity of the parson.

In a mind-numbing flash, the ceremony was over, and Jo and Baron turned to face the audience.

Jack stepped up beside them, winking at Jo. "It gives me great pleasure to present to you Mr. and Mrs. Baron Hillborne."

A cheer rang out, followed by Jamie's loud, "Mama!"

Jo smiled and stepped forward with her new husband, eager to begin married life.

August 4, 1893

Jo glanced up at the cloudless sky as she walked back to the store after eating lunch at Maureen's house and then putting Jamie down for a nap. Maureen loved Jamie and had proven to be the perfect solution to her need for a babysitter while she worked in the store. Though she loved spending time with her son, she was eager to get back to her new husband.

As she stepped into the back of the store, the familiar scents of spices, leather, and coffee greeted her like an old friend. Her heart did a little flip when Baron's gaze met hers. It amazed her that she loved him more now than when she married him a month ago. Excited voices pulled her through the supply room and into the store.

Luke stood with his back to her, waving one arm through the air like a bird's wing. Something white bounced up and down in his hand. Jack leaned against the counter, looking a bit bored, while Baron listened with interest.

"It says right here in the *Wichita Times* that more land will be opened in the Cherokee Outlet land run than was in the rush of '89. I'm gonna get me a claim this time."

Jack shook his head. "I don't mean to discourage you, but there's bound to be thousands more who want land than there is land to go around, just like before."

"That's probably true." Jo reached out her hand. "May I see the paper, Luke?" She quickly scanned the information. "Did you read this part that says the officials aren't going to let anyone who rode in a land grab before ride in this one?"

Luke's head jerked toward her. "Where does it say that?"

"Right there." She pointed to the paragraph and handed the paper back to him.

Luke blew out a loud sigh and crossed his arms. "Well, that sure is disappointing."

Baron tapped his lips. "I imagine participating in such a historic event must be mighty exciting."

"It's like nothing you've ever done before," Luke said, his voice awestruck. He looked over his shoulder. "Tell him, Jo. You know how exciting the rush can be."

She walked past Luke and her brother and took hold of her husband's outstretched hand. "You forget. . .I didn't ride in the run. That was Lara. I was too young and stayed with Grandpa and Michael back at our campsite where the run started."

Luke's gaze swiveled to her brother. "Ain't you never ridden in one, Jack?"

"Nope. I was living in Texas when the land rushes took place."

Luke slapped the paper against his leg. "I can understand them government people not letting a man who won a claim ride again, but it don't seem fair to not let those ride who didn't win land. I've got a hankerin' to get some land of my own."

Jack clapped the cowboy on his shoulder. "You've got things good at Gabe's place. Maybe you shouldn't be lookin' for greener pastures."

"I know, but it's so much fun to ride in those land runs. The excitement beforehand is like nothing I've ever experienced. Then it gets all quiet when everyone's waitin' on the race to start. Then they shoot guns or a cannon, and the loudest cheer you ever did hear rises up, and the race begins. I sure was lookin' forward to ridin' in another one."

"Wait a minute." Jack eyed Luke. "You couldn't have been old enough to ride in one of the other races. What are you, twenty?"

"Twenty-three. Just had my birthday last month." He grinned, looking proud. "I rode in the 1891 land run to settle the Sac and Fox land."

"I do remember the excitement." Jo nodded. "I've never seen so many people in one place. The rows and rows of men, and a few women, lined up for the race ran as far as the eye could see in both directions. And there was such a blithe atmosphere—a hopefulness—that is hard to explain if you weren't there to witness it."

"I'm sure that's true, but think what things were like for those who didn't get land." Jack pushed up from the counter. "We probably should be gettin' back. Gabe'll be wonderin' what happened to us."

Luke nodded and turned toward Jack. "I don't suppose I could talk you into riding in the race for me, huh?"

Jack shook his head. "No, thanks. My poor old horse would never make it."

Baron cleared his throat. "My father and I have been discussing trying for a lot in one of the towns, like Mark did. It worked out well for him."

Jo lifted an eyebrow. It was the first time she'd ever heard Baron compliment something Mark had done. "You're not considering opening a new store, are you?"

Jack glanced at her, grinning, and pulled his hat down on his forehead. "C'mon, Luke. Time for us to go. You don't want to witness a lovers' spat."

The young cowboy glanced from Baron to Jo then to Jack. "Huh?

What are you talkin' about?"

Jack gave Luke a nudge. "Outside, cowpoke."

Wearing a baffled expression, Luke waved good-bye.

Jo crossed her arms and stared at her husband. "So, that's what you and your father have been powwowing about. You really expect me to up and leave my family again?"

Baron shrugged. "Not necessarily."

"You do know that if you win a claim, you'll have to live on it for five years to get ownership of the land."

"Hmm. . .I was thinking if we won a claim, we could start a new store and hire someone to run it for us."

"Not unless you're willing to put the land in their name. As I said, *you* have to actually live on the claim in order to own it. I remember hearing Grandpa say there's a provision where you can leave for up to six months, but then you have to return to the land or lose the title to it." She returned to the storeroom and grabbed the broom then started sweeping. She never expected Baron would catch the land run fever as Mark had.

He reached for the broom. "Jo, we were merely discussing it. I wouldn't make such an important decision without talking to you about it, so don't get upset."

His reassurances warmed her. "I'm not upset."

He lifted a brow. "I've been married to you long enough to know when something is bothering you." He took the broom from her hands and leaned it against the counter then wiggled his finger. "Come here, wife."

She was tempted to run and make him catch her, but sure enough if she did, a customer would walk in. She moved closer, her heart picking up its pace. "What is it you want, dear?"

"I missed your company. You were at Mother's for a long time. And I'm hungry."

"Ah. . .now we get to the crux of the matter."

"Not true." He narrowed his eyes, giving her an expression that stirred her insides. "I missed you far more than I hunger for food." He tugged her close, glanced over his shoulder at the door, and then kissed her soundly.

Jo loved his kisses, which were gentle but possessive. But they shouldn't be expressing their affection in the store, where anyone walking past could see. She loosened her hold on his neck, causing him to relax his hold on her waist. "As much as I'd love to continue, we shouldn't be doing this here."

He blew out a sigh. "I know." Then he grinned and waggled his eyebrows. "We could always close early."

Jo smacked him on the chest. "You goose. Your mother has your lunch ready. When is your father due to return?"

Baron stepped back. "He went to the barbershop and to run several errands. He should be back anytime."

"Well, you go ahead. I want you to eat before the food gets cold."

"All right. If you're sure you don't mind running the store alone."

"I'll be fine. Run along."

He nodded, stepped close, and stole another kiss. Grinning wickedly, he grabbed his hat from the hook in the storeroom and placed it on his head; then he winked. "I'll be back in a half hour."

"No rush. I'm sure your mother would enjoy spending some time with you."

He waved as he exited out the back.

Jo smiled, feeling more contented than she could ever remember. She picked up the broom again, sweeping the dust out the front door and off the porch. She leaned against a post and surveyed the town. Guthrie had grown and done well for itself since it was established in a single day. Mark had told her the story of his train ride to Guthrie the day of the land run and how he thought he'd missed out on getting land. He'd been fortunate to find a claim in a good spot that had somehow been overlooked by the other Boomers.

She remembered the early days of the store and how hard it had been to sell stock out of a tent. It had been impossible to keep dust off their wares back then. That was one thing she wasn't looking forward to if Baron decided to ride in the run and start a new store.

Footsteps sounded behind her, and someone turned into the store. She pushed her feet into motion and went inside. The man stood in front of the rifle case.

"Can I help you?"

He glanced around then turned to face her, a leering smile tugging at his thick lips. "Well, howdy there, Sapphire. Ernie told me he'd seen you, but I didn't believe 'im."

Jo's stomach knotted at the same time her shoulders and neck tensed. She recognized Frank Bennett from the bordello. He'd been one of Ruby's regulars, but he'd often eyed Jo from a distance. She shuddered at the memory. Her gaze darted to the counter where Baron stored his gun. Forcing herself to relax, she smiled, praying she could edge closer to the gun without him noticing. Denying she'd been Sapphire would do no good. "What do you want, Frank?"

He grinned. "So, you remember me."

She casually moved to the end of the counter and slid behind it, putting a barrier between them. She prayed her father-in-law would return, but then, she didn't want him to get hurt if Frank got rough—and after witnessing Ruby's many bruises, she knew he could. "Of course. But you didn't answer my question."

His grin widened, and he slithered closer. "I reckon you know the answer."

Jo picked up a pad of paper, hoping to distract the man, and sidestepped closer to the gun. "I'm a married woman now. And my husband is due back any moment."

"Ah, ah. Lying doesn't become you. I saw that fellow you was spoonin' with go out the back." He rested his hand on his gun. "Lock the doors and turn the sign to Closed."

She glanced down at the revolver.

"If you've got any funny ideas of pulling a gun on me, forget it. I'm a fast draw." Then to prove his point, he yanked out his gun, spun it around on his finger, and shoved it back into the holster.

"Get on over there and lock the doors—and turn the sign to Closed while you're at it. Ya don't want no one comin' in and disturbin' us or gettin' hurt, do ya?"

Jo sucked in a breath. *No, Lord. This can't be happening.*

Chapter 26

Baron strode down the alley, eager both to eat lunch and to get back to Jo. He couldn't believe how happy she'd made him. No wonder his mother had pushed him toward marriage for so long. He'd just needed to find the right woman. Yes, his wife was stubborn at times, but he was patient and flexible. There was generally more than one way to do something, and oftentimes, Jo's way made more sense than his.

He stuck his hand in his pocket and felt a piece of paper. He stopped suddenly and withdrew it, realizing he'd forgotten all about filling Finn Mulligan's order. If he continued on to lunch, the man would probably return before Baron did, and he wouldn't be happy that his order wasn't filled.

Sighing, he turned back to the store. Jo could tend to the order while he ate, and they would have a satisfied customer. And he might just steal another kiss while he was there.

He jogged up the steps and entered the supply room. Thinking to surprise her, he quietly stepped through the door they left open because of the August heat and to allow a cross breeze. But as he neared the door to the store, he noticed the front door had been closed.

"Now shut the back door."

He sucked in a sharp breath. Had he walked in on a robbery? Quietly, he backed into the corner where Jo had hung several ready-made dresses so that he could assess the situation and see how many people he was up against.

Jo entered the room, walked to the door, and closed it. A stranger followed.

Baron struggled to come up with a plan. If only he could get the spare gun he had hidden in the inventory desk. But what if the man had a gun drawn? He couldn't see one in the man's left hand, but most men were right-handed.

Jo spun around, her face white. "All right. I've done as you asked. Now what?"

The stranger stepped another foot into the room. He was shorter than Baron but a bit on the stocky side.

The man nudged his chin toward the stairs. "What's up there?"

"Nothing much. Mostly only a few things we're storing. Look, my husband will return any moment. I'm also expecting his father to come back soon. You'd better leave while you can."

Grunting, the man shoved Jo. She stumbled backward, falling onto the stairs.

Baron clenched his fist and gritted his teeth, waiting for the right moment to jump the man.

"Get on up there, Sapphire."

Baron's heart lurched. The man knew Jo from before.

She glared at the stranger but turned and trudged up the stairs. The stranger followed closely on her heels. Baron slipped out from behind a bright pink dress with a full skirt and held his breath as he grabbed a cast-iron skillet that sat on the inventory desk. He tiptoed toward the stairs.

He swung the skillet, ramming it sideways into the bend of the man's knees. The man cried out and fell backward down the six stairs he'd climbed.

Baron pivoted toward the desk, yanked open the drawer, and

pulled out his gun. When the man opened his eyes, he was staring into the barrel of Baron's gun.

"Jo, get the marshal."

She cast him a grateful glance, hurried down the stairs, and slipped past the man and Baron into the store. He heard the door open and fast footsteps retreating.

The stranger sneered at him. "You the husband?"

Baron nodded.

"How can you stand to marry the likes of her?"

He ground his back teeth together. "I suggest you keep quiet and move into the store."

The man rose and shuffled into the other room. "That marshal cain't take me in. I didn't do nuthin'."

"Bob's a friend of mine. I'm thinking he won't see things that way."

The confidence disappeared from the stranger's face, replaced by concern. "Listen, let me go, and I won't never come back here. A few minutes alone with her ain't worth going to jail for."

"That's my wife you're referring to." He'd never wanted to shoot someone before, maybe with the exception of his own brother for what he'd done to Jo.

Heavy footsteps came their way, and the marshal rushed into the room, his gun drawn. "What's goin' on here?"

"That man tried to kill me," the stranger cried.

"That's not what his wife told me." Bob's expression changed. "Did he tell you I stood up with him at his weddin'?"

Baron noticed the man's Adam's apple moved as he swallowed, and he was looking less cocky than before.

Bob waved his gun toward the door. "Let's go."

Baron's pulse returned to normal as Bob escorted the intruder from the store. Jo ran in as soon as they were gone, and straight into his arms.

"Thank the Lord you returned when you did. I didn't know what to do."

"God knew you needed me." Baron kissed her temple then trickled kisses along her cheek until he claimed her mouth in a long, slow kiss.

Clapping and hoots sounded outside the open store door. Baron and Jo jerked apart. Heat warmed his neck, burning a trail to his ears. He'd been so relieved that Jo was safe that he hadn't noticed the crowd growing outside.

"They's still newlyweds, y'know." Elmer Baxter poked a man in the ribs.

Chuckles echoed through the crowd as people turned away, returning to their own tasks.

Jo giggled. "I guess they'll all have something to talk about at supper."

Baron wasn't quite ready for levity. "That man remembered you. . .from that place."

Jo nodded. "We knew this could happen."

He rubbed the back of his neck. "I sure didn't expect it would happen so soon."

Jo walked over and closed the door, standing there for a long moment. Finally, she turned to face him. "I think we need to discuss the land run idea."

He had mixed feelings about the subject. The land rush had been what brought Mark to Guthrie and into Jo's life. But then, on the other hand, if his brother hadn't come here, Baron never would have met Jo, and Jamie wouldn't have been born.

"What are you struggling with?"

"Many things. My parents only recently settled here. Your family is here—the store."

"That's true, but we can always come back to visit them. Right now, we need to think of our family—you, me, and Jamie."

"You're right. The Cherokee Strip run is next month, so that doesn't give us much time."

Jo took hold of his hand. "No matter what, we need to pray about our decision."

Baron smiled. He loved that Jo had turned her heart to God and saw the wisdom in seeking Him when an important decision needed to be made. "Once again, you're right, dear."

Jo cuddled against his arm, smiling up at him. "I'll never tire of hearing you say that."

"Which one? You'll never tire of hearing me call you dear or saying that you're right?"

She cocked her head, giving him a sassy grin. "Both."

Baron chuckled and pulled her into his arms, so thankful to God for protecting her.

September 16, 1893
Orlando, Oklahoma Territory

Jo stared out the tent door at the huge crowd. The dust that had been prevalent for days finally began to settle as most everyone had stopped milling about because they were waiting for the race to begin. People had gotten into position at the starting line days ago. She remembered the same excitement that surged through the mass of Boomers right before the land run of 1889. Like last time, about ten minutes before noon, the noise of thousands of excited people eerily quieted to an occasional horse whinny, dog's bark, or baby's cry. All was quiet so no one would miss the starting gun.

Baron was somewhere near the front of the line. She smiled, thinking about how he'd been so excited that he hadn't slept but a few hours last night, even though Luke had relieved him where he and his horse stood in line. She stepped through the flap of the tent that held the store they'd operated for the past week.

Luke hammered the lid on the last crate in the tent—half-filled with vinegar bottles, just about the only liquid that remained from the rush this morning. He shook his head and chuckled. "I still can't believe anyone would buy castor oil or vinegar to drink."

"I suppose if that's all they can find, they're happy with it, but it turns my stomach to think of it." She shuddered. "I hated castor oil whenever Lara made me drink it when I was young."

Luke grimaced. "Me, too. I'm sure glad we filled those extra barrels with water as Gabe suggested."

The flap snapped, and Jack walked in. "It sure got quiet out there." He glanced around the near-empty tent. "What else needs to be packed?"

"Not much." Luke lifted the crate and headed out of the tent.

Jack moved toward a row of tables still standing.

"We're almost done. Just the tables, counter, and then the tent." Jo examined the empty area, amazed they'd accomplished so much in the hour since they'd closed. While her back was to the men, she scratched at a trickle of sweat that ran down her chest. She longed for a soak in a tub, but that wouldn't happen for days, not with the drought they were experiencing.

Jack folded up a small table and carried it and another toward the exit. "I have to admit that husband of yours sure has a head for business. I never expected y'all to sell so much before the run."

"I was hopeful. I'm glad he ordered another trainload of supplies to arrive in Perry tomorrow, though, or we wouldn't have enough for our store there—if we have one. Now we just need to pray Baron is able to get a town lot."

"I've been prayin' all day. It's in God's hands." He winked at Jo. "It always has been, sis."

"I know. I'm learning that to be true." Jo lugged one of the heavy tables toward the exit, following her brother. Though she was learning to trust in God more each day, her life was once again in turmoil. After that last encounter with a man who knew her from the bordello, she and Baron had made the decision to move, but where they were going to live still had to be decided. If Baron won a claim in Perry, they would make their new home there. If not, they'd return to Guthrie and rethink their plans. No matter what, she didn't want to be too far from her family. She'd already spent enough years away. If they made their home in Perry, they'd only be a short train ride from Guthrie.

Luke grabbed another table and carried it out while Jo attempted to drag the last one toward the exit. Jack nudged her aside and easily hoisted up the table then stood with his shoulder holding back the flap for her to pass through. "So, are you missin' that little scamp of yours?"

"Of course. And the big one, too."

Jack grinned. "It sure was nice of your mother-in-law to offer to keep him so you could be here to support Baron."

"I hope Jamie is behaving. Could you imagine trying to keep him corralled in a tent now that he's walking?"

He chuckled. "It sure would have added to our workload, especially since that scamp didn't just start walkin'. He started runnin' almost at the same time."

"I suppose I'll find out what it's like if Baron gets a claim. I can't leave Jamie with Maureen for months until we get a house and store built." She blew out a breath. "It makes me tired just thinking of chasing after him all day."

Jack chuckled and handed the table to Luke. "You might have to rig up some kind of pen to keep him safe."

Jo tapped her lips. "That's not a half-bad idea." She turned and cocked her head. "So, are you missing that pretty wife of yours?"

"You know I am." Her brother's ears turned red. "It worked out well for her to return home with her folks to fetch the rest of her belongings while I helped you. But after takin' so long to decide to marry, I'm wantin' Cora by my side again."

"I understand. I miss Baron, too—and I just saw him a few hours ago." Jo wiped the new layer of dust off the top of the sideboard that had served as her checkout counter. "If things don't go well with the startup of your church near Gabe and Lara, you might think of coming to Perry—that is, if we end up there."

"I'll consider that, but I imagine things will go fine since Gabe donated the land and is building the church. Besides, staying there means I can also work some for him."

Jack handed another table up to Luke, who loaded it on the wagon. Covering her eyes against the near-noon sun, Jo looked toward the start of the race as the eerie silence continued. For as far as she could see through the settling dust, people on horseback and in wagons and buggies of all kinds lined the horizon, stretching out for miles. "How much longer until noon?"

Jack pulled out his pocket watch and popped open the cover. "It's about five till."

"We'd better be ready to hang on to the horse when the race starts." Luke jumped down from the bed of the wagon, stirring up a cloud of dust.

Jack turned toward the tent. "Let's pull down the tent stakes real quick—"

The sound of gunfire erupted, and a thunderous cheer rang out. Jo jumped. "It's too soon!" she cried, but she doubted the men could hear her over the deafening roar of the crowd.

Luke spun and ran to the closest team while Jack rushed to the other one. The horses' heads jerked up and they pawed the ground, but neither team broke free.

Clouds of dust filled the air, making seeing difficult. Jo covered her face and hurried into the tent, thankful it was still standing. "Lord, please guide Baron and let him land a claim."

Finally, after weeks of preparation, days of waiting in line, and several tense hours, Baron kicked his horse and yelled, charging forward with the rest of the horde. A gun had gone off early, but there was no stopping thousands of anxious people. He rode with the leaders, urging his horse as fast as he could go. He hoped he hadn't made a mistake by choosing to ride a horse rather than taking the train, but it was too late now to change his mind.

He held on as his horse jumped a small creek and then he angled the bay toward the east just a smidgeon as the leaders spread out. He hadn't ridden this fast since the day he searched for Jo. The wind whipped his face and clothing, blowing off the layers of dust that he'd collected. He hunkered down, leaning slightly forward, like he'd once seen a jockey ride a racehorse. The horse's mane slapped his face, but he kept the position.

The horse's hooves thudded against the ground as Baron searched for signs to let him know he hadn't veered too far off course. He'd started the race in Orlando, which was close to fourteen miles due south and a short way west of the Perry town site.

After a mile or so, he slowed his horse to a trot and looked over his shoulder. He could see several riders on either side of him, but thanks to the fine horse Gabe had loaned him, he was one of the leaders, best as he could tell. Riders coming from the north had to ride farther, so he should be in good shape. *Thank You, Lord.*

Now, if only the town wasn't filled with Sooners who managed to slip past the army's guards and sneak into the Cherokee Outlet early, he might fare well.

Mile after mile passed by, and he knew he had to be getting close, but finding the town site on virgin prairie wasn't easy. A distant train whistle sounded, and Baron jerked his head to the right. He could see the smoke in the distance. "He-yah!" He kicked his horse from a lope to a gallop. He had to beat the train to have any chance to win a town lot.

Hooves thundered, matching the frantic beat of Baron's heart. The train whistled again as it drew closer. Never had he participated in anything so exhilarating.

Up ahead, he saw people milling about. He frowned. So the Sooners had made it to Perry before him—and they had already staked out their tents. He slowed his horse as he reached the first of the claims. Man after man waved him on, some with flagged stakes, others with rifles and guns. He rode on, continuing his search for an empty lot.

The hiss of the train as it slowed echoed across the plains, followed by the roar of the riders. He saw people jumping off the top of the train and the platforms and climbing out windows. Baron reined his horse away from those running toward him and encountered more men waving rifles and flags.

And then—praise God!—he saw the last man in line before the barren prairie opened up again. He clucked to the horse to increase his speed once again. "C'mon, boy. We're almost there."

As he reached the last claimed lot, he drew the horse to a halt and slid off. He pulled his blue flagged stake from his saddlebags and surveyed his land. It wasn't much, just dirt and grass, but soon a new town would spring up where only nature had been. Baron couldn't stop grinning. He glanced at his neighbor and nodded.

"Howdy, friend. You're fortunate you made it before all them train folks got here."

"Just barely did." Baron walked his horse around his lot, both cooling the winded beast and surveying his land. If Jo, Jack, and Luke arrived tomorrow as planned, he'd have his store open in less than twenty-four hours. It boggled his mind to think of all the changes that would soon occur here.

As the train riders ran by, Baron held on to his horse with one hand and waved them on with the other one. It sure was a glorious day—one that dreams were made from.

All he needed was for Jo and Jamie to arrive to make things perfect.

The train whistled and slowed as it approached the Perry town site. Jo wiped the dust from the inside of the window with her handkerchief and tried to look out, but too much dust coated the outer glass for her to see details. All she could make out were the forms of people nearby but not faces.

She sat back, her handkerchief against her nose, waiting for the train to stop. Her car was filled with sweaty, smelly men, still hoping to get a claim, but she feared that by now they were too late and their hopes would soon be dashed. Jo understood their excitement—and even their disappointment. Once again, she'd been too young to ride in the land rush. Just another year, and she could have ridden at Baron's side, but it wasn't to be.

She laid her head against the seat as the train stopped and fanned herself as the eager men forgot their manners and battled one another to get to the door. Pushing, shoving, and curses filled the car. She was more than ready to get out in the fresh air again.

She prayed that Baron would be waiting. Getting a claim meant a new start for them—a start farther away from Badger's clients—and made it less likely she'd encounter one of those heinous men again.

Anxiety and excitement made her limbs quiver. Had Baron gotten a claim? Was he even here? What if his horse had stumbled and fallen? It might be days before they knew anything. "Please, God," she murmured, "let him be safe."

Finally, the last man rushed from the car. Jo stood, picked up her satchel, and made her way down the aisle. The late-afternoon sun shone in her eyes, and she could hardly see past the steps.

"Jo!"

Her heart jolted. "Baron!"

He reached up and tugged her from the last step, swinging her around in a circle. Jo laughed like a giddy schoolgirl. He must have gotten land, or he wouldn't be so happy.

But she had to know. She smacked his shoulder, creating a shower of dust. "Put me down this instant."

Obviously surprised, he did as told, although his smile dipped. "What's wrong?"

"Nothing, except I have to know. Did you get a claim?"

He looked wounded for a moment, but his grin broke forth again. "You doubt me, fair wife?"

Jo stomped her foot. "Don't tease. I'm dying to know."

"Yes, I got a claim. On the prettiest speck of prairie you ever did see."

Jo smiled, more than a little relieved. Now they could build a store of their own, as well as a house that she hadn't shared with Mark. It was a fresh start in a brand-new town with the man she loved.

The road that led here had been scary and difficult, but she'd met God and He had washed her clean and given her a wonderful husband and a precious son to share her dreams.

She tugged on Baron's shirt. "Well, what are you waiting for? Kiss me, husband."

About the Author

Bestselling author Vickie McDonough grew up wanting to marry a rancher but instead married a computer geek who is scared of horses. She now lives out her dreams in her fictional stories about ranchers, cowboys, lawmen, and others living in the Old West. Vickie is the award-winning author of thirty-five published books and novellas. Her novels include the fun and feisty Texas Boardinghouse Brides series, as well as *Gabriel's Atonement*, Book 1 in her Land Rush Dreams series.

Vickie has been married forty years to Robert. They have four grown sons, one of whom is married, and a precocious eight-year-old granddaughter. When she's not writing, Vickie enjoys reading, antiquing, watching movies, and traveling. To learn more about Vickie's books or to sign up for her newsletter, visit her website: www.vickiemcdonough.com.

Land Rush Dreams

Book 1 & 2
Available now!

Sarah's Surrender
Coming 2016

Wherever great Christian books are sold!